Stengrow's Dad

Stengrow on his journey in search of his One True Dad, meets and falls in love with the beautiful **Daphne,** becomes a master of subliminal advertising, gets one of his Dads elected President of the United States, and almost loses his life. In the course of his innocent, comic, ultimately tragic pilgrimage, Stengrow becomes an American Everyman, seeking his own identity, seeking a way of life he can believe in, as he makes his way through a nation that has become, here at the end of the millenium, a maze of conflicting truths, often - like Stengrow himself - at war with itself.

Elia Katz

ELIA KATZ 's stories have appeared in such journals as *The Chicago Review, Carolina Quarterly, Deathburger*, and *The New Directions Annuals.* He has also published *Armed Love*, a non-fiction novel about America's commune movement of the 1960's and 70's; *The End-of-the-World Chapter*, and *The Buster Booklet*, two science fiction novellas; and the long poem, *Christ in the Bronx.*

He created and produced the ground-breaking video series, *Authors on Videotape*, and is an award-winning tv writer, his work having appeared on *Hill Street Blues, Tour of Duty*, and *Simon and Simon*, among many other shows.

STENGROW'S DAD

a novel by

ELIA KATZ

Wavecrest Books
Venice, CA

Published in 1994 by
WAVECREST BOOKS
124 Wavecrest Avenue
Venice, California 90291
(310) 396-1194

First Edition.

ISBN: 1-881053-02-4
Library of Congress Catalog Card #:94-61534

This book is dedicated, with much love, to my brother
Fred Katz

Stengrow's Dad

STENGROW'S DAD
TABLE OF CONTENTS.

Chapter 1.   See and Raise.

Six years ago. The night I made the discovery that tore me from my family, and the life I had known, and threw me onto the dark, broken road that ends at the door to this plaid room where I write, on my Executive Writing Tablet, in the light of this brown TV...

I was 17 years old.

I was sitting at the kitchen table with my mother and father, and my sister Tule, playing poker. We were in the family condo, in Santa Monica. Outside, the tree-bats flapped through the trees, and sat on the condo patios, among the bicycles and hibachi grills.

All night I had been the winner. The table in front of me was covered with mounds of red, white and blue chips. There were so many it became a chore to stack them, and my father had already told me a couple of times to get them organized. Once, he even refused to deal the cards until I had carefully gathered up all my chips and put them in neat piles. I did this, feeling that he might reach out and swipe at me across the table, in his anger. Not that my father had ever hit me, but on this night, and in the weeks and months preceding it, I noticed more and more that my father's feelings toward me had changed, in some way I didn't understand. It was as though he was trying to communicate to me, in all kinds of ways (except by telling me) that I had done something wrong. I couldn't figure out what it was.

My mother was looking at him as though he were a plate she had balanced precariously on a coffee cup while she stretched for the phone, as though she were ready at a moment's notice to drop whatever she was doing and catch him before he slid off the coffee cup onto the floor. Her hands were nervous, ready to cover his mouth. Her mouth was ready to talk loudly and drown out whatever he said, if she should find it necessary. Once or twice I looked up from my hand and saw the two of them exchanging looks. My father finished his babka with butter and his cup of coffee. He sighed. We played another hand. The spirit of mischief came over me. I had nothing in my hand, but instead of asking for three cards, I only asked for one. This made it seem there was something about the four cards I had kept that I liked. When everyone had taken the cards they wanted, and the betting began, I raised the pot over and over. Finally, my sister and mother both folded. My mother said somebody had better just settle down, but my father and I sat there, betting against one another.

In these games, money changed hands at the end. We weren't betting for much, but it was real money. There got to be about eleven dollars in the pot, and my father finally listened to the gentle voice of my mother (I wouldn't) and he said "I'm out," and threw his cards on the tablecloth, (I can still see the golden plastic of that tablecloth, and feel the stamped smoothness of the translucent flowers around the border) and smiled at my mother, who touched his hand supportively, because he was being a mature person, and she was relieved, and he didn't seem to hate me any more, but instead was looking at me lovingly.

I put my cards down, face down, and started to gather up the sea of plastic chips, chortling as I did it, in that family style of chortling, when you know everyone is on your side and everyone loves to see you happy, and you feel like acting up. My father reached in over the chips, between my gathering forearms, and flipped my cards over, saying, "Let's see what the boy had."

I had nothing. The fifth card had not matched any of those in my hand.

My father said, "Not even a pair of deuces. The boy has zip."

"Heh," my mother said in an attempt to laugh, or at least to indicate laughter, and she leaned against him in a playful way. But he was looking stranger and stranger, his eyes all lit with waters and lights I was not to understand at all for the next few seconds, and I was not to fully understand ever, even up to this moment, as this dragon fly hops across the wall over the TV, distracting my eye.

"I had three nines, but I gave him the pot," said my father to my mother, "because you conned me into it."

"I didn't con you, darling..."

4

I watched them. My sister slunk away into the kitchen.

"I guess it's his highly-prized intelligence," said my father, and when I looked at him he was smiling at me. "Our son, the genius... You're a great genius, aren't you?" he said to me. Then, to my mother, he said, "The great genius. The great genius."

"Shut up, Nick," said my mother, at the same time looking frightened, tired ...

"He must get it from his wonderful parents," said my father. "It's 85% of the battle if you have the right parents, right, son?" he said, with that big smile and those wet eyes, like you don't want to see your father's eyes, except in a situation where the two of you are in agreement, and united.

"Did you ever hear of the genie from the bottle?" my father then asked me.

I said, "you want to play that hand over again?"

"That's what *you* are," he said to me, "the genie from the bottle."

"What is that supposed to mean?" I asked, wishing he would go for a walk or something.

"It doesn't mean anything," said my mother. "It means your father is a sore loser."

My father turned to my mother and wiped away a tear from his own eye. "His father?" he said. "His father's a glass tube. His father's some anonymous stain in some beaker somewhere, that's all we know about that illustrious individual. His father!"

My mother said, "Reynold, go down to Wilshire, I need something at the store," and she reached across the table and started tugging at my arm, to make me go. I didn't even look at her, I couldn't hear what she was saying. I was staring at my father's hands, which now covered his face. I watched him make rubbing, washing motions with his hands. Finally, he put them down, and he looked at me. He said, in a voice that sounded as though he were speaking from his death-bed - croaking: "Your father isn't me. I want you to know that (and here he said my name, which I may not honestly reveal to you, but must transcribe as) Reynold. He isn't me."

"Oh, my God!" said my mother, and she grabbed his throat

5

as though attempting to strangle him. His chair fell over backwards and they both hit the carpet shouting with surprise.

The secret was out.

But not all of it.

Later, as the three of us sat around the coffee table in the living room, and I toed at the magazines with embarrassment and anger as they both talked to me (they were together again in their love) I discovered the rest of the secret, which concerns things done to me, and even things done to the components of myself, prior to their combination into the person I know as me, and everyone else knows as my pseudonym, and effects.

Perhaps, telling this will help you understand how I came to do the things I have done since the night I made this discovery. Things which the Government and the media have portrayed as crimes, and which probably *were* crimes. Perhaps, it will have no bearing on my case at all. I want to tell it anyway, the story of my creation.

They sat side by side on the white couch. Above their heads was an oil painting of the four of us, Mom, Dad, Tule and me, painted when I was five or six. We all still looked like the people in the picture. My mother, hands pressed together on her knees, began by telling me she and my father were very, very sorry I had learned the truth this way.

She said, "We've talked hundreds of times about how to tell you, Reynold, but we could never agree on a way. I am sorry to say that most of the time, I think both of us intended never to tell you at all. Certainly not like this... In this traumatic... "

She reached out and put her hand on mine. My father put his hand on hers. They looked at each other and kissed. She was crying. She sat back, pulled some tissues from the mother-of-pearl box on the side table, blew her nose, wiped her eye, and put the tissues in her dungaree pocket.

She said, "A little over twenty years ago, your father and I decided we were ready to have a child. We were in love, we were optimistic about the future of the world, or some such nonsense, and we felt, in a way, obligated to contribute something of ourselves for the sake of the future. Typical, and if not praiseworthy, at least not

entirely evil, motives for having a child. Maybe, not even true.
Maybe, with our teaching careers going well, with both of us having
travelled to most of the cities and nations in the world, and with me
facing the prospect of starting the novel I had always told everyone I
wanted to write, the only way out I could see for myself was to
become a mother. Whatever the spark actually was, we tried. We
tried and tried and tried. Three, four, five years went by. 'We're still
trying,' we told our parents and friends. Nothing. We saw doctors,
one after another. Nothing. We were about to give up, when the
cleaning lady who cleaned our rental units to get them ready for the
summer, told me about a doctor in Burbank. This doctor could work
miracles, she told me. His name was Dr. Lord, Hamish Lord. At
first, we didn't really think about going to him. We were tired of
doctors, of hoping, and trying."

"Then we saw him on TV," said my father, joining in really
for the first time, the muggy look of guilt starting to clear up on his
face, and the strength coming back into his voice. He even laughed,
though dimly. "He was in handcuffs, and they were leading him into
the District Central lockup!" He laughed again, and I could see he
felt a certain admiration for this Dr. Lord, and especially for the fact
that he had been arrested.

I was smiling, but wary, as I always am when someone
discusses a period in my life when I was not yet a conscious being.

"What was he being arrested for?" I asked my Dad.

But my Mom answered. "That was for the genius thing."

When I looked perplexed, my father said, "He promised
people a genius for a kid, and somebody didn't like that and they
complained or something, and Dr. Lord had to stand trial..."

"But for what?" I asked.

"For nothing. Envy," my father said, and swiped the thought
away with a strange dance-like movement of his right arm. Then, the
strength that had carried him through that gesture, carried his hand to
the serving tray, where he gathered more of the rich bakery crumbs
from the babka we had had for dessert, and brought them to his
mouth, which was still smiling. He was beginning to enjoy the story.
They both were. I realized they had never told anyone before.

"We thought, shit. A genius! That might be interesting to

7

have in the family," said my Dad through the dry crumbs.

"I remember we went out there early in the morning," my mother said, as she fed my father more small pieces of broken-up cake and cookies, those yellow cookies with the chocolate icing in the shape of oak leaves covering their top halves. He was shaking slightly as she fed him, as though he was cold.

"He lived across the street from a little airfield, for those small planes, you know," she said.

"We should have spit on the ground and turned around and walked away," said my father. My mother fed him a piece of cookie, and pushed a crumb from the corner of his chalk-white lips into his mouth. She said, "Be a man about this, Nick." He looked at me, peered at me like a man waking up from a long sleep, recognizing a face he feels he should know, not wanting to admit he doesn't.

"He had a little California Craftsman," said my mother, referring to the house of Dr. Lord. "Remember, Nick? How lovely it was, with those strange flowers growing all up the fence around the porch?" She looked at me. "The flowers - you would have thought you were in South America," she said. "There was a chain link fence across the street, and little planes were pulling up to it, like they were looking at us through the fence."

"He doesn't care what was across the street," said my father, pushing her hand away, even though she had bunched up her fingers and was about to transport to his mouth a large mound of crumbs.

"We had a 1954 Lincoln," she said to me, as she first held the compressed thumb, crumbs and fingers toward me, asking with her eyes if I wanted any. I shook my head. She ate the crumbs herself and continued. "It was blue and grey, with a green interior. The seats had a diamond pattern in white leather cutouts along the top where you rested your head." Here, she brushed my father's thinning brown hair back with her hand. She got some crumbs in his hair, which she quickly picked out and threw on the floor behind his chair. "I remember it so well," she said, "that street he lived on, so white, white - like talcum powder was covering the whole road, and the sidewalk, the lawns, everywhere. It was six-thirty in the morning. Dr. Lord had told me on the phone that his office hours were from five-thirty to seven, every weekday morning. He said by the time

most people were getting to work in the morning, he was back in bed
- "

"Weird hours," I said. I had a feeling of foreboding,
concerning what was coming, but I wanted to keep things as normal
as possible for as long as possible. I felt I should make comments. I
also felt I should make those sounds you make when you want to
indicate to somebody that you care about what they are saying, and
want them to continue. and that I should have some sort of facial
expression, while she was talking to me, but I was too tense for any
of these things. I sat like a stone, after I had squeezed out the words,
"weird hours..."

"It was fine with us," said my mother. "We wanted a child -
we wanted you - so badly, we would have gone there at midnight.
Anyway, we were able to drive to his place on the way to work; and
then we stopped at Du-Par's when we got through there, before we
went to our respective schools. Remember that, Nick?"

My father said, "Du-Par's," and brought a crumb down from
his hairline by pressing his forefinger against his face as the crumb
slid all the way down to his mouth, and then he ate it.

"So we got out of the car, and it was total quiet. When we
shut the car doors we felt like somebody was going to scream at us
from a window for waking them up. We scuffled across the road, up
the stairs to the doctor's house. He had a porch, covered with
flowers. On the mailbox it said, Dr. Hamish Lord, M.D."

My mother's face had assumed that trancelike appearance
she often got when remembering things from her past. She was
travelling through the past in a diver's suit, walking through the
aquarium of bygone scenes, speaking into a tiny microphone,
recording everything that floats by her, for those listening to her story
- in this case, my father and me - to hear, at their posts on the surface
of the ocean, bobbing in their boat, waiting for her to return to them.

"Your father turned to me," she said. "There was dew on the
wood, on the mailbox. Your father kissed me. That was so sweet.
He touched my waist. We kissed again. Then, he kissed me on the
forehead, as though he was worried, so I said, 'Don't worry. It's in
God's hands,' and he said 'OK, baby.'

"There was a cheap, plywood door, painted red. It didn't

9

even look like the door to a house. It was like a door from one room to another, inside a house, but not a door to the street. I didn't like that. Your father knocked on the door. We watched it, but nobody answered, nobody came to the door. So your father said, 'What would General MacArthur do in a case like this?' You know, it was a joke we had."

"Luana," said my Dad, rolling his eyes and then his whole head.

"Just then we heard a voice, calling - remember, Nickie? Calling: "I'm here! I'm on the way!" And there he was - Dr. Lord - coming up over that hilly street, that powdery sidewalk - "Thirty more feet! Here comes Dr. Lord! Coming to you now!" This roly-poly little muffin. Like a round, golden corn muffin, chugging up the hill. He had these big hips and tiny little feet. I thought at first it wasn't a man, but a small dog on a unicycle, wobbling up the hill, about to fall off the unicycle at every moment... possibly with a man behind him. But, of course, that was the man. That was Dr. Lord himself.

"When he got up the stairs, and he came right up near to us, and I could smell his breath, I coughed."

"The man was a drunken pig," said my Dad. "Still is."

"Shh!" said my Mom, quickly, so that I was clued to the fact that my father had revealed something (even in those few words which fate and my mother had allotted to him) that he shouldn't have revealed to me.

I realized that what my father had said, and my mother's reaction to it, meant they still saw this Dr. Lord, or at least had some contact with him.

"He could hardly find the keyhole of his door," said my mother. "He could tell I disapproved of the fact that he was obviously drunk as a skunk at six in the morning. He could see how I felt, a potential patient after all. So he kept looking at me, instead of the door, and scraping the key all over the place. 'Madam,' he said to me,' if you had discovered, even as a child, that you were of an order of intelligence not dreamed of or hoped for by the rest of the people with whom you had daily contact; and if you, further, found the picture did not improve no matter how close to the border you

10

allowed yourself to look; that is, if you found, even as a child, that you were desperately alone in this world, and if your attempts to use the natural intelligence with which you had been blessed, were met, from the start, with the scorn and laughter of humanity, that tree of old foam - I ask you - hic - as a fellow individual - what would you have done that I have not done? Would you, do you think, have resigned yourself to a lifetime in your own company, made pleasant only by the addition of some drug or stimulant to the daily routine? Well, so did I.' That's when I took the keys out of this cool, plump little hand - like a white cupcake coming out of his sleeve - and I opened the door, and we went in. First I went in, then Dr. Lord, with his breath, and then your father. Your father closed the door before anyone had turned on any lights. Dr. Lord put his hand on my behind, under my dress, and goosed me. I gave a little yell, because it was so surprising. Your father asked what was the matter, and I said, "Oh, nothing." Of course, I told him later, when we were thinking everything over - thinking over whether or not to go back to Dr. Lord, and have the procedure done."

"What procedure?" That was me, rubbing one of my eyes vigorously as I spoke, and closing the other one.

What was this procedure doing in the story of my birth, and how could I get rid of it, without hearing what it was?

But it was too late. A thing like a procedure can either be totally forgotten, never mentioned, or, once mentioned, must be entirely brought out into the open. The procedure in my past had put its foot in my door, and I knew it wouldn't leave me alone until I had bought the whole encyclopedia.

"That's what we're getting to," said my mother. I heard the tinny, hopeless melody of the ice cream truck outside our little cream-colored building.

11

Chapter 2.
"In Vitro Veritas."

The doctor took my parents into a back room of his house.

As my mother recalled it, when she was telling me, the room was covered with white dust, everywhere, like the dust in the street outside the house. The doctor had to kick aside small piles of dirty laundry. Then, he bent to shove against the wall a leaning stack of magazines, so my mother could pass by them with ease. In this back room, he had a collection of used furniture, and medical diagrams, that made it look like an examination room. There was a dentist's chair in the center which Dr. Lord said he was using as an examination table, because his real examination table was being used as a lawn chair by his nurse, one Lilly Bakoff, who waved to my parents from the back yard, where she was relaxing on the table at that moment.

On the walls, Dr. Lord had a series of medical drawings with thick arrows leading the viewer's eye from one to the other - all on a series of ivory oaktag sheets around the walls - representations of the stages of Dr. Lord's procedure.

These days, *in vitro* fertilization is fairly commonplace, but you have to remember this was 1973, and my parents had never heard of anything like it before. They were amazed as Dr. Lord showed them how it worked - the egg cells taken from the woman, then combined with the sperm of an anonymous donor, in a round, low-sided dish called a petrie dish, then placed in an incubator for a few days, to start the embryo's life on its way, then inserted into the mother's womb for the rest of the foetal journey, with its dividings and expandings into the formal nest of eights called a human being.

"But who's baby will it be?" asked my mother right away.

"Yours, dear lady," said Dr. Lord. "Yours and your husband's child it will be, completely."

"You mean, the egg cells will come from me and the sperm cells will come from Nick?"

"I didn't say that," said Dr. Lord, putting his hand up like a traffic cop. "Each couple is different. In your case, the fact is, you are perfectly capable of reproducing, but Nick isn't. According to what you told me on the telephone, his sperm - possibly because of genetic reasons, possibly through some excess in the way he has led his life - it doesn't matter, really - his sperm has about as much life in it as a bag of drowned puppies. No offense."

"No offense taken," said my father, "but if the sperm isn't going to come from me, who will it come from?"

The doctor said, "Here is the real beauty of the method I have hit upon. In cases like this one, where the husband can't provide it, we get the necessary masculine component from one of a limited number of men, all thoroughly tested by me, all completely known to me. Not only they, but their families, going back as far as anyone in each family can remember, are included in the information bank I require for each sperm donor before I will consider using his sperm for the delicate, personal, and holy purpose to which it is intended. As a result of this careful research, I can guarantee that the biological father of the child will be, with one hundred per cent certainty, a total and complete genius."

"Well, good bye, Doctor," said my mother. She was ready to leave. She had thought the famous procedure would allow her to have my father's child, and she didn't want to be the mother of anyone else's child, she said.

"Not so fast," said my father, and held onto the belt of her raincoat, so she couldn't get out of the room. He was still looking up at the oaktag diagrams, fascinated. "Who are these, uh, genius donors, Dr. Lord?" he said.

"The greatest minds of our time and place," said Dr. Lord. "The goal of my work is to improve the genetic material of the human race. In order to do this, I have prevailed upon a few men of acknowledged brilliance in their respective professions, to donate their sperm. This seed, the raw material of a brighter future for all mankind, I then match with carefully chosen couples, who want and can provide good homes for, the next generation of geniuses."

13

"But who are they, specifically?" asked my father. "Do we get to meet them, and pick the one we want?"

"I'm afraid that is a matter between myself and my donors, Mr. Stengrow," said the doctor, "but you can rest assured these are the sort of fine, high-class individuals you yourself would choose to impregnate your wife, if you met them. Which I would love for you to do, if it weren't for my strict rule, keeping the donor and the receiving couple totally unknown to each other. I'm sure you understand. But I assure you that, as the District Attorney has so accurately written in the complaint against me, I only accept the seed of geniuses. That is the purpose of my clinic. Not to fulfill your dreams of parenthood, noble though I am sure they are - but to increase the number of geniuses in the world! Let them call me an elitist, let them call me...' and here he drifted off, to total silence and a period of wobbling on his feet, with his eyes closed, before he started up again, loudly calling: 'The biological father - '

"'Which one is that?' I asked him," said Mom.

"'That's the sperm donor,' said Dr. Lord. 'He will be a man with at least a 150 IQ. That is my breakthrough. That is my service to the nations and peoples of the earth, little regard though they have had for me,' he sniffed. 'Mr. Stengrow will be the legal father, however, and the biological father will have no rights at all over the child. You can understand why. Except for the physical reality of his high I.Q. health-filled sperm, it will be as though the biological father never existed. As a person, he is not. As an individual, you can forget him completely. Don't even think about him -'"

"But I want a child who looks like me, my family - or at least has a chance -" said my father. He is light-colored, with light, long eyelashes and pale blue eyes that sometimes, especially in the bright sunlight, make him look insane. My mother is even lighter - with white skin and light red hair. The doctor assured my father that the child would look like he, my father, did. In this, he lied. As I look at myself here in the mirror, I see a large man with black hair and brown eyes.

"But you're sure the procedure will be safe for my wife?" asked my father.

14

"I've done over a hundred of these fertilizations, and so far not a single problem for a mother since the twenty-fifth, if you don't count the thirty-eighth -"

"Over a hundred?" said the young husband, his renewed hope allowing him to touch his wife for the first time since they had arrived there. He pressed his thigh against hers.

"Well," said the Doctor, looking around the room, and out the door into the corridor, for his nurse, "not all of them were human females, of course. But still, they were primates. Mammals, anyway, most of them - Lilly!"

And the nurse, who had been sunning herself in the rising sun, on the former examination table, came into the house. According to my mother, she was a large, beautiful woman, around two hundred pounds. She showed them the rest of the set-up while Dr. Lord went into the kitchen and resumed the drinking he had evidently interrupted somewhere else in order to get to his house in time to meet my parents.

Nurse Lilly told my parents again about the high calibre of the sperm donors, and in order to dispel any corners of vagueness that might still exist in their minds concerning this event, she showed them the room where the sperm donors, inspired by Dr. Lord's historic collection of girlie magazines and pornographic novels, donated their sperm into glass beakers, which they gave to Nurse Lilly, who marked them with the doctor's secret code, so no one except Dr. Lord would ever know which father had fathered which child or children. Did Nurse Lilly know? I don't know.

Anyway, my parents were worried, because of the way the doctor drank, and because of the dust that seemed to cover everything in his house. When my mother asked him about the dust, he tried to reassure her by telling her he washed the few glass implements needed for his work, and that so far none of the offspring produced in his house had been particularly dusty. As for his drinking, he defended himself, saying, ""What can a true man of science do in America today, where all the funding goes to the herd, and the lone man fends for himself, but drink?"

My parents went home. My father convinced my mother that he would love the child as though it were his own. That they

15

would raise it together, and their love would grow on account of the child.

They went back to meet with the doctor one more time, this time in a cocktail lounge near his house, and said they would go ahead with the procedure.

That night, the night of the card game, my mother spent a good deal of time comforting my father, and they did a lot of low talking, that I couldn't hear, until I decided to wander off to bed. There was a little residual kissing and touching among us, and some time spent assuring me that my father had always loved me, even though I was not, strictly speaking, his son, and even if my sister had been born a couple of years after me, (much to their amazement) a true child of the two of them, and had thereby linked them in a strong union, which I, they told me, had failed to do in the first years of my life, although they had given me every opportunity. Still, I never made the grade. They would sit together and watch me playing in my play pen, or taking my first leaden steps, and they were filled with admiration for the workings of nature, in making children develop and change, and do this and that, but they never felt drawn together by the shared experience of being my parents. Instead, as Mom said with sadness, just having me around made them feel estranged from one another. They were happy and relieved when they got a woman to watch me, while they locked themselves in their room, watching television.

True union had not come to my parents until the birth of my sister.

Not that they had ever hated me, they said. Especially not Mom, who had after all put up fifty per cent of my genetic stake. It's just that the main fascination I held for them, so powerfully as to make them forget some of the other nuances of parental love altogether - namely, trying to see in my attributes the attributes of the man who was my biological father - the medical student or lawyer, or chess wizard, that anonymous donor of me - that man they had never met and did not know the name of, but a man who had been described to them in the most glowing terms, by Doctor Lord, that genius my parents loved to look for, so to speak, in me... I looked a

16

certain way when carrots were placed in my mouth, I made a certain noise when I banged my head against the porcelain, maybe the brilliant doctor or oratorically flamboyant lawyer, and his wonderfully hidden genius-generating family had given me that look, or that particular skeletal resonance...

At first, it seemed to my mother that, amazingly enough, I was the spitting image of my father (by whom I mean the man who raised me, Mr. Stengrow). He agreed, at first. At first, they tell me, it seeemd a miracle had been given to them, a son in the image of the father who would raise and support him, even if he had not contributed any gametes to the lad. However, my father said the only important thing, as far as he was concerned, was that the two of them had a child to raise, and teach, a biological child of my mother, who was, my father said, the same person as he was, because doesn't it say in the Bible, husband and wife are one flesh?

They tell me those were good days in the history of our family. I don't remember them very well, except for the linoleum on the floor of my room. My recollections only go back to when I was about 5 or 6, maybe, and when I take myself through a mental review of those times, even the earliest I can remember, I think they must already have started that practice of theirs, of looking for the qualities of the unknown donor who was my biological father, in my qualities...

"Look," my father would say, pointing his finger at me, "he loves the mud!" Then, my Mom and Dad would look at one another, and if someone else were there, they'd say nothing. But if they were alone, or if they remembered later how I had loved the mud, one of them would be sure to say to the other one: "I wonder if the Donor is clean?"

"Anyone in your family a mud-lover?" my Dad would ask my Mom. She'd put her hand under her chin and squint her eyes. "None that I can recall," she'd say. Then they'd laugh together, fondly, thinking of the Donor, and the Donor's childhood, when, they were sure, he probably dove into mud at every slight opportunity.

Sometimes, my Mom told me, they used to praise the Donor. For example, when I got good grades in school, and when I beat up another boy because someone said he drew horses better than I did.

17

My Dad got a kick out of that, partly because no one in his family had been in a fight for three or four generations, as far as anyone could remember, and because it pointed out the fact that I was so large. The largeness inherent in myself, which some might call "my" largeness, is one thing for which even now I thank Heaven, for it brought great happiness to my Dad, and some cause for satisfaction to my Mom. Much do I wish there had been more things about me that had brought them joy. I tried my best. But I was not originated rightly, and there was nothing I could do that ever could correct what had been made wrong in my beginnings. Maybe you've done better with your beginnings - you who will never read my story - I hope you have - As for me, my beginnings are up before me each morning, and they see me to sleep at night, softly tearing each day's creations, so that by the next morning I am back once again where I was, with them - my beginnings, my cold spark, the birth of the blues...

And sometimes, my Mom said, they would speak meanly, or make dirty jokes, about the Donor.

They sometimes felt he was a fool. After all, a man who gave away the seed of his loins for twenty-five or thirty bucks, never knowing or caring about the fate of his own offspring. My father used to suggest that the Donor would one day wake up and want to find all the children he had fathered in this disembodied way, but it would be too late. "The records are sealed. End of discussion!" my father would cry out triumphantly, making a grabbing motion with his hand that ended with the hand in a fist against his chest, like a Roman legionairre, secure in the knowledge that the Donor, my true father, would never find me, and would die tormented. All this, as I say, took place out of my earshot.

Years later, when my mother was telling me the story of those years, she said she had soon realized the habit of looking for the qualities of the anonymous Donor in my qualities, was not a healthy pasttime, and she could see the deleterious effect it was having on their marriage. She was happy when my sister was born, and they had something else to think about. She was happy when my father lost his job in a recession, and he had to search for a new one, because it gave them something else to occupy their minds.

Chapter 3. Estrangement.

The night my Mom and Dad told me the story of my conception marked the birth of a new attitude on the part of both my parents toward me. From this night on, I was no longer really a part of the family.

It was only two days later that they said they needed my room for a sewing room. They said I would be able to live in the basement, though, and I would love it. My father said, with a laugh, "you'll have the run of the place."

"Except when I do the laundry, you'll have complete privacy," said my mother.

My father said, "This will be great for you, Reynold. Now, you'll be able to practice that damned hobby of yours all night if you want to, without bothering anybody."

"I don't think so, Dad," I said. "It's hard to get maximum use from a telescope in a windowless basement."

"You could get a new hobby," said my mother. "That's not the point."

She was right. The point was, we had all changed. They had come to see me as a stranger. And I had changed, too.

From that night on, I was determined to learn the identity of my true father, Our Anonymous Donor. Because now I knew he was there, written on my face and my physical features, and in my thoughts and deeds, but I couldn't see him. He was a shading over known things, but not himself a known thing, and therefore impossible to judge as to the extent of the shading. He was a hidden writing written through me... my true father, the Donor - He was off the books, like one of those day-workers you pay, but you don't want to pay their unemployment insurance, and you don't want anyone to know you even had the money to pay them, so they are off the books.

I wonder if my parents, while they were watching me and I was failing to unite them, (even though I was succeeding in providing them with many hours of wholesome fun looking for the True Dad shining through their son,) ever thought of the things you can inherit from your father, or your mother, that are not in the flesh at all, or even in the mind, or the spiritual qualities of yourself, but just words that have been said over the fates of your parents, or words that have been said over the fates of their parents -- the blessings and curses earned by ancient people, or more recent people? And is there an inheritance called "Off the Books," and is it a curse or a blessing to inherit this? It seems that all my life I have been off the books. I have been seen but not recognized as having been seen - I have been the shadow too pale to show up on the x-ray, the meaningful breath too soft to feel on the sleeping face of the one I love.

I moved my things into the basement. My mother had cleaned it out for me, and it was nice, but it wasn't the same as my old room. I still ate dinner with my family, and for the most part, we all acted as though nothing had changed. One day my father and I were out in the front of the house, after dinner. He said, "You think you'll do well in your math exam on Tuesday?" and I said, "No problem."

He looked at me in a strange way, as though the sun were over my shoulder instead of his, and as though he was the one with the trouble seeing me instead of me being the one having trouble seeing him, which was the truth of the situation. He said, "I hope there are no hard feelings between us."

I said, "Of course not, Dad. You raised me, you fed and clothed me."

He said, "You'll always be my son. I'll always love you."

At this moment, my mother came out of the house, and we all stood together in the small vegetable garden my father has always kept there, from which all the residents of the condo were welcome to take vegetables. The earth was steaming up at us, along with the smells of tomatoes and peppers, hot, as though we were standing on a heated griddle in the sunset light, between the long shadows of the palm trees outside on Fourth Street. My mother put her arms around my father and me, and some people came along the street, and we called hello to them, and they said they were going to the movies on Santa Monica Boulevard, did we want to come? My mother said no, we were going in to have coffee in a minute. The sun was shining on her beautiful face. I kissed her cheek. My father clapped me on the back, reaching around from the other side of my mother. I knew I would always love these people, pioneers who had brought me into the world, settlers who were here in the world before me, and made a place for me. But still, the next day, I started to search for my other, my biological, father. My True Dad.

My parents told me that they had long ago lost track of Dr. Lord, and that they believed he was dead, or in Europe. I knew they were lying, but out of respect for them, I decided to leave them out of it, to search on my own.

I thought my best bet would be to read books and scientific journals, looking for Dr. Lord's name, and some account of his experiments, so I went to the UCLA library, and the main branch of the Los Angeles library, downtown. I couldn't find his name anywhere. I couldn't find any mention in the newspapers of his arrest. I went to the police department, and the office of the District Attorney. There was nothing. I enjoyed the feeling of driving around, searching, getting out of the car and having a building to go into and a reason for going into it. I enjoyed asking directions of the guards, and getting help from the librarians. I even told one of the librarians, a young woman with large brown eyes and curly brown hair at the UCLA Graduate Library, the purpose of my quest. After I told her, she cried with me, and held my hand on the yellow-wood table. She then went to work, checking every library in the state, it seemed to me, and staying after her work hours for a whole week, just to help me. But even she couldn't find any mention of Dr. Lord, or his work.

I also went through the newspapers from 1970 on, jotting down the names of all the men in Los Angeles who were prominent in the fields of medicine, mathematics, law and academia. My mother and father had told me in no uncertain terms that my true father was a great genius - as a matter of fact, he had only qualified to be my true father because of his genius. The problem here was that there were so many geniuses, when you took into consideration all the endeavors of mankind, each having to itself its proper quota of geniuses, that the possible population of fathers for me quickly became too large ever to explore.

I drove around Burbank, all around the airport, because of the description my parents had given me of the place where Dr.

Lord's house was supposed to be. When I told Mom and Dad, they got upset, and said I should forget about finding my biological father, because it wouldn't do me any good to find him anyway, and would only bring me misery. An hour later, my mother told me she thought they had made a mistake about the place where Dr Lord lived. She said it was opposite an airport, but not necessarily the Burbank private field. She thought it might have been further east, inland, in the Inland Empire. She was sad for me. She kissed my hands. She said she hoped I wouldn't make myself unhappy, searching for the Donor. Then she asked me if I had told anyone about the fact that I had been created through artificial insemination. I said I had only told the librarian. She got angry, and my father heard her, and he came in chewing on a turkey leg, and they both told me forcefully that I wasn't to tell anyone the facts of my conception. My father said my mother would be sent to jail if anyone knew. My mother cried. My father shook his head with a look of wisdom. "That's the sad thing," he said, looking at me with a look freighted with meaning, "because no matter what happens, I won't be in any trouble at all. I didn't do anything wrong, after all. But your mother did. She was the one that was artificially inseminated. She's the one that committed adultery."

My mother made a noise of protest, and looked at him. He said, "Sorry, it's true."

I felt terrible about it. The fact is, not only had I told the librarian about my condition, I had also made the mistake of telling my best friend at school, Marty Rothenberg. I had told him one day when I was feeling low, and he had told everyone else in a mood of high spirits, over the next two or three days. Kids were coming up to me in the cafeteria, or while I was crossing Pico to the Taco stand, and saying, "Hey, Reynold - are you feeling ok? Your eyes have kind of a glassy look," and then they would crack up. Or, they would ask me if I had a navel. A lot of their fathers were thinkers in think tanks up and down the Pacific Coast Highway, and in Malibu, so they didn't really have as hard a time believing the story of my conception and birth as the kids at another high school might have had. In a way I guess this made it easier for me. Still, I knew that soon I would have to leave school.

Then, one night I was supposed to go to the movies with Rothenberg, but when I got there, he drove up with his father, and they said they had to go on to the Cedars-Sinai, where Rothenberg's grandmother was lying sick. I looked again at the cards in the lobby advertising the film, and decided I didn't want to see it, after all. Instead, I walked home, very slowly, listening to the televisions in all the apartments along the way, and the sounds of people clearing up after dinner. When I got home, I went in the back door, and right to the kitchen to get a sandwich.

I heard my parents' voices through the kitchen door, and another voice, and before I opened the refrigerator door, I could hear my name, and I knew they were talking about me. Instead of opening the refrigerator door, which would have made noise, I stood in the dark and listened to the conversation in the living room.

"You never should have told him," said the stranger's voice, which was high and strained, like wind coming through the crack in a wall.

"It was my fault," said my father. "I lost my temper. I felt estranged from him, and I wanted to show I knew something he didn't. I feel like a fool."

"Oh, Doctor Lord," said my mother, "will he be able to adjust?"

So, this was Doctor Lord.

It didn't bother me that my parents had lied to me, and told me they were out of touch with the doctor. I knew they had done what they thought was best, for all of us. However, it was obvious from the things they were saying that throughout my entire life, my mother and father had been making regular, detailed reports to Dr. Lord, concerning everything from my appetite to my moods to the notes I made in my school notebooks when I was not writing my assignments. For example, Dr. Lord said at one point that I had seemed so happy when he had last observed me, "at the bowling alley on Pico." Then I knew why my parents had urged me to take up bowling in the first place, and why they had insisted on the three of us joining a family league, even though it was so out of character for them - especially, for my father, a man totally unathletic in every other respect.

23

I smiled at the thought of my father's selflessness - allowing himself to look ridiculous (as everyone agreed he did, every time we went bowling) for the good of science, and probably for my good, too.

Also, I found myself wondering whether the doctor had done his observing from another alley, or from the snack bar that overlooked the entire place from its raised platform. Or was there a camera set up in the crawl space over the alleys, or behind the alleys, to film me? I wondered if there were other artificially inseminated boys and girls, all living in this general area, whose parents also dragged them to the Pico Lanes one night of every month, for observation.

I gathered from their conversation, as I stood at the breakfast bar, that Dr. Lord had a girlfriend who was an Administrator at Santa Monica High School. This girlfriend had heard about the controversy over my origins. I'm not clear on whether or not the girl also knew about Dr. Lord's work, but for whatever reason, she had obviously thought I was worth mentioning to the doctor. He was very upset. He said he didn't know what the consequences would be, but as for himself, he intended to leave Los Angeles.

"Unfortunately," said the doctor sadly, "the current climate in the world of science is unfriendly toward the real pioneer."

"But you've given barren couples babies," said Dad.

"Yes," said the doctor, "and a generous spirit, such as you possess, will concentrate on that fact - the good a man has done - the families he's helped to complete. However, the sad state of the world is such that others will tend to dwell more readily on the unavoidable tragedies and errors that (any innovator will be glad to tell you) must precede even the most glorious new step in the scientific progress of mankind, ah, me - The babies who never got born - the few, and sadly remembered women who - " and here his voice became so low that I'm sure even my parents, sitting directly in front of his face, could not have heard what he said next - Then, a bit louder: "They'll fixate on the fact that I guaranteed geniuses, and their envy - the non-genius press, the non-genius public, the non-genius agencies of government - will cause them to find every possible fault with what I, we, have done... But still," he picked up volume here, feeling better about what he was about to say than about that which he had already said, "still, one day we'll all be able to tell the things we know, to a humble and waiting world. I'm sure of it. However, until then, I think it would be best for all of us, if we changed our places of residence. In the future, I don't know exactly when, you will hear from me. I will write, and send instructions on how we may continue our acquaintanceship, and continue the vital work of observing young Reynold, how he develops in the months and years to come. Until then, good luck, dear friends - "

Then, I carefully looked out between the plantation shutters that separated the kitchen from the living room. I had to lean painfully across the breakfast bar, and I felt the doorknobs of the cabinet push into my groin. I saw my parents standing with a short, plump man in a brown tweed jacket with leather patches on the elbows. Awkwardly, my mother walked forward and embraced the doctor. Then, my father did the same. They said they didn't see how they could leave Los Angeles on such short notice, but that they would be sure to keep his secret, and not admit to anyone how I had been born.

He said, "The press has its ways - " but they reassured him. He said, "The police, the FBI..." but they said there was no way in the world anyone could get them to betray him. My father (Mr. Stengrow, that is) said, "When the world is populated with geniuses, they will appreciate what you have done."

Dr. Lord sighed, fumbled with his fingers in a twirling gesture I have never been able to duplicate, and said, "I sincerely hope so, my dear Mr. Stengrow. The problem is, geniuses, just by the fact of their existence, are a standing insult to the rest of mankind. This is the one problem I never counted on. I am afraid that my life's work, when all the facts are known, will have been wasted, wasted."

"No!" said my mother.

"Never!" said my father.

They walked him to the door.

Chapter 4. The California Craftsman.

I peered out at them, surprised to see how my mother towered over both Dr. Lord and my father, as they stood by the front door.

When Dr. Lord went out, I ducked out the back door and ran around to get my car, which was parked on Montana Avenue, so I could bring it around to Fourth in time to follow Dr. Lord. He had a 1969 Impala; I, a 1964 Pontiac LeMans with a white convertible top, a black body, and red leather seats. He pulled out, his car hoisting itself to the central mound of the street like a waking lion, and I followed at a distance, trying to keep one or two cars between us at all times. The streets weren't as bright at night as they are these days, but I remember the blue-white lights under which we drove, out to Burbank. I had only been in Burbank those times when I was looking for Dr. Lord's house, and I didn't know it very well. I had never been there at night, except if you count that long-ago time when I was conceived there, and I couldn't be expected to remember much about the place from that time, because after all, I didn't even have eyes then, or a nose, and I was really nothing more than a rapidly dividing clump of cells and a soul (if you want to give me the benefit of the doubt) and so, I was pleasantly enjoying the sights of the clean restaurants and ghostly auto repair shops, most of them lit and glowing within.

Then, the Impala swept around a corner onto a wide, downhill-running side street, with a long chain link fence running down one side, as far as the eye could see. And a row of single-family dwellings made of wood ran down the other side. And I saw the white dust, as my father and mother had described it to me, puffing up in clouds around the Impala, and around my car.

Dr. Lord pulled his car into the driveway of a house I assumed to be his. A white, small California craftsman, with trapezoidal posts in the corners of the porch. It was only then that I noticed his headlights were off. Yes, I thought, he turned them off when he came around the corner onto this street. I wondered why. I also noticed that he got out of the car very fast, and when he shut the door, he didn't let it slam, or even drop closed. He guided the door instead to a position where it just rested against the car. He looked over the top of the car, all the way up the street. I was parked by then, against the chain link fence, but my lights were out, and I was sitting as low as possible in the seat, looking over the dashboard. For a moment, I thought he was looking right into my eyes, but he kept rotating his head around on his neck, so I suppose he didn't see me. He looked behind him, too, all down the other way. There was nobody in the street. Once he saw that, he seemed to relax, and breathe more naturally than he had been. He even looked up at the sky, and just stood there, nodding at it for a while. Then, he appeared to remember the mood he had just been in, and it was like an electric current had been shot through him, the way he leaped into action, patting the top of his car decisively and then running in through the garage door of his house. I saw a light go on inside, and I could see that the garage door hadn't closed all the way. I got out of my car, played the same trick with my car door that he had, so that it would not make noise when it closed, on this silent street, and I walked up to his house, trying to look calm as I went. Just in case I was being watched from one of the houses up or down the block.

What did I do? Walked along the fencing, as I recall, pretending to be studying it for some purpose - what a fool I must have appeared to be! What a fool, not to recognize those early warning signs of being a fool! What did I do? Approached more closely, walking with my hands in my back pockets, looking at the ground, as though I was looking for a dropped quarter - yes, I engaged in two or three separate ruses to give myself the confidence that just in case anyone was actually watching me go (as it turned out, there were many people watching me, but all of them knew where I was heading, from the time my LeMans wobbled around the corner at the top of the hill, behind the doctor's Impala) that just in case anyone was actually watching me go, they would not know why I was here.

I noticed there were words written in paint on the outside of the house and on the pavement, and what appeared to be gashes across the front of the house, and burned places in the front lawn. The one tree looked like it had been set on fire. Most of the branches were burned off, and whatever leaves there had been, were on the ground, black. I tried to see the words from under the shelf of my brow, as I kept my head down. I saw the words "Hell," "Love," "Nazi," and "Bottle," all sprayed on the walkway, the public sidewalk, and the three steps to the Doctor's porch. I don't know if they were parts of sentences, or were supposed to stand by themselves. The words were too big to take in, as I was going forward.

I went into the garage, and slipped through the slightly opened door to his kitchen. I heard voices from the back of the house, so I looked down a long corridor, to see the layout of the rooms. I had to look around the doorway from the kitchen to the corridor. The corridor was dark. There were two or three rooms off to the sides of it, but they were all dark. The living room was out the other kitchen door, and didn't come into play, because there were no voices coming from there, and no lights were on. The main activity seemed to be in the very back room of the house, which was lit up. It was at the end of the corridor, and I could see people's bodies crossing from one side of the room to the other past the narrow doorway. One of the bodies I knew was Dr. Lord's. The other person there seemed to be a woman, much taller and bigger than the doctor. Then I heard the doctor say, "Faster, Nurse Lilly - I don't know if we even have an hour, and all the files are still -- "

But the woman, Nurse Lilly, interrupted him, with a beautiful, comforting voice I still remember, after all these years, saying: "Don't worry, Doctor - I've already packed the petrie dishes and the micropipettes - also, your diaries and notebooks, at least all of them since Lisbon, and only you know (as you know) where the pre-Lisbon books are - far be it from me to pry into a matter obviously so tender in your - but that's neither here nor there -" (sigh) "- and the diagrams are all rolled up neatly, along with your diplomas and skiing awards; and your entire medical library, and those treasure hunting magazines, are all in the boat, completely wrapped in waterproof cloth, just as you instructed -"

28

"Fine," said the doctor, as he streaked and blurred around the room, seeming always to be rising from some scooping motion as he went from the left to the right, and seeming always to be swooping, or scooping, down, as he went the other way. "That just leaves thirty years of files, thirty years of photographs - Did they come around today?"

"I didn't go to the door," said Nurse Lilly. "I could hear them banging away, and they tried to see me through the windows, but I stayed out of sight."

I supposed they were referring to the people, whoever they were, who had written the words all over the house, and set the fires that had created the unmistakable signs of burning which I had noticed on the way in.

I decided this was as good a time as any to make my presence known to the Doctor and his Nurse. I think I was emboldened by the new knowledge that there were other people obviously interested in them, people they were afraid of. I walked down the corridor. I clapped my hands to get the dust off the palms, and also to announce my presence to the two people. Nurse Lilly peered at me a long moment down the corridor, and then started screaming, "Out! Get out! We didn't do anything!" She dropped two stacks of files, that she had been carrying pressed into her hips and supported by her forearms at the moment when she had seen me. The files fell away like some rubbery animal being sliced into a pan, and some of the pages fanned out into the corridor, blocking the path of the door when Nurse Lilly tried to close it in my face. I took advantage of my good luck to throw myself against the door with all my might, and try to push it open. She yelled with pain, but she held the door shut, or almost shut. The files were still in the way.

"I don't want to hurt you people," I said through the door. I'm Reynold Stengrow. Ask Dr. Lord. He knows who I am."

"Get away, Stengrow," I heard the Doctor call through the door to me, "there's nothing for you here."

I said, "I want to know who my real father was." I didn't immediately throw myself against the door again, because I wanted to try first to appeal to the Doctor's sense of fair play.

"That's confidential information," said Dr. Lord, through the door, sounding like he was pressed close to his side of it, probably standing right beside Nurse Lilly, helping her hold it shut. "I'm a responsible man of science," he continued. "Go away, and be grateful for life. Don't screw up everybody else's life by asking a lot of questions."

"The Doctor is a man of great intelligence," said Nurse Lilly, "Listen to him, young man -"

There was something about the way she said the words "young man" that made it sound like she wasn't quite as strong at the end of the final syllable, as she might have been at the beginning of her speech, so I took advantage of this moment of weakness, and pushed with all my might, fast and hard. "The throw rug!" I heard her say, with a sound of despair, just before her feet slid out from under her body, and when I was able to get my head around the corner of the door, I could see she was being glided across the floor by the motion of a black and white hook rug in the shape of a baseball. By the time I got inside, she was hanging onto the doorknob with both hands, trying to pull herself back into an upright position. The Doctor, on the other hand, had abandoned the door completely, and he was concentrating on shoving his files into a bunch of sturdy-looking cardboard boxes that said "Whitehall Moving and Storage Co., Inc., Worth Street, NYC."

He looked at me, like a golden retriever standing defensively beside something he has been chewing, which has been unjustifiably, as far as he can tell, claimed by some human... He said, "Your father is a prominent man - they all are - or were - or, in the case of one or two, could have been -" and he gestured around the room, causing me to look around, and see the refrigerator units lined up against all the walls, even blocking out most of the light of the two small windows in the room.

"Now," he said sadly, "how can I take it all with me? The seed of the one tenth of one per cent, here is an entire future for mankind that mankind never will know, because its concentrated form is in this room, and soon will exist no more." The Doctor saluted the refrigerators, and gave them a lingering look, that made me sad, and almost made me forget what I was there for.

"Still," said the Doctor, turning to look at me again, with a look of courage, "I had a pact with these men - anonymity for their sperm - and I intend to keep it." And with that, he tossed the files he had in his hands, into a cardboard box, and walked sort of heavy-footed to the row of refrigerators.

He opened one of the refrigerator doors - an old Kelvinator of lime green - and I could see it wasn't like a regular refrigerator inside, but more like a freezer, and a lot of smoke came out of it when the door was opened. Inside, there were four shelves, made of ice-covered metal, and on every shelf were wire and wooden racks. Dr. Lord took one out and I saw it was a rack of glass test tubes. "Good-bye, men," he said. It seemed he was talking to the test tubes. "No one will ever know the contributions made by every one of you, every dear one."

"Please," I said, "I want to know the name of my True Dad."

Nurse Lilly was still loading the boxes, frantically. She said she wanted the Doctor to hurry up, and help her load, but he didn't hear her. He turned to me, or rather, peered at me through the row of frosty test tubes in his hand, and said, "Think of what you are asking me to do! These are important men, men with something to lose. These are men with families."

"I'm family," I said.

"Families that love them," said the Doctor, "that share their names. Is it fair to the families?"

"But that's who I am," I said, louder. "The family! I'm a child of the man who donated. Half of me is from him. It's not as though I were some stranger."

He said, "You'll be a meteor colliding into the planet of some poor fellow's life - "

"I'll be discreet - Please, Dr. Lord!"

At this moment, I started to see lights criss-crossing outside the windows, like the lights at a premiere. Flashlight beams, and maybe car headlights, lighting up different sections of the sky and the building next door, and the wires that ran over the street. I could also hear voices outside. Dr. Lord whispered to me, "News of your search somehow reached my neighbors, confirming suspicions they have long held about me, and about Nurse Lilly, and our work. that is why we must now leave."

Then, it was silent for a few seconds. Nurse Lilly, the Doctor and I all stood still, listening. Then, the voices again. I could hear the ends of a couple of sentences - then, the way a voice sounds at the end of a question - then, there was a rock through the window. Then, there was screaming, and a shrieking voice over everyone else's, yelling, "How many years I been saying this guy's crazy? Since he moved in here!" Then I saw a little old lady poke her face in the window. The lights were criss-crossing behind her, and over her head, and she peered around the room from behind her little wire-frame lenses. "What kind of a man needs twenty five refrigerators was the very first thing I remember saying to anyone about you, Mister -" she said straight at the Doctor. Then she pulled her head back out and said. "It's just like I thought - they're gettin ready to pull out, takin all the evidence with em..."

"Oh, no they ain't," said one of the men outside. They crowded up to the window and one of them said, "You better hold everything in there, and we'll be right in..."

The Doctor threw the rack of test tubes at the face in the window. They missed him, but shattered against the wall above his head, and he had to pull back to avoid being showered with glass and gel-like, near-frozen sperm. I could hear people coming in through the front door and through the kitchen door, and down the corridor I had come down. Some of them were laughing, even while the others sounded angry, and for some reason it was the laughers that made me feel the most afraid. The fact is, of course, if there had only been laughers, and none sounding angry, I might not have been as scared, or at least, I might not have been scared in the same way - but the presence of the laughers in that sea of dull, low-voiced rage, gave me that rare taste of metal in the mouth you get when you're terrified, if you're like me, and why should you be now that I think of it, but still -- that sound -- the easy laughter of the ones in the crowd who know that whatever hideous events may occur on this night, they will not be held personally responsible for any of it, even if they enjoy it as much as, or more than, anyone else.

Nurse Lilly took a file cabinet and pushed it in front of the door to the corridor, just in time. As the people outside smashed against the door with their shoulders and flashlights, she pushed another cabinet, and an old wooden desk in front of the door. Dr. Lord was emptying the open refrigerator-freezer of test tubes, throwing them all at the window, to keep the crowd at bay.

"We've got guns out here, Doc," said one of the men.

"No!" a woman screamed, and all the other women seemed to agree with her. I had a short glimpse of the crowd in the yard when Nurse Lilly overturned one of the refrigerators, sending it crashing across the room, opening up another small corner of the window for me to see through. I saw the people were mostly in their bathrobes and slippers, or barefoot, and there were children, running around in pyjamas, carrying toys and playing with a small dog in the background there, against the next house. There were also people on top of that house, and its garage, pointing in the Doctor's window. A young boy on the roof lit a rolled-up newspaper with a cigarette lighter, and threw it at the Doctor's house, but one of the women leaped in the way, and caught it. She and her friend stomped out the fire, and I heard one of the women call out, "Be careful, all you men! We've got to get that simmen in there and make him tell us who it all came from!"

"Good people," said the Doctor, "of what possible use could that information be to you? You're trampling on the work of a lifetime here, dear neighbors -"

The ceiling broke open and a man's legs dropped into the room in front of my face. The door to the corridor was also broken by now. Only the height of the furniture piled in front of it prevented the neighbors from storming in through that opening. The man in front, who had his arms stretched over the surface of the file cabinet, found he couldn't slide over the cabinet into the room, so he settled back to his feet and tried to reason with the Doctor from where he was. The man had a long face, like a beagle.

"Listen, Doc," he said, trying to sound sensible, "we know you been collectin the simmin a' some real smart men. It's been a rumor around the block here for ten, fiteen years already, I guess you know that. But now, well, it seems like the news is all over town, and you been sellin this simmin all over Beverly Hills, Santa Monica, Brentwood, to them that can pay, but what about us?"

"What about who?" asked Dr. Lord. He had stopped

throwing things and he seemed interested for the first time, even more interested than terrified. I was still more terrified than interested, but there was one thing I was interested in - the identity of my True Dad - so I kept my eyes open, and looked for an opportunity, having no idea what form that opportunity might take.

"Us! Us!" two women shouted through the window, in answer to Dr. Lord's question. When he looked confused, the man at the door said, "That simmin you got in there is from the best, right? Your prize steers, if we hear correctly in these matters. Now, is that true?"

"Why," said Dr. Lord, "that's it exactly. It is all from geniuses. The genetic cream of the United States."

"And we all know what kind of a world we have out here, with these smart Japanese and Koreans and who all, and the kind of world we're going to have, come the future -"

Here, many of the people murmured agreement.

"A world," said the man, "where, if a kid ain't smart, he's gonna be left right out. And, well, if a kid is smart, then he can be expected to scoop up the best jobs, and make all kinds of money. Am I right so far?"

"Sure," said Dr. Lord.

"But us whose neighborhood you lived in, and who were civil to you every morning, even after Tom Stiller found all that porno in your garbage cans that day - what shot have we got for any kids with that kind of brainpower? None at all. Combine my brainpower with my old lady's, you got enough brainpower to think of what to have for dinner tonight, just about. How much can we give to our kids, then? And the proof of it is, our kids themselves! Why, we got three and all three of them haven't got enough sense to face the table when they eat, let alone the intellect to be ready for the Twenty First Century!"

People started all talking at once, telling heart-rending anecdotes of how stupid their children were.

"But you sell that simmin all around Brentwood, Beverly Hills, and where else, but around here, we're parched. What's the matter, ain't we good enough? Who's gonna support me and my wife when we get old if we can't have us a little computer kid or somethin

34

like that - or like a painter-genius-type kid, or some kind of kid who can make a dollar in the Twenty-First Century, you know? Because I can tell you as sure as I'm standin in a doorway with the door all busted apart, my three kids I got now, they ain't gonna support one ounce of me, let alone support all of me and all of my old lady. No sir, that simmin ain't leavin this area till we come to some kind of an understandin here - OK. Doc?"

"You don't know what you're asking," said the Doctor, and he took the moment to resume stuffing his files and photographs into the cardboard boxes. "I have to study the prospective parents, I have to observe the home environment, I have to be sure that each child is going to have a home commensurate with the potential inherent in his conception itself, or it would be better not to do the thing at all..."

"Then you're tellin us we gotta be poor just like we are, forever," said the man. "And our kids'll keep gettin dumber and the kids of the people that can pay you are gonna get smarter and smarter, and probably better lookin', and whatever you can throw in there, like extras on a new car, they'll get, and our kids won't get - "

"Please," said Dr. Lord, "go back to your homes, my good people." He was imploring the young women at the window, and the man at the door, and he turned back and forth between them as he spoke.

"One day," said the Doctor, "the techniques I have pioneered will be available to all people. Yes, even the poor, even the ignorant. Even to you! Now, it's too soon. Science starts by ones and twos, before its magic blossoms to the millions and billions. But hope, dear neighbors! For I see a day when your children, and your children's children, will be able to assure themselves that not one bit of any of you will survive in their children, and their children's children! Hallellujah, well you may say! There is indeed a brighter day a-coming! When the apple will fall so far from the tree, you'll think it's a red red rose --"

"Now!" said a woman at the window, "We need it to start now! You can't keep these blessings from our kids - it just isn't right!" She was a lovely woman, I still remember, with beautiful blue eyes, and those long hands and fingers that make you want to be touched. I remember thinking, God has done so well by this woman, why does she think Doctor Lord can do any better? She was crying, reaching out to the broken test tubes of the semen of geniuses, trying to touch them.

Chapter 5. "I'm Seventeen, Ma'am."

As for me, I took advantage of the fact that the Doctor and his neighbors were busy having their conversation. Moving slowly, so as to attract as little attention as possible, I went to the cardboard boxes and started rooting around in them, until I saw a stack of ledger books, taller than average notebooks, and thinner than you'd expect books of that height to be, and each one had a white label on the front of it, with a blue border, and a year's number typed on the label... 1946, 1947, 1948...

The man hanging through the ceiling was stuck there, with his feet dangling between the faces of myself and Nurse Lilly. His friends were on the roof, struggling to free his shoulders, so he could drop the rest of the way into the room. Now, just as I found the ledger book for 1973, which I hoped would tell me what I wanted to know, although there wasn't time for me to open the book, because I didn't feel confident enough in the situation to lower my eyes even for a second, to see whether I had an accounts book, or a personal diary, or whatever - but just as I found this ledger, the man came down from the ceiling, with cracking noises, right in front of me, and you could see he was injured. This caused Nurse Lilly to scream, and run to him, while he was trying to stand up. She looked around frantically, as she stood over the man, then found what she wanted, a toaster, picked it up, and holding it in both her hands, smashed it down on the man's face.

The toaster was still plugged in, and the wire stretched over the black stone table that had a sink in it, and a lot of bunsen burners and glass beakers on top of it. The wire stretched to the other side of the table, then back a few inches to the wall, where it had to go behind a metal bureau - not a file cabinet, but the kind of cabinet that has two doors that can swing open, and shelves inside - before it reached the wall-plug. When Nurse Lilly hit the man from the ceiling, who was covered with white dust, and seemed to be trying to spit some of it out of his mouth, he raised his hands in a natural defensive measure (even today, I don't blame him, or even Nurse Lilly, really) and sort of caught the toaster along one side with his wrists, and the lower portion of his hands, and he pulled his hands violently over his head, to deflect the toaster away from his face (you can't blame him) and his motion pulled the wire attached to the toaster, out straight. It stretched to its full tension, over the black table, behind the black table, and behind the metal cabinet with the doors. The wire behind the cabinet was low where it met the wall-plug, but it had to go higher on the other side, to stretch over the table, and that height, on that side, was sufficient so that the wire, when it was stretched tightly, pushed the cabinet forward, away from the wall.

At first, the doors of the cabinet held. Then, bulges appeared in the doors, on the lower left hand side and the upper right hand side, so it looked for a moment like a beige man with one knee raised and one hand pressed outward from the level of his chest, to break his inevitible fall onto the sharp edge of the black table. Then, before the cabinet could reach that sharp corner, the little lock attached to the two lever-shaped handles on the doors, snapped open, and the doors swung down and open. From the shelves of the cabinet, like waves of neon-throbbing, multi-colored oil, poured several thousand, or possibly several tens of thousands of magazines, all with naked women on their covers. The top ones slid first, down to the surface of the table, then skidded over the table, and cascaded to the floor. The ones from the lower shelves dropped to the floor and the others mounded up in piles where the magazines collided with one another.

Everywhere you looked were brightly colored, vivid photographs of naked women, women in bikinis or underwear, sometimes, but mostly naked - winking, laughing, looking surprised, looking angry, looking frightened or casually allusive - the naked women of thirty years of publishing history, to judge by the covers I could see, that lay around my legs and were piled almost to my knees, holding me in my place.

Everyone stopped where they were. The women at the window, the three men who had shoved the cabinets away from the door to the corridor, and were crawling over the cabinets into the room, the new people, including an old man with his glasses hanging

38

from one ear, wobbling above me in the hole in the ceiling, where he and his buddies were staring down at us, the Doctor, and even Nurse Lilly - all stopped and were silent, in homage to the overwhelmingly seductive effect of all those magazines, those smiles and shoulders and breasts and bellies and fingernail polish.

Many in the crowd no doubt scanned the images for a favorite hair color, or a favorite style of lipstick, or a remembered shape, or part of shape, when the sea of color came to a rest, after its long slippery disgorgement from the cabinet.

Finally, one of the women said, "Why, you filthy old bastard." Then there was a continuation of the silence.

Nurse Lilly said, "You fools - how in the hell do you think we get the geniuses to give us their sperm? You think we give them one of the Doctor's monographs on the effect of chocolate syrup on sex-selection in the Feather River Frog? Ladies, we have to get this stuff when we need it - we have to catch it quick to freeze it good - is that really so hard to figure out?"

But, while I would have answered her question, "no," the people who were assembled there evidently would have answered in the affirmative, if they had given any answer at all, which they didn't, because the sight of those magazines had changed them from a mindless, angry crowd into a furious, violent mob, almost European in its ferocity, and they were so busy tearing at the confines which held them back, trying to get their hands on the Doctor, and Nurse Lilly, and probably on me, if they thought about me at all, that they didn't even hear the end of Nurse Lilly's question.

Nurse Lilly, the Doctor and I stood in the widening sea of the girlie mags, pulling our legs from the pulp quicksand, then stepping carefully to stand atop the thousands of beautiful girls, balancing our feet on their faces as though they were a conquered race, forced by some decree to smile up at us.

Two of the the Doctor's neighbors, both women, got in through the little window. Then, three men got into the room, the first one helping the other two over the tilted cabinets, and they ranged out behind Dr. Lord.

I took this opportunity to glance into the ledger I held in my hands, and saw that there was every possibility it was the one I

39

needed. I saw the words, DONOR and FAMILY and CHILD, at the top of the first page, and a wobbling, meandering line drawn down the page between each of these words, from top to bottom. I must say, the way those lines had been drawn, without a ruler, and looking so wretched, as they did, brought me up short. I thought, here is this scientist, the man responsible for bringing me into the world, when I would have been well out of it if he had minded his own business in the first place, and he can't even take the trouble to find a ruler, when he's setting up a new notebook. A ruler isn't always available, I realized that, but even then, he could have used the edge of the page itself, which was straight, or folded the page in three. Well, fuck him, I thought, now he's in the middle of a hundred people who want to kill him. Until that moment, I had been sure that nothing bad would happen to the Doctor, Nurse Lilly or myself, because, the fact is, I have faith in anyone with the word Doctor in front of his or her name. But now that I saw the first page in that ledger, with its wobbly lines, I began to feel weak. I saw with new eyes the people crawling into the room from top and sides, and for the first time I wondered if science had an answer for the problem they posed to my safety.

One of the men pulled a knife out of the back pocket of his blue jeans. He was barefoot, and as he walked, the bottoms of his feet stuck to the girlie magazines in a series of smacking sounds. He started positioning himself like a fighter, leaning from side to side in front of the Doctor, as though looking for the right moment to lunge forward with the knife and cut the Doctor's throat. He said, "Now, a man that keeps this much pornography has got something seriously the matter with him, and I don't care if he calls himself a Doctor or a Dentist, or a Priest. Of course, any redblooded American man likes to thumb through em in the drug store, maybe buy one or two and read em, but shit... You got to throw one away before you can buy another one, or else you cross right over the line and you become a psychotic insanity case."

"Yes, sir," said another guy, who dropped in from the hole in the ceiling, and slid around on a couple of piles of those slick, flapjack-like magazines, "or else you start to fixate on these girls, and the next thing you know, you're out there stalkin' em and rapin' em and all that evil shit, just because you got fixated. Fixated by pornography."

"Yeah?" said the first one to the second one, seeming rather surprised, and maybe a little worried by what he had heard.

Then, recovering his poise, this first one, the barefoot one, turned to the Doctor and said, "That's it for the gum-flappin'. Now, Doc, we want you to get that simmen into our women. Then we'll let you out of here alive. If you won't do it, I can't guarantee these women won't tear your head off, rather than see you beat it outta here in that car o yours, with all this simmen and the secret to how it gets used. Well, what do you say?"

"Sir," said Dr. Lord, and he gave the impression of losing all strength, and will to argue, and he looked like a beaten man. "Sir, you see me surrounded. I have chased a dream, since 1945. Since before that, if you want to know the truth, but that was in my native land, and I never think about those days, and anyway, as I said to the man at the State Department, when I had to answer all those questions - and for what? for the privilege of bringing civilization and knowledge to a nation of gum-chewers? - as I said to this pitiful man at the State Department... science doesn't ask... science doesn't..."

He paused to inhale, and it took on a withery unhappy sound as the air rushed into his lungs. But the people standing around didn't feel any pity for him, or if they did, they didn't let it show. The Doctor seemed to be trying to remember what he had been saying. Then he said, "Oh, yes -- and so the point is, here we are, nineteen whatever, and I have brought many children into the world -- one -- " (he flung his arm in my direction, and everyone glanced at me for a moment) " -- stands here with us tonight. Reynold Stengrow."

They looked at me in a more serious way. The women looked me up and down, as though trying to see if I had turned out all right, despite the strange circumstances of my conception. But perhaps I am wrong about that, considering how excited they were to have the process tried on themselves. Maybe they were too far gone in their dream of more perfect children, even to care for any evidence concerning the Doctor's methods. I felt as though I were standing in a spotlight, having come a long way to deliver a speech, but I had forgotten the words to my speech. I felt somehow that I should have been able to say something to these people, something that would do them some good, and even have the sound of a thing that would do them some good, so it would save me and them at the same time, and even Dr. Lord, and Nurse Lilly, but I couldn't think of anything to say.

One of the men who had come down through the ceiling grabbed me by the upper arm, and gave me a hard squeeze. "Feels normal," he said, and then gave the Doctor a little involuntary look of approval and respect. The guy with the knife stepped back, too. Everyone seemed to catch, like a premonition, the sense of the importance of this moment. They were actually standing with a boy who had been created by artificial insemination. He had hair, features, height, weight, and all things, as far as they could see, that you might look for in a boy.

"How old are you, son?" asked the beautiful woman with the blue eyes who had crawled through the window. I could see now, as she dusted the dust off her flanks, that she wore one of those cotton dresses with a pattern of tiny flowers on it, and she had sneakers on and no socks.

"I'm seventeen, ma'am," I said.

The woman said, "Well, tell us, son, we're dyin' to hear about it, can't you see?"

I said "Tell you what, ma'am?"

"Why - how it feels - how it feels to be the way you are - unofficial seminated - you know -"

"Well," I said, "for a long time, I didn't know."

Those that could hear me, whispered what I had said to the ones behind them, out across the lawn and on top of the roof. I felt better, because the people really seemed interested in what I had to say, and they didn't look like they wanted to kill me any more. Also, I kept looking in that one woman's eyes, and their beauty, along with the fact that they looked so interested, and even concerned, as though they had seen me hit my head against a wall, gave me a way to go - they let me calm down enough to answer her question -

A lot of the people were saying awww, because they pitied me for not having been told I was artificially inseminated. The woman asked me when I had found out, and I told her about the card game. Then I told her I was looking for my True Dad, and that was what had brought me to the house of the Doctor that night. Some of the men settled down on the floor, and were leafing through the colorful maazines. Other men crawled into the room, and some of the magazines were passed out the door and the small window, to those who couldn't get into the little room.

The beautiful woman took my hand, and held onto it with both of hers, as I talked. She started to cry. I told her there was nothing to cry about. I was perfectly happy, except for the curiosity to learn the identity of my True Dad. Still, it didn't satisfy her, and she seemed very sorry for me.

She said, "This is something we didn't think about. Whether we're gonna tell these kids they're unofficial seminated, or not. Now, this young man never was told, until it came out in the most embarrassing way, and tore his family apart. But on the other hand, if we tell these kids as soon as they're able to understand, then they'll know right away they're better than their daddies, like this one does - "

"I don't - " I started to protest, but she kept on talking through the sounds I tried to make. "And they'll have lots of problems, and they'll always be off looking for their semminator daddies, and be a royal pain the behind, if my imagination's not playing tricks on me. Then, they might not even want to support their parents that raised them and cared for them, when their parents are old, and need that support from the kids with all that scientific know-how, and computer training and so on - "

And the Doctor, looking over at her from where he had returned to the job of stuffing the cardboard boxes with files, a ceramic frog, and a calendar with pictures of different breeds of dogs on it, said, "Now, you're treading on an area known as thinking, dear young woman - You others - listen to her! She is thinking clearly now! Go home - leave well enough alone - these processes are not for you - not yet - go home -"

But the men on the floor, some of whom were now leaning on one elbow, with their hands propping up their heads, as they read the magazines all around them on the floor, now began to get angry.

One man said, "Don't start a lot of talk-talk with this guy - he'll hypnotize us and get away clean, and take the simmen with im."

Then the man, and a couple of the others, got up, and approached the Doctor. The one who had the knife, put it under the Doctor's chin, and said, "Now, Doc - start telling us how to get this simmin stuff rollin' - "

The Doctor was very brave. He said, "For your own sakes - I can't do what you ask - please leave my home right now - "

But the man with the knife made an animal-type noise, and raised his hand way above his head. The women screamed, one way or another, and the men inhaled, or made a ratchety sound with their throats. The man with the knife brought his arm down, with the knife pointing toward the top of the Doctor's chest bone. I thought the Doctor was a goner, but the force of the knife-man's movements caused the rubbery, slick magazines under his feet to slip and slide in a lot of different directions all at once. The man's feet slid with their separate piles of periodicals, in opposite directions. They slid out to his sides, and the man was split at the crotch. Because of this his knife missed Dr. Lord, and he drove it through a red headline on an old issue of Cavalier. ("The Aztec Love Goddess Expedition to Hell.") He followed the knife down, and landed on the point of his chin, at the Doctor's feet. Blood from the man's nose flowed over a glossy picture of a naked blonde woman looking at us over her right shoulder from the balcony of an apartment in a place that seemed it might be south of L.A., along the coast somewhere. The woman had her hand under her breast, and she was holding it up, smiling, until the blood covered her face. Another man made a dive for the Doctor. But this second man also had his feet pulled out from under him by the frictionless texture of the covers of the pornographic (although, who can define pornography?) magazines.

As the second man went down, the Doctor reached down to the floor and picked up an electrical outlet, attached to a thick black wire. I could see it was attached at the other end to one of the large freezer-refrigerators, one that had a green glass bulb at the top, about the size of a basketball, glowing yellow-green, and having a sort of fluid consistency inside its surface. Then, pulling another wire from a place under the black table, the Doctor attached the two wires through a plug and socket mechanism. There was a small red button on the side of the plug end of the wire from under the table, and the Doctor put the side of his thumb alongside this red button. He called out, "Nurse Lilly, I cannot see you, but if you can hear my voice, respond please -" and Nurse Lilly, behind me now, and on the floor herself, gave forth with a muffled sound. The Doctor recognized it as her voice. He said, "I am forced to go to Plan B..." in a tentative, but loud way. The Doctor's attackers were struggling to regain their upright positions. Others stood by with sheepish expressions on their faces, some of them pushing the toes of their sneakers through the porno lilly-pads, looking for things to look at.

"I understand, Doctor," said Nurse Lilly. "It can't be helped."

"And, are you ready, Nurse Lilly?"

"Ready, Doctor - I remember every step - " said Nurse Lilly

And hearing that, Doctor Lord may have looked at me for the briefest of moments, or he may not have, but he looked around, the way men do in the movies when they are about to die. Then, raising his face to the ceiling, and saying, "I have done nothing to them," he pushed the side of his thumb upward until it was pressing flat down against the red button, and when it got to the position where you heard a tiny, tinny click, the lights went out. A moment later, the refrigerator with the green bulb at the top exploded.

Red, yellow, black, white. That's all I remember of the explosion, all I really noticed at the time... That, and the impression of compressed light, bursting around the outline of the refrigerator door. Then, the impact of something hard and wide across my chest. The force of this object, the identity of which I have never been able to learn, along with the expansion of the air in the room according to the laws of gases, threw me across the room, through the paper thin walls, into a blue bathroom with Spanish tiles on the walls in the shape of Aztec faces, with their tongues stuck out, and down. I was wedged into the sink, with my legs hanging over the edge. I still held the big ledger book in my hands. The force of the explosion had put a gash in its cover.

45

I got myself out of the sink, without letting go of the book. I stood, at first bracing myself against the sink to avoid falling. When I had the strength, I searched my body for injuries, and found none, except for a couple of tender spots, one in the center of my chest. Then, still holding the precious ledger, I exited the bathroom into the long corridor by which I had come to the refrigerator-room a few minutes earlier.

I looked into the refrigerator-room. The doctor's body was face-down on the floor, not moving. Nurse Lilly was swinging a broom at the men and women who filled the room, as she made her way through their dazed, or preoccupied forms. No one tried to stop her. They were like sleep-walkers in the dust. One man had a rolled up girlie magazine coming out of his mouth. The beautiful woman in the blue dress with the little flowers on it, sat up and wiped her forehead with her forearm. At first, I thought she wanted to fall back down to the softish surface of magazines spread out beneath her on the floor, but she shook her head and forced herself to stand up. She helped herself up with her hands.

She looked out through the back of the room, to an area of the back yard that was now covered with the debris of the room's wall, as well as thousands of pages of manila files, old photocopies of documents, black with white lettering, the still-ripe-looking pages of the magazines, an exploded chair, and two or three men's bodies, who may have been dead, I didn't know - and she evidently saw there what she was looking for.

"There it is!" she screamed, and staggered out through the hole in the Doctor's house, to the place where broken test tube glass was glinting in the moonlight, and the searchlights. Another woman saw where the woman in the blue dress was heading, and she took up the cry -- "There it is - the simmin -" she said - "The simmin's over here - " The younger women converged on the test tube fragments with a respectful but playful look in their eyes --

Some of the men were pointing at me. I could see them over the bent backs of the women. I turned and ran down the corridor, to escape.

The men didn't follow me. I had thought they would.

After a while, I turned and saw the yard scene from

a further distance. The women, crowding together, were trying to salvage what they could of the test tubes. They poured the contents of the broken test tubes into fruit and jelly jars that were brought to them by other women. The men were hanging back from the center of the action, passing a bottle of whiskey back and forth.

I crawled low up to the driver's side of my car, so as not to be seen, and opened the door and crawled like a snake into the seat. I threw the ledger onto the front seat, and put the key in the ignition from an angle I had never seen before. I pushed down on the gas pedal with my hand, and then with my knee, as I changed positions, and the car rolled away from the Doctor's house.

I was covered with white dust when I finally sat upright in the seat, and pulled the door closed, and drove normally onto another dark street, then another, then into the peaceful glow of Burbank Avenue - and there were lights in the Luther Burbank VFW - and there were clear lights all the way to Barham Boulevard, like the lights at a night ball game... I felt good... You'd think after the explosion, I might not have, but I did.

Chapter 6. My Uneventful Escape.

I drove directly back to Santa Monica, to my parents' condo, which I no longer thought of as my home, thanks to the pride that was in me. Possibly this pride is the legacy of my True Dad. Anyway, when I got to the condo building, I had to circle the block a couple of times, to find a parking space. About the second or third time around, I began to resent the fact that my "father," Mr. Stengrow, had never allotted me a parking space in our basement. He and my mother had their cars there, and there were two or three spaces available, because a couple of the condo owners were too old to drive, but my father had never thought it was worth paying the owners' association an extra hundred dollars a month so I could put my car somewhere secure and covered. Before I found a space, I realized I didn't want to go into our condo that night. I didn't want to see my parents, or tell them what had happened. I just wanted to be alone with the ledger book. So I drove down to the beach parking lot on Navy Street, and parked facing the ocean. There were some abandoned cars there, and some vans with people living in them. Also, one of those old Volkswagen buses with a mural painted on it, from which I could hear the sounds of old music.

I sat in my car, with the interior light on, and I looked at the book I had taken from Doctor Lord's house. It was the first chance I had had since the explosion.

The pages smelled old and had none of the sharp smell of new paper, but the smell of dark dirt mixed with sand, inhaled under the warm sun. I liked the smell. In between the first and second leaves of lined dried-out paper there was a photograph of a little blond girl, sitting in front of a snow-capped mountain, on a stone bench. On the back, it said "Connie." On the first page was written: "The Property of Dr. I. Lord," and then the Doctor's address, Burbank, California, U.S.A. And under that was the date: January - December, 1973. And under that were the words: "Record of Donors and Recipients." And under that were the words: "If Found, Please Lose."

The book was an alphabetical list of the names of men. Each man's name was at the top of a single page, written in ink, black or blue or green. Under the name was a record of the man's age, a brief physical description of the man - for example: "black hair, green eyes, 5'4", mesomorph -" followed by some phrase indicating the man's profession, field of study (or intended field), and an estimation (presumably by Dr. Lord himself) of this particular donor's level of intelligence. Level of genius, I should say, because none of the men in the book was said to be anything less than a genius, a master, a future pioneer, or something equally awe-inspiring, in his specific job or course of study.

Under these few sentences, most of the page would be empty, except for a series of dates: month-day-year, with each date followed by the letter "M" or the letter "F". Across the page from this brief entry, would be the name of a city and state, or in a few cases, a province in Canada. There was also a parenthetical underneath the city and state, which would say, "See Book A11," or "See Book V34."

I went through the book, page by page, and circled all the birth dates that were the same as mine. I went back again, and rechecked. I had them all. There were six. Then, I read the names of the donors who had donated the seed that had gone on to become those six births... Jonathan Elam, six foot two inches, blonde, slim; Business Administration - "Best mind for math I've seen since Canter..." David Peterson - even taller, at six three, but with red hair and kind of fat - a big fat physical engineer; Dwight Hoff - a squat, light NASA scientist; Abraham Steinstein; George Faroun (a strange notation appeared under his name. It said: "As for this Donor, I may have to apologize to someone at a later date - couldn't exclude George, owing to his rhetorical brilliance/ logic of his thought"); Michael Popper - about whom more later - the six. They, who might be my True Dad.

I sat in the car and studied their descriptions, matching my own qualities to those of my possible fathers. I had this one's height, that one's coloring, another one's interest in nothing in particular. It gave me pleasure to imagine that I was the son of each of them, first one, then the next, until I had imagined myself as the son of each one.

I had my hand on the open pages of the book. The interior light was still on in my car, but I didn't notice it, as I drifted off to sleep, thinking of scenes from several lives. All the lives were mine, but in each of them, I had a different family, and different surroundings. In each life I was happy in a different way. The words I said to others sounded the same, but they meant different things, because they were said in the six different worlds, to the faces that inhabited each one. All night, I dreamed of these worlds. I will not bother to describe the fragments I can still remember of these dreams, except to say that by the end of my long sleep, I was convinced that my father, for some reason, needed me to find him. I woke with a sense of urgency, as though I had been called by my mother, to wake up for a test at school. I knew that one of the worlds in my dream was incomplete because I was not yet in it. My head was on the back of the seat, and my neck felt broken. I heard the sharp sound of a knuckle on my window.

"I need I need I need a weed," said a grey, watery-eyed 40 to 50 year old man, when I rolled down the window. Then, he smiled at me. His teeth were broken. His lips were cracked and bleeding. He leaned in his brown overcoat on the door of my car. I got the pack of Marlboros out of my glove compartment that I kept in there for when I went to dances, and I needed something to hold onto as I tried to stand upright in a room full of women. I shook it out and gave him two cigarettes. He said, "Hoo! Two for the price of one," and kissed the two cigarettes, and winked at me, before pushing himself away from my car door, and heading toward the ocean. He lit one of the cigarettes with a plastic lighter, and inhaled it deeply. He coughed, over and over, and used the coughing to say a few words to someone who wasn't there, words bitter and long-suffering, as though this person who wasn't there had kicked him high on his back, and made his coughing jag start.

I slid lower in my seat, to give my head the support of the seat-back for a few seconds, so I could gradually bend my neck back into motion. Then, I got out of the car, got a bathing suit out of the trunk, and changed beside the car. I ran across the bike path, onto the sand, and ran diagonally toward the ocean, veering away from the ocean enough so I could run until my legs got tired.

I jumped into the ocean and swam for a few minutes. I laid out on the sand until I was dry. The sun by then was coming through the morning fog. I went back to the car, and got some money. I went to the Indian grocery a half a block inland, on Dudley Avenue, and got a container of milk and two cruellers. I was going back to the car, intending to drive to my home, so I could change my clothes and go to school. But when I got to Main Street I saw a metal newspaper machine with a picture of Dr. Lord looking at me from the top newspaper. The picture had been taken twenty years ago, according to the caption, but he looked exactly as he had the night before. I put a quarter into the vending machine, and despite my agitation, and the million images going off in my head, still had enough emotional energy in me to feel gratified when the rickety machine actually opened, and I was able to pull a paper out. Police were speculating, the paper said, that one of the doctor's experiments had led to the explosion at his home-and-lab. So far, the remains of seven people, all neighbors of Dr. Lord's, had been identified. Dr. Lord's body, and the body of Nurse Lilly, had not yet been positively identified, but the police were still sifting through the rubble and feared the worst.

I thought of the people I had seen the night before. The Doctor, Nurse Lilly, their neighbors. The newspaper referred to a "thin layer of broken glass" covering the area of the ruined house. A police lieutenant, interviewed for the article, complained that the neighbors seemed to know a lot more about the night of the explosion, and the goings-on in Dr. Lord's house, than they were letting on.

He also said investigators were looking for a young man who had been seen entering the Doctor's house a few minutes before the explosion, and who had been seen emerging from the black and red smoke, and running to a black Pontiac Le Mans with a white rag top. This individual was not a yet a suspect, said the lieutenant., but most certainly knew something about what had happened. Those same neighbors who had been so unhelpful about everything else in the investigation were more than willing to describe me and my car, (which descriptions, inaccurate and unflattering one and all, the lieutenant passed on to the reporter) and to ascribe to my face a "crazed look," and to talk about me in ways that would lead people to dislike and distrust me. I looked over my shoulder. I looked up and down the street. A man was walking into an alley, one half block to my north, and the side of his face was to me, but I had the feeling he had just been looking at me, and turned when I looked up from the paper. I realized I had to get out of L.A. I went back to my car, and read the rest of the article, as I drank my beverage. I continued reading the paper, to put off the necessity of serious thought.

Dr. Lord was called an eccentric scientist. He was said to be the heir to a huge fortune, left to him by his mother, who was a member of the royal family of an Eastern European nation (which shall remain nameless). The Lord family had escaped to Germany when the Communists took over their country. There were still, I read, many citizens and exiles of that country who looked to Dr. Lord's mother, and when she died, to Dr. Lord himself, as the only legitimate rulers of their nation. However, Dr. Lord had never shown much interest in politics, being obsessed with his scientific experiments, about which very little was known.

He had no survivors. When I read this, I wondered if I might consider myself a survivor of his. After all, I thought, staring at the lifeguard tower a hundred yards in front of my car, in a way, he had been my father.

But when I had that thought, it triggered once again in me the idea of finding my True Dad. I picked up the ledger book, which had fallen to the car rug. I put it on my lap, under the newspaper. I kept my right hand on the ledger, while my left hand rested on the newspaper, my arm and hand encircling from above the photo of the Doctor. I closed my eyes and said in a whisper, though there was no one near enough to hear, "Rest in peace, Dr. Lord. Thank you for bringing me into the world."

When I opened my eyes, I saw in the rear-view mirror that a police car was just entering the parking lot. It was moving slowly, past the few abandoned hulks of cars, past the vans and the painted bus. The cops were turning their heads as they passed each vehicle, to look into all the windows. I fumbled with the pages of the fat newspaper, attempting to fold them. Finally, I just shoved them onto the rug. I nervously ran my hand along the top cover of the ledger, pressing down on its pebble-like surface. The police car passed behind my car and the cop on the passenger side looked me over carefully. But the car didn't stop. It rolled slowly down to the far southern side of the lot, then back through, in front of the vans again, and then out onto Navy. They probably weren't looking for me on the Westside yet. Or, it occured to me, even if my description was given to them this morning, before they left the station house, and the description of my car, these cops might not connect me with the description, because they already knew me. They were the police of my neighborhood, after all, and had probably been watching me, around school, or around the bowling alley, or when I had my paper route, for the Outlook, for many years. So even though I hadn't recognized them, they might well have known who I was, someone who, once they saw him, merited no further thought. Still, I knew that one day, the police would stop me, and I would be taken in for questioning. After that, I might be arrested, for the murder of Doctor Lord, and Nurse Lilly, and the others. If that happened, I thought, my story would be in the newspapers, and everyone would know the story of my parentage. In order to protect my mother and father (Mr. Stengrow) I could not allow myself to be arrested. I knew I had to leave the city of my birth, that I had never left before, within a few minutes.

I went back to my parents' condo, and went in through the basement door to my room. I think they were asleep. Anyway, I didn't want to talk to them. I got some of my things together. I put some of the things in a nylon suitcase, some more in a duffel bag, which I used for laundry. This green duffel bag had been my father's during the Viet Nam war. I mean, it had been Mr. Stengrow's, and it had his name on the white address tag under the thick cellophane sheet. Even as I zipped it, to take it with me, I knew that in a way the thing I had loved most about this duffel bag, I had already lost, for all time. That connection I had felt, to the entire history of the world, through thoughts of my father in Viet Nam, in that losing war, and with his friends, performing that extreme act of citizenship - I had taken so much glory from the thoughts of his deeds, the deeds he did before I was born, the loyalty and courage he had shown. He

53

was my pride, and now my pride was gone. Instead, I could only lean on my own mediocre history of accomplishments. That army that had always stood behind me, and the armies behind that one, they were gone now. As I touched the duffel bag, I thought of all the things my father had done for me, the excuses he had made for me, the things he had paid for that defined me now, my education, even the straightness of my teeth. Still, I didn't want to talk to him or my mother, and I didn't want to see them before I left. I wanted to go out on my own, with the notebook I had found at Dr. Lord's house, and find my true father. After I did that, I thought, I would be able to return to the house of my parents.

How could I have been such a fool? Which chromosome on which strand of DNA, from which biological parent led me to be such a moron? Please step forward.

I decided to keep the name of Mr. Stengrow, and call myself Reynold Stengrow, as I had been called as long as I could remember, in honor of Mr. Stengrow. I was alive because of his sacrifice, and his efforts, and I knew that I had only reached the age of seventeen, because Mr. Stengrow had refrained from killing me. After all, he could have smothered me with a pillow when I was asleep. Either when I was an infant or more recently. He had known he wasn't my father, even if I had not. In that way, he had had the advantage over me year after year, but still, I was alive.

Before I left, I looked up at the ceiling of the basement, in my mind's eye seeing the floor of the upper rooms, to see my father, Mr. Stengrow, mentally, and I silently thanked him for letting me live and for feeding me, and for hiding his anger from me for all those years. Now, I knew I must find my True Dad, but that would only bring me closer to Mr. Stengrow, my false Dad, because I would be able to return, and need nothing from him (because I would have my True Dad, and my true identity, and I would be able to face him as an equal) and I would be able to deal with him in a more dignified, more loving way than had been possible up to now.

I thought of my mother. It was too painful. I wanted to see her before I left, but I did not dare. I kissed my hand, and travelled the ceiling with it, and said, "I love you, Mom." Then I took my radio and left.

I looked over my shoulder as I went back to my car, and looked at the old building. I didn't know how far away I would have to go or when I would be able to return there, so I stopped at the corner, and looked at the dew starting to bake off the old boards, the old lawn, and I listened to the sputtering of the electric wires that ran over our street.

I knew I should head out onto Wilshire, and then drive down to the Pacific Coast Highway, and start driving north or south, but first, I drove around past my old schools, and some of the streets where I used to play. Where I used to play with Heavy and Baker, when we used to skateboard from the Santa Monica Mall to the bluffs, up past San Vincente, and those low trees, rolling down the hill to the Pacific Coast Hwy in the pitch black four a.m. cold air.

Then, I drove to the ocean, and headed north. I had forty seven dollars and three cents. I had some clothes in the backpack which I had been using to carry my books to school for the past three years or so. I had my radio. I had my toothbrush. I'm just trying to be back there, and remember every detail, for the calories of warmth in every item, that it can still send to me, even at this great distance, even to the place where I am now. I had that plastic case for my student I.D., and library card, and social security card. I had a receipt from the purchase of my telescope. I did not have my telescope, nor have I ever bought another one - even when I started making money, that huge amount of money I was making from tricking the public, even then I didn't buy myself another telescope. I still say hello to the stars, but I do it from between the buildings, or under half-hiding branches out in the country, but I still say hello, and I still use the stars to travel through, into past times, and future times, as I always have done. I lie on the ground, and look at a star, and I imagine that the beam of my sight is bouncing off the star, like the path of the billiard shot, off the cushion, and it bounces into another time and another country, and I look down on scenes full of people I have never seen, wearing clothes unlike the clothes I have seen, in life or in pictures, and sometimes have watched these scenes until I fell asleep. But when I was fleeing, that morning, with the ocean speeding by beneath my left elbow, I didn't have time to think about the stars. And then, in later years, even after I became rich, the stars themselves, in some way that I couldn't describe, but had the sensation of, were telling me not to buy another telescope. I think they wanted to keep me at a distance.

Chapter 7. "French Fries on a Stove."

I drove up the coast, and then inland. I saw a sign that said Redbird, and another that said College Avenue. I had been thinking of applying to Redbird College, before my life had been so totally changed. I had been there for an interview with an Admissions Officer the year before. I thought it might be as good a place to hide as any other.

I soon found myself in front of the Administration Building at the center of the campus. It is the only really old building of the College. The other buildings are mostly yellow and white, covered in ceramic tiles, built in the early 1960's, but the Administration Building was originally built as a hotel, in the 19th century, when Redbird was a gold-mining boomtown. It is four stories high and covered with redwood siding.

I felt miserable, watching all the college students walking in and out of the building, and greeting one another beneath the leafy trees. I knew I would never be a part of their carefree world. I got out of my car and went into the building, where it was cool and smelled of sun-warmed floor wax.

I had to get a job, unless I wanted to become a panhandler. I also needed a place to stay, in Redbird. If I continued north, I would only reach a large city, and if I drove east, I would be in the desert. I liked the air in Redbird. It was small, so I felt I could handle it.

I saw a bulletin board, with jobs and apartments advertised on index cards. I wrote down the details and phone numbers for all of the jobs, and the cheapest apartments, or guest-rooms.

I went to the basement of the building, passing the students and teacher of a drama class on the stairway. They were coming up from the small theatre in the basement. There was an unguarded telephone, attached to the wall behind the stage, and I was able to make free calls to all the numbers I had copied onto my piece of paper.

Reasoning that I would not need a place to stay if I couldn't find a job here, I first called all the employment possibilities. A job at a copy shop - filled just that morning - a job at a pet grooming establishment, pizza delivery person, companion for an elderly invalid, tutor in tennis, salesman of magazine subscriptions, clerk in a comic book store - all of which were unavailable, for one reason or another. This left me with one remaining hope, the card that had said:

> YOUNG PERSON REQUIRED,
> LAB ASSISTANT
> FOR   IMPORTANT
> PSYCHOLOGICAL EXPERIMENT
> $6 PER HOUR
> CALL DR. CROSSE
> 396-1194 AFTER 6PM

I had four or five hours to 6 PM. I walked around the campus and the town. I could have gotten back in my car, and continued north, even leaving California, going through Oregon and Washington, escaping to Canada. But the beauty of the campus, the freshness of the air, and, to be perfectly honest about it, the loveliness of the female students, in their pleated skirts and fat white sneakers, or their torn jeans and thin t-shirts, made me want to be a part of the place, to be one of the men they knew by name, and spoke to. Does this mean that later, when I fell in love with Daphne, the moment I saw her, in her father's garden, I might have fallen in love with any female of approximately my age? I don't think so. It is just as possible that I had such a heightened appreciation of the beauty of women, on that particular day, because the Universe, (or Spirit of the Universe) was preparing me, gathering my attention in gradual pulling motions, to those emotions and thoughts whose only possible conclusion, I now have the perspective to realize, was my first sighting of Daphne. During that day, however, I only knew I didn't want to leave the town of Redbird.

I went to the small mall market and bought a carton of milk and a package of hamburger rolls. I parked the car on a dirt plateau in some canyon, got out and ate the rolls and drank the milk staring into the purple shadow growing over the canyon like a flood, and down toward the invisible sea. I got back in the car when I was through with my meal.

I went to the college research library and read until six. Then, I went to the front desk and asked the Librarian, a middle-aged man with a blue suit on, and a head of slick grey-yellow hair, to help me find a certain back issue of Telescope Monthly. When he went into the large room behind the Librarians' Area, where the back issues of magazines were kept, all on tan metal shelves, I carefully slid the telephone across the desk, until it and myself were out of sight of the Librarian. I called the number for Dr. Crosse.

"Hello," said the voice of a man with food in his mouth.

I said, "Hello. Is this Doctor Crosse?"

"It is," said the man with food in his mouth, and he went back to chewing.

I said, "I'm calling about the ad you had on the bulletin board in the Administration Building."

"What's your name?" he asked.

I had not remembered to supply myself with a false name, although it was obvious that sooner or later the police would connect me to the events at Dr. Lord's, and my own name would be useless to me.

Now, I said, "Elam," taking the name of one of the six men who might or might not turn out to be my biological father. "Jack Elam."

"Are you a Redbird student?" asked the man, and then evidently drank something from a wide-mouthed glass or pitcher, that hid most of his face from the mouthpiece of his phone.

"No, sir," I said.

"Well, do you live here in town?" asked Dr. Crosse.

"Actually, sir, I just got here. If I can find a job, I do plan to stay in the area. Yes, sir."

"Do you have a car?"

"Yes, sir."

He gave me directions to his house, amid the sounds of what may have been a vigorous after-dinner flossing.

I drove along a narrow road that ran around and around through the steep mountains. The sun was almost down, but it still flashed out at me from between cliffs, momentarily blinding me now and then. Finally, (after a hand-lettered sign on cardboard that I almost missed, that said, "public road ends, make u-turn at earliest convenience,") the public road ended at a set of high gates, made of white boards about two stories high, with wooden cutouts at the top of each gate. On the left gate was a cowboy, on a bucking bronco. On the right gate was an Indian, riding flat out on his pony, while holding an arrow high in one hand. Beyond the gates, the road continued, but it was no longer paved. It was made of white gravel, and grass grew through the stones in small clumps.

There was a metal post standing in the road, with a red box at the top of it. There was a white button and a speaker on the box. I pushed the button. I expected to hear a voice come through the speaker, but instead, the gates just swung back, slowly. When they were far enough apart, I drove through them. About a hundred yards up a winding road, past meadows where horses stood in the evening's colorless air, was a huge old ranch house - all white with a blue roof - and surrounded by barns and outbuildings, all painted the same white with the same blue roofs. It took a moment for me to realize that the rooftops were made of stainless steel. In the front yard, there was a neglected pond that seemed to have reddish-white hair over most of it's surface. Standing to the left of the pond was a tall pole with an American flag whipping softly in the wind.

Running the width of the front of the house was a wide porch, with several groups of furniture on it. I went up the four steps to the porch. I remember the triangle hanging from the porch roof, with the metal pipe hanging next to it. Pointed at the triangle from a few inches away was a video camera, that moved slowly from side to side, covering that part of the porch near the front door, and keeping an eye on the triangle, as though the ranch had been plagued by some criminal who liked to sneak up onto the porch and ring the triangle, summoning everyone to dinner.

I knocked on the door, and waited. I didn't know if I should try to look into the house through the narrow bands of clear glass around the ovals of frosted glass set in each of the double doors at approximately eye level. I thought it might be rude. On the other hand, it might be rude to stand back and spend my time swivelling to look at the mountains and meadows, beautiful as they might have been. I wanted to make a good first impression, because I wanted the job.

The door opened, with no tell-tale squeak or squeal. Standing there was a man of approximately, I didn't know - forty? fifty? He was about six foot one or two, or five foot eleven. He had thick brown hair with a good amount of gray in it. It was parted on the side and the front of it kept falling in front of his eyes, and he had to drag it back with his left hand, back to the top of his head, where it waved and wavered for a while before crashing back over his forehead to cover his eyes once again. His eyes were what you would have to call "merry," unless, under extreme torture by someone who denied your right to use that word, you were forced to choose an appropriate alternative and that would have to be "miserable." Many years later I was to realize that these eyes of merry misery are very often the result, or at least the sure sign, of a lifetime spent in the faithful service of Science. On that evening I just thought he had gotten dust in his eyes, or smoke from the cigar he held in his right hand.

"Jack Elam," he said. He transferred the four inches of cigar to his left hand and stuck out his right. We shook hands. "Yes, sir," I said.

"I'm Dr. Crosse," he said, and then his head tilted slightly to the left as he lifted one corner of his mouth in a self-deprecating manner, as though to say that all the wonderful things I had heard about him were not necessarily true. This had the effect of making me feel as though I had heard many praises of him, though I had never heard his name spoken before. He stood away from the door and ushered me into the house, saying, "Come on in, Jack. Let's shoot the shit."

I entered the house. It took a moment for my eyes to adjust to the darkness. Then I saw that we were going through a set of doubled-doors, with the Doctor's hand guiding me by the elbow, entering a cavernous living room. It had a floor made of one massive

61

stone. It was the weathered surface of a boulder or meteorite, that looked like it had been in the sun for thousands of years.

"Is that the floor?" I said. It made you feel like you wanted to reach down and touch it. Actually, I was feeling bad, because I thought that someone had sliced the top off of a magnificent boulder, probably somewhere in Africa, to bring its smoothe lid all the way over to California, to be the floor in this rich doctor's house.

He stopped, took his hand from my elbow, and held it poised over the floor like the hand of an angel in an Italian painting. He said, "The house was built directly on the existing rock. My father never let anyone so much as put a nail in this rock. When he was building this place, the contractor told him, 'Dr. Crosse, at least let me put grooves in the rock, to anchor the timbers.' But my father told him to lay the timbers loose on the existing contour, and fill the spaces with mud."

Dr. Crosse bent down and ran his hands over the smoothe rock, just as I had wanted to do. "Feel how cool it is," he said. I bent and touched the rock. It was like a rock in the middle of a flowing stream. Like glass, but secure, glass you can lean on.

Now, I felt differently about it. Better, because the rock had not been disturbed and brought here from somewhere else. But also, worse, because I felt I was standing on the head of a giant. As I scanned the surface around me, it was like the forehead and brows of an elephant, and the groups of furniture around the room were like tufts of hair coming out of the elephant's head. I wasn't sure I was standing in a place that might not uncomfortably touch on a nerve or soft spot in the brain of that gigantic elephant on whose top surface we were walking.

There were slight hills and valleys in the floor, and the red Turkish rugs that were laid down here and there, making a path into and through the living room, were allowed to lie unflat, following the curvature of the floors, even if their corners stuck up into the air, or they were permanently creased by the positions they had to assume. There were groupings of furniture in four separate places in the living room, each with its own fireplace and television set, making the place look like the lobby of a hotel. We went to the dining room, with its long window looking out on a garden. I could see through the window that the contour of the rock continued a few feet beyond the house. After that, grass grew, and in the grassy area was a small vegetable garden, marked out with wooden stakes.

I saw a blur of motion in the garden, as someone turned and went out of sight, behind a tree. All I could see of the person who had been there was the heel of her foot, and the back of her ankle. "My daughter," said Dr. Crosse, with a movement toward the window through which we had both perceived that golden blur, as though he was introducing us. Then, he went to the side wall, to a table covered with plates, silverware and silver-topped serving dishes. He lifted one of the silver tops and laid it on its back on the white tablecloth. He spooned some huevos rancheros onto a plate, told me to get some for myself, and sat down at the table to eat. I went to the serving table and took some eggs. I sat down to the Doctor's right, facing the window. I dug into the food.

The Doc chewed on a tortilla covered with hot sauce for a while, then took a swallow of beer.

He said, "I was expecting to hire a psych major."

I sat there. He said, "You have to live here. You have your own car, which is good, but you'd still have to be here 24 hours, six days a week."

"What is the job, exactly? It said 'assistant'."

He said I would have to help him with his experiments, when he was too busy with teaching, or with his other experiments. He said he was almost continually running tests on various subjects, to test aspects of the human mind. "You might be able to pick up some extra cash acting as a subject now and then," he said with a hopeful smile.

"What kind of experiments are they?" I asked, employing my own interpretation of a hopeful smile.

"All kinds," said Dr. Crosse, swallowing about half his glass of beer. "You'll see one tonight.

"Most of the time, I'll expect you to help around the house, the yard. Shopping. My daughter has all her schooling here at the ranch, and one or two of her tutors don't drive, so you'll have to pick them up at the bus stop on Ocean, bring em back there. Do you cook?"

"No, sir," I said.

"We have a cook, Maria, but she's off two days a week."

"I can make french fries on a stove," I suddenly remembered.

"The job is yours, if you want it," said Doctor Crosse.

At this moment, there was a knock on the door. The Doctor called out, 'Come on in!' then stood up and walked toward the front door, shouting again. The door opened, and a group of men came in. Five or six. Surrounding a tall quiet woman with black hair, and a scarf over her head. One of the scientists stood at either side of her, holding her arms. Dr. Crosse greeted the woman, Mrs. Welby, and asked if she was feeling better. She smiled, very exhausted, and said she felt a lot more relaxed. Dr. Crosse said, "Who knows? If all goes well tonight, we might be able to take you off drugs entirely,"

"I hope so," said Mrs. Welby. Dr. Crosse patted her on the back. He said, "First, everybody eat. Then, we'll go out there."

All of the scientists, and Mrs. Welby, ate in impromptu groupings around the table. Then, we all went out the kitchen door, to what looked like a barn.

Inside, the former barn had been refurbished as a modern, steel and formica laboratory, with an acoustical ceiling and walls panelled in golden wood. The room was divided into two halves, by a wall of glass. We all sat on folding chairs. Dr. Crosse told me that we could see through the glass, but the subject, on the other side, could not see us. As he said this, the light went on in the other half of the room, which had been dark up to now, and Mrs. Welby was sitting there, in the middle of that part of the room, with two wires coming out of the top of her head. Her hands were folded in her lap, her legs were set solidly on the floor. On our side of the glass wall, one of the scientists, (*NOTE: I will not here reveal the identities of the other men who were engaged, along with Dr. Crosse, in these scientific studies. They have not done anything wrong - if, in fact, anyone has, even Dr. Crosse, even me - but they would certainly be embarrassed to be mentioned in these memoirs, without the opportunity to tell their stories, each in his own way, in his own time. However, to assure myself that somewhere there would be an accurate history of the ranch, these names are all mentioned, in documents deposited by me with a law firm in New York, to be*

opened and made public no sooner than 30 years after my death),
the scientist who had thought of this experiment, sat at a small table
set right against the glass wall. He fiddled with a set of dials, and
tabs that he moved up and down the table. He looked at Mrs. Welby
and gave her the OK sign. She gave him the thumbs up.

Dr. Crosse turned to me and said, "Mrs. Welby fell off a
horse eighteen months ago.   Since then, she has been depressed.
Tried to kill herself twice. Responds to medication but complains
she isn't herself any more. The tranquilizers make her tired all the
time, she can't relate to her husband and kids. Her husband agrees.
Dr. --------- here (the scientist at the table), one of the most brilliant
students of the great Dr. Jose Delgado, out of Madrid, wondered if a
variation on Delgado's implanted electrode technique might give Mrs.
Welby a better way to control her moods than by using drugs."

Dr. Crosse went to a drawing on a blackboard, a drawing of
a brain, with two wires sticking out of it. The wires came together in
a little housing, that looked like a bullet, and that was stuck into the
center of the brain.   "An electric current, sent through the wires,
through the electrode, to the right spot in the medulla, should
brighten anybody's day," said Dr. Crosse, to me, because everyone
else in the room already knew it. "The problem is, everyone's spot is
in a slightly different locale, and responds to a different wattage, and
more or less slips around so you don't really know when you've got it,
if I'm not getting it too far wrong, am I, Ernesto (not the real first
name of the scientist at the control panel)?"

"Si, senor," said Ernesto.

Dr. Crosse said, "So Ernesto is going to be searching for that
spot in the brain of Mrs. Welby, in the hopes we can one day give her
a little button to push whenever she feels down, and it will cheer her
up." All the other men nodded at Dr. Crosse's back. "But first," said
the Doctor, I'd like you to show this young man the phenomenon we
observed last week, Ernesto."

"But Doctor Crosse," said the man at the control panel,
"would that really be fair to Mrs. Welby?"

"Of course it would!" Crosse said, swiping backward to
punch the blackboard as he spoke, "She's a member of the human
race, isn't she? She's a citizen of the twentieth century, isn't she?

She's already got the hole in the top of her cranium, and the wire in place, hasn't she?"

"But she is a patient of mine, Dr. Crosse. She has consented to an experimental procedure for one reason only, to improve her health. The, the display, you ask for - that has no bearing on her emotional condition whatsoever."

"Look, Ernesto," said Dr. Crosse, sitting down, and settling back in one of the folding chairs, "I'm sure Mrs. Welby would be thrilled to participate in a harmless demonstration to a gathering of esteemed scientists, and would give her consent in a flash if she knew about it."

"Which she doesn't."

"Which is what makes it an experiment," said Dr. Crosse. "That, and the fact that all of her responses will be recorded by that camera over there, and those heat meters over there, and the computer under that knotty pine table over there, all paid for by me, I hate to mention."

Ernesto shrugged, and hung his head over his controls and jiggled on one of the wheels. He said into a microphone on the table, "Injection number one." He then gave the date and the time, and the strength of the shot, and the direction, given in map co-ordinates. Finally, he gave a number indicating the depth at which the injection had been fired into the brain, measuring in centimeters from the top of the brain.

A split second after he said "injection number one," Mrs. Welby turned around in her seat, and looked behind her, over her left shoulder. After a moment or two, she turned again, to her original position, seated squarely on the seat, facing forward.

Ernesto, speaking to me, because of the way he had seen Dr. Crosse speak to me, explained, "When I throw this switch, she can hear what we say in here. Up to now, she has not heard a word." Then, he threw the switch, and said into the mike, "Mrs. Welby, why did you turn around?"

She thought, and then said, "I felt a draft behind me."

Ernesto said, "You could have said something to me, if it was bothering you."

"No," she said, "it really wasn't important. When I turned around, I saw the door was closed, and I didn't feel it any more, so I didn't say anything."

Ernesto threw the switch controlling the loudspeakers, so she couldn't hear him, and said "Injection number two." Again, after he sent the current through her, she turned around in her seat, and faced the back of the room. A second later, she turned to face forward again.

Ernesto asked her, "Why did you turn around, Mrs. Welby?" She answered, "I thought I heard someone calling my name."

A few seconds later, Ernesto shot her another jolt, and once again she turned in her seat, making almost exactly the same motion for the third time, not too rapid, very little expression on her face. Over and over he did it. Every time she would turn around. Every time, he would ask her why she had turned around. Every time, she had a reason. Every time she gave a reason, it was a different reason.

The current was the same strength, it went to the same spot in her brain, and stimulated that spot in the same way, every time. Therefore, she turned around in her seat, every time. So far, so good. But the amazing thing is that when you asked her, a few seconds after she turned around, <u>why</u> she made that motion, she had a completely reasonable explanation for what she did. She heard her cat... she thought something fell off a shelf behind her... she thought there was a clock back there (there wasn't) and she wanted to know the time... her neck was stiff and she wanted to stretch it... she was doing a yoga position she had been taught twenty eight years ago in South Carolina... the list was infinite. She always had another thing she had heard, or another notion she had gotten in her head, to explain that one motion, turning in her seat. A motion which we all knew had been caused by a shot of electricity.

Ernesto shot Mrs. Welby with fifty-eight jolts of electricity during this demonstration, in the space of about one hour and ten minutes. After the first four or five times, there was a short space in there when I thought it was funny, and I wanted to laugh, but I didn't. Then, after the twentieth time or so, I didn't want to laugh any more.

I didn't feel comfortable, seeing what I was seeing. The way Mrs. Welby turned every time, so simple and natural. That was the weirdest thing about it. And the way she answered when Ernesto asked her to explain why she had turned around. Again, natural and simple. She never even remembered all the other times she had turned around. She never even said, "Gee, it looks as though I've been doing quite a bit of turning around here tonight." No, because every time, her mind supplied her with a reason, a cogent, logical reason, for what she had done.

"There's the rub, boys," said Dr. Crosse, when he had told Ernesto he could stop what he was doing, and recalibrate the electrode for the original medical purpose for which Mrs. Welby had thought she was here - that is, to make her more cheerful - and while Ernesto was doing that, Dr. Crosse and the others were discussing what we had all just seen. "There's the rub. When we shoot her with the jolt, and she turns around - fine. We're scientists and she's a subject, and fine. But it's after that, when we ask her why she turned around, and she gives us a reason. That reason is a *mem*ory, of something that preceded her turning around, something that preceded the jolt, but something that never happened. You get a stimulus you don't feel, (which is the case with a brain implant - there is no feeling in the brain at all) and since you didn't feel the stimulus, your mind comes up with something else, to explain to itself what you have just done. And you have to admit, when you hear the reasons, one after another, supplied by Mrs. Welby to explain her turning around, that our minds are no different from hers, when we think of any event in the past - even the most recent past - even ten seconds ago - and try to remember what made us do such and such a thing. Like Mrs. Welby, we may just as easily be making it up, so we can explain our actions to ourselves. In other words, we are separated at all times from the past by a solid wall of ignorance. There is, in fact, nothing I can say with certainty about any moment of my life before this very present one in which I am now speaking. I may remember that eight seconds ago I was also speaking, but how does that differ from Mrs. Welby's recollection of all 72 of the things that never happened, each one of which she remembers with utter clarity, that caused her to turn around in her seat?

"We are in a state of exile from our own past. Always. Every moment sends us once again into exile, and blocks the way back, and we can never again see clearly the place we have just been thrown out of. And this is done with the active participation of our own brains, the gatekeepers that keep us out."

After this, Ernesto was ready with the controls, and we watched for a while as he tried to find the pleasure center, or the optimism center, or whatever it is, in Mrs. Welby's brain. That night, he never found it. But I wasn't really paying attention, anyway. I was thinking about the demonstration, the turning around. I was trying to think of a way to catch the past, so I would be sure my memories were accurate, and not lies told to me by my confused or conspiring brain. And wondering, if the things I remember from a few seconds ago are so susceptible to being total fabrications, what is *not* susceptible to being a total fabrication? What I see and hear? Ha! What I believe with all my heart? Double ha!

After the other scientists and Mrs. Welby had gone, Dr. Crosse asked me where I was staying in town. I told him I had been planning to sleep in the car, or on the beach. He took me to a room in the main house, and said it was mine. He said I would get two hundred dollars a week, which I thought was very generous, and he took a wad of bills out of his side pocket and peeled off three hundreds and two fifties. He said it was an advance. He said he would tell me more about the various jobs he needed done, tomorrow.

I liked the room, which had a picture of an Indian family in front of their tee-pee on one wall, and a lamp with a spinning shade, with a picture of a train on it, and the headlight and smoke from the engine kept moving all night, giving the room a good feeling. Still, I slept in my clothes, in response to the flood of new impressions that had washed over me since I had left my parents' condo in Santa Monica. No, since before then - since I had learned the terrible secret of my birth.

In a way I could not explain, Mrs. Welby and myself were the same.

I dreamt of a garden, where I was walking naked, listening to a disembodied voice. The voice came through the branches of the trees, from high above my head. The path was deeply shaded, and my footsteps gobbled it up at an incredible rate of speed. I came down to a lake, and stood knee-high in one of the side-pools. I was trying to catch frogs. They popped out of the water, over my outstretched hands, and back into the water, on the other side of me. I couldn't catch one. They bounced around in all directions, even landing on the top of my head, or resting for a moment on my shoulders, but I couldn't get my hands around fast enough even to touch one. I got very tired, and I fell into the water. I was sitting in the mud, but my back still hurt, because I had to stretch in every direction, after the frogs. I didn't give up, until the sun was completely down, and far away the screen of a drive-in theatre suddenly lit up the sky. Then (I think) I forgot the frogs, and the rest of the dream was the movie on that screen. In it, I met Dr. Lord, and he took me to see my True Dad, who looked a lot like the father on "My Three Sons." When we shook hands, I saw that we were on a platform, overlooking a city park, and millions were watching us, cheering.

Chapter 8. Embeds.

In the morning, I changed into my other clothes, which I got from the duffel bag. I went downstairs to the big dining room, and had eggs and waffles from under the silver lids. No one else was there. It was about six a.m. I found a note from Dr. Crosse. "Elam - eat breakfast, then mow the lawn down by the front gate."

I got the mower from the garage. A guy named Raphael showed me how to drive it. He said he was from El Salvador. He told me how to lower the blades, and how to follow the curve of the hillsides. I drove down to the front gate and was mowing happily until I saw a police car on the road. It seemed to be skulking around the sides of the hills, about five miles away, coming slowly. I thought they were looking for me.

I turned the mower and drove it back up the hill, away from the gate. I remembered too late that I had left the blades down, and I looked behind me and saw I had mowed a straight swath across the decades-old pattern of the hilly lawn. My destination was a stone wall that enclosed the back and one side of the house. I drove the mower out of sight of the road, behind the wall. I parked under an African pepper tree, and stood on the seat in order to raise myself up to the top of the wall. I wanted to be able to see the road, the front gates, and the path leading to the house, without being seen. I lay down flat on the grey slabs of granite stone. The police car came right up to the front gates of the ranch, but then used the turn-around, and headed back the way it had come, going just as slowly.

Relieved, I raised myself up to a slightly more comfortable position, resting on my elbows, and turned to look into the enclosure.

I saw that it was the same area I had seen the evening before, through the dining room window. Through the branches of a tree that stood beside the wall, I could see the small vegetable garden. The marking stakes and mesh fences glittered in the sunlight. Then I saw a flash of gold through some other branches, and realized there was someone sitting at the edge of the vegetable garden, at a filligreed white-metal table. The gold was her hair. I saw the heels of her feet as they bounced up and down in a rapid, concentrated rhythm under the cast-iron bench on which she sat. One of them was the same as the heel I had seen on the previous evening, which Dr. Crosse had said belonged to his daughter, Daphne.

The police were gone, and I knew I should climb back onto the mower, but I wanted to see the face of this girl. I crawled forward along the wall. Her hair was long, and spread over her shoulders, so I had further to crawl than I   might have if she had worn her hair in a bun, or if it had been cut short. Soon, however, I saw the first suggestion of the outline of the side of her face. It was still mostly hidden by the branches of the tree, and the stray strands of her hair, but already I could see how beautiful she was.   "The future Mrs. Stengrow," I said to the back of my hand.

Her long lashes, the quiet, studious set of her back, the way her lips moved, mumbling something I could not hear, all these conspired to hypnotize me, and draw me closer, closer along the wall, until I was almost to the point where if I had gone another inch she would have seen me in the corner of her eye. There, I stopped, and re-focused my eyes, to see what she was doing.

She was writing. No, she was etching something onto a thick sheet of glass, using an implement that was shaped like a fountain pen, but made out of soft lead. Instead of an ink-producing point, it had a sharp needle at the end. It scratched the glass, making a sound like tires crunching over gravel, and leaving piles of dust, which she bent now and then to blow away, then resuming her murmuring. It looked like she was speaking to the glass.

Seeing the concentration on her face, and in her every motion, I thought it might be safe to move myself forward a few inches, and then raise myself from the waist like a failed push-up, to see between her shoulder and the soft swell of her dumpling-like cheek, what she was etching onto the sheet of glass.

At first, though the sheet faced me directly, and I could see at least half of it, the light was wrong, and the glass just looked like a rectangle of black and silver mercury. However, as she ran her long, tapered forefinger (with a delicate scar on the first joint) from left to right along the surface of the heavy glass, I followed the finger with my eyes. As it moved, it changed the level of light that fell on the glass, and in the moving shadow of her finger, I could see, for the first time, that she was writing words in the glass. The words were arranged in lines, but the lines weren't straight. They went up and down like gentle hills. Also, the words were of different sizes, some huge, some tiny, some words written through the holes in the letters of larger words. As I saw the words, I realized for the first time what I had been hearing, almost, in the air coming through her lips. She was reading the words as she wrote them.

I hesitate to mention the words she was writing, but for the purposes of this narrative, I must. She was writing, and saying aloud, the words *fuck, prick, cunt, shit, cock, asshole, death, cancer, suicide,* and *murder,* in an unbroken sequence, rising and falling across the page of glass, never in the same order, and at the same time saying to herself, "Fuck shit fuck fuck cock cunt asshole fuck death cancer fuck death shit murder fuck," and so on.

"Fuck, fuck, sex, fuck, prick," all in gentle hills of writing, line upon line on the glass. The same words emanating from her pink lips. The tip of her tongue coming out to sit on the corner of her lips. I stared at her. Somehow, my hand slipped over the edge of the granite wall, and I fell into the enclosure. On the way to the ground, I went through some branches, which cut my face, and I was slapped by the leaves. I landed on my hands and knees, but my elbow buckled, and I fell further, until my left cheek was against the ground, and my mouth was filled with dust.

The beautiful future Mrs. Stengrow turned, and screamed when she saw her future groom. She stood up, and the sheet of glass slid off her knees, and off the edge of the table, where its top third had been resting, and glided to the used brick patio, making a clinking sound, followed by a moment of silent indecision, followed by a resounding, cavernous sound of shattering, as it fell full on its back on the bricks. She turned from me to the glass sheet, and surveyed the damage. She sighed in a helpless manner. I raised my head, wiped the mud off my cheek, and said, "I'm sorry. I was... I fell..." I said, giving nothing away.

"What were you doing there?"

"Well, I was, the mower... and then I, I saw something, cleaning, something that needed cleaning in the tree, so I had to get up on the, so I..." I stood up, and checked my clothes for tears and rips.

A woman in a light blue uniform, like a maid or nurse, appeared at the long dining room window, saw me in the garden, and put her hand over her mouth. "It's all right, Maria," said Daphne. "Everything's fine."

Maria disappeared, not seeming satisfied.

I felt I should climb back over the wall, but I couldn't stand to leave the presence of this angelic person, so I took a step or two toward her, attempting to magnify the extent of my injuries by limping as seriously as I thought might be believable, considering the height of the wall. I hobbled forward, and bent down to pick up the pieces of the glass. I held one large piece at arm's length, and read it, and acted as though this was the first time I had known what she was writing on the glass. I silently mouthed a series of the words before my eyes: fuck fuck shit fuck cunt shit fuck. "Well," I said, "I've had days like that myself."

She laughed and her eyes twinkled. "That's not the way I feel."

"What is it, then?" I stacked the broken pieces of glass one on top of the other and put the biggest pieces on the table.

"It's an embed," she said.

"An embed?"

"For an experiment of my father's. Oh, by the way, I'm Daphne Crosse." We shook hands. Hers was cool and soft. A few stones that had been imbedded in my palm, and the heel of my hand, fell out.

"I'm Jack Elam," I said. "Your father hired me."

"I know," she said, "I saw you yesterday, when you got here."

I must have been looking at her too intensely, because she turned her gaze from mine, and looked down at the pieces of glass. "This was an embed for hair," she said.

I looked at the words on the shards, over which she was then sliding the tips of some of her fingers. I looked at her hair. I didn't understand what she was talking about. I said, "I don't understand one word of what you just said." I was looking at the side of her throat where it disappeared behind the rolled collar of her pink cashmere sweater. She smelled like the earth after the rain.

"It's called 'subliminal marking,'" she said. "My Dad has a grant to see if you print these words on top of a picture in a magazine, will more people buy the magazine. At least, I think that's what he said." She shrugged, and shook her head as though to show that her head was filled with something filling and numbing, and that therefore she was not the person to ask about complicated matters like her father's experiments. But I wanted to know more.

"You mean," I ventured, "I'll start to see magazines on the newsstand with... with these words... written all over the covers?"

She laughed, and said, "No no no. They print the letters very lightly, so you *can't* see them. Or else it wouldn't work. That's why I write on glass, so they can put the glass on top of the pictures, and then take one picture of the two things together."

"I still don't get it. If you don't see the words, you don't see the words. It's the same as if they weren't there. What good does that do?"

"Well," she said, "that's the experiment. My Dad wants to find out, if these words are all over the picture, but you can't see them, but they're really there, does your *mind* see them? And if it does, will that cause you to act differently than if the words weren't there. Like, would you be more likely to buy the magazine? Less likely? Whatever."

I was beginning to get the idea.

"Like," she said, "You'll have a picture of a girl or a guy with a big wad of dark hair, right?"

"Right."

"And a plate of glass goes over the hair, when they duplicate it for the magazine. A hair embed. This - " she pulled another plate of

75

glass to her, from across the wrought iron table - " - is a flesh embed. It's for naked arms and legs - see? The words are bigger, and I etch them lighter because they would be too easy to see if I didn't."

I could read the words in the shadow of her breast. It showed the same relentless string of obscene words as the other plate of glass had shown. Fuck and shit climbing hills and sliding down into the valleys, line after line.

She said, "Actually, it was my idea to use different size words for hair and skin. My Dad was real proud of me."

I touched the glass, putting my hand near hers.

"I also have a different style for the folds of dresses and shirts and stuff."

I touched her hand. She pulled it away, but only after a third of a second of stillness.

"These words, " I said. "Does it ever bother you?"

"What?" She looked at me. I felt warm. Her eyes were light blue, her eyebrows and hair were yellow and red. Her lips, after her pink tongue had travelled through them and back into her mouth, were glossy and pink. Her father, she later told me, would not allow her to wear lipstick.

I cleared my throat in order to start time moving again, and said, "Does it ever embarrass you to write all of these dirty words?"

For a moment, her expression was frozen. Then, her cheeks became pink and her eyes welled up with water, and her lips opened slightly. "This is science," Daphne said.

I realized at once how disgusting I had been, to say such a thing, to bring the attitudes and thoughts of the locker-room into a matter of science. I felt ashamed.

I said. "I'm sorry, I didn't mean to upset you. "

"Oh no, " said Daphne, lowering her gaze and smiling at the floor, "I just forgot how these words seem to most people."

"Seeing your lovely hand, writing those words - your mouth," I said, not sure where I was heading with this line of thought - whether toward a sad tone of voice, or a hope-charged trailing-off of talking. I noticed that we were standing very close to one another. I sent my hand forward once again, to find hers, below the level of my sight. We were looking each other in the eye when my hand found hers. I grabbed it, and she didn't move. I heard a motion several yards behind her, and shifted my focus, to see her father, Dr. Crosse, coming through the dining room, into the garden. He wore a tan-colored cowboy hat that shaded most of his face, but I could see the grim look on his face. In his right hand, he carried a long-barrelled nickel-plated revolver. He raised the gun to shoulder level, pointing it at my head. He said, "Stand away from him, Daphne."

She reversed our hands, so that hers now was clasping onto mine. With her other hand, she grabbed my shirt, and stood closer to me. She said, "It's all right, Daddy. I just yelled because I was surprised. That's what Maria heard. I told her there was no problem."

"I was working on the tree, and I fell into the garden, sir," I said. "I'm sorry."

"Stand away," he said to his daughter. To me, he said, "You weren't working on any tree." To his daughter he said, "Put an arm's length between you and him, or I'll shoot him right now. You know I won't miss." I felt her release the grip of her hand on my shirt, and the energy went out of her body. She moved away from me, looking at the ground.

Chapter 9.
I Am Offered a More Important Job.

Dr. Crosse held the gun on me, as I led the way into his study. Daphne walked behind him. He said, "I'm sorry to treat you this way, Jack, but I have to ask you a couple of questions so we can see where we're at here and what's what." He told me to sit in one of the leather armchairs. Daphne stood at the door. Dr. Crosse set one haunch on the edge of his desk, and now held the gun on me more casually.

"Maria came in here and told me there was a murderer in the garden with my daughter. She saw your picture on TV, son."

To his daughter he said, "His name's not even Jack Elam."

Daphne looked at me. I couldn't tell whether she was disappointed in me. I said to Dr. Crosse, "Sir, I am the one they're looking for, but I didn't do anything. I was just there, and that place blew up. I didn't kill anyone, I swear it!"

"What were you doing there?" he asked me.

I found that to explain, I had to tell Dr. Crosse and Daphne the whole story of my life, from the night I beat my father at cards, and discovered the true story of my origins.

I told them that I had gone to Dr. Lord's simply to find out the identity of my biological father, had been caught up in a neighborhood riot that had probably been building up over a period of many years, and now suspected I had been falsely accused by the very neighborhood people who had perpetrated the riot, in order to cover up their own activities of that night, and even more probably, to avoid having to answer any questions about what had happened to the thousands of test tubes filled with the semen of American geniuses. I told them how I had escaped, and the scene of pandemonium that existed at the time. I told them about the ledger book. I told them I planned to find my biological father.

Dr. Crosse put the gun down, soon after I mentioned the name of Dr. Lord. At that time, he completely relaxed, and rubbed his temples with his thumb and fingers, his hand spread across his forehead. He massaged his eyes. He sat down in the other leather chair in the visitors' section of the study, and nodded knowingly at many of the things I said. However, he let me finish my story, and only when I was silent, waiting for his response, did he say, "As a matter of fact, Dr. Lord was a very good friend of mine. A mentor, really." He paused. "Everything you say rings true," he said. "I knew of his experiments years ago, at Berkeley. Before he was forced to resign. Very controversial back then. Not just the in vitro fertilization, it was the eugenics, the fascist overtones. Breeding for intelligence! Of course, there were rumors he carried on, even after he lost his university affiliation, but he kind of dropped out of sight. None of the journals would publish his stuff. I must admit, even I stopped thinking about him... So *you're* a product of that experiment! What do you know! I feel honored!"

He got up and came over and shook my hand. He said, "Don't worry. I'll tell Maria she was mistaken. You can stay here as long as you like."

"I don't know if she'll believe you," I said.

"Trust me. She's illegal. The last thing she wants is to see or speak to any representatives of any law enforcement organization."

Dr. Crosse continued, "In a while, they'll find out what happened at Lord's place, and you'll be in the clear. Until then, I have a proposition to put to you."

He went around to the other side of his desk and sat in his swivel chair. "But first, what is your real name?"

"Reynold Stengrow," I said. "Stengrow is the name of the man who raised me."

Crosse said, "Reynold, I have to ask you a couple of questions. First: what were you doing on top of that wall? Were you looking for my daughter?"

I told him about the police car.

He said, "OK, so then you were on the wall, and what? You saw Daphne making her embeds? Or you heard her?"

I didn't really remember which had come first, so I hesitated. He said, "Come on, Reynold, no need to be shy. We're scientists here."

So I told him the truth, which is that, after all that had happened, I couldn't really be sure if the murmur of her voice, or the vision of her sitting there, deep in concentrated work, had been my first contact with his daughter. I said, "The way she was speaking - now that I think of it - I might have started hearing her voice before I saw her, and actually before I realized I was hearing a human voice, or even hearing anything at all."

To my surprise, this answer seemed to be the very answer Dr. Crosse was looking for. He raised his cowboy hat off his head high in the air with his right hand and shouted, "Yee-ha!" then he said to his daughter, "What did I tell you, Daff? Subliminal!" Then, to me he said, "And it was the low sound, the unclear words, the sense that you were missing something of importance that drew you along, wasn't it? That kept you on that wall even after the police car was gone, and you knew you should have climbed back on to your mower and gone back down that hill. Am I right?"

I didn't know what to say, but he didn't seem to need me any more, to answer the questions he asked me. "It works!" he said to Daphne. She smiled weakly.

"You saw the words on the glass, then, didn't you?" he asked me.

Then, he answered, before I could, "Yes! At first, you didn't know what you were seeing. Was your mind playing tricks on you? What was the force drawing you forward? Maybe the sun was playing tricks on your eyes, as it bounced against the glass plate. You had to know. You had to know. Before you even knew what it was you had to know, you were compelled to read, and hear, the words.! Right?" I nodded. "See!?" he said to Daphne, and she nodded, too.

At this point, Dr. Crosse explained to me the theory of subliminal messages. Telling me, in more technical terms, what Daphne had already told me. While the conscious part of your brain doesn't even know it saw the words, "fuck, cock cunt shit" written subtly over some news photo, the sub-conscious part of your mind does know it.

I liked Dr. Crosse. I appreciated the fact that he had put down his gun, and even more, that he had offered me sanctuary, but I must admit, at first I had my doubts about these experiments in the world of subliminal messages.

Daphne went to the kitchen to re-assure Maria and some other people who were evidently out there, and to get us some snacks.

Dr. Crosse said, "If our preliminary tests are any indication, subliminal images are going to be a big, big part of life in this world for the next several centuries." He sighed, as though he had reached the end of a big desert, and found himself a spot of shade.

Why was he smiling so happily? Was it only the understandable pleasure and relief we find at successfully explaining something new to someone who seems to care? Or was he envisioning on the screen of his thoughts a world filled with subliminal fucks and sexs, and the rest of that titillating troupe?

This made me ask Dr. Crosse: "Why these words in particular? I mean, if you want someone to buy a magazine, wouldn't the words "buy me," or "get this," or "you'll love this magazine," written in this same half-invisible way work better than..." and I didn't want to finish my sentence, because Daphne was in the room. Dr. Crosse knew what I meant, though, and he answered:

"Fuck and dick and cunt and sex and cock and death and suicide and cancer are the powerhouse words. We've tried all kinds of other things - but these are the "big triggers," I call em. For one thing, less guilt-laden words don't seem to hide as well as the big triggers. The word "love," written just as lightly, sitting in just the same clump of hair or hidden in the same sweater weave as the word "sex" will be spotted by the casual observer more than twenty times as readily. It seems the big triggers are the words we all have a lot of conflicting feelings about, a lot of things we'd rather not think about mixed with a lot of things we can't stop thinking about. That's what makes a good subliminal. But we're always looking for new ones. This is a virgin field, Reynold. Any and all suggestions cheerfully accepted and tested. Right, sweetheart?" This last, to Daphne.

81

"Yes, Dad," she said, looking at the floor.

"Who are the people who asked you to do the study?" I asked, filled with interest.

"The less you know about them, the better all around, Reynold," said Dr. Crosse. "Even Daphne doesn't get told the details of our sources of funding. Let's just say, they're people who love America, and who have to know, no ifs ands or buts about it, any technique that might be used by an enemy of our country, foreign or domestic, to infiltrate the thoughts of our people. Good enough?"

"I won't ask again," I said.

"Good, becuase I want you to work on the project. You're the first person outside of Daphne that I've told about it. None of the other scientists who come here, and none of the people at the college, are aware of this particular aspect of my work, and I am going to ask you to promise me you won't blab it around."

"I wouldn't do that, sir," I said. "I'm grateful for your help, and the faith you've shown in me. I would never do anything to hurt either you or your daughter," I said.

"You're a good man, Reynold," he said.

Then, he clapped his hands together and said, "You'll work with Daphne most of the time. Most of the time I've got to work on other things - not to mention my teaching load, which is pretty heavy this year - so I'll be counting on the two of you to keep good notes, and fill me in every few days as fully as possible on whatever you've been doing.

"What else? Oh, yeah. This is a well funded experiment, so your former salary is hereby doubled." He took a roll of bills from his pocket, peeled off four hundred, and gave it to me. "One week in advance," he said.

He said, "One more thing. The money's good, but it has to be off the books. You will be completely off the books. Another little peculiarity of my funding situation, you understand. Again, this is for your benefit as well as for mine. There might come a time, though we hope it will not happen, when you will want to be able to separate yourself in every possible way from the work we are doing here. If that day comes, the lack of pay stubs will help you inestimably."

Daphne served us our snacks, and we toasted my new job.

Daphne seemed glad to hear that we would be working together. As for myself, I felt comforted. I liked the idea of having my well-being in the hands of Dr. Crosse.

I told Dr. Crosse that I would assist him for as long as he wanted me to.

"Good," said Crosse. "I must tell you, I have great hopes for these subliminals, and for our work in this field. I have been a psychologist all my life, but this is a different realm for me. The fact is, we are artists in this new form, more than scientists. We - Daphne has been the pioneer for most of what we've done up to now - I just suggest ways to go forward - we are a new art form."

He got us three glasses of red wine and said, "Pale, pastel in tone - we are the Los Angeles of artistic forms - so vaguely defined, so modest in the sphere of things, between the sky of the viewer's eyes, and the ground, which is the page, the colored photograph itself, on which we lay our humble, invisible efforts - calligraphy and crude drawings (Daphne will show you later) that call no attention to themselves, and yet stay in the mind of the viewer for as long as he lives. And who will be the Michaelangelo, or the Rodin, of this new form? It may be you, Reynold."

I thought of myself creating works of art whose purpose was to hide themselves. Working on glass so that even I couldn't see what I was writing unless the sun hit it just right. I raised my glass to the Doctor, and then, shyly, I turned to Daphne and raised my glass to her, also. We all drank our wine, and I became drunk, although it was only ten in the morning.

When the Doctor went to another part of the house to continue giving tiny electric shocks to student volunteers who failed to correctly identity large photos of people in the news, Daphne took me outside again, and showed me how to scratch the words on the glass sheets. We did this until lunchtime. I chattered on and on about myself as we worked, but she didn't say much in response. Finally, I shut up.

That day, we didn't relate to one another like human beings for the rest of the day. I don't know why. After lunch, Daphne received her tutors in the living room, and I took a nap in my room.

83

I had a strange, tired dream, where there was a long table, dusty lights along its length, with florescent bulbs. And I was scratching words in white dust.

After dinner, the Doctor left me again alone with Daphne.

I had an uneasy feeling, and made a comment on the work we were doing. I asked Daphne whether or not she ever had thoughts of the acts and objects represented by the words we were writing on the sheets of glass. She said she only thought of the shapes and lengths of the words, and the sounds of the words.

She said, "I set up a rhythm. You see? When I write the words, I say them to myself, like a poem or a chant. That's what they become - after a while."

She looked thoughtful as though deciding whether to reveal a secret to a friend; weighing the pleasures of the secret versus the pleasures of telling. Then she said, "Listen, it's like this - are you listening?"

"Yes." I was very still.

"Ok." And she pretended to write in the air, with her hand shaped as though it was holding a pen, as she closed her eyes, and spoke in a quiet, deep voice, saying, "sex, sex, sex, fuck, sex, dick, fuck, prick, fuck, sex, dick, cunt, fuck, cunt, fuck, cunt, prick, sex, shit, sex, prick, cock, dick." She looked at me, to see if I was following what she was saying. Then she said, "Death, fuck, shit, ass, death, dead, suicide, suicide, dick, suicide, death, asshole," and again wrote the words in the air. Finally, I took her plump hand in both of mine. I kissed her wrist, and the palm of her hand. "Fuck, sex, sex, fuck, fuck, death," she said, in a whisper.

"I love you," I said.

She withdrew her hand, and went back to scratching diligently on her glass tablet. We wrote until the sun went behind the Western hills, and turned us into giant shadows on the pasture that faced the Indian Head Rock. We walked to the edge of the incline and looked down into the grey valley, the meadows fenced and cross-fenced, here and there a man or woman leading horses into the barn for the night. A car on the valley floor turned on its lights. The strong profile of the Indian, with full headdress, was the last surface on which the sun blasted full and blazing before it fell into the sea. I thought, in the golden dizziness of it all, that someone had written in big crude letters across the face of the Indian Head, S-E-X S-E-X, from just under the eye, all the way to the rear end of the headdress.

I thought of asking Daphne about it, but I didn't want to spoil the mood of the moment, which lasted until Dr. Crosse called me to assist in an experiment, part of another study entirely, concerning the speed with which people make friends with other people they meet in the dark. This other experiment took place in the converted barn, and kept me busy until well after midnight, when I fell into bed, exhausted.

Chapter 10. Working with Daphne.

There followed many happy days, working beside
Daphne, in that big house with the skulls of steers hung against the
white Spanish walls, along with ancient saddles, and antique sample
sheets of barbed wire, framed and encased in glass.   In those early
days, we stood or sat side by side as we wrote on our embed sheets,
or Daphne would take the sheets into her photo lab, and shoot the
combination shots of photographs-plus-triggering-words. She kept a
careful record of the f-stop, and duration of each exposure, and could
match this information with its negative.   Already, she said, her
father and the men she referred to alternately as his "friends" or his
"backers," had been including samples of her work in various
magazines and newspapers around the country. For example, she
showed me a picture of a little girl sitting in the dentist's chair, with
her head back and her mouth open wide, as the dentist, a white-
haired, chubby-cheeked gentleman of about sixty vibrant, productive
years probed around her molars with a steel pick and a mirror.
Behind the little girl's head, through the half-open window of the
dentist's office, you could see other children playing happily in a
school yard. The dentist's window had delicate blue curtains. Under
this pleasant scene were the words: "Fewer cavities. Don't you owe it
to your family?" And below that, in smaller letters, a short sentence
of praise concerning the brand of toothpaste whose ad it was.

I said, "Nice picture."

Daphne said, "This ad was in Time Magazine six months
ago. "In certain test markets - four towns - we only sold copies that
had an embed over the picture. Here is the same picture, in a print
made from a mistake - I exposed it too long, so you can see the
embed."

She handed me the print, and I could see the same picture
with the words SEX and FUCK clear and black, exactly as I had
seen them scratched on our sheets of glass. I saw that the words
were scratched in such a way that they followed the patterns of the

little girl's skirt, and the folds of the curtains, and the creases in the dentist's shirt. There were other words, a train of COCKs and CANCERs written small, following each other in a rush along their irregular paths. Even smaller SEXes followed the strands of the little girl's hair. A variety of larger words covered her bare legs and arms, and followed the soft outline of her chin against her throat.

I said, "You mean these very words were also in the magazine?" By this time, I should not have had to ask, but seeing the picture of the little girl, juxtaposed with those already mentioned words, or as Dr. Crosse preferred us to say, "phenomes," bothered me. It seemed to me there might be a moral murkiness attached to this whole science, or art, or whatever it was, in which I was beginning to involve myself.

I said, "I hate to disagree with your father, but it does seem to me that people who are thinking about buying toothpaste for their families, are not the sort of people who want to see fuck sex fuck fuck in tendrilly, hand-scrawled letters running up some little girl's legs. Can we agree on that much, at least?"

She said, "In the four towns where the picture ran with the embed, sales of this toothpaste doubled."

I held the picture away from me. I tilted my head.

"And they don't see, see... what you said... tendrilly anything... " she said. "They just see the picture, and they buy the toothpaste because they want to keep their families healthy."

"But you've proved that they are responding, at least in part, because they like the dirty words."

"No. If they actually saw the words, of course they'd be disgusted. They'd never buy that toothpaste again."

I did not continue to argue, although I probably should have. I myself was laboring under the subliminal forces created many thousands of years ago for the propagation of the human race, and many words, etched by spiritual, non-physical hands, seemed written on the surfaces of the face, hair and clothes of my beautiful Daphne. I was too grateful for the chance to be near her, so many hours a day, and to talk to her. Instead of insisting on what I had been saying, I bent my head over my glass, and wrote the words. She touched my hand, and turned to her own work again.

One day, to help pass the time, I told her about my goal of finding my True Dad. She said she could understand why I would want to do that, because she knew how wonderful her father was, and wished all children and their parents would have as good a relationship as she did with him. Actually, the glory of her father was just about the only topic of conversation that really interested Daphne. His incredible youth on entering Harvard, his youth and fame on leaving it, the gift he was giving to the State of California by his presence among its unworthy populace, bringing wisdom and reason from the East. Etc. Other than these tirades in praise of her father, she was the quietest person I had ever spent any time with. She never said what she thought about anything, apart from its effect on her father and/or his work. She never seemed to have a thought with herself as the center of it.

She said her mother had died giving birth to her, sixteen years ago. She had travelled all her life with her father. Because they moved so often, she had never been able to go to a regular school. Her father got tutors, wherever they stopped, and the tutors taught her at her own rate, instructed by her father not to speed her up or slow her down in any subject.

I attribute to the solitudinous nature of her education the fact that many of her emotional responses were like the responses of tourists, who aren't sure of the language, or the customs, and sometimes don't know whether something is supposed to be funny, or insulting, or nothing, or what.

Here is this grave girl - shy, sheltered - having a conversation with her Dad, about a week after we all started working together:

"Father?" asked Daphne.

"Yes, my girl," said Crosse.

"What about a fuck through the u in a cunt or the o in a cock?" asked Daphne.

"If the fuck is horizontal, and the cock or the cunt is at an angle off the horizontal --"

"Forty-five degrees?" she asked, as she sipped her soup.

"No - at most I'd say fifteen..."

"How about a shit, right on top of a fuck?"

88

asked the Daphne next, as she looked at me, and gestured that she would like me to pass her the basket of rolls that was near me on the table.

"A big shit is generally preferable to a little shit," said Crosse. "According to Liebermann and Guttmann in Detroit, and Anselm in Massachussetts, people will detect a small shit, or if not actually see the word, will be left with a distinguishable negative feeling after exposure to the word, which they seem to attach to the product being advertised. On the other hand, most subjects studying subliminals of shit, written large... report feeling wonderful, exhilirated, somehow 'lighter,' 'free-er' -- the conclusion is self-evident - Big shits are preferable."

"I see," said Daphne, as she spooned a few bright vegetables along with the clear broth into her pink mouth, and then stuck her tongue out a bit to gather in some of the moisture she had left on the lower left-hand ledge of her cushiony lip. "Cocks?"

"The smaller the better," said Crosse, helping himself to a spoonful of mashed potatoes.

"What about cunts and fucks?" asked Daphne.

"According to Guttmann..."

Overhearing this, some people might think Daphne and Dr. Crosse oddly ignorant of the normal uses of our language, but in fact theirs was a self-imposed ignorance that aimed at forgoing the "standard" responses to words and ideas, in order to push through to the essentials of language.

When Daphne worked, she seemed to have no sense of the meaning of the words she was writing on the glass. Hearing her say fuck fuck cunt cock all day was enough to keep me in a state of perpetual straining rigidity, as far as my emotional life was concerned. But she was not emotionally affected at all. Hour after hour, she wrote, and guided herself with her low mouthing of the words. Her narrow lips, her pink tongue, her white translucent teeth, the surfaces of which I would stare at sometimes, losing myself in the fantasy that obscene words had been etched on them.   Often,   I found myself alone with Daphne in the lab or garden - sometimes we would accidently touch. Sometimes I would take her hand. Once, we almost kissed, while waiting for cheese sandwiches to heat in the toaster oven, but before our lips met, the buzzer on the oven sounded, and Daphne opened the glass door and took out the sandwiches.

We were excited by one another but stayed apart because we didn't know how Dr.Crosse would react to our being lovers, and neither one of us wanted to test that out. Thus, more and more, both Daphne and I directed all our thoughts toward Dr. Crosse. The enjoyment we shared in one another's company had little to do with one another, and everything to do with making Dr. Crosse happy. That was our joy.

And I was happy in those days. Etching on the glass, spending my time with Daphne, reporting every day or so on our progress, to her father - were all pleasant things to me. Still, when I felt enough time had passed, since the explosion at Dr. Lord's, I told Dr. Crosse that I wanted to head out, to continue looking for my biological father. I said, "I don't want to leave you, and Daphne, but I feel - and don't ask me why - that my True Dad needs me. I have to find him."

Dr. Crosse thought about what I had said, and the next morning, he told me I could go and then come back again. He said my job would still be there. Not only that, he said he would help me as much as he could, help me to find my True Dad.

He asked me to give him the ledger book, with the names of my six potential Dads, and he hired a detective (something I never would have thought of) to locate them. A week later, he handed me a manila folder with pictures and information about Mr. Jack Jerry Elam, the first name on the list.

Mr. Elam lived in New York.

Dr. Crosse very kindly gave me a round-trip ticket for New York, and again promised that my job would be waiting for me when I came back. Before I left, he sent me into town with Daphne, and she helped me pick out some clothes for travelling, and a suit in which to meet Mr. Elam. Dr. Crosse suggested it might be a better idea for me to phone ahead, but I didn't want to do that. I wanted to meet the man face to face, and tell him of our possible connection, and take it from there.

Dr. Crosse reserved a room for me at the Hotel Pierre, on 60th Street and 5th Avenue. It was just a few blocks from Mr. Elam's house, which was on 65th Street.

They drove me to the airport on a Thursday morning. Smog was coming up the coast from Los Angeles. Dr. Crosse said, "Wait till you get above all this shit, you've never seen anything like it." He knew it was to be my first time in a plane. We shook hands, and he said, "You've only been with us a while, boy, but I consider us to be good friends. You're smart, and a good worker, and if this doesn't work out with Mr. Elam, or any of the other possible fathers in your book, you know you can always come back here, and I'll try to be a good employer to you, which is all the dad a grown man needs in this world, as far as I can tell." Then he told Daphne, "You walk Reynold to the gate, hon, I'll wait in the car."

"He thinks we're in love," she said, when we were standing at the window of the terminal, waiting for my plane to board.

"I am," I said. I put my hands around her waist.

"How do you know?" she said, pulling away, and smiling mischievously. "Couldn't it be the effect of the triggering phenomes?"

I was insulted, but I didn't let her see that. I said, "No. I love you, anyone would love you."

"But why?" she said.

"Because you are you."

She looked at me sadly, and we kissed, for the first time since we had met. We kissed for a long time, and I had the impression she was trying to decide how she felt about me while it was going on. She said, "What if it's all part of the experiment? What if you love me, and I love you, because of something we know nothing of, but my father has set up?"

"But why would he do that?"

"He puts us together, we write these words on sheets of glass, we are near each other." She said it as though she was accusing *me* of something.

She said, "You'd probably be better off if you never came back here." She touched the side of my face, she gave me a small kiss on the lips. She turned, before I could think of what to say, and ran down the corridor away from my gate, back to her father.

Chapter 11: At the Home of Mr. Elam.

I read about Mr. Elam on the flight.

Jerry Elam had a very impressive history. High I.Q., showing itself early in his school career, as he won award after award for writing and drawing. Skipped a few grades, entered college at seventeen - Johns Hopkins - graduated at twenty - then, Medical School - after which, internship and residency at the Johns Hopkins Hospital - looked like he was on his way to a big career as a brain surgeon, when he got involved with a scandal at the hospital. He found out some of the staff were stealing and selling pain killers from the hospital supplies. According to the file, these doctors were handing the drugs to local police, who were selling them in the slums of Baltimore, and splitting the profits with the doctors. Elam went to the head of the hospital. A month later, fearing that nothing was being done to stop the activities he had reported, he called the Baltimore <u>Sun</u>, told his story to a young reporter there - a woman named Barbara Filter - and then co-operated with her fully to get the evidence she needed to expose the situation.

Their series of articles won Ms. Filter the Pulitzer Prize, and was instrumental in getting a lot of doctors and policemen fired. After that, Elam quit medicine. He and Barbara Filter were married, and they started a newspaper together. This was the sixties, and their paper was called "Deathburger." It was a sort of underground publication, filled with muckraking about the city government and horror stories about the chemicals in the food people were eating. There were also advertisements for clothing stores and shops that sold drug paraphernalia, and there were personal ads. Now, these ads are everywhere. You can even call phone numbers announced on TV to hear messages from men and women who want companionship. But then, "Deathburger" was the only place in Baltimore where you could find such messages. For this reason, "Deathburger" became a huge success. Five years later, the Elams sold their newspaper for two million dollars, and moved to New

York. There, they founded a couple of free newspapers, that were left in the lobbies of apartment buildings and the entranceways of supermarkets. The personal ads in the back attracted readers, and the readers attracted advertisers. Soon, they were making so much money they were able to buy a small book publisher specializing in bird and flower guides. The guides, one for each State, were steady sellers, but the real reason they bought the company was that it had its own printing plant. The Elams started publishing reprints of classic novels and works of poetry, the kind of books that were old enough to be in public domain, and good enough to be on the reading lists of colleges and high schools. They managed to carve out a niche in the textbook market, because their prices were low and most students didn't mind the cheap paper and runny ink they used to manufacture the books.

They continued thus, the small millions rolling in, through the seventies and into the eighties, when a wave of religious fundamentalism crashed over the formerly peaceful beach of academic publishing.

Groups of parents in Texas and California started to notice that their kids were learning from textbooks that taught, of all things, man was descended from the apes! This was, the parents felt, in clear contradiction to the words of the Bible, which tells us God created man from dust, and woman from his rib. They brought their concerns to the administrators of their schools, who passed them along to the boards of education in their various towns and counties, who duly informed the textbook publishers, at the next buying season, that they would like Darwin left out, and the Bible taught. The publishers, most of them located in New York, were not very quick to see the threat this posed to their business. They issued statements that here at the end of the 20th century, it was time we all took responsibility for making sure our kids got a complete and correct scientific education, so they weren't going to change their textbooks, just to please a few crackpots in Texas and California. The problem with that stand, principled as it was, is that between Texas and California, you have about 40 per cent of all your textbook sales. You can't successfully publish a textbook without selling it in these two States.

The Elams understood. They rushed into print with a biology text that came complete with artwork of the Adamic dust standing up in the Garden of Eden, and of naked Adam and Eve seeing their nakedness for the first time, and being ashamed. Darwin and his ilk were consigned to a small, red-bordered box on pages 143-144 in which the Theory of Evolution got two short paragraphs, starting with the words, "Some people believe..." and illustrated by drawings of bearded Darwin and a chimp with eyeglasses staring at one another across what looked like a small island, with one palm tree on it.

The Elam book was a big hit. They now had a 2,600 acre hunting preserve in Colorado, 4,300 acres of prime grazing land in Montana, and a 32,000 acre ranch called Zinjaire in Northern California. They also had property in Southern France.

My prospective father, and his wife (I wondered if she would like me) spent most of their time in New York, guiding their publishing empire, and doing charitable works. They had been the subjects of many articles in such magazines as *Time* and *Newsweek*, *Business Week*, and the New York *Times Sunday Magazine*. The file noted that Jerry Elam was considered to be a possible candidate for President of the United States.

I thought of it. Me, Reynold Stengrow, or rather Reynold Elam... son of the President of the United States! Or maybe my father, Mr. Elam, would prefer me to have a different first name. Possibly, Jerry, after himself. Jerry Elam, Junior, the Son of the President of the United States! I thought of myself allowing people ahead of me in line, in department stores and supermarkets, even though I was the Son of the President. I could feel the admiring gazes of the other shoppers. Of course, they knew who I was. I thought of the word getting back to my father, in the Oval Office, how democratic I had been, letting people ahead of me in line. He would send for me. He would tell me how proud he was of me. He would make me one of his advisers. Daphne and I would sleep together. She would be proud of me. I would gladly share my new status with her, and with Dr. Crosse, and with the Stengrows, whom I intended to call, as soon as I was settled in my hotel room.

95

However, I did not call them. I decided, once I was in the room, to wait until I had made contact with Mr. Elam.

I wanted to be able to call them with good news. After all, they had nurtured me, and one of them was a biological parent of mine. I wondered if my mother would get along with Mr. Elam. I resolved myself to attempt to bring about their meeting and foster in every way I could, their friendship. I looked out at the city of New York, wet with rain, people running home from work. I felt warm and safe in my room. The rug was thick and soft, after the hard stone floor of Dr. Crosse's ranch.

While I was waiting for dinner, I called the ranch, and talked to Daphne. "My father's got his friends over, they're zapping that Mrs. Welby again," she said.

I told her I missed her, and she said she missed me. I told her about the food on the flight, and the movie. Then, I told her what I had read in the file her Dad had given me on my possible Dad. I didn't mention anything about his being a possible candidate for the presidency, because I didn't want her to feel I was getting a swelled head over it. We laughed and talked about nothing for several hours. My dinner came, and the steak got cold, and I watched the ice cream sundae melt, and then the ice in the outer cup in which the sundae was sitting. We couldn't stop talking, until two a.m., New York time.

The next day, I slept later than I had intended to, and left the hotel about nine a.m. The day was cool and sunny, and the air was fresh and crisp against the sinuses. I stopped at a florist's on Madison Avenue, and bought a dozen red roses for Mrs. Elam. I felt wonderful, striding along the rain-cleaned streets to 65th. I was wearing my new suit, I was wearing leather shoes for the first time in approximately ten years, and my hair was combed with Vitalis. I liked the look of all the small houses in a row, with brightly painted railings in front, and the two or three steps down to the front doors.

I was vaguely aware of one or two people standing around in the street near the house. A man in a tan blazer, if I remember correctly, and a very pretty woman of about 30 years, also wearing a tan blazer, twirling a microphone on the end of a wire, around and around, as she leaned in a bored manner against the railing of the house one over from the Elams'. I also vaguely remember that a minivan pulled to a stop at the curb, as I reached the house, and it parked in front of a fire hydrant. I remember looking in to see if the driver knew what he was doing, but the look of the driver, large and zombie-like, with silver wraparound sunglasses, dissuaded me from offering him any parking tips. Instead, I smiled in passing, and turned, and went down the stairs to the Elam house.

I knocked on the door. Mrs. Elam opened it, a moment later. "Mrs. Elam," said. I would have continued, but she stopped me by shouting, "More flowers!? More!?" She shook her head, and put her hand out, against my chest, to bar my entrance. Then, she looked at the flowers, and thought, and said, "Oh, well - never mind. Put them in the library."

"Mrs. Elam - " said with clearly preparatory intent, but before I could go on, she reached behind her, to a black woman who had been walking by, with her arms full of saucers. She grabbed this woman by the upper arm and said, "Gilay, show this young man where to put his flowers." Then, she wheeled around Gilay like a dancer around her partner, and propelled herself out of the doorway, through the hallway, and into some distant room, to the left. Gilay and I watched her disappear, then Gilay looked at me, angrily. "Wait," she said. Then, muttering to herself a series of complaints, she found a place to set down her saucers, looked at me again and said, "All the flowers were supposed to be here before seven."

She turned her back on me, before I could explain. She led me down the corridor, and finally opened the door to a large room. There were dark-brown bookshelves covering all the walls, to the ceiling. There was a single large window, with sunlight coming through it, and in front of the window was a long, heavy table with a row of chairs behind it. Four microphones stood on the table, in front of the four middle chairs. There was a white cloth covering the table, and on the part that hung down in front of the table, there was a picture of a donkey. Several large American flags stood between the chairs and the window, and there were small American flags in water-glasses, in bunches, tied with rubber bands. Near the small flags were floral arrangements. There were six floral arrangements, six waterglasses filled with flags. I was trying to decide where I might best put the roses I had brought when I heard a man's voice. It was high, squeaky, like the voice of a movie gangster when he gets defensive about something. At first I couldn't see where the voice was coming from. I heard it say:

"I consider myself to be the Daniel Boone of American intellectuals," and then it sounded like he was inhaling strenuously with his mouth open, as if trying to swallow a man's head. After what seemed like about eighty seconds, I heard a sound indicating someone had breathed outwardly. Instantly, the room was filled with gallons of smoke. From the currents in the smoke, I traced its source to a place behind the library ladder. I went over there, the flowers still in my hand, and saw the man I recognized as Jerry Elam, curled up in a small chair, over a small table, smoking a filter cigarette and reading from some sheets of paper. He continued, "Like ol' Dan'l Boone, I like to build my cabin where I can't see the cookfires from the chimneys of my nearest neighbors. Speaking intellectually, of course. I try to search out new ideas, blaze new trails, neither liberal nor conservative, neither hawk nor dove, neither bleeding heart nor heart of stone. In other words, I'm kind of a, well I don't like aggrandize myself, but I think of myself as a, well, a pioneer of the mind." He smoked some more, and coughed, following that by saying, "Shit."

Then, still not seeing me, he put down the papers and thought of what he had just said, saying to himself, "Daniel Boone. I like it." Then, he saw me. "Aaa," he said, in a kind of muffled panic.

I said, "Mr. Elam, I'm..."

"How did you get in here?" he asked, at the same time struggling to get up, while at the same time hiding his cigarette. He threw his whole body and face toward me across the desk, for no other reason than to hide his cigarette. Finally, thinking I didn't see it, he dropped it down the inside of his leg, and crushed it with his shoe. In doing all this, he knocked over the small yellow table at which he had been sitting.

"Your wife sent me in here," I said.

"She did?"

"With these flowers."

"I see. There, on the table. Thank you."

I said, "I can see I got here on a pretty hectic day."

"All right," he said with injured dignity, "so you saw me with a cigarette. Fine! Blackmail me! Expose me! I'm a hyprocrite, so fuck you!"

I said, "I'm not here to catch you smoking."

He said, "You're not?" Then, he obviously believed me, because he became very relaxed, and took a pack from his pants pocket, along with a lighter, and lit up another cigarette. "I'm announcing my candidacy in about a half an hour. President of the United States. But the American people won't elect a smoker. That's what my wife says. And all my advisers. So what are you, from the florist's?"

I said, "Actually, I came here to see you, Mr. Elam. About something."

He was putting the table back on its feet, and I put down the flowers, and picked up the chair he had been sitting on. When he heard the personal tone of my speech, he became flustered once again, and moved around to put the table between us. "About what?" he asked.

I said, "Well, I think I should have planned better how to say this. I did have some idea, but everything's different. The room looks different from the way I thought it would look, and there's so much excitement here today."

He said, "Please, tell me what it is you want to see me about. Do you want to work in my campaign?"

I said, "Well..." I wanted to say yes, because it sounded like a good idea. But, I decided to leap immediately to the main purpose of my visit. "I guess the best way is to come right out and say this," I started. "I mean, the thing is, do you happen to remember a Doctor Lord? Doctor I. Lord?"

He thought about it. "Lord? Lord? Why I... Yes, of course I do! Used to pay ten dollars a shot for..." Suddenly, his face lost its nostalgic upward gaze, and he was looking straight at me. "What is this about, young man? Why have you come here? Today, of all days..."

I said, "I just got to New York, yesterday," as though that were an answer to his question. After a moment of silence, from both of us, I added, "I think I might be your son."

He stood staring at me. Then, he sat down. Slowly, his face transformed itself into a warm and friendly smile. It was a friendliness not primarily directed at me, but at Dr. Lord, I soon learned, when he said, "That old psycho. I never thought he'd really go ahead with that clinic of his. The Genius Sperm Bank. I thought when they kicked him out of the UC system, that was it. Heard he was running a plant nursery in Glendale. So, he did it, and you are the product. Well well. Step into the light."

I did so.

"But the children weren't supposed to learn the names of the donors. I'm sure that was part of the deal. Even the parents who got the donations weren't supposed to know."   I   answered,   "I managed to get a ledger from Dr. Lord's office, that listed all the children born in my year, and their fathers. I really don't know if you are the one. There are five more possibilities. But I wanted to meet you, and speak with you, and see if we might be related."

He laughed a choppy laugh, and said, "I hate to get technical with you here, fella, but here's where I have to say, I do not for a moment admit that I was ever a sperm donor for Dr. Lord, but even if I were, which I do not admit, as neither do I admit I ever met the man, or even heard of him, although I might under duress confess the name is not unknown to me, so, considering all of that, what would make you think that I might under any circumstances want to admit to being your, or anyone's, father?" He seemed to be struggling not to crease too visibly the line directly between his doe brown eyes that indicated, all too visibly a former time when Mr. Elam was really unhappy.

I said, "It's not a question of admitting anything. I was just interested in finding out. I thought you might be interested, too. I don't want anything from you."

He looked at me with renewed interest. "From the look of simple, plodding honesty on your face, I could almost believe you mean that. However, as you may or may not know, I am a very rich man. Being my son might reasonably be expected to put you in the

way of quite a chunk of change. You might want nothing now, but
you might want a lot later on. Or, you may want a lot now. You
may have heard about Dr. Lord's experiment, possibly you were his
prison cellmate, if he ever went to prison, which is not what I would
call unlikely."

"No, sir," said I. "Nothing like that." I told him about how I
had gone out to Dr. Lord's house, and about the explosion. Though I
hesitated to give him any more reasons to think badly of me, I even
told him that I was being searched for by the police.

He said, "All these things you say, they make me want to
believe you. Also, that look of simple potato-brained honesty I spoke
of earlier. This intrigues me not because it makes me think you are
honest, but because I too have always been able to summon that look
to my facial features, when I need to, whether I am telling the truth or
not. Seeing you with that same expression I have so often seen on
my own popular mug, makes me think there might be some truth in
what you say - you might really be my son, my offspring." He stood
up and leaned very close to me, to study the features of my face one
by one, this eye, that eye, the sides of my nose, saying "hmmm" and
"rrnnrr" now and then.

As for me, I had no doubts that this was my True Dad. As
far as I was concerned, no test was necessary, there was no reason to
search further.

"We don't look too different, do we? " I asked hopefully. He
brought me to a mirror, and I had to squat down a few inches, so that
my face and Mr. Elam's could both be in the mirror at the same time.
I grinned at Mr. Elam, full of love, and playfully twirled my fingers
at him in the mirror. Mr. Elam, you might say, broke open a
pleasant little smile he seemed to have been saving for a special
occasion and which he thought, considering the unusualness of my
visit, and the biological and emotional issues involved, he could
probably go ahead and decant at the present moment.

"Uncanny" said Mr. Elam. "Although not decisive, I'm sure
you don't have to be told."

But I couldn't believe he didn't see the resemblance. To me,
we were like peas in a pod - one much bigger, it is true - one with a
long face (me) and one with a round face (him) - one with brown hair

101

and one with formerly red hair - one with straight hair and one with curly hair - one with brown eyes, one with green eyes - but the similarity, I still insist, from the vantage point of my current objectivity, was striking.

"Look at the way both of our faces are compounded of interlocking eights, all with their centers at the same point, and their top and bottom circles rotating like the hours on a clock!" I suggested.

"Sorry, can't quite-- maybe it's the light--" Temporized Elam. It occurred to me that he might be feeling warm and uncomfortable in the crook of my arm, which I had thrown casually around his neck in order to get our faces closer together, for comparison in the mirror. I took my arm away, perhaps too quickly. My hand brushed against a lamp shade and knocked the lamp off its table. I apologized, as Mr. Elam picked it up, and set it back in its place.

He said, looking at me with one eye half-shut: "In fact, I do see some resemlance between you and me, Mr. Stengrow. And what's more, I like you. I have three sons, and I must admit I have always thought of my children
as the worst set of betrayers, constantly changing their personalities, even their forms and features, until you can't remember what you started with to get the mess you now see before you at the breakfast table. Eruptions, is a word I have used to describe my sons, I'm not proud to admit. When you meet them, later on, you may judge for yourself." He smoked, and stared into the problem of which he spoke, with an intense look. Between massive inhalations and life-saving exhalations, he said, "The word, "offspring" has always carried the right sound to my ears, the ring of truth. I think of huge children springing on and off parental trampolines, parents laying prone in the back yards of their homes, each set of parents, lying side by side -- with paperback books over thin faces, and their children jumping on their bellies, higher and higher, and -- But I like you. A son I never had a chance to spoil. I want to know all about you, later. I can't wait to tell my wife of this incredible thing! Why, I could be your brother," exalted Mr. Elam, checking his pockets, as

he went over to the tiny alcove covering a sink and a small refrigerator, and shelves containing bottles of every known liquor---

Seeing Elam, and noting that the man looked old, weak, unhappy, pasty, dry, asthmatic, dandified, expensively but uncomfortably dressed in clothes that he seeemed to cringe from as from an iron maiden, I still thought we looked alike. More than that, I was sure that Mr. Elam saw the likeness, too, and that it made him happy. I was at the age when we think older people want to look like us. I couldn't know that Elam considered me to look like the large, clown-faced golden retriever he had once, on a hillside in Virginia with the sun going down over the ocean side hills, shot in the head with an automatic pistol to cure it of flatulance.

He mixed a drink, and held the glass out toward me. I took it and quickly gulped.

Mr. Elam mixed himself a drink and sat down in one of the large, leather chairs. He put his feet out on the leather footstool.

I paced back and forth in front of Mr. Elam, with my characteristic appearance of lurching forward as I walk, and leaning forward so that to many observers it sometimes seemes I am toppling forward with every step. I was very excited about being here, face to face with one of my prospective fathers.

I stopped pacing, faced Elam, and said, "I want to tell you things about myself -- would that be ok? And then you tell me if any of these things remind you of things you have noticed about *your* self. Maybe that way we'll both be able to see the effects of our relationship. Could I do that, Sir, Please?"

"Absolutely," said Elam, "After the press conference. And I'll do my best to help, in any way."

"Just tell me if any of this sounds like you?" Mistakenly, I thought he looked fascinated. "For example," I said, "I have no social gyroscope. I say things in all sincerity and people think I'm joking. I try to tell a joke, they think I'm being critical. I -- "

Elam was too polite to stop me, but from behind me I heard a woman say, "What's going *on* here?"

I turned and it was Mrs. Elam. She ignored me and said to her husband, "They're gathering in the street, for God's sakes. You have to get ready."

He assured her that he was as ready as he would ever be, and then introduced me to her, and her to me. He told her who I was, and the purpose of my visit. He reminded her that he had mentioned Dr. Lord, once or twice, and he asked her if this wasn't great. He said, "Here I thought I was only capable of fathering louts and slugs, and along comes this quite presentable young person." Elam held his hand in my direction, like a figure in a painting whose purpose is to draw the viewer's eye to the center of interest - me.

She looked at me, blank. Blink, then blank. Then, she took her husband by the upper arm and led him toward another entrance from the one I had come in through. She said, "Jerry will be right back." I smiled at her. I heard her shouting from the adjoining room, and I heard his voice, trying to soothe her. Soon, they both came back. He studied the floor. She said to me, "Mr. Stengrow. As you know, Mr. Elam is about to announce his candidacy for the presidency of the United States of America. America needs Mr. Elam."

I nodded.

"The problem is you."

"Me?"

"If the press discovers, and broadcasts, the fact that my husband was a sperm bank donor, I doubt that he will ever sit in the Oval Office, or that America will ever get the benefit of his vision, his ideas, and his strength. Perhaps this should not be. Perhaps it is unfair. But as a woman who has seen a good deal more of the world than you have, Mr. Stengrow, I have a feeling that the thought of my husband jerking off into a glass bottle with a copy of Gent open across his knees, is not going to spell landslide for him or the Party, no matter how well you have personally turned out, and I do not say that you haven't."

"My wife's kind of a pessimist," he said, not looking up from the floor.

"All I'm saying is, if you sincerely like Mr. Elam, want to help him, ever hope to gain anything of material value by your fortunate association with this family, you will not spread the story of your birth before the election."

I breathed a sigh of relief, and said, to both of them, "Of course! Anything I can do to help, I will do. I don't mean to disrupt the lives of any of my prospective fathers, only to learn the truth of my origins. The fewer people besides myself who know this truth, the better I'll feel."

Hearing this, she turned to her husband, and said, "There. I told you the young man would want to help." Soon afterward, she said it was time to go. She straightened Elam's clothes, and sprayed him, so he wouldn't smell like cigarette smoke.

She said, "Mr. Stengrow, you come, too."

The three of us went through a door and I saw we were about to descend a flight of wooden stairs, into a basement. I said, "I thought the press conference was going to be in the room we were just in." Mrs. Elam said, "Mr. Elam wants to greet the press in his office, and then walk them to that room. By coming down here, we can come up again in his office, and they will think we've been there all along."

We walked about fifty feet, when three men, in their early twenties, met us, coming out of a small cellar room where I could see bikes and pinball machines and clothes all piled up. They were all dressed up for the press conference. These were Mr. Elam's sons. They greeted their father and mother. Mrs. Elam gestured toward me, and said, "That's the one." The three young men looked at me. "Our new brother," said the largest of the three Elam boys. I thought I detected a note of sarcasm, or was it only a slowness of speech? We continued walking, toward another set of wooden stairs, which I assumed led to the office. We went past heating ducts and stored furniture, and the boiler. Mr. Elam climbed the stairs and opened the door to his office. Mrs. Elam started after him. I remember the back of her shoe as I started up the stairs. The lights went out in the basement. I felt a breeze, I knew not from where. A moment later, I was struck on the top of the head, by some heavy object. I remember the pain, a moment of fear, then nothing.

Chapter 12. Subway Subliminals.

I woke up. I was lying on the floor. From the feel of the concrete, I was still in the basement. At first, the place was pitch black to my eyes. My head hurt when I tried to move. I grabbed it with both hands, and screamed in pain. One side of my face felt sticky and wet. I was sure I was bleeding. I heard the sound of whispering, somewhere high above my head. I looked in that direction. Gradually, as my eyes became accustomed to the light, I realized I was looking at a cinder block wall. I noticed that where the wall met the ceiling, there was a small rectangle of light, coming through from another room. I looked toward the light, trying to focus my vision, at the same time finding some position in which my head could be comfortable (there was none) and attempting to figure out what had happened to me. As I was looking at the rectangle of light, it got smaller.

"Wait," I said, or rather tried to say. No sound came from my throat. I now understood that I was in a small, enclosed space, behind a brick wall, and that someone was closing me into this space. A moment later, the area of light high on the wall got even smaller, as another brick was shoved into place.

"Hey, I'm in here!" I attempted to shout. It came out as a dry rush of air.

The whispering voices on the other side of the wall stopped for a moment, then started up faster and more urgent than before. I tried to stand up, but fell on my back. "Please! Help me!" I tried to yell. Another brick was shoved into the tiny area of light. One more, and that would be it. I felt a moment of panic, then I gathered my strength, and made one more try at standing up. I rose a few inches before the pain in my skull overwhelmed me and I passed out again.

I don't know if a half hour passed, or three hours, or two days. When I again awoke, there was no light at all in the place. I crawled around, feeling the walls and floor, searching for a way out. Three of the walls were of rough stone, and the fourth was the new cinder block wall. Nowhere could I detect a doorway, or any possible opening. This time, I was able to shout loudly, but no one answered me. I listened at the brick wall to try and hear the whispering voices again, but I couldn't hear anything. I shouted. I stopped. I thought of what had happened to me. I would have liked to believe that the Elams and myself had been the victims of an earthquake, or even a bomb plot, that had caught us all off guard in the basement. But that would certainly not explain the hands bricking up my little room, or the whispering voices. Then, I thought, perhaps the Elam home had been invaded by terrorists, who had smashed me on the back of the head and done whatever they wanted with the Elams, and being humane terrorists, had decided not to shoot me, but to give me a fighting chance by suffocating me to death in a tiny coffin-room. But that idea didn't hold water, either, because I had not heard any scuffling, or shouting, or anything behind me as I had prepared to climb the cellar stairs. The three sons of the Elams had been behind me, and certainly, any terrorist would have had to get through them to get to me.

Finally, in the many hours I had there, to think things over, I came to the reluctant conclusion that it was the Elams themselves who had smashed me on the top of the head, thrown me into this place, and sealed me up. I remembered what Mrs. Elam had said about Mr. Elam's race for the Presidency, and how concerned she had been that the public knowledge of my existence might harm his chances. It's true, I had given Mrs. Elam my word not to tell anyone the truth until after the election, but if she was an especially suspicious or careful woman, perhaps my assurances had not been enough for her.

I realized I was hungry, and incredibly thirsty. I slept again, drained of energy, and when I woke, again I felt along the walls for a way out. I discovered a place on the wall where it was wet. A rivulet of water, probably the sweat from some household pipe, made its way down the irregular stone surface of the wall. I put my mouth against it and let the water drip against my lips and tongue. It might have been sewer water, for all I knew, but I had to quench my thirst.

As I enjoyed the sensation of the water on my lips, I felt, then heard, a tremendous rumbling on the other side of one of the stone walls. The rumbling got louder and deeper, until the walls and floor of my coffin-room were shaking. Then, suddenly, it stopped. I thought I heard human voices. I strained to hear the voices, but the rumbling started again, deafening, making my stomach turn with its rattling movements. When the rumbling once again died down, I was sure I did hear people. I yelled, but I was still very weak, and no one heard me.

I can't remember how long it took for me to figure out what would have been obvious to a native New Yorker, but sooner or later it occurred to me that what I was hearing must be a subway train, and that just on the other side of this stone wall from me must be a subway station.

Whenever I heard voices, I would yell, "Help, I'm in here, I'm trapped" But the train would come, drowning out the sound of my voice with its great rumbling, followed by its tremendous grinding noises. Or, sometimes even long before the train came, the people would simply move away from the wall behind which I was shouting, and their voices would stop.

As the days went by I got to know the train schedule. I got to know the rush hours, and my hopes would rise before every one. But each rush hour, the last train would leave and there would be no one left on the platform. Sometimes, I would be positive that someone out there heard me. A voice would stop mid-sentence, or feet would move toward the wall, and I'd hear a tapping on the wall, as though someone on the other side was trying to decide if the wall was hollow. But even then, if I would shout louder, "Help! Help!" or speak more clearly, saying, "Please, get the police to come and break down this wall. I'm trapped, I'm starving!" no one stayed for long at the wall. They left when their trains arrived. They didn't come looking for me. Were they afraid to help? Did they think they were imagining the shouts from behind the wall?

I needed a way to get the attention of someone who would help me. All my shouting wasn't helping me, and since I was getting weaker with every hour, from lack of food, I was sure my voice would get softer and softer, and no one would ever hear me.

Also, I had to admit to myself that several of the people in the subway station had almost certainly heard my cries. Still, none of them had done anything to find out where they were coming from, or if they might do something to help the person making the cries. Sometimes, I thought I heard fear in their voices or in their motions, the sounds of their shoes on the station platform, a brushing sound. Sometimes they seemed to laugh. But in either case, they were gone when their trains came. And those brought to the station by the arriving trains, always went right to the exits, passing my wall without stopping.

Then, suddenly, as I was laying with my face near the wall at the place where the rivulet of water slid down, I remembered what Dr. Crosse had said about the strange motivations people have for doing certain things -- "That's it!" I realized. "My job is to make these people *want* to open this wall and let me out. If, for some reason, the sound of someone calling 'help' from behind a tile wall doesn't have that effect on them, it is my job to find something that will! If they want to get me out of here, they will find a way to do it, and they'll knock down this wall. I've been doing this the wrong way. After all, who would want to interrupt a journey, perhaps after a hard day's work, or before an evening appointment, just to go search behind the scrawled-over walls of some forbidding subway station for the source of a loud voice, that advertises by its tone, its tremor, the few words it says -- that it can only lead to an evening filled with difficulties, sorrow, filling out police forms. And you know if you did find out where the voice was coming from, you would still have to knock down a wall, or look for someone with the authority to knock it down. And who can begin to redress the grievances of everyone -- even of all those with grievances in the subway! So, how many would care to start the job while waiting for a subway, at night, on the self-same Manhattan Island I had often seen on TV? Few, if any. And none of those, as my efforts of the past few days had proved to me, ever came within hearing of my cries for help.

How then could I get one of these passersby to feel a strong, even overwhelming, desire to remove me from this place?

I heard a man and a woman scuff their feet on the gritty platform (it sounded gritty) as they stood talking a few feet from me, on the other side of my wall.

I thought of the subliminal words Daphne and I had drawn on our sheets of glass, and the way they had increased the sales of certain magazines and products...

Suddenly, my new plan devised itself in my brain.

Instead of yelling, I put my lips about five feet up near the cold cement wall, and said in a distinct but very low voice, so low that even I, speaking the words, could hardly hear them, "Sex, sex, sex sex, prick, cunt, sex, sex, cock, pussy, mmm."

I moved around to make my voice come from various heights and places on the wall. I tried to say the words cleanly, like a mechanical bell, cold, and yet forgiving. I wanted the man and woman to hear without hearing, the way Dr. Crosse had said we could get people to see without seeing, or to obey without having been commanded.

I kept at it for a long time. The people on the other side didn't seem to notice. Still, I was pleased to note that they didn't run away from the immediate area, like the people had before, and to that extent, I thought, the new subliminal technique was already proving itself superior to the traditional manner of getting help from other people.

However, when I had yelled, even though the others ran away, I knew at least that they had heard me. I did not have even this small comfort, using my new method. Before, when I yelled "Help!" and they ran away, I could always imagine they had gone to get others -- professionals, to help me. Even though they never did, I had a few minutes, or hours, of thinking I might soon hear a crash and see a jagged shape of light as the sledge hammer breaks into my prison. With this new way, I had to forego the old, comfortable false hopes, and try new hopes. I thought the air must be running out in my room, so I kept at the new way. "Fuck, suck, sex, suck," I whispered to the stone wall.

The people on the other side started to linger longer at my part of the wall. As the days and nights went by, I thought I could detect people touching the wall. Sometimes, they would run what sounded like the tips of their umbrellas across the white tiles of the station wall directly over my wall, back and forth--ratcheting along the wall, as I wooed them.

Sometimes I heard arguments on the other side of the wall. I couldn't make out the words. I heard tones, attitudes. One time I heard a lot of men arguing, and I knew they were arguing about the sounds coming from me. At this time, I might have switched from my subliminal mutterings, and said "HELP," as clearly as I still could, considering my weakened state, but I decided to stick with the subliminal method. It was that method, I reasoned, that had put men out there arguing in the first place, and that method, if any, would cause them to free me from my room. I kept saying, against the wall, "fuck fuck sex death cancer cock fuck cunt, etc." After a while, someone hit the wall. Then, I heard laughter, and then gunshots, as one of the men shot at the wall with what sounded like a pistol. Then, there was more silence. Then, I heard them leave.

I couldn't tell how long I had been there. The water kept me alive. Evidently, air came into the space around the water pipes far above my head.

Finally, one day, I was muttering as usual, my subliminal litany against the wall, and I heard an angry voice in the subway station, shouting very clearly and distinctly: "That's it! That's it! Fuck you! Fuck you! You!" Then, there was a smashing blow against the wall, directly opposite the side of my face. The wall buckled inward, and knocked me back. I was in terrible pain. I didn't know it at the time, but a shard of the inner wall had come loose and stabbed me in the temple. Again, the wall shook. Again, the furious, pained cry: "Fuck you! Not me! You! You're the cock! You're the cunt! You get cancer! Not me! You!" and so on. From the sound of things, someone was responding to my efforts. I didn't exactly understand the nature of that response, but there was no doubt that I was experiencing a level of success previously unknown. I felt my best course of action was to continue saying the words, just as I had been. So I did. "Sex sex fuck suck cock death, etc." The wall shook, again and again.

Finally, a small chunk of the wall fell out, and I could see the shadow of a large man, and then tiny sections of him - face red and bathed in sweat, swinging a huge mallet. He swung it sidearm, wham, into the wall. Then, pulled it back and smashed it into the wall again. "Fuck cunt sex cock fuck," I said, my voice barely above a whisper.

"You! Fuck you!" screamed the man, as he smashed the wall one final time, with all his might, and a piece the size of a legal pad fell out, letting in such a block of light that I had to cover my eyes with my arm. Under my arm, I peered through the wall, to see this man, the first human being I had seen in weeks, as he reached back to hit the wall again, and then, with an air of total defeat, dropped the mallet to the platform. He raised his hands before his face and looked at them. He shook his head in misery, and said to himself (though out loud): "It's happened. I've gone insane. Oh, my God, what am I going to do?" Then, he brought his hands to his face and covered his eyes with them. It seemed as though he wanted to push his palms through his own head. He let out a loud sob, and sank to his knees on the platform, weeping.

I crawled around as best I could on my side of the wall, lifting my face a little closer to the open section. I said, "Hello? Hello?" as my eyes got used to the light, and I could see the crying man clearly for the first time. He was wearing coveralls and work boots, and besides the mallet, he had a tool case with him. He didn't hear me, because he was still sobbing.

I gathered together all of my remaining strength and said, "Could you help me, please?"

He unstuck one of his hands from his face, and looked at me out of the corner of his eye. The eyebrow of that eye came down in a frown, for just a moment. Then, it shot up suddenly, like a parking meter saying Time Expired - shot up with interest, concern, relief, brotherhood, friendliness, and most of all, understanding. He said, "You were in there. I thought I was hearing things. I thought I was going insane!"

I told him what had happened to me, as far as I knew. I told him I had seen hands bricking me in. He said, "Shit... no wonder you were sittin' in there cursin'. Thing like that happened to me, I'd curse, too!"

"No, you don't understand," I said. I started to explain the theory of subliminal suggestion, by way of explaining the words he had heard coming from the wall, but he interrupted me, telling me to crawl back away from the wall. I did so. He picked up the mallet and smashed the wall a few more times, opening up a hole large enough for him to step into. He carried me out of the room, and put me on the floor of the station, leaning me against the wall. I was shocked by the appearance of my arms and legs. It looked as though I had lost about 50 pounds.

The man who had rescued me said he was a maintenance worker for the Transit Authority.

Every morning, he said, he came to this station at five-thirty, to meet his crew. The crew came down the track on a hand-cart, and picked him up, and they went down to 14th Street, to plaster up some wall that was falling onto the tracks. Generally, they were a few minutes late, and he would stand on the tracks, sneaking a smoke. Then, one day about a month ago (this was the first notion I had of how long I had been in the room) he was standing there, and he thought he heard someone curse at him. The hand-car came along, and he got on, and forgot about it. But the next morning, again he thought someone was cursing at him. He looked behind the pillars, to see if someone was hiding. He went through the short side-tunnels, and up the stairs and across the upper platform and down the other stairs to the uptown side of the station, to see if anyone, any kids or anything, were hiding there, but he couldn't find anyone. When he got back to his usual spot, there was that voice again.

"That was me!" I exclaimed with joy. I was then chewing on a candy bar the man had kindly bought for me, along with a package of 'Nilla Wafers.

"That was you?" he asked, slowly. "Cursing at me?"

"I wasn't cursing at you," I said. "I was saying triggering phenomes. I was introducing triggering phenomes into the environment."

"What are those?"

"You know: fuck, sex, cock, death, etc."

He said, "That *was* you! You was cursin me. Why, I ought to..."

"No!" I shouted, getting my voice back at last. "I wasn't cursing you. I didn't even know you were there."

He said, "That's true. But why didn't you just yell for help?"

113

I told him I had tried that, but it didn't work.

He said, "Sure. I could of told you that."

I told him about the work on subliminals we had been doing at Dr. Crosse's ranch. I informed him it was the triggering phenomes which had caused him to smash open the wall and save my life.

"Well," he said, looking at the hole in the wall with new respect, "it sure worked."

He said his name was Dan. He took me to a hospital. It was a filthy and frightening place. I told him I wanted to call Dr. Crosse, in California. Dan asked if we should call the police first, to tell them what had happened to me at Mr. Elam's house, and to swear out a warrant against the Elams. I said I didn't want to do that.

"Why not? Shit, they tried to kill you. And this man is running for President!" He held up a copy of a newspaper and I could see Mr. Elam's smiling face, and large hand, as he waved at the camera taking his picture. The headline said, "'If democracy works in Russia, maybe we should try it here,' says Elam, to cheering garment workers."

I told Dan, "In the first place, I don't know if Mr. or Mrs. Elam even know what happened to me. Their three sons could have hit me, and then told the Elams I stopped to go to the bathroom. Then, later they could have said I just walked off, or told them I didn't want to interfere with Mr. Elam's candidacy, so I went back where I came from. Or, there could have been someone else in that basement, perhaps someone hiding. Perhaps, a squatter, or a political enemy of the Elams."

"Doesn't seem likely," said Dan. "But still, you want the cops in on it."

"No, I don't. If we tell the police, the newspapers will find out. Any news about this, about a man found bricked into a wall below Mr. Elam's house, a son by artificial insemination, any of that, though it need not reflect badly on his ability to hold high office, or the ideas which he would set into motion once he got into office, still, might sway some voters to vote for his opponent. Unfair though that might seem. I don't want to be the cause of Mr. Elam's losing something that obviously means as much to him as does the Presidency of the most powerful nation in the world. If I thought,

114

that by my actions, or worse, just by my very existence, I had brought sorrow into the life of my father, I'd feel lower than a snake's belly in the bottom of a dry well. As we say out West. I would wish I had never started my search for my True Dad."

I gestured with my face toward a plastic cup with a bent straw sticking out of the lid. Dan held the cup so I could drink from it.

He said, "Well, whatever you want. I guess I'd just as soon not have to explain to the Transit Authority how I came to smash in all those tiles, anyway. What with the budget the way it is, I don't think they'll be too happy with me for givin' em a wall to replace."

I said, "You saved a man's life. You would be hailed as a hero, for getting me out of there."

He shook his head, saying, "It might be different if you were an actual passenger, but the way things are, you not even buying a token or anything... I'd just have to explain to Mr. John Walsh, my superior, and to Otis Washington, Pedro Matilla, and Paddy Loubert, my crew, how I heard curse words comin' from the wall, and how I came back there, with a mallet, to destroy the wall if it cursed me one more time. I can hear the howls."

"But you were right," I reminded him. "You weren't imagining the words, I was saying them."

"Yeah, but you don't get it. You said you and this Doctor Crosse found out how you can get people to do things, with these dirty words, right?"

"Triggering phenomes."

"But they don't know why they're doin' it, right?"

I nodded, as well as I could.

"So they did it for the dirty words." He looked at me in a direct way, that seemed to indicate that he had been injured. "No," he said, looking now at his hands, which were latched in his lap, facing upward, "if you had been yellin' help, and I helped you, I'd be a hero. But the way things are, I'm just as happy to let the whole thing slide, if you know what I mean."

He called Dr. Crosse for me, and Daphne answered. By this time, I knew I had been in the wall for four weeks.

Daphne said, "Where are you? Who was that?" referring to

Dan, who had only said, "Is this the Crosse residence?" I told her I was in a hospital, in New York. I said, "That was Dan. He rescued me." She told me she and her father had been very worried about me.

"When we didn't hear from you, we called the Elams. They said you'd been there, but left."

The Elams' assistants (for they never talked directly to the Elams) had said no one in the family knew where I had gone after leaving their townhouse. Daphne said she and her father had called the New York Police Department, and all the hospitals in the area, to see if anyone had been brought in with a concussion. They had also tried the morgues of the City.

"Where is Dr. Crosse now?" I asked. She said, "He's in New York. He went there to find you, two weeks ago. He's staying at the Pierre Hotel, because you left your things there, and he thought you might come back for them, or send for them."

I was amazed and gratified to hear that Dr. Crosse had gone to all that trouble, just to find me, and I told Daphne so. She said, "You should give up all this searching for your True Dad, Reynold, and let my father be your father."

Within an hour, Dr. Crosse was with us, in the hospital room. It was wonderful seeing his smiling, tan face, and his kindly eyes, and the hair that fell in a pile over his eyes from time to time. I introduced him to Dan. After assuring himself that I was all right, or would be after a couple more days of rest and good food, Dr. Crosse questioned Dan and me closely. He said, "Reynold, I think you've just made a great discovery!" He asked how I had said the phenomes. He asked me to duplicate the volume of my voice, and he taped what I said on a portable tape recorder. He asked how long and how often I had intoned the words. Then, he asked Dan about the nature of the material through which my words had come, in order to arrive at Dan's ears. Dan, thanks to his expert knowledge of subway construction, was able to tell Dr. Crosse the precise specifications for the tiles, and the stone wall behind them. Then, Dr. Crosse asked Dan about when he had first become aware of the phenomes coming through the wall. Dan said he couldn't say exactly when it was, but it was several weeks before he had broken through the wall. Dr. Crosse asked him if he had noticed any new feelings or thoughts about that particular spot on the platform, before he had first heard the words. Dan said the only thing he could think of was that he noticed he liked to stand closer and closer to the wall every morning, while waiting for his crew to come in the hand-car. He said he used to stand right by the tracks, to step onto the car without it having to stop, but in the weeks before rescuing me, had been backing up maybe a step or two every day, until he found himself waiting right against the wall, and he had to run across the platform to jump on the hand-car when it came.

"Wonderful!" said Dr. Crosse.

Over the next two days and nights, he continued to question Dan. He also rented some electronics equipment I couldn't recognize, so he could test Dan's hearing and brain waves.

Doctor Crosse had his own reasons for thinking we should not tell the police what had happened to me, which he told me after I told him my reasons. "Reluctantly, I agree to keep your secret," he told me one time when Dan had gone home. "Of course, this man Elam, and the members of his family, deserve no consideration. I cannot go along with you there. However, the story of your escape would bring our work into the eye of the public, and I'm sure you'll agree, especially now that your impromptu stroke of genius has opened new realms for us, and given us the extra assurance to carry subliminals to the next step, I'm sure you'll agree that we need continued anonymity to continue our studies." I was flattered that Dr. Crosse thought so highly of what I had done. He said that when the final records were written, and the story of the subliminals was finally a part of the history of science forever, that the "Stengrow Auditory Annoyance Effect" would assure me of immortality. As for Elam, he said he would not vote for him, even if he did somehow (unlikely though it was) turn out to be my True Dad. More than that, he said he would keep "tabs" on Mr. Elam, and if the day ever came, and secrecy was no longer required of him and me, and it should happen that I changed my mind, and decided to rescind my anonymous forgiveness of the Elams (for after all, they didn't know they were forgiven, not knowing I was alive) then he would, he vowed, have enough on them to bring them down from whatever height they might have attained by that day. I said I was sure I would never give the go-ahead for anything like that. "Honor thy father and mother..." as my father and mother used to tell me.

When I was a bit stronger, we said our goodbyes to Dan, who had become a good friend, and Dr. Crosse brought me back to California, to the ranch. Before leaving Dan at the hospital curb, Dr. Crosse gave him a check, and Dan, not wanting to take it, was trying to shove it back at Dr. Crosse, when he happened to see the amount, and said, "Twenty-five thousand dollars?! What for?" Dr. Crosse said, "For saving the life of one who is like a son to me." That made me cry, as the limo slid into the traffic, and I turned around in the seat, to wave at Dan.

Chapter 13. The Work.

"Over a period of several decades, America's advertising agencies and some of their client corporations [have] engineered subliminal techniques into a fascinating new technique of behavior modification through a direct communication with the brain's unconscious systems." (Dr. Wilson Brian Key, *The Clam-plate Orgy and Other Subliminal Techniques for Manipulating Your Behavior*, Signet, NY 1980).

"They came to me, as I told you," said Dr. Crosse, "the people whose identity I keep to myself, patriots, is all you have to know, and that is why Daphne has been etching on the glass, and that is why you and she have been making the photographs with the embeds, and that is why now I ask you to write up, in some detail, the story of your experience locked in that basement room."

He said that thanks to the earlier work done by Daphne and myself, and thanks to the story of my miraculous escape, which he had told to his sponsors, they had decided to expand the funding for our experiments. He said that only he and I and Daphne, of all the people on the Redbird campus, knew what we were doing. He praised me, and gave me a tremendous raise. Now, I was earning two thousand dollars a week. The only problem, said Dr. Crosse, was that I still had to be off the books, my name couldn't be officially linked with the project, and we didn't want to leave, he said, a "paper trail." That was fine with me. I found a hiding place on the ranch, and when Dr. Crosse gave me my pay every week, in cash, I went out there, to my place beneath the pine tree by the seasonal stream, and buried it in a green tin box with a picture of Gene Autry on the cover.

Dr. Crosse and Daphne ate their meals in my bedroom while I was still weak, and fed me, and we happily plotted our future research in this wonderful new field, subliminal mind-control.

When I was well again, Daphne and I resumed our experiments in the field of subliminal suggestion.

We tried out our ideas in the little town, and around the campus. We gained access to the student newspaper, and the textbooks, to cover them with embeds, and study the effects they had on the grades of the students, or their opinions on various issues of the day.

For some reason, drawings of cute animals, and little drawings of skulls, ghosts, monsters and/or decapitated men and women are also very effective. For certain purposes, such drawings are even better than the words - for example, in advertisements for cake mix and cigarettes designed for women. We caused a certain brand of cigarette to dramatically improve its sales in Redbird overnight after an ad appeared in the program for a school concert, showing a pack of these cigarettes, and subliminals of decapitated bodies and skulls all over it. According to Doctor Crosse, this is because death is as attractive to most of us as sex is, especially to cigarette-smokers.

I remember those days, walking and talking with Daphne. Sneaking into the office of the student newspaper together, and substituting the embedded photographs for the ones the newspaper had been planning to print. Sitting together in the malt shop, sipping sodas and watching the kids thumb through the magazines we had planted in the racks. The nights we shaved subtle "fuck's" into the turf of the football field, or circlets of "pussy's" and "sex's," cutting the letters into the grass with pinking shears. Then, the Saturdays, the crisp autumn air, cheering Redbird on, while Dr. Crosse operated the video cameras we had set up around the stadium, to watch both purchasing behavior, and romantic behavior on the part of the fans. Our spirited discussions about which words had caused the fans to buy too little and make love too much, and why. Creating these subliminal words and pictures with Daphne, on the only sheets we shared for many months, our sheets of thick glass, and photographing the glass along with all those magazine and newspaper pictures. This was the best part of my life, to that time.

But my thoughts turned once again to finding my True Dad. It seems, as a matter of fact, that each increase in my good fortune, each new sign of the power of my work, made it that much more important to me to find my True Dad, and through him, my entire ancestry and affinities.

I felt a growing need to benefit some segment of humanity, and glorify it, and I felt it should be that slice of the world pie that came to a crumbly, rich point in myself, Reynold Stengrow, or whatever my name might eventually turn out to be.

Chapter 14.
True Dads # 2 and # 3.

Dr. Crosse and I decided that if I was going to search for the rest of the possible True Dads in my ledger, it would probably be better to find a new detective agency to help me. We didn't want to answer any embarrassing questions from the man who had located Mr. Elam for me.

I went to L.A. quite often in those days, because we were doing business with a printer down there, and on one of my trips, I went through the L.A. phone books and found the names of detective agencies. I called one, and went to see them. They had an office in Century City. It was modern, with grey, pebble-textured furniture.

I was led to the office of my Personal Investigator, MacDonald "Mac" McDonald, a man of approximately fifty, thin, with blonde hair and a blonde mustache that drooped over the corners of his mouth. I gave him the list of names I had gotten from Dr. Lord's ledger. I didn't tell him why I wanted to locate these men, though he asked. He said I didn't have to answer, as long as I could assure him that I didn't intend to break any law once I had the information I was looking for. I said I didn't. I paid him a couple of thousand dollars in cash ($400 a day, five days in advance) and three days later, Mr. McDonald called me to tell me he had located the first name on the list - Mr. Merle Persson - and asked if I could come in to talk about what he had found.

Merle Persson, as it turned out, was as rich as Mr. Elam, my other putative Dad, but unhappily, for him and for me, he was dead. He had died two years before, as the result of a shootout with a Los Angeles Police Officer. Mr. Persson had been unarmed, but according to the police officer, "it looked like he had a gun." Police experts testified at the hearing, that men with hairy wrists, (as Mr. Persson evidently had), when they raise their hands in the air, (as Mr. Persson was doing when he was shot), sometimes, in certain light, at certain times of day, can give an appearance of having a handgun snapping out of the sleeve, into their waiting fingers. "The officer sees the hair on those wrists," the expert said, "and he doesn't know if it's a gun, a knife, maybe a grenade launcher. Could happen to anyone." The fact that the policeman fired eight shots into Mr. Persson (six after the man had died) was explained by the fact that the officer had been under a great deal of stress recently, having been dropped from the Department's weightlifting team when traces of steroids were found in his urine. In any case, the officer was exonerated of all wrong-doing, and given a stress disability leave at twice his normal salary. However, said Mac, Mr. Persson was also exonerated of all wrong-doing, because he had not had a gun, and more than that, he was judged to have been correct in the argument he was having with the police officer, about the expired parking meter.

"He was killed over an expired parking meter?" I asked in amazement, grieving over the loss of the man who could possibly have been my True Dad.

"He said the meter was free," said Mac.

"How can there be a free meter?" I asked.

"Well," said Mac, "it seems that Mr. Persson was something of a philanthropist. Where other men might endow the city with a symphony orchestra, or an art museum, to improve the lives of their fellow citizens, Mr. Persson, who made his fortune in parking lots, incidently, decided to use his money giving people what they really could use - he endowed parking spaces."

"I didn't know you could do that."

Mac nodded. "He did it. Made a deal with the Municipal Courts, eternally endowed about two hundred meters around the city. Way they did it, the meter just always says there's an hour left in it. That way, Persson avoided unwanted publicity. The meter maids were supposed to know which were the endowed meters, by this blue stripe they all have around the bottom the pole. Evidently, this one cop was a recent transfer from Glendale, didn't know about the endowed meters, had driven past this one meter all day and seen it always had the one hour on it, assumed it was broken and that since this one car had been there all day, the owner of the car must know it was broken, started giving the guy a ticket, at which point Mr. Persson comes along --"

"You mean it wasn't even his car?"

"No, he died for another man's free parking," said Mac sadly, "Another man's free parking and those damn hairy wrists."

I took a walk in Century City, thinking about Mr. Persson. Thinking about the soaring joy of the people who had found and would continue to find, as long as Los Angeles existed, those free meters, with their eternal one hour periods of grace. And I knew he must have been my True Dad. How like me he had been - how generous, how thoughtful - and that touch of secrecy about his generosity - how like me, with my subliminal etchings! I sat in one of the endowed spaces, in a cool concrete multi-levelled lot in Westwood, studying the pictures of him given to me by Mac. Except for his coloring, eyes and hair, chin, cheeks and nose, and ears, Merle Persson and I could have been the same person!

I went around for days, feeling good about myself, reading the Constitution and Declaration of Independence, underlining inspirational passages and muttering them over and over to myself as I thought of possible gifts I might one day give to my city, in emulation of my True Dad. Perhaps, I would endow oxygen, water, underwear... It was hard to decide what endowment might be worthy to continue the tradition of my True Dad, but I knew I would find something.

Then, just as I was settling into my new identity as the surviving son of a great social benefactor, proud heir to a rich man's gracious urges, Mac McDonald called me again, and said he had found the next name on the list.

Although I was sure we had already found my True Dad, I felt I should go and meet Mac, if only to take a glance at the photos he might have of this new candidate for my paternity. Then I would know in my own heart that the new man was not a possibility.

We met at a Denny's Restaurant, on Pico Boulevard, because Mac said he had a stakeout near there. He ate hash browns and bacon while we talked. He tossed a manila folder across the table at me, that said, on a tab at the top of the cover, JEFFREY POPPER.

"What do you know about him?" I asked.

"Popper's a pauper," said McDonald.

"A pauper," I thought. "A pauper named Popper? How was it possible for a genius - which is what Dr. Lord had promised the Stengrows after all - to turn out after a lifetime in America, the land of the greatest opportunity known to the human race, a pauper?"

"He's a writer," said McDonald, by way of explanation. "I brought you some of his stuff... it's pretty weird..." He held a paperback book over the file. I took the soiled paperback from his hand - a publisher I had never heard of - paper of an inferior quality - no comments whatsoever on the front or back cover, about the book or the author - filthy dirty covers and pages - McD. had found it in a used book store on Lincoln Boulevard. "Only book he's ever had published," said McD. "Only came across it 'cause the owner of the bookstore happened to remember Popper's name, remembered he had this book since 1969, down on the bottom shelf in the back room somewhere. Not difficult to see why Mr. Popper isn't better known. Just take a gander at a page or two..."

I opened the book, which was called AN HONEST BOOK, and read the first page. I had already, I'm ashamed to say, concluded that Mr. Popper was my True Dad. I think I decided the moment my hand touched the manila folder. I felt it in the pages of his book, in the letters of his name, in the face of McD. seated across from me on his vinyl fat couch. This was a flaw in my character. I can see that now. This instantaneous acceptance of each subsequent candidate for my True Dad, on the basis of almost no evidence at all... I hadn't even opened Popper's file. But something about the way the sun was slanting in over the hash browns, and the fly-speckled covers of Popper's book, gave me a genetic twinge...

It was not hard to understand, reading a page of the book, why Mr. Popper was less well-known than, for example, any other writer of all time. Here is a sample of his work:

"I will make good laws, for the
sustenance of many nations,
and of the world.
I will reveal that the cure for cancer resides

in corn, and the silk threads
around the stalks of corn.
I will put a wooden table in the middle of the street
in order to create Peace
in the place where I was born and raised -
Who will make this possible?
How will a way be made for me,
*   here on Earth?*
Only by Your Grace, and that of the Beautiful Lady. "

"You sure you want to meet this guy?" said McD., and of course I said I was. He gave me the address. He asked me if I wanted company but I said I'd rather go alone.

Mr. Popper's apartment was in Venice, across from the beach. One room and a kitchen in an old pink house.

According to Mac's file, Popper wrote from six in the morning till noon, then he sold jokes for 25 cents on the beach. I waited on the street between the house and the beach, and when I saw the man whose pictures Mac had shown me, I leisurely followed him down to the boardwalk. He looked both older and younger than the 42 years old I had been told he was. Older, because he was overweight, with a stooped walk and ragged, torn clothes, and because he had a balding head of black and grey hair. The remaining hair flew in all directions and looked dry, as did his mostly grey beard. However, he also looked younger, much younger, because his face and eyes were almost childish. His skin was smoothe, with no wrinkles on his brow or under his eyes. His eyes themselves, large dark brown eyes, seemed innocent of all intention or experience. To everyone he passed, he called out, "How ya doin'?" and shot his hand in the air in a formless salute, as he moved on. His neighbors, who were working in their gardens, or sunning themselves on the concrete aprons in front of their houses, seemed to like him well enough. They all shouted something back to him. But none of them asked him to stop by their stone fences and tell them anything. From the way he was moving, I could see he didn't want them to. He sped up when he passed the houses with people in front of them, and only slowed down when there were no people. Then, he liked to study the flowers and weeds that grew through the fences, and he spent at least a few moments (while I had to hang back and look inconspicuous on that tiny walk-street) touching and talking to any cats he happened to pass. I could hear him say to them, "Tender Vittles?" and reach into his pocket for a white envelope from which he would pour out a couple of spoonfuls of semi-dry cat food. Then, the cats would stand and stretch their muscles, and gobble up the food, and Mr. Popper would move along.

At the beach, he bought and consumed a container of coffee and a danish. Then, he stood up from his bench, and unfolded a large white sheet of paper he had been carrying. I saw that it opened into a garment - like a tunic - that he slipped over his head, and fastened with a rope around his middle. The tunic came down to his knees. On the front and back, in large, hand-written letters, were the words; "Jokes - 25 cents. Laugh, or You Get Your Money Back."

I, sitting on one of the benches, watched as he walked alongside the passing tourists, generally choosing a couple or a family, and offering his services. "Just a quarter," he would say. "Three knee-slappers for a half a dollar." Most of the time, the people kept going, sometimes drawing up their shoulders against the presence of this big, obviously destitute individual. But sometimes, a child might say, "Oh, Daddy, let's buy a joke! Please!" and the father, with obvious feelings of pride and benevolence would dig into his pocket and take out a quarter or two, and say, "OK, let's have a joke."

Then, Mr. Popper would generally start with: "A man walks into a psychiatrist's office, says, 'Doc, you gotta help me, I don't know what to do, wherever I go, people ignore me!' The doctor says, 'Next.' "

Then, if they liked that one (stolen from Henny Youngman, if I'm not mistaken) he would go on to: "Man calls an attorney's office. Goldbloom, Goldbloom and Goldbloom. Says,'May I speak to Mr. Goldbloom?'

'Sorry, he's passed away.'
'Then, I'd like to speak to Mr. Goldbloom.'

127

'Sorry, he's not in the office right now.'
'Then, can I speak to Mr. Goldbloom?'
'Speaking.' "

Also stolen from Henny Youngman. However, I am sure Mr. Youngman never had to give back the quarter. On the other hand, Mr. Popper, confronted with the stoney faces of those to whom he had told his jokes, would often have to give back their money, and watch them walk away arguing about what the jokes might have meant. Sometimes he might yell after them, "*Speak*ing. *Speak*ing. Don't ya get it?" but most of the time he just veered toward a new family or couple, with his odd style of walking, which made it look as though he were about to topple forward with each step, his wild hair and beard, and his hard-to-believe offer of laughter.

Finally, I stood and went toward him. I tried to introduce myself to him, but he was so intent on selling me a joke, that I gave him a quarter and he told me about the man and the psychiatrist. I pretended to laugh, not wanting him to know I had heard the joke at a friend's wedding, where Henny Youngman had entertained, and not wanting him to feel as though he had to give me back my quarter. Then, before he could sell me another joke, I said, "Actually, I wanted to talk to you."

"I don't get it," he said. "Are you making a movie or something?"

"No," I said, "I read your book, and I liked it. I wanted to meet the writer.

Since my experience with Mr. Elam had been so disappointing, from a family point of view, I had decided to keep my possible relationship to Mr. Popper a secret, until I got to know him better, and had a chance to see for myself if we resembled one another in any way.

He was amazed that anyone had ever seen that book, let alone read it. He said, "I was very embarrassed when that book came out. It was published by a girlfriend of mine. Her father was some kind of rich golf pro or something. She did it without my permission. It wasn't ready."

Again I told him I had liked, actually loved, his book. I was lying, I am sorry to say. My only excuse is that I was almost positive that after many false leads, I had indeed found my True Dad. Perhaps it was the toppling-forward walk, so much like my own. Perhaps, it was because he was the only candidate so far who had not tried to kill me, or died before I could meet him. He was both non-threatening, and available for perusal. Many have offered their children less and been fathers anyway. I was sure Mr. Popper was mine.

I remembered the money I had in the metal box in the ground at Dr. Crosse's ranch, and I decided, there and then, I wanted to use some of it to publish the works of Mr. Popper.

I said, "Do you have anything you think might be ready for publication? I'm a fan of yours and I have some money in a metal box buried up in Redbird, and I want to use some of it to publish your books."

He stood frozen for a moment, then his arms dropped to his sides, and were buried in the tunic. His mouth hung open for a moment or two, then he closed it, and focused his eyes on me. "Published," he said, "are you joking?" I assured him I was not.

Now he sat down. He sank his head between his knees and covered it with his arms, like a dog expressing shame in a movie.

"Are you all right, Mr. Popper?" I asked him.

He raised his head and upper body slowly, and looked at me through his sad eyes. He said, "I don't know if anything is ready."

I asked him, "Have you written anything since the book I read?"

He said, "Have I written anything! Come with me!" He stood up quickly and for a moment I thought he was going to fall over on his face, but then I realized he was merely walking forward, and I had been fooled by the toppling-forward style of walking which he and I shared, obviously a characteristic of our Popper blood. I reached out to catch him, but he was already past me, and I had to hurry to catch up with him. He strode back to his apartment, and I followed him up the wooden stairs.

Inside, there was a living room-bedroom, a kitchen and a bathroom, all filled with Mr. Popper's manuscripts. They were all in dusty manila folders piled from floor to ceiling along every wall in every room, their titles written on each folder in pencil, along with the date of completion. There were even manuscripts in the refrigerator, and the freezer.

He said, "I used to have furniture, a TV, records, a record player. I had to get rid of all of it, to make room for my books."

"Don't you ever send them to publishers?"

"I did, once," he said. He took from the top of one of the manuscript piles a small yellowed piece of yellow paper, folded in three. He unfolded it and showed it to me. It was a rejection letter from *The New Yorker*, dated thirty years ago. There was a picture of a man looking through a monocle at the top of the page. The letter said, "The manuscript you have sent us, "The Search for Wilhelm Reich," defies ready classification. Is it a story, is it a work of non-fiction, is it a prose poem? One of our editors thought it might best be characterized as a "prophecy" of some kind. Especially that part about the survival of only two-sevenths of one-eighteenth of the population of Europe, after that worldwide cataclysm caused, as far as any of us can tell, by salt. The one thing we could all agree on was that, no matter what genre your work may belong to, it is certainly a bad example of that genre. It is, in fact, a bad example of writing in general. It makes us question the whole transition of mankind from an oral to a written culture, because anyone who had to communicate what you have written face-to-face would certainly be smacked many times before he had had a chance to finish talking. Only through writing could such a spurious mind follow its own impulses for a long enough period of time to create this hideous abomination. Thank you for thinking of *The New Yorker*. Good luck in your future writing, if you should be foolish enough to do any. Yours very truly, etc. etc. etc."

I said, "This was thirty years ago. Look at all you've written since then. Haven't you submitted anything else for publication?"

"I will," he promised. "As soon as something is really ready. Then, I'll send it to *The New Yorker*, and they won't hate it. But I have to have something that's ready. Then, I'll ship it right out."

He said he wrote every day and with the money he made selling jokes on the beach, he wanted and needed for nothing, except some more room, so he could store his novels and poems.

Riffling through some of the dusty manila folders, with their pleasant heft and motion, I asked him if he didn't mind not being famous. He said, "All writers want to be famous. But it's no good if it happens before you're ready. I want to be ready."

I wanted to change his mind, and give him reason for hope, so I said, "But I'm a member of the new generation, and I love your writing!" I waved in the air the thick novel I was then holding and said, "This book here... It's ready, and I want to publish it." I was even brash enough as to take a bunch of hundred dollar bills from my pocket and push them towards him. "This is an advance," I said. "Just give me your manuscripts, and I'll publish them."

He was tempted, I could tell. "But not that one. Wait a second and I'll find one that's almost ready. Maybe not totally ready, but possibly with a quick polish... maybe a new first chapter... Now, let me see here..."

He turned to the wall and started searching up and down the tall piles of folders, shaking his head as he read each spine, lovingly running his hand along the dust of his life's work, and touching many of the titles with his fingertips, as he read them. But each time, he shook his head, and moved on to the next title, and shook his head again.

"No," he said, "they're not ready."

"Well, what would make something ready?"

"If I thought I could send something to *The New Yorker*, and they would publish it, then I'd know I was ready. They're the last word, you know."

A couple of times he seemed about to lay his hands on some folder, and pull it from the endless wall of manila, but he always stopped himself, with a small sound from his throat, a warning croak, telling him the work wasn't ready.

I said, "I want to help you, though. You're my favorite writer. Can I be your assistant?" He said he didn't need one and couldn't afford one. I said I would do it for free, but he said he still had no use for me.

As for me, I found him strangely loveable, though I couldn't really approve of him because he had wasted his genius and hadn't made any money with it. Also, his writing was not to my liking or

131

indeed to anyone's. But he had a good time doing it, and I felt by then it was obvious he was my True Dad, and I wanted to help him. I wanted him to assume his rightful place in the literary life of America, along with my favorites, J.D. Salinger and Tom Clancy. But how to help this pitiful pencil-pusher? He wouldn't even take the hundreds of dollars I tried to give him. When I left him, he allowed me to give him two dollars, but only on condition that I listened to a dozen jokes.

I returned to the ranch, and told Daphne that I had gone to see the old man, that there was no doubt in the world he was my True Dad, and that I wanted to help him, but he wouldn't let me.

She said, "Why don't we rent him some storage space for his writings? That seems to be the only thing he needs." I said I didn't think he'd accept, except on the condition that he be allowed to tell us six jokes for every dollar of the rent, and that was too much of a sacrifice, I suggested, even for one's own putative flesh and blood.

Finally, she and I secretly bought a one-story building a block away from his apartment, and told him it belonged to a friend of ours who needed a house-sitter. We said if he would work there, and spend a few hours a day there, he could have free storage space, and a small salary. Daphne and I arranged the building as a perfect, climate-controlled storage facility. We put in a desk and chair, some plants, snack machines that took no coins, file cabinets, copy machines so he could have triplicates of every page...

He accepted the use of the place when Daphne and I convinced him his manuscripts were in danger of crumbling from exposure to the sea air. "You can keep them safe and secure until they're ready," I said.

Popper and I and Daphne arranged and filed all his writings.

Still, I wanted to help him more than that. Daphne again hit on the solution, suggesting a way we could help him get his writings published.

One day when he was out, giving Tender Vittles to the cats on his walkstreet, Daphne and I retyped two of his short stories on typing paper which had been embedded with subliminal words, (sex, fuck, death... the usual anthology) and sent them to *The New Yorker*.

132

A week later, we arrived at the storage facility to find Mr. Popper sitting on the cot he had set up, to spend some nights there, as well as for naps. He was still in his pyjamas, and was weeping into his open hands. A letter lay on the floor at his feet. Daphne picked it up, and read it. I read over her shoulder. It was from the editor of *The New Yorker*, telling Mr. Popper they were accepting both stories for publication.

He looked up at me and said, "Without a plot, without sympathetic, antipathetic or even recognizable characters, without a hero or an equally powerful but evil villain, without a celebrity name attached and without the use of one single line from Henny Youngman's act, I have done it... I have sold a story to *The New Yorker!* Home of Truman Capote, John Hersey, A.J. Liebling, Gilbert Rogin, J.D. Salinger, Vladimir Nabokov, S.Y. Agnon, Mr. Luria, Whitney Balliett, John Updike! Pauline Kael! Ved Mehta! And you, you have made it possible!"

He stood up and kissed me and Daphne with gratitude, for having been instrumental in bringing about his time of good fortune, after all his desert years.

Daphne and I clasped one another around the waist and dried our happily weeping eyes with paper tissues we got from a box on the nightstand beside the cot. We all went out for lunch at a place called the Queen of Cups, and talked about the future. I asked Mr. Popper if he thought Daphne and I could send some more of his novels and stories out to publishers.

He said, "Not a bad idea. If I'm good enough for *The New Yorker*, who shall say me no?"

I went to Dr. Crosse, and told him what Daphne and I had been doing to help Mr. Popper. I thought he might be angry at me for the unapproved use of subliminals. I told him I was sorry to have gone so far without telling him beforehand, but "once the idea popped into our heads, we just did it. I guess we didn't really think that magazine would take his stories, but now that they have, I'd like to continue helping him."

Dr. Crosse thought about it for a while, then asked, "Did you tell him about the subliminal paper you sent his manuscript out on?"

I said, "No. Both Daphne and I know the necesssity for secrecy."

He said that was good, but he asked, "How do you think Mr. Popper would feel if he knew that magazine accepted his stories because they were reading 'fuck', 'sex', and so on through the typed letters, written in the weave of the paper?"

I said, "He wouldn't like it, but that doesn't mean he'd be right."

"How so?" asked Dr. Crosse.

I said, "It's like you said about the people buying the toothpaste. If they want it, they need it. If those editors want his stories, they need them, too. I just helped them focus on the stories long enough to realize that."

"You're learning, boy," said Dr. Crosse with a grin. He slapped me on the back and said he had to go to a class. He said, "Send Popper's novels and stories out, if you want, but remember - keep notes. Above all else, keep notes!" Then he ran out of the house.

Daphne and I doctored the manuscripts, and Mr. Popper sent them out, along with a cover letter, also embedded with triggering phenomes.

The editors gobbled them up. At first, the advances were small. A few thousand dollars for a novel, or a few hundred. But almost everything sold, on the first submission. Finally, Daphne and I could not devote any more time to the submissions, having work to do at the ranch, so we found Mr. Popper a literary agent. This agent had the idea of having an auction for one of the books, and it sold for a hundred thousand dollars.

Soon after that, we went down there, and he had gotten a haircut, and his beard was shaved off. He was moving his manuscripts into a new condo in Santa Monica, "North of Montana," as he proudly said, and he had a lovely young girl helping him pack. Her name was Genevieve. She quoted passages from some of Mr. Popper's works as they packed: "In Russie, Czeck, and the Ukraine, they think they have abolished inheritance, but they are inheriting yet," and "This is a prayer for the people living in cities, O Lord, the nations gathered in Your town," and so on, issued forth from her lips, pushing aside bubble gum to do so. I was surprised to see that Mr. Popper sighed deeply, and a little hopelessly, whenever he heard a quote from his works.

As he looked around his apartment, and out the window at the walkstreet, and the beach down the block, he shook his head, and sighed once again. He said, "I had my picture on the cover of the *L.A. Times Book Review*, Genevieve and other young people have memorized passages of my works, I'm on TV two or three times a week, giving my opinions about the latest movies, insurance plans for the State of California, censorship, gays, abortion and James Branch Cabell, everything the publisher thinks of for me to do."

"Isn't this what you wanted?" I asked him.

"My work existed to be hidden," he said. "I didn't realize that until I saw it in other people's hands, like a hostage. Now, I have to write more, to ransom the old stuff back. But how can I ever write enough, how can I get my pages safely back from the thoughts of other people?"

I slapped him on the back, to buck him up, perhaps help him inhale more oxygen.

Then, we packed my car with the stuff that wouldn't fit in the van he had rented, and we all drove North of Montana Avenue, to Mr. Popper's new condo, where he would live with Genevieve. It was a large place, four bedrooms, plenty of room for the collected writings of the man I considered to be my True Dad.

He was so busy, or so conflicted about his good fortune, he hardly noticed when Daphne and I drove away.

Chapter 15.
The Church of Marilyn.

Mr. McDonald called me periodically to assure me he was still working on the remaining names on the list, but I didn't really care, because I was so sure Mr. Popper was my True Dad. I had not decided when or how to tell him about our relationship. I was in no hurry. I was just glad that Daphne and I had been able to help, and glad that Dr. Crosse seemed to like our written report of the subliminal help we had given Mr. Popper. He told us we were doing 'valuable work.'

We continued our glass etchings, and I continued helping Dr. Crosse with his other work, when the subliminals didn't require my full attention. Daphne and I continued our innocent flirting, but I could tell she didn't want it to go any further than that, and I tried to forget my desire for her, and concentrate instead on the lab work we did, with our shiney new Mackworth Camera, among other items. And our Pupilometer, observing the movements of volunteers' eyeballs over pictures we would place before them. We had to plot the movements their eyes made over the pictures, to know how people look around in a picture, first looking here, then over here. How interested they are with each part of the picture, indicated by how long their eyes rested on that spot, and how wide their retinas opened when looking at each spot. That way, we knew how to design a photograph or drawing, best to draw the viewers' attention over the subliminal story we wanted to tell them while they thought they were looking at the visible picture. All these things are linked forever in my own brain, with the simple pleasures of standing next to Daphne, or feeling on the hairs of my arm the same molecules of air that had a moment earlier been passing among the hairs of her arm, or seeing through the side of my vision the tip of her nose, or the forwardmost loops of golden hair from the top of her head, as we bent over some apparatus together.

Inspired by our success with Mr. Popper's work, we devised another experiment on our own. Of course, we couldn't carry it out before we had the permission of Dr. Crosse, and we were very happy when he heard our plan, and approved of it. He said, "You're thinking like real scientists, now," and Daphne and I looked at each other briefly, trying not to show our pride.

Our experiment was in the field of religion.

There was a student group on campus - a small group - called the Church of Marilyn.

Really, it was just three or four girls, who lived in adjoining rooms in one of the dormitories. Their leader, a History major named Maya Quantrell, had been obsessed with Marilyn Monroe since she was five or six years old. She said had first seen Marilyn Monroe in "The Seven Year Itch," on TV, and had fallen in love with her. When the film was over, she had asked her mother who that lady was, and her mother told her the story of Marilyn Monroe. How she had been an orphan, and always dreamed of being a movie star, and became the greatest star in the world, but was hated for being beautiful and sexy, and was killed by unknown members of the Kennedy family, to cover up her love affair with John Kennedy, then the President of the United States. At least, this is what Maya's mother told her, according to Maya. Then, one night, a vision of Marilyn Monroe came to Maya, in her room, a beautiful vision in the dress from the film, that blows up when the subway goes under her, and the dress was billowing upward, as in the film, and Marilyn told Maya that she was very special to her, and that she loved her.

This experience led Maya to seek out every Marilyn Monroe film, and to read everything written about her, and collect her autographs and publicity photos, and finally, eleven years later, to found The Church of Marilyn, which had, as I say, just the four members. She and her roommate, and their friends.

The four Church of Marilynites had tried to proselytize Daphne, and she, who could never bear to disappoint anyone, had agreed to go to one of their services. I drove her there.

I had never before been to a religious service. I had played basketball in the gyms and basements of churches and synagogues, and I had peeked in, and seen the layouts of the houses of worship,

137

but until I saw the Mass of Marilyn, I had seen no faith at the moment of its worship.

The service started with all of us sitting in a circle on the floor. There were two posters of Marilyn Monroe on the wall over Maya's writing desk. One showed Marilyn in that scene from "The Seven Year Itch," and the other was the Coroner's photo, of her dead body when she was on the autopsy table.

Maya stood, covered her head with a shawl, and said: "Forgive us Marilyn, for we are the misfits. We were born in asphalt jungles. Our life here is a wild river toward the Niagara that leads to death..." and words to that effect, which I cannot remember after all this time. I remember one part where she said, "You offered them love, but they used you as a whore."

After the prayer, Maya acted out what she called "The Passion of Marilyn." This was a representation of the last night of her life, from the time she was awakened from a nap by a call from Robert Kennedy, begging her to cancel a press conference she had announced for the following day. Maya, pretending to be talking on the phone, refused Robert Kennedy's plea, complaining of the way the Kennedys have treated her. She threatened to reveal certain secrets Robert has told her while they were in bed together, among these the fact that the CIA and the Mafia had a deal to kill Fidel Castro. Robert Kennedy, (played by Maya's roommate, who played all the non-Marilyn parts) tells her she doesn't know what she's saying, she's playing with fire, she could get hurt. The Mass then goes through several more telephone calls from and to Marilyn, until the Kennedys and their doctors come in the middle of the night, and forcibly inject her with barbiturates, which they assure her will settle her down, but which kill her... Maya laid herself flat out on the floor, whispering to John Kennedy: "I have hidden our daughter where you'll never find her. You and your family will never get a chance to kill her, as you have killed me." When she died, we were all crying.

The other girls then stood, one at a time, and told stories of the ways in which the Spirit of Marilyn had helped them throughout the preceding week. One girl was blessed with a passing grade in Social Science class; andother was cured of a bad cold, after praying to Marilyn.

Finally, Maya stood, and led us in a final prayer to the movie-star. We all kissed, and Daphne and I departed.

Leaving the service, Daphne and I passed a redwood tree with notices stapled to it, and she noticed one announcing the upcoming Campus Faire, at which all the student groups on the campus - clubs, teams, religious groups, fraternities and sororities - would be represented. Each group was going to have some kind of game booth, either gambling, or games of skill, to raise money. And each group had a scheduled informational lecture, to get people interested in the group. We noticed that the Church of Marilyn was not listed as one of the participating groups. This is when Daphne had her idea, and we talked about it, and went to Dr. Crosse with it, and he said we were thinking like scientists.

"We want to see if we can get people interested in the Church of Marilyn," we told him. "We have two months."

We returned to Maya's room, where we found the four adherents to the Church of Marilyn.

"People aren't interested in the Church of Marilyn," said Maya, sadly. "We try to tell people all the time, but you two are the first who have ever taken us up on our invitation to come to the service."

"Just sign up for the Campus Faire," Daphne said to her, "and let us handle the rest."

We took some of Maya's Marilyn Monroe photos, and re-photographed them with specially etched overlays. We decided on an embedded web of delicate fucks and sexes, and I etched some pictures of small dogs and cats, rabbits, drowning men and women, and images of broken windows and shattered metal and torn limbs, as might be seen after a terrible car crash, since early research had given us reason to believe such negative pictures would enforce our message in the minds of the viewers. Our posters were pictures of Marilyn, covering the whole sheet, and the words, "The Church of Marilyn. Come see us at the Faire." We put them all over the campus, and I bought space for a full-page ad in the student newspaper, and a smaller one in the local advertising sheet. We also made a three-minute video about the Church of Marilyn, which we sent to TV stations all around the area. Some of them ran all or part of our tape, sometimes re-cutting it to make it seem like their local newsman was interviewing Maya. Of course, we embedded the tape with subliminals.

One day, after a long afternoon of working on another of Dr. Crosse's experiments - tachistoscoping pictures of a woman in a fur hat and coat, with her arm plunged into a fur muff, at a variety of sophomores who were asked to write down whether or not the room seemed hotter or colder every thirty seconds - Daphne and I put away the projector, folded the portable screen and put it behind the accordian-like vinyl room divider. We both rubbed our eyes, which hurt from the long hours in the darkened, flickering room.

I said, "You work too hard. I don't like to see your eyes burning like that."

"I don't mind. I'm working for the fulfillment of my father's work," she said. "When he asked me to help with his research, I was so grateful that finally there was something I could do for him."

I said, "I'm just grateful to spend time with you."

We took our flickering consciousnesses in her Jeep, down to the Redbird campus, to visit the Alumni Auditorium, for this was the day of the Student Faire. The booths were set up in the lobby of the auditorium, and the lectures given by all the groups were upstairs, in the classrooms.   We went up the stairs, to look for Maya, because we knew her lecture was about to begin. Since there were so many campus groups - racial, religious, sexual, hobbyist, political - many of them had to have their lectures at the same time. As we went along the corridor on the second floor, we passed the rooms set aside for the Chess Club, the Square-Dance Cotillion, the Sewing Circle, and others. Their representatives stood in the doorways of their lecture rooms, looking forlornly up and down the corridor to see if anyone was coming. We heard a sound, as of many voices, but we never seemed to come to the room where the voices were. We went to the end of the corridor, and the lean, dark, angry-looking speaker for the ROTC sneered when I turned to him and said, "Church of Marilyn?" and he jerked his thumb toward the ceiling and his shoulder toward the stairwell. I opened the swinging door to the stairwell and immediately saw the solid crush of students climbing to the third floor in one undulating line, like a dinosaur's stuffed intestine rising to the third floor. Daphne and I entered the stream, and were carried along. It was impossible to tell if all these people were happy or sad. Angry? Curious? They merely were going, all going.

On the next floor, the corridor was jammed with people, trying to see down toward the far end, where in the doorway of a double classroom, I saw Maya climb on a yellow chair and shout to them, "The Church of Marilyn lecture will be down in the auditorium, people. We just can't stay up here. We'll be crushed."

For a moment, the crowd did nothing, then they began heading for the stairwells, peaceful but, in their way, frightening. We caught Maya's eye, and she made her way to us.

"You were right," she said. "I never realized the amount of interest there is in our Church. It's wonderful!" and she thanked us for encouraging her, and rushed off to give her lecture. That day, the Church of Marilyn received 300 new members.

We couldn't tell her what we had done. Not that I am saying our subliminals were the only factor in getting all those people to the Church of Marilyn lecture. They helped, but there is no way to determine how much, based on this one test. And the subsequent tremendous growth of the Church of Marilyn, which today has chapters in all 50 states, and in 134 nations, I attribute more to the power of the Service, as written by Maya, and to the life and works of Marilyn Monroe, than to the magic worked by myself and Daphne. Also remember that the Church of Marilyn devotes its special attention to the care and nurturance of orphans, and children without fathers, because Marilyn Monroe was raised fatherless, and was sent to live in an orphanage, and because she spent the final days of her life in a city park, wearing sunglasses and a shawl, watching children at play. Since we have become a nation of children without fathers, is it any wonder that the women of the Church of Marilyn have had so much work to do, and found themselves a part of so many lives?

Nevertheless, at that moment, Daphne and I felt that we had greatly benefitted our friends, Maya and her three co-religionists. We walked away from the auditorium, holding hands. We climbed into the Jeep. As I started to back up, I looked at Daphne, and her eyes were shining like prisms of mercury, if there are any such things. My excitement arose from the power we had had over the lives of others, from seeing that power. Daphne, I think, was excited for another reason: because she saw the fulfillment of her father's science, career and reputation, dreams left in her care by the death of her mother.

We returned to the ranch. She ran into the house ahead of me, calling to her father. "Dad! Dad! We've done it! You'll never believe what just hap..." Then, she stopped, and turned to me, just bounding through the front door. "This is Dad's weekly behavior modification field trip," she said, and I remembered it almost a moment before she said it. We were both disappointed.

"Well," I said, "we might as well write up our results, and show him when he gets back."

"Right," she said, cheering up.

We went into the room we had been using for our makeshift lab. It was mostly empty, except for a wooden door laid out on two sawhorses, as a desk, and two folding chairs, where we sat as we did our etchings on the glass. We sat in our chairs, which were on opposite sides of the door-desk, to write our reports, but after a moment, I got out of my chair, and stretched out on the soft rug, in the long parallelogram of sunlight that was barrelling through the windows from the west. I put my hands under the back of my head, and set the heel of my left shoe on the toe of my right shoe, and let the sun hit me in the face. I thought of the posters we had done for the Church of Marilyn, and the crowd of people we had drawn to the lecture, and smiled to myself. At that moment, Daphne turned in her seat, and burst out laughing.

"What's so funny?" I asked her, casually.

Instead of answering, she got up and went to the door of the room, and closed it. On the back of the door, was a full-length mirror, and when she closed the door, I could see myself in it. I saw that, along with the sunlight, my face and whole body were also covered entirely in swirls and eddies and lines and crowds of fucks and shits and cocks and cunts and deaths and so on. I was momentarily startled, thinking perhaps that the content of my thoughts had found some way to seep out and show themselves on the surface of my flesh and even on my clothes.

Then, I saw that the pattern was being caused by the passage of the sunlight through a stack of our etched glass sheets, which were standing on the radiator, leaning against the window. I covered my eyes and allowed myself to fall flat on my back. Daphne, still laughing, came and sat down near me. Then, she lay down on the rug, beside me, and took my hand away from my eyes.

"Look," she said. She put her finger against her own cheek, then her neck, to show me the words there. I grabbed her hand, and kissed it. She took it back, and opened the top button of her shirt. She pulled the shirt back, so I could see the top of her breast. She moved, so the words (or triggering phenomes) floated across her breast, over her white skin, covering and uncovering the delicate blue veins just under the skin. I was sad - I didn't know why - seeing those words on her skin, but I couldn't turn away. I put my hand on her breast, following the words (which were in her handwriting) as though I were reading braille. She looked at my face, above my eyes, and started running her fingers along my forehead, I suppose following a similar path of words.

I took my hand from her breast, and put it around her thin waist, pulling her toward me. As her body moved, huge SEXes and FUCKs rushed over her face and hair. We kissed for a long time, then we clumsily took off our clothes and made love, (the first time for either of us) sending the patterns of the shadows of the words on rolling irregular waves of motion, up and down our bodies, over our curves and limbs, as we moved together, until the sun set and the room was dark.

Chapter 16.
Faint Signs of Secret Success.

The next day we made love again, outdoors, a.m. No words floating along our skin surfaces. Near the stakes in the small vegetable garden. After which, I said I thought we should probably be married. She was buttoning her dress. She asked me if I was in love with her, and I said, "Yes." I asked her the same and she said "yes," too.

"Therefore," I said, "unless we want to reserve the right to change our minds, and start looking around for other people, and get all kinds of sexually transmitted diseases, and die, if we're lucky, or if we'e unlucky live alone and miserable to age one hundred, we should probably get married, is what I'm saying." She nodded silently. She looked around on her clothes for signs of dirt, and whisked them away.

Finally, she said, "But I don't want to tell my father. Not yet."

I said, "You mean you want to elope?"

She said, "No. I want to hold our wedding off for at least a year, and during that year, not tell my father."

"I feel funny about keeping a secret from your father. He's been so good to me. He's always treated me honestly." Then, after a while, I said, "Don't you think he'd approve of our getting married?"

She said, "I think he would approve. He likes you. The thing is, all my..." and then she couldn't go on.

I said, "It doesn't matter, Daphne," and touched her shoulder, "anything you want. I don't mind."

She seemed to gather her strength, and go on, saying, "All my life, I've wanted to have a feeling my father didn't know about, a thought he couldn't read, an idea he neither agreed nor disagreed with. I have always wanted to have a secret from him."

"A secret? Why?"

"Do you know how it feels to have a psychologist for a father? A man whose life is based on his ability to understand what other people's minds are doing at any given moment? A man who understands, who makes allowances, who sees to the heart, who comprehends the big picture, who analyzes the minutiae and heals the sick? It drives you nuts, Reynold! Nuts! It's like having a piece of glass where your forehead is supposed to be." Here, she put her hand on her forehead and wiped it across roughly. "Just once, once - I want to have a feeling and not hear what he has to say about it. A feeling I don't have to change for his purposes or pleasure, as so many times I have had to do. Do you understand what I mean? Do I sound like an ungrateful child? I feel ashamed to say things about my father. It's just that falling in love," and here she touched my face, "has created new feelings in me, that I don't want to share with my father. Not yet, anyway."

I said, "I owe him a lot, but I'm willing to keep our relationship a secret, if that's what you want. Even if he winds up hating me, or thinking of me as a betrayer, it doesn't matter."

We kissed once more, settling into the loamy, aquifer-moistened earth for a few moments, before returning to our work, typing on Daphne's computer the results of our Church of Marilyn experiment. We sat closer than we had before, except when Daphne thought she saw the shadow of her father across the table, and moved away from me. Then, she laughed at her mistake, and took my arm, and pulled her chair closer to mine. I didn't like the feeling of having a secret. I remember that, clearly. But still, I knew that she had been suffering, and I would have done anything to alleviate her pain. I knew that she loved her father, and I trusted her to see the three of us through this time. We had our affair in secret. Many times, I was on the verge of telling Dr. Crosse, but the memory of Daphne's intense feelings rose before my eyes every time I was about to tell him, or hint in some light way, that his daughter and I were in love, and stopped me. In all other things, I was his follower, but in this secret, I obeyed her.

We hardly ever made love, or acted like lovers at the ranch, even when Dr. Crosse was not on the property. Instead, when Daphne and I went on our field trips, to meter the shopping habits of the local housewives, or monitor the beer-buying at sports events and taverns, we would stop in parking lots, movie theatres, or empty apartments which we would rent for the purpose. Sometimes, we would go to the next town over, Beltrone, and rent a room at the Hilton., and several times, after thinking up some elaborate excuse, we were able to spend a few days in L.A. together, where we got a bungalo at the Beverly Hills Hotel, and everyone thought we were the children of important producers.

We could afford these luxuries because Dr. Crosse's backers were so pleased with our results. Dr. Crosse came to our work-room one morning when Daphne was in the garden and I was alone, etching fucks in the glass. He said he had been able to force the backers to change their deal with him, from a grant, to a contract for services. According to Dr. Crosse, his fee for these services would be twenty-six million dollars the first year, increasing by fifteen per cent per year for ten years.

He raised my pay to just under a million a year ($80,000 a month). As before, I was paid in cash. Dr. Crosse reminded me that I was, and would remain, off the books. If anyone asked me what I did around the ranch I was to tell them that I was the groom.

"Everyone but you, sir," I said, having a slight private joke with the word "groom."

"Excuse me?" said Dr. Crosse.

"Well, you know why I'm here," I said. "No sense lying to you." He looked at me strangely, sort of sideways and a bit downwards. I laid out a thin plank of a smile and my eyes attempted to walk across it, from myself, floating and lost, to Dr. Crosse, the dry land. He smiled at me, and I felt relicved.

Daphne came into the room, and looked from her father to me and back again, wondering if I had betrayed her confidence. I tried to show her by a look that I had not. She sat down beside me and he told her about the new deal. He then told us both that we would start to see the subliminals showing up in national magazines and on TV commercials. He said the unqualified success of our early tests had convinced his backers the time was right for total public saturation with subliminal messages.

STENGROW'S DAD

"One fascinating sidelight," he said with a shrug and a laugh, "You know those glass sheets full of embeds? They're copyrighted now. I put them in Daphne's name you understand Reynold. But there it will be, on the bottom of every page and photo using one of our embeds. A subliminal copyright notice."

Daphne said, "It should have been your name, Father, you're the scientist here. We're just your assistants."

"Darling," he said, and hugged her. The three of us were all crying within a minute or two. As for myself, I was very moved over the love between Daphne and her father, and by the idea that the woman I loved had these copyrights, because it was a sign of her blessedness (I think) and also, I should admit, the knowledge that I was about to become a millionaire made my head light, and it felt like wind was rushing through my brain. I felt all-powerful, all-energetic, and yet at the same time I had never been so filled with fear. Because in your mind, something incredibly good happening, suddenly, can cause the same doubts concerning the stability of the universe as can something incredibly bad happening suddenly. I felt I might be hit by a falling rock, or lightning, and it took many weeks for that fear to pass.

Perhaps it was that fear, the natural outgrowth of unlooked-for good fortune, that caused me to experience the first doubts I ever had, about the work itself.

Before, I had thought all our work was for the benefit of America. Dr. Crosse had said we were working for "people who care about America." People who didn't want to let others control our minds. When he said that, I had lain in my bed, my chest rising and falling with pride, with love for my country. I had felt like I was a part of law enforcement. Don't ask me why. But now, when all this money came to me, I felt like I was not a part of law enforcement, but of some secret group of sneaks. I realized I knew nothing about our backers. I was beginning to worry about my effect on society.

If it is true, I asked myself, that my actions have such a profound influence over the lives of others, then what influence is this? Is it a good influence, or a bad influence? And, having this power, or any power, one must ask oneself - How can I best use this power? I wanted to use whatever power this might be, for the good of other people.

"Are we doing good when we add these scratched images over the photos in this magazine?" I asked Dr. Crosse at dinner that night, getting a magazine from the sideboard, one of the ones Dr. Crosse had brought to the work-room before, to show us our embeds covering the face of the Prime Minister of Canada standing next to Senator Peeny, of Massachusetts.

Then, I turned the pages of the magazine until I arrived at the picture of a beagle, advertising a radial tire. I remembered when Daphne and I had carefully lowered a thin square of glass over a large, glossy photo of a beagle, and on the glass was an intricate, finely wrought pattern of FUCKs and SEXes. As I laid the magazine down, rolled back to the page with the beagle, and nudged it in his direction with the inside of my thumbs, Dr. Cross reached into the inside breast pocket of his cowboy-styled sports coat and pulled out a jeweller's loupe, through which he appreciatively studied the overlay.

"A great job you kids did," he said with a congratulatory sweep of his right hand through his thick brown hair, and a laudatory shake of his face back and forth.

"But are we doing good, by doing this, or are we doing bad?" I asked him again.

He said, "I don't think I understand your question. We're certainly doing something useful, which I think can be seen from the enormous amounts of money people are willing to pay us for doing it. Usefulness is a quality I would have to ascribe to any action or product of man before I could in good conscience call that activity or product a quote good thing unquote."

"Harmlessness is a quality *I* would have to ascribe to any action or product of man before *I* could in good conscience call that activity or product a good thing," I said, using as much of Dr. Crosse's sentence as possible in order to show him that I had not lost respect for him, even if I did find myself in the unusual position of having to question something he had said.

"What could be harmful about what we are doing here?" he asked me. He pushed his soup bowl away and grabbed a roll.

148

I looked at Daphne, to see what she thought of our discussion, but her head was bent over her bowl, and I couldn't see her eyes. However, her face was bright red. I didn't really want to go on, but having started the discussion, I felt I might as well express all of my doubts.

I tapped on the magazine page where a certain complexity of swirling DEATHs closely followed the soft, naked sweetness of the exposed inner ear-flap of the adorable beagle.

I said, "If a man, hurrying home from a day at the office, and it's snowing on his shoulders and face, and he steps under a tent of plastic on West Broadway, to buy a copy of TIME magazine, with the face of this beagle on it, not because he needs domething to read, not because he loves or even cares about beagles, but because his subconscious mind, independent of anything true to him, the man, the customer, himself- just because his sneaky, silent, subconscious mind, responded to a bunch of hidden words, then..."

"Triggering phenomes" Dr. Cross corrected.

"A bunch of triggering phenomes, then, that stole a part of his mind from him, that whispered suggestive phrases to him in his weakened tired state. Can he really be said to want that magazine?"

"Well," said Dr. Crosse, staring at his roll, "I have thought about what you're saying, and I've come to the conclusion that yes, he does really want that magazine. Yes, even if he only wants it because he has been seduced by triggering phenomes - we still can say that he wants the magazine, because he buys the magazine."

"But..."

"Possibly, in the future, we can hypothesize a society where each man and woman gets his daily requirement of triggering phenomes at home, in the marriage bed, perhaps. In such a society, people would pass by this magazine like so much dogshit in the street. Even if we agree, that the man who buys this because he's been drawn to it by that clever nest of fucks and cancers and shits you kids wrote over the beagle, does not know why he is buying it, we still have to admit that he did have a reason for buying it. If you deny him the pleasure of his attraction to pale, shadowy obscene words, you might as well deny him the pleasure of his attraction to his wife. For we have no idea what attracts us to one another as men and women, while we do have ample evidence to suggest that whatever it is, we do not find it when we do find one another. If that makes any sense."

"So, you're saying, since Nature attracts us subliminally, making us do things for reasons our conscious mind never suspects, why can't people do the same thing to one another. Is that it?" I asked, respectfully,

"Exactly," said Dr. Crosse. "And another thing. As for your scruples about working for people whose motivation might be commercial, rather than patriotic, as you thought before, I ask you: is it not patriotic to help the American economy grow?"

"Yes, sir," I said, though I did not really know what an "economy" was, since I was so young.

Perhaps sensing my ignorance, Dr. Crosse popped a bread-ball into his mouth, smiled at me as he spiked it with his side teeth, and then said, "You see, the more people buy things, the more manufacturers can produce, and sell. This gives jobs to people in manufacturing, sales, service, advertising and so on and so forth. People make more money, they buy even more, there is a general improvement of the conditions of everyone in the society, and that's called prosperity, and that has always been considered a good thing."

"Even if people spend all the money on things they don't need?"

Dr. Cross said, "Who's to judge need? Does a man need another drink? Does he need a new car when the old one still runs? Does he need a chocolate bar? If he wants it, he needs it, as far as I'm concerned. That's good enough for me, even if he doesn't know why he wants it and even if I do."

Dr. Crosse continued, growing enthusiastic: "We're artists here, that's all we are. How is what we do any different from what any artist does? They play a game with sex and death, that's all. Truth to be told, religion does the same thing, no different. Every religion gets into your reproductive behavior and your death thoughts like a leech, and sticks like glue to these two areas of your mind, till you follow it like a zombie. Every religion I've ever come across has had one hand on a man's balls and the other on his tombstone."

I didn't know if Dr. Crosse was right, but I didn't like the effect this conversation was having on Daphne, who seemed to be choking silently. I was too confused, and secretive, even to reach out and slap her on the back in case she might be choking on food. In a moment, she was all right, and she looked at her father and me over the lip of her water glass.

"We're artists. You kids, especially," said Dr. Crosse, smiling at Daphne. "Yes, we hide our art, that is true. But can you tell me the name of one single artist whose work has not been driven more by his secret concerns than by his open concern? They all have their secret stories, they're all writing secretly about their Mom and Dad, or little Becky, the girl who wouldn't kiss them 30 years ago, it's all a secret ocean, Reynold! For the past three thousand years, they've been hiding God in paintings of orgies, or orgies in paintings of God-- How have we overstepped any boundaries not already kicked over by the entire tradition of the Western world?"

I said, "I don't want to steal people's free will."

"Don't worry," said Dr. Crosse. "If you broke into a house, and there you found and stole all of the free-will there is in the world, you'd still crawl out the window empty-handed."

After our conversation, I threw myself again into The Work. Daphne and I making the glass sheets, for pictures that were now sent to us from New York, twice a week. When we weren't etching, we would be in town, or down in Los Angeles, studying shoppers and making love.

As it happened, we had a series of innovative ideas, most of them after making love, that led to what you might call the "super-expansion" of the field of subliminals, and possibly this is the place to mention that you, the reader who will never read this, are probably reading it in an environment almost totally drenched in subliminals, thanks to Daphne and myself.

Your wallpaper, if it is from any of the five largest wallpaper manufacturers, is covered with obscenities. You might have yoghurt in the refrigerator with FUCKs and CUNTs and COCKs written on its surface tension. Cookies with FUCK in the frosting. Cookies and crackers with SEX written thousands of times in the dough. We drew up the plans for subliminal weaving of fabric, so your shirts and suits can suggest sex and cancer, and get you that big promotion. These fabrics have been blamed (by the Senate Investigating Committee before which I testified, about which, more later,) for the current plague of sexually transmitted diseases from which the world now suffers. I hope that is not the case. If it is, it is one more thing for which I shall be tortured throughout eternity, in hell. Or so I have been told, and believe.

Then there were the subliminal building materials to help the stagnant construction industry, subliminal patterns on aircraft control panels to keep the pilot staring where he's supposed to be staring, subliminal patterns in the bulbs of tanning lamps, so you can have SEX and DEATH written all over your face and body, invisibly. We made these tanning lamps for the leaders of industry, and later for American diplomats, who met with their Russian counterparts, with SEXes and FUCKs written in Russian on their faces, hair and clothes. Some day, the full story of the role subliminals played in the collapse of Communism, will be revealed to the world. At present, however, the documents are sealed in the archives, not to be opened for seventy-six years, and the only people who know what happened - Daphne, Dr. Crosse, and myself - are here, along with so many others, in One Corner, Maryland, our existence denied by those who put us here.

But back to those early days:

Sales of cigarettes advertised with the word "CANCER" written over their packs shot up, seats on airlines advertised with the word "CRASH" etched on the faces of the passengers sold like hotcakes.

The question I asked myself changed.

It had formerly been: "May we justifiably steal the free will of our fellow citizens?" Now it became: "Do people with subconscious minds that would respond to this stuff even deserve to have free will?"

As I saw the spread of our techniques, to more and more magazines and newspapers, to the TV, to products and flesh, I felt satisfied, for I thought I was increasing the prosperity of a nation and a people who would be lost unless they were fooled.

152

STENGROW'S DAD

I buried my salary in the hiding place I had prepared at the ranch, in the metal box, and I felt like a benefactor of all mankind.

Chapter 17.
The Blessing and The Curse.

In the next year, we saw subliminals on television, in the movies, secretly embedded on baby clothes, to make fathers love their children. On telephones, the largest corporate clients of Dr. Crosse's backers would regale all callers with a constant stream of inaudible obscenities, burbling through the wires while they were on hold. We saw the introduction of subtly sperm-flavored milk, cereal, bread and cake, and the very successful marrying of steak sauce, spaghetti sauce, and salad dressings with a slight vaginal odor. Fluorescent bulbs that threw sex grids over a room to impart a general air of low suggestiveness, which caused workers to bend more assiduously over their desks, for many more hours, and feel less like workers than like individuals looking for love. On the bars of prison cells and etched into the cinder blocks of each cell, under the blood-grey paint, FUCK and SEX, to make the prisoners want to stay.

According to Dr. Crosse, these things happened in such a way as to involve the smallest possible number of conspirators.

Only the following groups had to know:

Our backers knew, of course. And the owners and managers of the cartels that owned all the natural resources, the materials on which the subliminals would be embedded. And the owners of three advertising agencies. Dr. Crosse reckoned the number of those in-the-know at less than two hundred. Each conspirator was pledged to secrecy, and they were all well pleased with the results of our work, because sales were up.

I felt like I was Thomas Edison. I had put my genius (the heritage flowing through me of my True Dad) at the service of my time and place, and for this I was being generously rewarded. Edison himself said, the test of any invention is its financial potential. Ashamed? I was proud. Ashamed? Well...

You see, my father, Mr. Stengrow, was a teacher, and my mother was a teacher, and I had always thought that I would teach. But what did I teach? Who would I ever benefit who wasn't rich before I met him, or her? I didn't know. I told myself not to worry about these questions, because I was still young. For now, I reasoned, I might as well continue under the direction of Dr. Crosse, who had shown faith in me, taken me in, and was paying me in cash, every week, which I buried in my hiding place, and took out to spend when Daphne and I took our increasingly frequent trips to Los Angeles and now and then, New York.

We pooled some of our money and bought two condos - one in Westwood, on Wilshire Boulevard, and the other on 63rd Street in New York. We also got two black Mercedes-Benzes, one for each condo. All people stared at us, especially at Daphne. Other women were attracted to me, partly I suppose because of my tendency to a vulgar display of wealth. I had Rolex watches, Cartier watches, expensive clothes, and manicured nails. Forgive me, I was young, it was like a joke to me, I had no sense of the gravity of money. I was a joker, so to speak. The class clown, suddenly laden with an ermine crown and robe. I was all over the place. You have to remember also that I had stopped my education, to work as a technician of deceit, so my thoughts grew more and more limited to the sphere of power and control and wealth.

At the same time, both Daphne and I were troubled by certain events that began to occur after the first mass publication of our subliminal embeds.

Some of the models used in our advertisements started to die. In spectacular ways.

The first, a girl whose name we did not know, until her death, was killed when a heavy glass coffee-table was dropped out of a second-floor window, onto her head, on Bleecker Street, in Greenwich Village. When I saw her face on the cover of the *Post*, I knew immediately it was the beautiful young woman who had appeared beside the Mitsubishi hatchback in six magazine ads, and two TV spots. I thought no more about it, but that it was very tragic.

Then, the second model was killed, a girl from Texas Daphne and I had met on one of our working visits to the ad agencies. She was run over by a motorist who, for no apparent reason, swerved his car in the middle of a busy street, to run her down on the sidewalk.

The motorist said he didn't know what had happened. He thought he might have had a heart attack, but he seemed healthy enough when the news lady interviewed him, only a few minutes after the incident. Then, the third model - a young man whose face and torso had been embedded by Daphne and me with FUCKs, COCKs and CANCERs for a new chocolate cookie - was knifed in broad daylight by two teenagers, whose only explanation was that they had "felt like killing him." I couldn't escape any longer the thought that there might at the very least be some connection between these deaths and the subliminals. Though I couldn't imagine what the connection might be, the third death made me tell Daphne of my fears.

Together, we approached Dr. Crosse. He agreed that statistically, the chances of three models used in subliminal advertisements being killed within such a short space of time, were slim. "But you have to remember, they all lived in New York," he said.

"I wouldn't want to think there was something about our work that got these people killed," I said.

Dr. Crosse said he would look into each of the cases, and tell us what he found out. "But I wouldn't worry about it, Reynold," he said. "You have to remember the embeds at*tract* people to the products and other items to which they are attached. If anything, the models in our ads should be experiencing enhanced social lives. I can't believe our embeds have led to their being slaughtered in the streets."

Unfortunately, about this one thing, Dr. Crosse was mistaken.

Chapter 18. Space Dad.

MacDonald "Mac" McDonald, my detective, called me to tell me he had found another name on my list. McDonald still didn't know the purpose of my search, or what it was that the men on the list had in common.

This entrant was named Mr. Huss.

"He was a bitch to find because the government keeps him locked up like a cat in the storage compartment of an airplane," said McDonald, when we met in the Denny's again, where he showed me Huss's file. As I looked at the file, and listened to what McDonald said, I tried to find clues that would tell me if this Mr. Huss was my True Dad. A day earlier, I had been totally positive that Mr. Popper was my True Dad. I had been happy to think of our similarities and tried to go through every day according to his words, inasmuch as I could understand anything Mr. Popper had ever said. I had felt like his son, and I had tried to be a good son. When McDonald had called me, the day before, to tell me about finding Huss, I almost felt he was intruding on me, and on my relationship with my Dad, Mr. Popper. But by the time I got off the phone with him, my mind was already beginning to send out tendrilly shoots of thought and hope, that the new possibility, Mr. Huss, was indeed my True Dad.

Now, sitting in the Denny's, I looked at Huss's picture. That was not at first encouraging. The man was short, with red skin and pale blue eyes, short blonde hair moussed and standing straight up. He had a pugnaceous, unfriendly and confused look in his eyes, as though he had just been accused of shoplifting and was bracing himself to oppose a body search. I noticed in some of the long shots, he was standing on one foot, with the other one tucked up behind him. I might have thought he was merely scratching an itch on his right buttock with the heel of his left boot, except for the fact that he held that pose at different times and in different situations. In one set of shots he was going over some plans with three Air Force Generals. The three Generals stood in what might be called the common way, with both feet on the ground, but Mr. Huss was always seen with just the one on the ground and the other up somewhere else. I might have thought one of his legs was not there, or crippled in some way, but he seemed to have full use of both legs, and both of them were long enough to reach the ground. But he never let them touch the ground at the same time. When Mac McDonald saw me frowning and shuffling the pictures, and deduced what I was thinking, he said, "You should see him walk."

He explained, "This fella doesn't put one foot down in front of the other one like the rest of us. He hops ten or twenty paces on one leg, then switches over and keeps going on the other one."

In answer to my unasked question, he said, "No indication why he does that." Could this really be my True Dad?

He was a rocket scientist. I liked that. According to McDonald, Mr. Huss was every bit the great genius Dr. Lord had promised the Stengrows I would have for a Dad. In this way, even though he did stand on one foot, hop, and have the face of a public masturbater, Mr. Huss made more sense as my True Dad than Mr. Popper did. I have to admit that, even with the growing public acclaim for Popper's work, and the improvement in his appearance once he got a hair stylist and new clothes, he never seemed to me a genius sufficient to the role of my True Dad. On the other hand, according to Mac McDonald, Mr. Huss was an important man in the United States Space Shuttle Program. Now that was more like it. I was soon imagining us sending off little rockets on open fields, that give out shoots of steam and fly in zig-zag paths as we race after them (Huss hopping, but so what?) and I could see us at the consoles in Houston, me standing over his shoulder as he is giving the order lighting the lights on the colonies of Mars. A rocket scientist! The fabled and traditional vocation of geniuses! My True Dad was looking out at me from those pictures! That rosy skin, that keen eye, that individualistic manner of self-propulsion, at odds with, yet oddly compatible with, his traditional Marine haircut. I couldn't believe the enormity of my good fortune. My True Dad was Mr. Huss! There was no question in my mind!

"He works out at Edwards Air Force Base," said McDonald, "but they don't seem too proud of him. Got him and his crew socked away a mile from the main buildings and landing areas - 'bout halfway to California City - on land that's supposed to be poisoned by radiation from all the rockets they've had to abort over it, the place isn't even supposed to have houses on it, and I can tell you it wasn't any picnic finding Huss's headquarters. Had to use infrared." He showed me a picture of a vast expanse of sand.

"What's this sand?" I asked.

"That's where he lives, it's his lab, that's where Dr. Huss has been for the past eleven years. See this?" He pointed to what looked like a sand dune, one of many, and showed me by circling his fingernail over the spot, a doorway, leading down beneath the desert.

"How will I get to see him?"

McDonald said he had done some asking around, and had learned that the Air Force was scheduling a shuttle landing for that weekend, and had issued an open invitation to journalists to tour the Base.

"My suggestion, you want to get near him," said McDonald, "we just go out there in a jeep and say we're reporters. My people tell me Huss is a publicity hound, but they've got a whole PR team out there whose only job is keeping Huss and the Press as far away from one another as possible. What we do, we start out lookin' at the other shit, and then kind of bank off, make a break for the lab."

The next day, I went with McDonald out to Edwards Air Force Base. We went in the main gate, and presented the false Press I.D.'s Mac had gotten for us. Then, we followed the press tour for a few minutes, seeing the centrifuge where astronauts are spun around and around, and the wall displays of the astronauts' food tubes. Then, Mac signalled to me, and we went out to the jeep. He drove as though heading back for the main gate, but then circled into the desert, and doubled back toward the vast many-miled interior of the Base. I daydreamed as we drove across miles of featureless sand, where there were no guards or vehicles.

After a half hour, we arrived at a large tin building, maybe the size of a football field, set in the desert three miles from the nearest road.

This tin building had a roof covered with sand, and sand was piled against the walls on all sides. I could see why it had been invisible from the air. We parked in front of a red iron door that sat like a navel in the mounds of sand, and Mac pounded on it with his fist. After a few minutes, he pounded again.

I took the opportunity to look around, and stand in the gathering airstreams, that blew tumbleweeds around us and our jeep. Soon, my face was covered in sand and grit, and small berries or seeds, probably from the tumbleweeds. Here and there I thought I saw a rock sliding toward me across the desert floor, but dismissed the thought as a fantasy. After a while, I heard someone clearing his throat inside the structure. Then, the sound of metal scraping against metal, as bars and latches were thrown around inside. The door opened, with a clutching, sucking sound, and out of the dimness and lowness of the doorway hopped Mr. Huss. He took two bounds in our direction.

He was smiling. "You fellas lost?" he asked, friendly enough.

"No, sir," said Mac, "we're with the press tour. They sent us out here to talk to you, if you don't mind."

"The PR guys sent you?" he asked, tucking his right leg, which was the one then off the ground, more tightly into his own rear end.

"They said you were doing some fascinating work out here."

At this point, appeared behind Huss, a gangly towering form with a blue New York Yankees cap on his head. Huss jerked a thumb back in his direction and said, "Larry Lindbergh, my assistant." Then, to Larry Lindbergh, he said, "What do you think, should I talk to these boys?" Larry shrugged so completely that his shoulders pushed his cap up on his head and supported it in midair. Huss reached up and set it back firmly on the young man's head and said, "I guess if we're gonna give em the tour we better do it right away, before General Stockey sends the fellas out to shoot em and bury em in the sand." Then, while I was still seeing that vision, he turned to me and said, "Because nobody sent you out here to see me, fella. That much I do know. But, seein as it meant so much to you to come, I might as well show you around." With that, he turned by hopping from one foot to the other, and then sprang himself back into

160

the gloom of the structure. Larry Lindbergh ducked to get through the doorway, and followed Mr. Huss, and Mac and I followed him.

Inside, there was a concrete floor with several cars and trucks parked on it. The enormous volume of the building stretched out a mile before us. The area we went through was covered with dust and cobwebs, and snakes slid over the floor. Mr. Huss took us to a small elevator and we took it down three stories under the ground. When the doors opened, the scene that greeted us was totally different from the one above.

Here, we walked along a red metal catwalk, down a narrow corridor, until it opened out onto what looked at first like a huge ball of light. As my eyes became accustomed to the brightness, I could see that we were standing over a bubble - a thin glass dome, containing a lush green garden, and some small houses, brick streets with yellow and blue flowers, and a lake, and what looked like farmland, deep furrows stretched out around the small buildings. We stood about fifteen feet up from the ground level inside the bubble, and looked down on the tops of the houses. As we watched, a man and a woman in overalls came out of one of the houses and kissed in the doorway. Then, she went to a well with two buckets and filled them, and the man threw the straps of a plow over his shoulders, and began to plow one of the fields.

"What you see before you is a complete Space Station. A biosphere, actually," said Huss. "I designed it. It's under the sand not just because we wanted to keep it secret, but also because this way we know exactly how much oxygen we're producing in the sphere."

"What's it for?" asked Mac.

Dr. Huss said, "Twenty astronauts have been living in that sphere for five years. Growing food, making their own air, recycling the limited water supply, and so on. We're learning amazing things about what it'll take to survive in outer space from this thing," he said, and hopped along the circumference of the bubble to the next point of interest.

"I don't understand," I said. "Why doesn't the Air Force want you to talk to reporters. This place is wonderful!"

"Can't understand it myself," he said, "given the fact that we're expanding the frontiers of human knowledge here and providing the United States with the best and surest escape plan yet devised to get us away from the nig..." And here, Lindbergh threw his large body in the space between Dr. Huss on one side and me and Mac on the other, waving his hands and shouting nonsense syllables like a guard in a basketball game, trying to block a shot.

"Dr. Huss," he said, "Please! Remember the work!"

Huss grinned sheepshly and scratched his head in a winning way, and said, "Disregard what I just said. Larry here reminds me that the only reason I haven't gotten a raise or been allowed to publish or even been asked to attend the annual Edwards AFB bar-b-que and dance is that I have what is generally considered though not by me to be a big mouth... OK? Spoke out of turn. Forget it."

I said, "Sure," though I didn't exactly know what the problem was. As we moved along, Huss resumed telling us about his space station, and then once again he veered from his topic to say, "And best of all, no nig..." at which point, Larry Lindbergh started singing "In a Gadda Da Vida" at the top of his voice, to drown out the rest of Huss's remarks, and Huss, catching himself, said, "Larry, you're right. You're right and I'm sorry." Then to me, he said, "Larry reminds me we wouldn't want to let what I just said get back to the Jew you probably work for, whatever newspaper it happens to be, they own em all. Don't want em makin a lot of trouble for the Base, do we?"

I wasn't really thinking about what he was saying. I was mainly interested, as was my wont with putative Dads, to constantly agree with him, and by my agreeing, to bring him joy, as also with the warmth of my gaze, the studious concentration which I gave to his every gesture and motion, his face and voice and hands and body language, the way I laughed when he said anything with a smile and almost cried when his face became squeezed up with the feelings of rage and protest that periodically coursed through his insides. All these acts of mine perhaps put Dr. Huss at his ease - because he gradually spoke less and less about the space station and more and more about the "*problems we have right here on earth.*" Of course, whenever he veered to these earthly topics, Larry Lindbergh would

162

go into his singing or shot-blocking behavior again, until Dr. Huss, with amazing dexterity for a man standing on one leg, finally grabbed Larry Lindbergh and hurled him into a mop closet and slammed the door shut on him. He locked the door. Over the sounds of Larry Lindbergh's protests and pounding, Huss led Mac and me to a small apartment, another floor below the level of the huge dome - a little chamber where, he told us, he slept and worked.

There, we saw a beat-up personal computer and lots of newspapers piled up around it. On the walls were pictures of Adolf Hitler, and rows of people saluting Nazi flags. There were pictures of burning crosses, of men, women and children in Klu Klux Klan robes, and cartoons of blacks, Mexicans and Jews being burned at stakes or being tortured. There were also pictures of blonde women being raped by black men, or dancing with them, and leaning on their arms, laughing.

As McDonald and I looked around at the pictures, Dr. Huss said, "Now I can tell you why I never let both of my feet touch the ground at the same time."

I turned from the pictures on the wall, to look at him. He said, "It's to show I have one foot on earth and one foot already in space. It's to show that this is not the true and final home of the white race. That home is above." So saying, he hopped and turned to look suspiciously at McDonald, who still studied the photos on the wall.

"You sure it doesn't mean you have one foot in America and the other one in Germany?" asked McDonald, scratching the side of his nose.

Dr. Huss said, "There! That's the very type of ignorant comment that has caused the administration of this Base, and the so-called "scientists" of the American space program, to stick me out here and try to to keep me silent!"

"Well, I just noticed all these pictures of Hitler," said McDonald.

"I am an American, born here, sir," said Dr. Huss. "Adolf Hitler was the Messiah, for American white men as well as for the white men of Germany. He was Jesus incarnate! Do you know Hitler could heal the sick, just by laying his hands on them?"

"You sure he wasn't just trying to pull out their gold fillings?" asked Mac, with a smile.

But Dr. Huss had a smile of his own, which he used to winning advantage as he told us that no matter how ignorant we might be, he was dedicated to building the space station, and helping in the effort to pioneer the exploration of the universe, so that white people could escape colored people, and leave them to this used-up ball of dirt called the Earth, which word seemed almost obscene in the midst of the fine spittle that accompanied its ejection from Dr. Huss's mouth. He said he intended to save the white race, "by taking to the high ground, the planets, the stars themselves. Then, we'll look down here and watch the niggers cut each other up with rusty beer cans," he said.

Mac blew air through his lips, making a harsh noise, and he left the room.

I liked Mac, and normally would have agreed with him, but since he was disagreeing (unpleasantly, it seemed to me) with a man who might well be my True Dad - I decided to let him go, and to hear what Dr. Huss, whom I considered, by that moment, to be almost one hundred per cent my True Dad, had to say. His concerns were mine, now. Sure, the racist and strange things he said were in opposition to all the teaching I had heard over the years, and they were opposed to my inner feelings. But after twenty or thirty minutes sitting at the edge of his desk, hearing Dr. Huss talk, I ached for the lost years, during which I had done nothing to hold back the advance of the black animal-people or the evil Hebrews. What fun we might have had, my True Dad and I, handing out leaflets, lighting crosses, wearing swastika armbands and badges, such as the ones Dr. Huss was wearing in the picture he showed me of the day he got arrested for protesting some minister who had said Jesus was a Jew ("He was a German, if you think about it," said Huss) debating brainwashed Americans at every opportunity... I felt so ashamed, that my True Dad had carried on his fight alone. And I wondered, when Huss told me about the callings of my aryan blood and various things like that, why I had not somehow sensed my racial duty even before hearing my True Dad delineate it. For by now I was certain that Dr. Huss was my True Dad. A rocket scientist - a hopper (I had loved to hop as a child) - a man with eyes full of suspicion and something angry and heavy behind the pupils (what more evidence did I need? what did it matter that no other human could have detected a single similarity between us? they were all strangers, to me and my True Dad) -

I felt I had betrayed Dr. Huss, been a bad son to him, because I had not hated the people he hated. I was ashamed. I could not bring myself to tell him that I was sure he was my True Dad.

I was grateful when Dr. Huss asked me for a favor. I agreed before he asked it. I hoped if I did this favor, and served him well, I would feel, some time soon, worthy of announcing to him our possible connection.

The favor he wanted was for me to leave what he called his "sociological" opinions out of the article I had (now, I was ashamed to think of it) lied to him and said I was writing for the California City *Sentinel* - a newspaper that did not exist - and of course I said I would - only concentrating on his work with the space station.

"They like people to think we're going to space for everybody, so they can keep suckin up everybody's tax money to get us there, but only the white aryan is going to the Promised Land. That's why a few of the boys had to teach everybody a lesson with that Challenger Shuttle."

I asked him what he meant, but he only said, "All in good time. But I'll tell you this much, the Challenger didn't blow up because of any faulty O-rings or any shit like that. It was exploded, from the Control Room, just like any rocket we send up that goes off course. That was originally gonna be the cover story - say the rocket was headin for Miami so we had to abort. But when we saw how weepy everyone got we figgered it'd backfire against us."

"You mean you..."

He smiled, twinkly-eyed and pure, "The idea was to send a message - no niggers, Japs, Jews, etcer etcer, in the Promised Land - Who'da thought people'd get so emotional about a bunch a mutts going up in smoke? I guess that's where bein' a dedicated scientist can get in your way of understandin' the public..."

165

He rubbed his chin, thinking of how he and his co-horts might make fewer mistakes in the future, and only roused himself from his reveries when we heard the sounds of many men coming down the corridor, toward his room.

"Here comes your escort out of here," he said.

Then, bending on the one stiff leg like a crane, he picked up a small stack of newspapers and asked me to hide them under my shirt, and take them off the base with me, to distribute them to the outside world - They were WHITEVILLE, USA - a newsletter he composed and printed on his pc, in this little room. I hid the papers.

The door opened and a Lieutenant stood there, looking at Dr. Huss as he might at a naughty child, who had tried to sneak out of the house, down a rope made of bedsheets.

"Hey," said Dr. Huss, "they surprised me as much as you. They told me PR sent em, what could I do but let em in?"

The Lieutenant smiled wryly. "I was busy with the dog and pony show back at the base," said the Lieutenant. "You got lucky." Then, he motioned for me to go with him. Mac was already standing under guard. Huss winked at me as we left his room. I told him that I would not only distribute the papers, but make more copies. He almost cried. So did I, looking forward to the day when I would tell him that he was my True Dad, and he would be proud of me.

Chapter 19.
A Few Minutes With Octo Rooney.

When we got back to Westwood, Mac said he would go to work finding the rest of the names on my list, and I didn't discourage him, but in my heart, I knew (as I knew with each new Dad) I had arrived at my True Dad.

Before going to meet Daphne, and return with her to the ranch, I took some of the newsletters into the streets of Westwood, handing them out. I was beaten up by some young Jews, one of whom carried a gun. They had white prayer shawls on under their sports coats, and fringes of threads coming out from under the fronts of their jackets. They left me, and I went into a clothing store to buy new clothes, because they had torn my shirt and pants to shreds. Then, dressed in a new suit, I tried to leave Dr. Huss's newspapers in the doorways of the stores on Westwood Boulevard, but the owners wouldn't allow me to stack them there.

That night, I went into the lab and re-photographed the pages of the newspapers with special embeds added. I used the small printing press at the ranch, to print two thousand copies. The next day, which was a day off for me anyway, I left the papers in the lobbies of apartment buildings and frat houses and on the doorsteps of single family dwellings. This activity took most of the sunlight hours, and when I returned to the ranch, there was a message from McDonald.

I called him. He wanted to see me right away, but I told him I was too tired. I asked if he could come up to Redbird the next day. I assured him there was a Denny's in town, and then he agreed to meet me there.

As I went to see him, I didn't know what to think. In a way, I almost hoped he had not found another putative Dad for me, but in a way, I was already preparing myself to receive the information that there was a new possibility, and to tell the absolute truth, no matter how ungrateful it makes me appear, as a son, I was getting a little tired of Dr. Huss as a Dad, and was ready for a new one. I wondered if Dads were like drugs, and if once you started finding them, you needed more and more Dads, to feed the habit. I hoped this was not to be my fate.

Mac was having a chocolate ice cream soda when I arrived. He slid a folder at me and told me he had located the next name on my list - a Mr. Faroun. At first, I felt almost as though this Mr. Faroun was an intrusion, trying to get between me and my True Dad, Dr. Huss. But then I reasoned that I didn't actually know Dr. Huss was the one, any more than I knew, or could know, it was Popper or Persson or Elam. Soon, I would learn a way to decide once and for all, but that had not happened yet. At least, I told myself, peruse the man's file, and then decide if you really are sure you have enough Dads. My career was going well, so there was no financial reason to limit my access to Dads. Why not, then, admit that Dr. Huss has been far from the perfect parent, and that, while we love and respect him, and will be thrilled if he does in fact prove to be our True Dad, he has not as yet provided any overpowering reason, by deed or appearance, for me to call off the search for my True Dad. I opened the folder of Mr. Faroun.

As soon as I saw the first page, a photo, I felt there must be some mistake.

I said, "But this man is black."

Mac McDonald said that was true, and went on eating his ice cream soda as though nothing unusual had been said to him. I stared at him a long moment. Then, I realized what the problem was. After all, I had never told him the purpose of my seeking the men whose names were on my list. He had asked, but I had told him I didn't want him to know. Now, however, I thought it was time to share my story with him.

I told him about Dr. Lord's lab, the artificial insemination clinic, and the list of geniuses who might be my True Dad.

I said, "How can this be my True Dad, when he's black, and I have such an extremely pale complexion?" I held my arm out over the table top.

Mac said he didn't know. He said he would think about it. As he continued drinking his soda, he handed me a small video player, and he put on a tape of Mr. Faroun - whose full name was the Reverend Minister Sharmin Kinshasa Torniquet Faroun - and the minute I saw him, I shuddered with strange feelings. The man was so different from Dr. Huss. Indeed, he was all that Dr. Huss had spoken and written so forcefully against. A black man. A black man filled with rage. With a large audience.

Faroun was not a darkly black man, but a reddish-yellowish color. He was tall, was practically bald, had red hideous eyes. I saw him on a stage, on the videotape, his face furious, his mouth rubbery and wet with rage, as he pounded himself on the head with a rolled-up newspaper. He was saying, "The white man is the devil! He was created one thousand years ago by a black scientist who had gone insane. Originally, they were created to serve us, and make our lives easier, but they got out of hand, and took over!" His audience said, "Uh-huh." He said that black people would never really be paid back for slavery until each black person in America had a white slave. His audience said, "Uh-huh," once again.

"Actually," he said, "we might need us each a few... Some fo the house, and some fo the field!" "Uh-huh," said the congregation.

I was fascinated by the Minister Faroun, and already growing to like him. A few moments ago I had seen a black man on my way into Denny's and I had looked at him through the eyes of Dr. Huss, hating him, and thinking ugly thoughts about him and his ugly thoughts. But now, watching the Minister Faroun on this videotape, that powerful force overcame me, as it did every time I was introduced to a new possible True Dad, and before I knew it, without the slightest intention on my part, I had convinced myself that the Minister Faroun *was* my True Dad. Twenty minutes earlier, I might have had bad dreams about him, but now I found myself lost in a fantasy of olden times. I saw the Minister Faroun and I working side by side in the cotton fields of a Southern plantation, cowering at the lash of a whip held by a man riding a horse. I wanted to kill that man, I wanted my pain and humiliation to be known and redressed. In the words of the Minister, I found some of the redress I sought. As the waitress slid a plate of food under my face, I started to cry.

Mac tried to get my attention, but I was hypnotized by the oratorical power of my Dad. Finally, Mac put his hand on the small screen. I looked at him. He was waving the other hand in front of my face. When my eyes focused on his face, he said, "I was just thinking here. I remember, I saw an episode on *60 Minutes* a few years ago about mulattoes, quadroons and octoroons, down in New Orleans. They said one out of every four white people down there is actually listed as black because they have some fraction of black blood." He took his hand off the screen and said, "Minister Faroun here is fairly light-skinned, he could be a quadroon, so that woould mean, as far as I can tell, you might actually be the man's son, and that might well make you an octoroon."

As I watched his tape - a series of speeches delivered before audiences of screaming, agreeing black faces - I couldn't help but see the uncanny similarities between us that might indeed indicate I was Faroun's son, and not Huss's. The way he paused at odd places in his sentences, places where no one would pause - I do that - the way he stalked the stage with a hitch in his step and a high kick when he changed directions - I did that on the basketball court - and to think of it what about my great talent for basketball, didn't that indicate also a possible connection to Faroun - so, in a short time, I had forgotten all the bad things Huss had said about black people - even the things written and drawn in his vile newsletter - as I grew more and more in love with my new candidate for True Dad - The Reverend Minister Faroun.

I said to Mac, "How do we get to see him?"

Mac said the Minister was impossible to see. "He's got round the clock bodyguards, he sleeps in a different house every night, doesn't answer his mail and won't talk to honkies."

"Who are they?"

"You and me," said Mac. Then added, "Me at least."

I said "There must be a way."

McD. showed me a flyer advertising Faroun's next speech, in downtown LA, and said, "He speaks at this place every month."

"That's it, then," I said excitedly. "We'll see him before he gives his speech."

"I don't know if that's a good idea," said Mac, but I didn't let him discourage me. I was determined to go.

"It's this evening," I said. "Let's go together."

Mac said he couldn't guarantee my safety. I offered him a bonus to come with me. He agreed, but only after I said I would go alone, if I had to.

"Octoroon octoroon octoroon," I said to myself as McD. and I drove down to the meeting hall. "I like the sound of that. It sounds like a word sailors might shout from the crow's nest in a heavy fog, to warn other ships of their nearness. Octo-roon! Octo-roon!"

I was already feeling octoroonish, too - kind of smooothe and impetuous, and cool, like the marble cutting surface in Dr. Crosse's kitchen. I was already beginning to love the Rev Min Faroun - already sure he was my True Dad - I thought of his jaw, like mine, knobbed with stubborn strength at the hinges, firm and square across the prow. Just as mine might have been if it wasn't round and somewhat soft, like the shape at the bottom of a sponge carved into the form of a duck. And our hair was the same, though his was black and tightly curled and glittering with grease, while mine was straight and dry - and our eyes were the same - though his were like balls stuck on the surface of his face and jutting out, while mine were set deep in my head, and couched in fleshy crinkles and creases.

It was near evening, the hour when the sun barrels into your eyes and makes you look like a quivering light bulb, when Mac and I arrived at the Fez and Crescent Meeting Hall, in South Central LA. As we drove up, we saw a crowd I estimated at ten thousand, crushing one another's backs to get into the Hall. They were all black people, the men dressed in suits and ties, the women in silk dresses with flowers over their hearts, or covered in Arabic-style robes and veils. To enter, they had to pass through a line of large men, also black, all of whom wore headsets through which they talked to someone who was not present, and heard instructions. These guards guided the crowd through five or six metal detectors that had been set up in the lobby. This slowed the progress of the crowd, but no one complained. They were orderly and quiet. As we came up near the entering crowd, a man of about twenty five saw us in our car, and spit at the windshield. Then another young man saw us, and smashed the hood of the car with his fist, and shouted something to his friends, who turned to look at us in what seemed to be amazement.

"Do you want to come in with me, to meet Minister Faroun?" I asked Mac, "Or would you rather wait in the car?"

"Now that I see the mood of this crowd, I think it might be better if the two of us went home for now, and possibly contacted the Minister at some later date, perhaps by wire."

"No," I protested. "Now that I'm here, I must see him. I think you've found my father for me, Mac, and I'm impatient to meet him, set my eyes on him, talk with him."

Mac shook his head, but said he knew a side entrance to the Hall.

We drove around to an alley, and parked beside a news van, where some news people were sitting in the open doors, having sandwiches. When they saw us, they ignored us.

Mac went to the small iron door in the side of the Hall and tested it. It was locked. He looked up and down the street, took something from his pocket, and started working on the lock, using his body to shield what he was doing from the eyes of the news people. When the door was opened, he indicated for me to go past him and enter. He followed me into the building.

We were behind the stage. I saw in the distance, some offices or dressing-rooms. I headed toward them. I saw a squad of young men that looked like the men guarding the front entrance, coming out of one of the rooms. There were six of them. After them, came a man I recognized as the Minister Faroun. I couldn't help myself. Seeing him, I rushed ahead, calling out, "Minister Faroun! Minister Faroun!" and waving my arm, so I would catch his attention before he went on the stage.

I was surprised when, the moment I yelled, the Guards rushed at us and crushed me and Mac to the floor. I found myself with one man's knee on my adam's apple, looking into the gun barrel of a second man, who leaned over my head. "Who are you? What do you want? How did you get in here?" were some of the questions I heard, but didn't have the breath to answer. After a moment, the Minister Faroun joined us, and was looking down at me and Mac. He examined our wallets. Mac's said he was a private investigator.

One of the Guards said, "I remember Mac McDonald. Used

to be a police officer."

"Assassins," said a voice from a face I couldn't see. In an instant, the word was taken up by other voices. As the men holding me started to rhythmically kick my ribs and legs, people chanted, "Assassins, assassins..." and someone added, "Kill them! Before they kill our beloved Minister. Kill them!" Hearing this, Faroun studied my face, then Mac's face, then he shrugged and turned to head for the stage, asking an Aide as he went: "Is there water on the podium?"

The Guards changed positions, to start the process of dragging us into one of the little rooms, and I managed to raise my head enough to see Faroun walking away. Then, I found the strength to speak, and I called out, in a voice that started as a croak, but got surer as it went on: "Minister Faroun - it's - it's about Dr. Lord!"

Faroun stopped on the stairs, as though he saw someone coming the other way. He just stood there. I shouted again: "I have to talk to you about Dr. Lord!"

Faroun turned and walked back to me. He said, "You know Doctor Lord?"

I said, "I have to talk to you."

Mac, from someplace on the floor I couldn't see, now spoke to the Minister. He said, "Believe me, pal, you want this to be a private discussion."

The Minister seemed to wrestle with himself inwardly a moment or two, then said to the Guards, "Stay with the other one." He reached down and grabbed my hand. He pulled me to my feet, and grabbed the fleshy part of my ear, with which he guided me into a small room. He closed the door and locked it. I had to tell him the reason I was there, because I felt it was the only way to to save my life. I said, "I think I am your son, sir, born from the experiments of Dr. Lord, which if I am not mistaken you took part in."

He just sat there, on a table, staring at me. Then, he sighed and said, "When I was at Berkeley, the Doc was the first person to give me an IQ test. I was a janitor there, but when he said I was a genius, the school gave me a scholarship. He changed my life."

"Mine, too," I said. But he looked at me skeptically, checked my ears, felt my arms and back, made me open my mouth for some reason he didn't tell me, looked around in my mouth, tested the up and down motion of my jaw, then just looked at me a while. Finally, he shook his head. "I refuse to believe a sickly, ugly white devil could be a son of mine. I'm sorry, but I see no reason here not to let the boys do away with you and your friend as a couple of paid assassins probably sent by the Federal Bureau."

I told him what Mac had said, about the people in Louisianna who look white but are actually the offspring of at least some black ancestors.

He said, as he had on the tape I heard, "White people were created by an evil scientist a thousand years ago, and they are all evil. You are white. That means you are woefully woefully evil."

I think he was surprised to see that no matter what he said to me, I continued to smile at him. Actually, I smiled more and more, for I was expressing love, and I was loving whatever he said. Even when he said octoroons like me would all be killed in the coming war of the races, I just couldn't get enough of it. I was so lost in admiration for the beautiful way he spoke, the rolling phrases, the songlike pauses, and all this, all this, from my own True Dad! I was in heaven. He told me he believed in a separate nation for blacks, comprising what is now known as Georgia, Mississippi and South Carolina, and said it was the only way to stop the approaching race war. He sounded so determined to stop this war, even if it meant having to start it, by invading the South, and taking it once and for all, that I could think of no better calling in life than to help him in any way I could. I told him that. He thought I was crazy. He said, "You're white, and you're the devil, but something about that trusting, moonlike, eggy face of yours makes me want to keep my bodyguards from killing you. Maybe - and if you tell anyone this, I'll kill you personally - maybe it's because I have no son of my own, and I have been thinking of that recently, and now, almost as though Allah Himself had..." But then he stopped himself and said, "Look, you have to get lost. Can't be no white kids around here calling me papa or we'll both be killed by my bodyguards. Believe that, son. They must never suspect the purpose of this visit."

I said I wanted to see him again, but he shook his head sadly. He said, "Leave me your name and address and phone number, and maybe some day, some day. But now..." he trailed off. Then he said, "You were brave to come here." He grabbed my shoulder fondly. "That's the way any son of mine would be." Before I left, we hugged fondly. Then, he opened the door and told his bodyguards I had brought a message from an old friend of his and that they should escort us safely to our car and make sure we got out of the area all right. We were soon on our way.

Later, I had McDonald send some black operatives to get me samples of the Minister's literature and the tapes he sends to his fans, and again, as with the newsletters of Dr. Huss, I secretly added sublims to all his material. Daphne carefully etched new fuck prick cunt shit death glass embeds for our task. Daphne suggested we just leave a bunch of phenome-embedded paper at the Mosque so whatever Faroun wrote from then on would have the necessary embeds. We had to sneak into his mosque at night, in blackface, to the composing room, to leave our paper. While we were there, I thought I heard his voice coming from one of the rooms, and I wanted to stop and talk to him, but Daphne said we had better not.

In the following weeks, Faroun started to rise, amazingly fast. His meetings were more full than ever, and more than that, his face started to appear on TV and in the papers all the time... Soon, he was starting to be considered a serious person by the same people who used to think he was a fanatical moron - even though he hadn't changed his opinions, or the way he said them. There was even an article in the LA *Times* called "Faroun - From Pariah to Pundit," which discussed the fact that Faroun was now on all the political talk shows, and had somehow become the African-American leader the networks and newspapers went to for a comment when anything happened. I saw David Brinkley smiling wanly at him and talking to him as though he were the leader of a foreign state.

Nobody could quite say what caused the change in the public perception of the Minister Faroun. Naturally, Daphne and I were pretty sure it was our subliminals. This, as it turned out, may not have been the entire truth. But at that time, I credited myself and Daphne with the miraculous and thrilling enlargement of the fortunes of Faroun, and I remember when she and I would lie together and bask in his good fortune, cheering him on from our place of secret watching. We were happy he would get his way in the world (me, because he was my True Dad - Daphne, simply because she was happy for me) - and we fantasized about the great new African-American nation in the middle of the present United States - where black men and mulattoes, and perhaps the occassional well-connected octoroon, would work and play among the native and imported people and animals of that veldt-to-be.

There was only one fly in the ointment. I began to see that Dr. Huss, too, was growing in importance. He was on Cable TV almost every day, sneering and fat thighed, attempting to cross his legs one way or the other, always seeming to be unable to do so, (possibly the result of years of hopping and standing unnaturally on one foot) as he imparted his racial theories and grinned with that innocent malevolence - that cuteness of tone - which I had used to admire so whole-heartedly, but now was forced to think of critically, to say the least. Now, of course, I had to question him and everything he stood for - because I had a new True Dad.

But this is not entirely accurate. It was worse than that, for me. The truth was, I found myself hesitating between the world-views of Dr. Huss and the Minister Faroun, as I alternately considered either of them to be my True Dad. Really, I was still searching for clues as to which the actual True Dad would turn out to be, and as sure as I was that Faroun was my progenitor, whenever I saw him or heard his voice, just that sure was I that Huss was my True Dad, when I saw *him*, or read *his* philosophizing. Sometimes I would be out in Westwood and see a stack of Huss's newsletters - "Marry an Aryan for Christ!" under one arm and a stack of Faroun's journal, *The Coming Black Militia*, under the other, carefully putting a few papers from each stack side by side in the doorways of Westwood. I wanted both of my Dads to succeed, though I was not fool enough to forget the fact that either one of them would have disowned, and possibly killed me, had he discovered that I was helping the other.

I told Daphne my predicament, and she suggested we tell her father, but I didn't want to bother him with my petty troubles.

There were intimations from him that the Subliminal Business was on the verge of a huge take-off, the exact nature of which he said he could not yet tell us. He gave me a raise just about every time he laid eyes on me, and soon my salary was in the range of 2 million dollars a year. I bought jewels and pearls and gold for Daphne, but she hid it all in a box under the earth, because she still didn't want to tell her father about us. Still. she and I travelled together, often leaving him at home on the ranch, and in many respects we lived as though we were a married couple.

Sometimes she would say, "I only wish you had never started looking for your True Dad. If it wasn't for that, I believe I could make you happy."

I assured her that I was happy, and that it was she who had made me so. But the truth was, I was worrying about Huss and Faroun more and more. I had taken on the emotions of both of them, in my attempts to be a good son, and now I found myself as the defender and saviour of both, though it was clear to me that the two men were totally at odds, were enemies, would have wanted to kill one another on sight if they ever saw one another. I wanted to identify with the triumphs of my True Dad, and to hate my True Dad's enemies, but how could I do that in my current situation?

Sometimes, in despair, I tried to reject both Huss and Faroun, and told myself that neither one of them could possibly be my True Dad. I tried to tell myself that despite my incomprehension of his writings, and the fact that he was by this time a rather old-hat True Dad for me, totally replaced in my family tree first by Huss and then by Faroun, Mr. Popper must be my True Dad. He was a good choice, also, because I had already helped him, enormously, and could justifiably bask in the reflected glory of his new fame.

Unfortunately, I made the mistake of going back to visit Mr. Popper.

Emotionally, he wasn't doing any better than I. As a matter of fact, he was in despair when I went to see him.

He was living in a fine house, and had recently married. His wife was about twenty-five years younger than he. The two of them smoked pot all day, and watched TV together. He tried to appear happy to see me. I smoked a joint with them. They told me they were expecting a child, and I congratulated them. I remember feeling a pang of jealousy toward the unborn child, but I knew it was unjust, and it went away quickly. What troubled me was that, at the end of my visit, when I walked out to my car, accompanied by Mr. Popper, I looked at him and he was crying.

At first I thought he was squinting from the sun, but when he saw me looking at him, he took the opportunity to break down weeping against my chest. I said, "Mr. Popper, what's the matter? You have everything you ever wanted. You are a famous and respected writer, you have a beautiful wife, and a child on the way. You live well, and have all the time you need, to write. You don't have to sell jokes for a quarter on the beach, and all your work is published, no matter that it has no plot, no characters, no point of view, no commas and damn few periods. Nobody dares to edit your writing because no one can understand it, yet everyone buys it because everyone buys it. You have succeeded entirely without compromise. In fact, while most writers want to be popular, in your case the world wants to be popular with you. Why, all this being true, are you sad?"

To which Mr. Popper replied, "That's just the problem. I have two billion people asking me to say something to them, and I have nothing to say. What advice, what beauty, have I come across that can be shared with half the world? None. None. My writing, I now realize, existed to be hidden. I was happy when every now and then somebody would come up to me on the boardwalk, and say he'd read that book, the one you read, or maybe one of my poems that my friends used to xerox and hand around at parties. Then, I would talk to that person, and sooner or later he or she would realize I was just an old crank, check out my ragged clothes for confirmation, understand that there was no reason not to call me an asshole and leave my presence, and do so. Those were my readers, that was my life, I was Popper, myself. Now, so many people come to me to talk about my work, and some of them have read it so carefully they understand it. And they are so clever they can make me understand it. Then, when I understand it, it becomes dim and grey in my mind. I used to love every word in every folder I had stacked in my apartment on Dudley Avenue. Now, page by page, the public is taking it all away from me, and sending it back with a haircut. Now who am I? Lost, lost in public."

I comforted him as best I could, but how well was that? All I really wanted to do was to get away from him, and pity myself because my attempts to help my True Dad had backfired.

Then, I was back to being torn between Huss and Faroun. Trying to decide which was my True Dad. Which, which? And how could I discern it once and for all, because all my reasonings and perceptions were wearing me down without giving me relief. I tossed in my bed, straining to find ways to vindicate my True Dad, myself, and all our ancestors, all joined to us, against my other True Dad, myself and all the ancestors that came with *that* True Dad. I found I was usually up in the mornings with different kinds of resentment flooding over me. Sometimes I would start muttering about the Catholic Church being the world house of torture. Sometimes it would be the Black people, or the Jews, or women, or men, or short men with white skin and tall women with black skin - or my mother, quite often - Or I'd resent people I knew - resenting things they had said. Sometimes I resented them as the son of Faroun, resenting their racism and smugness and plottings, sometimes I resented them as the son of Huss, resenting their race and numbers.

Then, I had just gotten another raise, and was strolling Westwood with a pocketful of variously styled Cartier watches for Daphne, inwardly volleying back and forth between hatred for blacks and hatred for whites, between weeping over the fate of the sainted African captives during the infamous Middle Passage and weeping for the fates of all the white women and little white girls raped and slain by the evil blacks, between snapping my fingers like a jazzman and clicking my heels like a Nazi, (or both at the same time, which produced a pleasing effect when I was alone, but seemed to attract strange gazes when I did it on public streets) between crying for a Christ who had been (as Faroun told me) a black man, living in ancient Israel, when it was a black land; and crying for Dr. Huss's Christ, an Aryan who lived in an all-Aryan ancient Israel; when suddenly I realized something. It was something important to me at the time, and when I realized it, I found my feet started to speed up, and soon I was running, running to meet Daphne, at our appointed dinner date, at Emilio's Restaurant, because I had to tell her what I had realized.   When I got there, I was out of breath, but very excited. I saw her, and slid into the booth beside her. She was so beautiful. We kissed, we ordered, we exchanged gifts - watches for her, a jewel-encrusted alarm-clock for me - and then she looked at me and said, "You seem very happy today. I'm glad to see your recent depression has lifted." She kissed the side of my face. I said, "I'm happy, I'm ecstatic, because I just realized, on my way here, that there is one thing on which Dr. Huss and the Reverend Minister Faroun actually agree!   Here, all this time, I have been torn, conflicted, between my two putative True Dads, not knowing which to please and which to hate, and now I see that there is one thing I may believe - clearly, unquestioningly believe - no matter which of them is my True Dad!"

"What is it that you may believe?" she asked me.

"That the Jews are no good," I said, with the very words serving to relax the tense muscles of my face and body. "They both agree on that one thing. Now, Faroun says the Jews aren't really the Jews but a bunch of Caucasians from Russia pretending to be the true Jews, who were really black geniuses who somehow forgot who they really were; and Huss says the Jews aren't really the Jews, but a bunch of mongrel niggers pretending to be the true Jews, who were really an all-white enclave in the Middle East that somehow drifted over to Germany where they too forgot they were the Jews and started calling themselves Germans for some reason, probably a Jewish plot. But however it happened, and whoever is right, I now know I can have a fulfilling and rewarding relationship with both my True Dads, if we confine our conversations to the errors and evils of the people who currently claim to be the Jews. No longer must I talk to one True Dad while insulting the other. I can avoid talking about whites to Faroun, or blacks to Huss, and with both I can agree on the single matter that binds the three of us."

Daphne thought it over, and said, "I don't like the fact that both of these True Dads of yours require you to hate other people to get along with them, but if this is what makes you happy, I'm glad you have found it."

I fairly shouted, "Happy?! I'm ecstatic! I am no longer totally torn down the middle. Oh, Lord," I prayed aloud, trying to see Jesus as I prayed, both as a black and as a German, which was easy when I allowed my mind to toggle between the positive and negative image of the same picture, at about ten beats a second, "Oh, Lord - thank you for this one thing, this bonding I may now have with both my True Dads!"

And just before the drinks came I started to say, "Whew! I'm glad I'm not a..."

Chapter 20.
Mr. Steinstein.

"...Jew!"

But before I had a chance to say the final word, the door of Emilio's snapped open, the sunlight of Westwood blasted into the place, and a hurrying overcoated figure I recognized as MacDonald "Mac" McDonald elbowed and shouldered its way to our table.

He said, "I called the credit card companies, got a list of your purchases for today, and Daphne's, put two and two together and figured you'd meet up in Emilio's to exchange gifts."

I told him that was just one more indication of what a fine detective he was, but in my tone I think he detected a touch of impatience, so he said, "Reason I interrupt you, is, I found the next guy on your list. Name's Steinstein."

I felt like telling him thanks very much but why don't you go home and forget this job completely, because I think I have all the Dads I need for the time being. But before the words were even out of my mouth, I realized that (strange though it might be to say so) I already had a feeling this man Steinstein would prove to be my True Dad. How can that be? I had no more evidence than the sound of his name coming from the lips of McDonald, and the light on the wall behind McD.'s head, a shade of parchment gold. Those things, the name, the light, McDonald asking the waiter if they had ice cream sodas at Emilio's, conspired in my brain to convince me that Steinstein was the one. Already, Huss and Faroun, Popper and Persson, and Elam, were dissolving into the mists of other tribes, not mine. I knew I had to meet Steinstein.

"Tell me about him," I said.

"Well, he's a TV producer. Jewish."

Daphne dropped her fork and looked at me, with tender concern. I smiled at her. She thought I might have been upset, since just a moment before I had been grateful that the one thing I was not was what I now was. She didn't know that the instant he said it, all my former anger at the Jews was passed away from me like a crease after it has blown through a sheet. Jewish was what I wanted to be. After all, I said to myself, if it's good enough for my True Dad - Steinstein - it's good enough for me! Think of all the Jewish ancestors I have. Generations of Steinsteins coming to a full rich flowering in me.

It seemed right in another way. As I may or may not have mentioned, Mr. Stengrow, the man who had raised me, and actually had brought me into existence by paying Doctor Lord to perform his fertilizations, was Jewish.

Perhaps, I thought, Dr. Lord took that fact into account when he chose my donor-biological-father... I liked the idea... It made simple sense, like a key and a lock... I thought of our life in the Stengrow home, where we were not so much Jews as devotees of the faith that might be called The Westside Religion - we celebrated all the holidays, Christian and Jewish, and Mr. Stengrow's attachment to the faith of his (our) fathers took the form of the sentence, which he said about once a year, usually after dinner, while turning on the TV, "I'm proud to be a Jew." When I asked him why he was proud, he said it was because the Christians and Moslems had learned the idea of a Single God from us, so it sounded like he was proud of the Christians and Moslems, like he had put them through college and was pleased with their achievements... Other than his love of Barbra Streisand and George Burns, that was the extent of the religious education I got from him. Certainly, I can say it now, I had been somewhat ashamed of myself for not standing up for Mr. Stengrow's people when they were criticized by the Reverend Minister Faroun or Dr. Huss, but I tried to drive that shame from my head in the interests of bonding with my True Dad. Also, I think I harbored some resentment against Mr. Stengrow, a resentment that any discussion of religion just brought to the forefront of my thoughts. This was because, as a child, I had sometimes had secret urges to explore further the world of Mr. Stengrow's religion, but whenever I talked about it to him, he seemed so tired of it, bored with it, humorously dismissive of it, that I gave up.

Now, as the son of Mr. Steinstein, I would be exposed to another interpretation of my ancient and venerable faith, and I looked forward to that.

I examined the folder Mac gave me, concerning Steinstein, and saw a man with completely white hair, covering his head in thick ringlets. His eyes were kind and dark. Except for his white hair, and the wisdom in those eyes, I thought, he might have looked no older than I did. And yet he must be twenty years older than me, at least.

Mac said, "Steinstein is super rich."

That made sense to me, because he was a genius. It made more sense, I thought, than the poverty of Popper or the middle-class status of Huss or the upper middle-class niche of Minister Faroun, where he dwelled with the takings of his church.

"He was a writer, like Popper, but unlike Popper, he fell into the world of TV and movies, where he has succeeded fantastically," said Mac, as he ate the hazelnut cake topped with bisque tortoni that was the closest thing he could get at Emilio's to an ice cream soda. "He was such a successful writer he doesn't do it any more. Now he's making millions as a Producer, and hiring other writers to execute his every thought."

"How can I get to meet him?" I asked.

"This is a problem," said Mac. "Since he has his name on so many TV shows, he's been the target of stalkers."

"Stalkers?"

"Psychos, nuts, weirdos, who read about celebrities and then try to contact them. They send letters, gifts, pieces of their bodies, threats - they call on the phone - they try to waylay the celebrities at home or work - Steinstein's not an actor or anything, but he's so successful, he's got a bunch of stalkers. So, I came up with a plan."

His plan was to get me hired to write one of Steinstein's many TV shows.

Over the next few weeks, we pursued Mac's plan. In order to assure me of the best chance for being hired, we employed very successful screen and TV writers, for huge sums, (I spent six hundred thousand dollars on the project) to ghostwrite scripts on which I could put my name, and then send through an agent to Steinstein. It took five Emmy winners and a two-time Oscar nominee, but we finally got one to Steinstein that he liked, and he called the agent, saying he wanted to see me for possible employment on his TV show -

"Kill a kid! Kill a kid!" I heard someone say through the door as I waited for Steinstein in his outer office.

The secretary-receptionist, an elderly alcoholic woman with a pronounced German accent, looked up from her tissues and said, "Sounds like the story meeting's almost over."

Soon the door swung open, and there stood Mr. Steinstein, glorious in ringlets of white hair, slim, tall, dressed in a knit golf shirt and pressed chino pants, wearing hi-top white sneakers. "Stengrow?" he said when he saw me. I stuck out my hand to shake his, and to touch perhaps for the first time, the flesh of my True Dad. He had a firm, dry handshake, and thin bones. "Thank you for seeing me," I said, "Mr. Steinstein."

I pronounced the word: "Styne-styne." I could see immediately that something was bothering him. He wiggled his nose as though it suddenly itched, and said, "If you're trying to make fun of me, I'll throw you out right now."

"No sir," I said, quickly, "Make fun of you how?"

He looked at me for a moment, as though trying to decide whether or not I was sincere. Then, he must have concluded that I ws, because his face relaxed, and he hit me softly on the upper arm.

He then took me into his office, where four young men were sitting in a couple of couches, watching the door expectantly, awaiting the re-entrance of Steinstein. He said to me, "Find a seat," then sat down himself, behind his desk and explained to me that many of the people he met mis-pronounced his name. "It didn't used to bother me but, well, I've mentioned it in a couple of interviews, and now I guess I figure everyone in the world must know how to pronounce my name, so when they get it wrong, I guess I figure they must be trying to be funny. I hear it all," he said, "Steen-steen, Steen-stein, or as you said Styne-styne. I guess everyone thinks he's a comedian."

I said, "How is it pronounced then, sir?"

"Pronounced? Why it's pronounced exactly as it's spelled! S-T-E-I-N-S-T-E-I-N! Styne-steen! Styne-steen!"

"Styne-steen," I said, this time saying it the correct way. He calmed down after that.

He introduced me to the other men in the room, all writers. They were working on the latest episode of their top-rated series, called "Alger House." It was about a small independent publishing firm, and the stories derived from the joys and difficulties of Mr. Alger, the founder, and the other workers there. The difficulty they were having, Mr. Steinstein informed me, was that the world of publishing sometimes didn't provide the kind of visual, emotional drama that viewers demanded if they were to stay tuned to the program through the commercial breaks. The most difficult of those breaks to write, so as to keep the viewers from straying, was the half-hour break, because that was generally the one with the most commercials. Mr. Steinstein explained to his writers and to me that over the years one of the sure-fire ways he had discovered, to keep audiences glued to his shows, was to have a child die, or be threatened with death, just before the break. Hence, the shorthand, "Kill a kid," which he felt should be the title of a chapter in any manual for TV writers. He had told these other writers of these facts, before coming out to get me, and now they shouted out to him ways they had thought of for killing a kid at the end of Act Two. I heard only, "Little Jimmy, Jack's son, skins knee, it doesn't heal, Jack takes him to a doctor, get tests, bing, kid's got AIDS, end of Act Two," from one eager scribe, and "Mary-Jo, eight year old daughter of Byron and Beth, shopping at the mall, comes out of Eddie Bauer's, passes a dark doorway, here comes a pair of big hands to pull her in, shwoop, will we ever see her again? Cut to commercial."

My mind started to wander, as I looked around the office, at the walls covered with placques of thanks and numerous awards.

I thought, I inherit these awards, on the genetic level. These Emmies will be in the DNA of my happy progeny forever and ever. When you're thinking genetically, you have a sharp eye for levels, distinctions and honors. You're looking for a pattern. You're fitting yourself into a great chain of being. I looked at the headlines displayed on the walls of Mr. Steinstein's office, the golden statuettes, and shapes of gold and silver, and of clear or textured glass on the tables, peeking out among the sandwich wrappings from the lunches of the writing team. I saw his awards from charitable and special-interest groups, for the taste and sensitivity with which his shows had dealt with them, and their groups. He was a benefactor of mankind, as I had always hoped my Dad would be, and as I wanted to be. This was good evidence to me, that Mr. Steinstein (his first name was Stu) was the one.

I was rollicking inwardly among all my Dads, so I knew I had to find out once and for all which was the true True Dad, but I wanted to give myself some time with Mr. Steinstein first, to see if I could decide on my own, from the evidence of my senses, and feelings.

I worked for him for two months. I started dressing like him, and had my fingernails buffed and manicured and my hair cut at the same studio barbershop where he went. We sat side-by-side in the barber chairs every morning, talking story. We wore the same Western shirts, with the milky snaps. I soon noticed our voice patterns were the same, and we both scratched behind our left ears in the same way, when we were thinking through a problem. And who else but Mr. Steinstein liked to look at the points of his sneakers exactly as I liked to look at the points of mine? Nobody. Not to mention the way we both told a joke, and were unintentionally hurtful approximately 50 per cent of the times we opened our mouths, all this served to bind me closer and closer biologically to Mr. Steinstein. Even the fact that, as I was forced to note, Mr. Steinstein didn't like me very much, when coupled with the fact that I didn't like him very much, seemed like just another proof of our family closeness. The unavoidable conclusion was, that this was my True Dad.

I cried with joy, relief and gratitude to Fate for two days when I finally came to this conclusion. I decided I must go to Mr. Steinstein with my story, to see how he would accept me.

After work on a Friday night, I found him in his office, and asked him if I could sit with him for a while. He seemed a little wary, but he said all right. I was made aware, as I had been on one or two previous occasions, of a certain physical revulsion felt by Mr.

Steinstein in relation to my proximity to any part of his body. He even seemed to turn his head a bit when I talked to him, to avoid being in the path of air expelled with my words. Still, what I had to say was so important, that I sat close to him, and told him the whole story, starting with Dr. Lord (a name he didn't seem to recognize, I was surprised to see) and continuing right through to that very moment, "now, here, when I can say, though I want and need nothing from you, and will gladly keep this secret for the rest of my life, if you would prefer it that way, that I accept and welcome you, Mr. Steinstein, as my father - my True Father! My True Dad!"

I reached out to grab and hug him, and perhaps plant a kiss on his forehead or cheek, but he slipped from my grasp, rising from the cowhide couch and falling toward the marble table covered with toys and awards. I was presented with a close-up (as I had learned to call it) of the palm of his hand, as he pressed it into my face, to push me back..

Then, he sat back down, and lowered his head. He scratched behind his ear, in that way I had learned to love, he looked up, he cleared his throat and said to me: "How old are you?"

"Nineteen, sir," I said, my eyes a little misty.

"I'm twenty-five," said Mr. Steinstein.

"But - ?"

"I'm prematurely gray," he said.

"But - ?"

"This business ages you, too," he said. "The pressures of episodic. Nobody knows who hasn't done episodic."

Then, shutting out the light, he left the office.

I sat in the dark, listening to some teamsters loading the lions and tigers for Mr. Steinstein's new circus show, "I Care About You Geeks" into the backs of their trucks, and I tried to think of where I had gone wrong.

Chapter 21.
A Superfluity of Dads.

I called Mac McDonald, to tell him what had happened. He checked things out and got back to me. "Little mix-up," he said, apologetically. "I got Steinstein confused with his father, also Stu Steinstein. The elder Steinstein died about ten years ago, and the younger one has done so much, and to tell the truth, looks so old, I just naturally assumed he was the right one. But hey - cheer up. Maybe Steinstein's your brother. Now wouldn't that be nice?"

He may have been right, but for some reason, I didn't care.

I knew I had to find out once and for all, who was my True Dad. I was nervous and exhausted from all the inward migrations I had done among all my Dads. The subjective criteria I had been using had obviously not done the trick. It became clear to me that I would probably, in my present state of mind, accept a chewing gum wrapper on the sidewalk as my True Dad, if its name was on my list, and I could come up with one or two areas of similarity between me and it.

I went to Daphne, and laid my head against her breast at the Beverly Hills Hotel, and wept.

She soothed me by rubbing my head and neck, and moving my hair around on my forehead. Finally, she said, "We have to talk to my father about this."

We went back to the ranch, where we found Dr. Crosse and Daphne told him about my problem. "Reynold can't decide which is his True Dad."

Dr. Crosse laughed with amused understanding, as psychologists will, and he told me there was a way to solve my problem, just recently perfected. It was called DNA testing.

He said that with a small sample of the blood, skin tissue, semen, or any other part of each Dad, we could do a chemical test that would determine, to a degree of certainty exceeding 98%, the identity of the genius who had long ago donated his seed to produce the human flower that he, Dr. Crosse, was proud to call friend.

"But I don't want to ask them all for a blood sample," I said sadly. "Maybe I should just forget the whole thing."

"Nonsense," said Crosse. "The three of us, together, have become what the layman might call 'filthy rich,' and what better use of money than to find the answers to puzzling questions? Leave everything to me. Give me your ledger book, the one you got from Dr. Lord's, and I'll find the right people, and hire them to surreptitiously obtain the samples of blood or skin we need, or hair, I think we might be able to use, until we find a match, and can confidently stand you next to your True Dad for an official photograph. How'd you like that, Rennie?"

I said, "Is that possible? To surreptitiously obtain..."

Dr. Crosse said, "Give me the ledger, and then don't worry about a thing. Your possible True Dads won't be hurt, I promise it. They won't even know we're taking samples."

Two weeks later, as I was sitting in the garden, watching Daphne plant tomatoes, Dr. Crosse came out to us, with the ledger book I had given him in his hand.

He said, "Slight hitch. Nothing to worry about."

"What's the matter?" I asked, standing to face him. He showed me that the notes of Dr. Lord could be interpreted in another manner from that in which I had been interpreting them. It gets a little technical. The upshot was, that by reading the notes, and the dates, slightly differently, the number of possible True Dads that might have been the donor of that particular seed that was me, increased. The six men I had isolated were still on the list. However, now, added to them were 30 more. Dr. Crosse said he had talked to Mac McDonald, and Mac had put on six new investigators, and together they had assembled thirty new manila folders, one for each of the new candidates. He led me into the dining room where, on the serving table, the thirty files were arranged in rows. I sat down and started reading them, and studying the pictures.

The reader probably knows by now, without having to be reminded, that I was certain that each of the men in these files, one after the other, was my True Dad. There was not one I didn't willingly accept as my progenitor, not one who didn't push the previous one from my thoughts and become, in the time it took to read his file, and until the beginning of the reading of the next man's file, my complete and ideal Dad. To each, I was a loyal son, until he was replaced by the next Dad's file. It took me almost three hours, but in that time I experienced, in my imagination, the sensations of being the offspring of an amazing variety of Dads, coming from a dazzling array of backgrounds. In those few hours, I felt the emotions of thirty lifetimes, thirty childhoods, thirty struggles to grow up and vindicate the lives of thirty Dads, whom I remember even now from the few moments I felt myself to be the son of each of them - an arsonist, a bigamist, a communist, a dramatist, an electrical engineer, a flutist, a gymnast, a hemotologist and a jurist. Also, a Kabbalist, a successful lyricist, one Maoist, one nutritionist, one opportunist, a purist, a Qumran relativist, a shootist, a Trappist, an usher, a violinist, a wooly wholist, a xylophonist, a Yin-yangist and a Zionist. Every mother's son of them a genius! This is not to mention those Dads who might be referred to as the aviator, bellhop, canned goods millionaire, deepwater diver, and exhibitionist (three-times-convicted). Also, all geniuses!

When Dr. Crosse came back into the room, with Daphne, and saw me sitting flabbergasted and itchy-eyed before the piles of evidence, he laughed. "The more the merrier!" he said with confidence. "We'll know the answer in two days at the most!"

"How is that possible, sir?"

Dr. Crosse said he and Mac had put together teams of operatives to go out and get blood and skin.

"It'll cost a lot of money, we may embarrass ourselves a bit along the way," said Mac, putting his hand on my shoulder and on Dr. Crosse's shoulder at the same time, and looking at me, "but this thing is driving you nuts, Ren, and Dr. Crosse wants to give you the truth. As a gift... Now, in the case of the Minister Faroun, we found out which of his wives he's scheduled to sleep with tonight, and we've got a gal over there waiting to scoop up the sheets and get 'em to the lab.

"As far as Elam's concerned, we've already got his hair and nail clippings, from his private barber. In the case of Mr. Popper, hope you don't mind, we're filling his house with a form of laughing gas, knock him and his wife out, as well as the maid, and we'll take a straight blood sample by needle. Steinstein, we gave him a little something in his Cobb salad, beautiful little salicilate, emulates a heart attack. They took him to Cedars Sinai where the surgeon on duty, for twenty thousand dollars, is getting us a blood sample, and a shot of spinal fluid just to be on the safe side..."

"But this is terrible!" I shouted, pulling away from Mac. "We're invading these men's privacy, we're assaulting their dignity, and for what?"

"For you," said Dr. Crosse. "And who has a better right? Conceived and deserted by one of these genius hotshots, you are back, to exercise some of your unacknowledged rights. Did these Dads think they could sell life for twenty bucks a pop?"

I must have indicated wih my eyes or body language that my objections had been sufficiently answered, because Mac continued to tell me some of the ways his men were collecting DNA samples from my putative Dads, all 36 (as they now numbered) of them. Some with staged accidents, some with nighttime home invasions, some through the use of prostitutes, who had been issued containers in which to save their semen. We also had dentists in our employ, I learned, who would be let into the rooms of sleeping Dads, to extract teeth.

When I considered what they were doing for me, I was very grateful to Dr. Crosse and Mac. That night, we drove into town and I bought Mac a huge ice cream sundae, and Daphne, Dr. Crosse and I watched him eat it.

However, the mood of sweetness and community faded the next morning when I went down to breakfast and remembered to ask about one Dad who had not been considered in the plans I had heard the previous day.

"What about Merle Persson?" I asked, remembering that that generous parking space donor had died a few years previously. "We can't test him."

Dr. Crosse said, "Nonsense. Easiest one of all. They are going to dig up his grave out in Westwood. They were gonna do it last night, but some kind of satanic cult had a permit to use the place, so they're going out again this morning."

I couldn't stand the thought of it. My Dead Dad - Persson - the Benefactor and Philanthropist - who had donated a thousand parking spaces to the people of LA - I had to stop them. I called Mac's office, but he and the team had already left. I called his car but the phone seemed to be out of order. Daphne and I jumped in the jeep and went to LA to try and stop this desecration, but we were too late - the grave was open, the coffin was open and a man in a green medical tunic was clipping off the tip of Merle Persson's little finger.

I sank to my knees in the grass beside the grave, and looked in, at the decomposing body, half skeleton, flesh in tatters where it still existed at all, and I said, "I'm sorry, I'm sorry. Please forgive me!" Then, from the hurried panic of the drive to the cemetery, and the feelings of sorrow and shame I felt, and the strong smell of the grass, which had just been cut, and the strength of the sun in the hot still air, drowned by the exhaust fumes of the cars going by on Wilshire and on Veteran, I fainted.

When I woke up, I was in my own bed, at the ranch. It was night. Someone had dressed me in flannel pajamas and put me under the cowboy-patterned sheets and covers. The railroad lamp was on, the the train was steaming ever onward. It took me a while to get my bearings. I realized I had been given something, a tranquilizer or sleeping pill. My face and hands felt thick, my brain was rubbery, wet and dark. There was a light knocking on the door, and Dr. Crosse stuck his head into the room. He said, "You feelin' OK?" Then, he picked one of my hands off the bed and measured my pulse. He said, "Exciting days. But, the mystery's been solved, that's one good thing."

I said, "You mean, you found my True Dad?"

He told me to get up and wash my face, then to come downstairs. He said the results of the tests were in, and the winner was in the living room. He said, "You might have conflicting feelings about the fella, whatever you do is up to you. But, I figured

193

you might as well talk to him, before you decide." Then, Dr. Crosse left.

I wanted to ask him what he meant by those words, but I was too slow. Wondering who might be in the living room, almost wishing the truth had never been discovered, I washed, brushed my teeth, wet and combed my hair, dressed nicely, and slunk downstairs to the lit living room... Overly lit... It hurt my eyes.

There, with Dr. Cross, were not one but several men, all of them in business suits, and it took a moment or two before I was able to distinguish their faces, and see them as anything but a mass of fabric arranged around the room. A moment later, I recognized that one of them was rising and (Dr. Crosse supporting him with a touch at the elbow joint) coming toward me. The rest were staying where they were.

Then, I realized the one coming toward me was Mr. Elam!

No! This could not be! The man who had thrown me into a dungeon, or dungeon-like enclosure, in New York, and walled me in, who had left me to whisper for my release into the subway station... Elam, the one Dad I had almost (though I could never entirely dismiss a possible Dad) decided wasn't mine, and now he was smiling at me shyly, and extending his hand to me, for a shake.

"My son," he said.

I looked at his hand.

Dr. Crosse, sensing my hesitation, smiled and tried to draw me toward Mr. Elam, by the cuff of my shirt. He said, "It's okay, Reynold - I told Mr. Elam of your suspicions concerning the night you visited him -"

"Suspicions?" I said.

"But he's explained the whole thing to me," said Crosse. "I think you'll forgive him, as I have, when you hear the truth."

I stood there, feeling I might fall to the earthen floor, from lack of energy, and lack of optimism. Dr. Crosse saw that something was wrong, and though I felt I was about to fall, he held me up. His face was close to mine, and he was smiling when he said, "It wasn't Mr. Elam who walled you into that dungeon - it was his sons - Caleb, Peter and Henry - who were afraid you would share in their inheritance."

"Ha-ha-ha-ha, oldest story in the world," said Mr. Elam, stepping closer to me, "Cain and Abel, Joseph and his brethren... "

I must have liked the sound of it well enough to stand on my own, because Dr. Crosse felt he could stop supporting me, and I became free-standing. I might have tottered a little, at least I felt it inwardly, but perhaps it was not visible to the others. I looked around, saw a chair, and managed to shuffle over to it and fall into it.

Then, Mr. Elam pulled a chair toward mine, and sat facing me. He said, "When Mrs. Elam and I went up the stairs, into my office, we thought you were right behind us. I did hear some kind of noise on the stairs behind me, but when I turned around, I was in the well-lit office, and peering down into the relatively dark basement, I couldn't see anything. A few moments later, my sons joined me in the office, and they said you had stopped off to go to the bathroom. I had no reason to think they would lie to me, although later I realized I should have suspected something, if only because of my experience over the years with those three louts.

"Anyway, I held my press conference, which went on for about forty minutes, and when it was over I remember I asked Caleb what had become of you. He told me you had said something about not wanting to get in the way. He said you told him you would call later in the day, to arrange for us to see each other again. When I didn't hear from you, I was disappointed, but I had no idea, no idea that..." Elam's face became complex and strange, as though the thought of my suffering was too overpowering for him. Soon, he went on: "A month later, Caleb came to me. He was just torn apart with grief, guilt, the whole nine yards. Told me what they had done. I couldn't believe it. Well, naturally, I made them show me the place where they walled you in, down there in the basement, and damn if I didn't make the three of them smash open that wall right then and there. Had to try and rescue you, give you a decent burial if it came to that. Oh, I was very definite about going right down there and getting you out!

"And I don't mind telling you we were all damn relieved to see your body, er - you - gone, and that hole in the subway station wall, through which we assumed you had burst, to freedom. I was going to institute a search for you, if you want to know the truth, but I was pretty sure you wouldn't want to hear from me or my family after what, well, happened."

He hung his head. However, soon his face brightened, and he told me how happy he had been when the detectives of Dr. Crosse had told him of the incontrovertible proof of our relationship. They had taken a sample of his blood from the blood bank where he had four quarts in storage for his own future use, should he ever need a transplant or other operation. He said the moment they told him, he had decided he must see me and express his sorrow over the misunderstanding we had had before, and his hopes that we would indeed join together as a family, as we always should have been.

Of course, I was swayed by his words.

I had never really blamed him for walling me into that cellar room, anyway. And hadn't I myself already come to the conclusion that it was the Elam children, not Elam himself, who had done that to me? And hadn't Mr. Elam told me on the very day I first met him, how disappointed he had always been in those three sons of his? How could I blame my True Dad, the man whose DNA I shared, for the unfortunate occurences of my brief taste of family life in the Elam household? It wasn't fair. I looked at the face of Mr. Elam, the eyes sad, the mouth turned down, the body half-turning away from me like the pitiful form of a beaten waif, half wishing to beg for food, and half afraid of encountering more of the rejection and pain he had already known enough of in his sad existence. I felt like a monster for the way I was treating him. Why have children if they are going to turn out like me? I wondered. How sharper than a serpent's tooth, I remembered from somewhere... Then, filled with the sudden need to forestall any more scolding of myself by myself, I practically hurled myself toward the arms of Mr. Elam, to embrace him. In my enthusiasm, I spun around the room with him, his feet flying out behind him. "Dad! My Dad!" I cried. As I went around I saw the happy crying faces of Dr. Crosse and all the suited men who were also in the room. These other men seemed to take a step or two forward, until Mr. Elam shouted out:

"I'm OK! I'm OK!"

When I finally put Mr. Elam down, some of these other men guided him to a chair, and looked at me and at one another. After we had all caught our breath, I learned that these other men were Mr. Elam's bodyguards and political operatives.

"That's right," I said, grinning widely and walking over to clap Mr. Elam on the shoulders one or two times, so happy was I to be united with him, "when I last met you, you were about to announce your candidacy for the Presidency of the United States.

"Yes," said Mr. Elam, "and I'm happy to say, I won the nomination of my Party."

"I saw it on TV," I told him. "I have to say, in spite of our misunderstanding, I was proud of you that day."

I congratulated him, wholeheartedly. He started to say something that started with the words, "As a matter of fact..." but Dr. Crosse made some kind of a sign to him, and moved forward, to speak to me himself.

Dr. Crosse said, "As a matter of fact, by an incredible coincidence, Mr. Elam's party (the Republicans) came to me only weeks ago, to discuss the possibility of our helping them in the coming election through the use of subliminals."

"But, I thought you were a Democrat," I said to Mr. Elam.

"I was," he said, "until I lost the New Hampshire Primary. It became painfully obvious that the Democrats have become the party of the special interests. Fortunately, there was just enough time to register in the Party of Lincoln before the Midwest caucuses. A lot of folks put me down as a dreamer, but then the frontrunner, Senator Eve, was unfortunately hit with that videotape of himself and his Chief of Staff shooting heroin, and voila, I became the compromise candidate."

"Now, your Dad is given a better than even chance of winning the Presidency," said Dr. Crosse.

"Oh," I said, happily.

"And as I was saying, he and his party have heard about the work we've been doing, and they think maybe we can help them."

"That's the truth," said Mr. Elam. "My Public Relations man took me to see Dr. Crosse here, and I'm saying how do I plug into this subliminal stuff, and what do you know, he tells me the only

197

man for the job is none other than Reynold Stengrow. 'The Subliminal Faust,' he called you. And that's when I said, 'Reynold Stengrow! You know Reynold Stengrow?' and I told him I was worried about you and then lo and behold, they do these blood tests, and shit... Isn't this the most incredible coincidence?" said Mr. Elam.

Chapter 22.
Elam's Election.

For a moment or two, I hesitated. Did I really want to use my skills to help Mr. Elam, the man who had (probably) been a party to walling me up behind that subway station?

The answer was: Yes, of course I would help Mr. Elam. After all, there he was, at long last - my True Dad! Who could have been such a terrible son as to refuse him?

We went to New York, and started working toward the election of Mr. Elam. Daphne, Dr. Crosse and I were assigned a suite of rooms at the Waldorf Astoria, where we lived and worked for the next six months.

We decided on a multi-pronged approach, including embedded campaign photos and campaign literature, as well as news photos and articles. Our party evidently had people on the payroll in every editorial office and pressroom to which we required access. Just as important as adding fucks shits pricks cunts cocks sexes deaths cancers to the reading material pertaining to my True Dad, was the necessity of keeping these powerful phenomes <u>off</u> the literature pertaining to his opponent.

The candidate himself wore writings on his forehead, cheeks, eyelids, ears, and the backs of his hands. We had a tatoo artist tatoo a colorless huge sex with the s on one cheek, the e on his nose and the x on the other cheek. His clothes were woven from pornographic fabric we made in Indonesia. For the TV debates, we had FUCK etched into his front teeth with a diamond drill. According to all the polls and comentators, he totally creamed his opponent.

Mr. Elam asked if we couldn't just use the words we wanted the American public to perceive, like - "Vote for Elam!" and "America the Innocent!" but Dr. Crosse showed him that our purpose was best achieved by using the tried and true; "SEX< FUCK< PRICK and so on. In the end, who could argue with the public opinion polls? Dr. Crosse and Daphne and I were treated by the Party, with the respect usually reserved for wealthy contributors.

The work was not difficult. It left me and Daphne a lot of time to be together, to explore New York, go to the movies, shop.

I asked her if I seemed any different, now that I had learned the identity of my True Dad, and therefore my own true identity. She said she could see no changes in me. Still, I was going through a period of re-thinking basic things, a time of being off balance, unsure...

My relationship with my three new brothers was uneasy. They showed me the grudging respect of a reputable but still untested witch doctor in a strange, new village - they apologized for what they had done to me, but they excused themselves, saying that they had thought I was an assassin sent to kill their Dad. They didn't entirely try to evade responsibility. Caleb honestly admitted that they had discussed the possibility I might be a true heir of their father's and that part of the motivation for what they did to me was clearly the protection of their inheritances - He hoped there were no hard feelings. He assured me that their Dad had punished them severely.

"He wouldn't even hire me a lawyer when that bitch Nancy accused me of raping her on the college hay ride," said Caleb, shaking his head. The others nodded in agreement. Then, they said they would like to start over in their relationship with me. They said they realized I had grown up without the advantages of being a fully acknowledged Elam, and offered to show me around New York, and introduce me to their wide circle of ex-girlfriends. I of course refused their offer of introductions, because I needed no woman besides Daphne. But I did want to be a good brother to them, and held myself to blame when I discovered in my heart certain fratricidal feelings toward the three of them.

As a matter of fact, whenever I saw them, I fantasized slaying them, in various ways. This being the case, could I really blame them for trying to get rid of me, back in those early days of our relationship? No, I couldn't. Still, I ate no food served to me by them, and tried not to be alone with them unless I had informed Dr. Crosse and Daphne of my whereabouts. I began to imagine their heads hanging from the wonderful old lampposts I sometimes saw in the city, severed from their bodies, twisting from a knot in their hair.

As for my True Dad, Mr. Elam didn't really have much time for me.

It wasn't, he said, that he didn't love me. He did, very much. And he was very proud of me for all my accomplishments in the field of subliminals. But he was running for the Presidency, fulfilling his pledge to visit every State at least once by election day. Our time together was necessarily short.

I tried to see him whenever he was on the East Coast, and many evenings I would sit by his dinner table in some Boston or Baltimore hotel telling him the details of the years of my life which he had missed. I told him about my first visit from the Tooth Fairy, my early troubles trying to ride a bike - everything I had wanted to tell my True Dad, since discovering that such a person existed. Sometimes I would ask him if he was bored hearing my life story, but he always said,"No, no, go on. I'm fascinated." I told him about my school friends, the weather at summer camp when I was eight, literally everything of note, little minding when I looked over at him, and saw that he had fallen asleep. I knew he was tired, and had a packed schedule the next day. I was happy to sit there, watching his sleeping face as it hung over the remains of his dinner, and listening to the ice melt in the water bucket. The next day I would be on a plane back to New York, to Campaign Central, again to work toward his election, along with Dr. Crosse and the team of psychologists he had gathered at the Waldorf.

I became fascinated with these other psychologists, all dedicated to finding every possible means of improving the public through psychology.... Those who used electrodes and LSD for their work, others who delved into the powers of loud noise and newly-invented odors to control the minds of their subjects. Often, in the long afternoons when there was nothing to do, I played cards with them. They liked to talk about their work, and insult one another, pretending to forget one another's names.

One day, two of the Electrode Experts, Merner and Marx, had a duel to see who had found the most interesting spots in the brain to insert their wires, and was therefore the better electrode psychologist.

To prepare, they shaved little bald spots onto one other's scalps, and each drilled tiny holes in the bald surface of the other's skull. They each placed three wires in the other's brain. Then, as the other psychologists and I looked on, they manned their buttons, and squeezed off jolts of juice into one another's medullas.

Merner pushed his button first. Marx lifted his left leg and lowered his head a moment later toward his crotch, which he sniffed. Merner laughed diabolically. So did some of the rest of us, sitting around the suite, watching the duel. After a moment, Marx lowered his leg, and shook it, as though to get the circulation going. He said, "Not bad."

As Merner was taking a mock bow, acknowledging the compliment of his colleague, Marx gave *his* button a twitch, and in that very instant, Merner was on the floor, crying, sniffling, and finally licking the carpet. Merner's hands flew out from under him, and his chin hit the carpet. He tried desperately to get to his button, but the small metal box had been knocked from his hands. He saw it across the rug and made a lunge for it, but Marx pushed and held his button down, as we watched Merner wiggle out of his pants, and stick his thumb up his ass. On his face, expressions of unconstipated bliss alternated with expressions of fury, directed at Marx. Merner scraped on his knees across the rug, followed by his pursuing thumb, until he managed to fall over his metal box, and press the button with his chin. Marx was forced to drop his metal box and drive the forefingers of both hands into his nostrils, while shouting, "My father used to say, the lost causes are the only ones worth fighting for," over and over, in a perfect imitation of the voice of James Stewart. Still, Dr. Merner was not released from the force of the electrodes implanted in his own brain, and couldn't stand up, or put any distance between his thumb and its target. This is the way they were when Dr. Crosse came in, and found them. He tore the buttons from both of them, and threw them across the room. Marx was all right, but Merner had to be taken drooling and covered with a tablecloth, to a hospital, where his electrodes were removed and he was finally able to straighten out in his bed, and rest, grateful to Dr. Crosse for having rescued him.

Aside from these pasttimes, there really isn't much I remember about the campaign, or the election. When the votes were counted, Mr. Elam had won.

Election Night was a thrilling experience for me, watching the returns come in on TV, the screen swarming with obscene words and drawings, that floated across the faces of the anchormen and anchorwomen, and across the commercials, and across everything in sight. Daphne and I sat together, allowing ourselves to be closer than we had ever before been with her father in the room, but he didn't seem to notice, so busy was he in pointing out to the assembled party elite the signs of our subliminal labors. He was drunk with knowledge, power, and hope.

The day after we won, Mr. Elam introduced Dr. Crosse and me to a man named Mr. Dominic, who he said was with the CIA.

Mr. Dominic congratulated us on our contribution to the great victory, and said the current President, President Ringer, who was of the same party as Mr. Elam, had expressed his personal good wishes to our team. Needless to say, I was filled with pride on hearing this.

"But we've got a problem," said Mr. Dominic. "We have obligated the President to a series of face-to-face meetings with the Secretary of the Russian Government."

"Hmm," said Dr. Crosse.

"The first meeting took place last week, at the Club Med in Pago-Pago. Seemed to go well, but when we analyzed the videotapes, we saw clearly that the Communists had hypnotized President Ringer. We think they use a low-frequency electronic signal, but we haven't been able to find it, or counteract it. The point is - when he is hypnotized, he tends to agree with everything the Secretary says, and what's worse, he loses the use of his own considerable powers of persuasion. Here, our President, our greatest voice for free enterprise, sits slack-faced and leaden-lipped, bubbles of water gathering at the corners of his mouth, while that suave Commie pours propaganda into his eyes and ears, telling our

203

President red lies while our dear old guy nods and chuckles at private thoughts."

"So, what you need," said Dr. Crosse, "is a way to make the President, even in a hypnotized, narcotized, semi-sleep state - as convincing as the Russian Secretary with all his considerable faculties at his disposal - is that it?"

"Exactly," said Mr. Dominic.

Daphne and I were assigned the task of working up a subliminal suntan for the Chief Executive, a lacey mask of fucks, shits, cunts and pricks, out of string and stretching the string words over President Ringer's face before his afternoon naps, which he now took under a tanning lamp.

We also had to be prepared for the possibility that the President's face would fall to the negotiating table, either because he forgot to hold it up, or because he had fallen asleep. Therefore, we gave President Ringer a subliminal haircut, so that if the Russians were left for any length of time in a position of contemplating the top of his head, or the back of his neck, they would still be subject to the mysterious rhetoric of the free enterprise system.

It worked. In subsequent meetings, the Russians continued to zap our President, and the Russian Secretary continued to practice his deft arts of persuasion on our nodding leader - but still, it was the Russians who came around to our way of thinking - abandoned Communism - learned to love all things American. Many people wonder why that happened, and all so suddenly. The truth is, they had no choice in the matter. As their Secretary and other leaders gazed at the face or neck of our President, representing as he did to them everything American - their subconscious minds were reading, "SEX SEX SEX" (in Russian) and they were helpless.

Who knows how differently history might have developed were it not for Dr. Crosse, Daphne and myself, and our secret arts? Yes, I say it here for the first time: Subliminals saved America! Subliminals broke up the USSR into smaller, more manageable states, better able to help their vicious, freedom-loving peoples join themselves to the free market!

Still, this triumph notwithstanding - for me, the period after the election was a tremendous letdown. I started to see things differently.

For one thing, Mr. Elam didn't seem to have much time for me. Though frequently during the election, he had expressed to what sounded like his sincere wish that he did have more time, so we could spend it together, now that he had the time, I was not the one he gave it to. Over and over, my request (silly, you may think) for him to have a game of catch with me, in Central Park, was denied. When he did consent to meet me, one of his Aides, or one of my three half-brothers would invariably call me and mumble about some political crisis that had come up, and tell me Mr. Elam couldn't get to the park. I began to feel blue. I longed for my time with my other Dads, our   talks,   my   helping them, their gratitude - it seemed the more I helped President Elam, the more his bodyguards were between him and me - his old CIA buddies - his dogs - the three brothers who had pushed me down the stairs and locked me behind the wall...

But there was a deeper problem -

Chapter 23. Looms of Hell.

The problem: you see behind people's faces. Once that starts, you're through as a friend, through as a relation, through as a lover, through as a human being.

I would go into the bathroom of some home I was visiting, and I see the Gleem toothpaste; immediately, I'd know somebody here (whoever did the marketing) liked our ad with the little girl reaching into the medicine cabinet, with fuck, fuck, screw, embeddeded all the way up her leg, from her socks to her jumper. Or I would watch their fingers stir their vodka and tonics and know, from the research, that they had been drawn to those pictures of decapitated dogs and long-chinned skulls that we drew on the ice cubes. I had a wealth of psychological data at my fingertips, which told me, after a moment or two of watching any individual, everything there was to know about his hopes and fears, his class and the glass he sees it through. Successful manipulation is its own hell.

And a good 40 acres of that hell is the knowledge that there are no laws governing what Dr. Crosse and I were doing. No bounds. I started to feel there were no real laws for our lives - no real rules - where is it written that we shall stay out of our neighbor's skull? After all, he doesn't own it, like his car. I found myself like the half-human mutation in that H.G. Wells story, calling out in my dark cave: "What is the law? What is the law?"

Average people never seeing farther than a child at a parade, crawling through a forest of legs, kept in ignorance by the powerful, but now I was one of the powerful - I saw to the ends of the earth, and as far as I could see, as high as I could see, as deep as I could peer, it was all me, and I hated it, and wished it dead. My father was a teacher. I mean Mr. Stengrow. And my mother was a teacher. But what did I teach? And how did I teach? My mother changed a student's life, so much that years later he came back, to thank her, for turning him into a success. What did I do, but lay in wait for souls, to trick them, for my own success?

Yes, I could excuse myself, and did. Saying I was too young to know any better. But, I couldn't get my brain to lock out the onslaught of the images which we had placed everywhere in the public space of America. The cornucopia of flaming swords with skulls for hafts, shoved into innocent flesh of bodies and faces and necks - the scenes of strange forests with animal faces peering out - the bucolic, the brutal, the hideous (women eating the legs of children) and comic drawings I now saw on every page of every written thing, and on walls, and pictures, windows, bricks, stones, on trees in the park and on the clouds, and in the clearest blue sky, and I would grab Daphne by the arm and say, "Look! Look! I told you! They're writing fuck in the sky!"

I tried to discuss the matter with Dr. Crosse, saying, "Have we gone too far? Have we stolen the private thoughts of men and women, to get them to buy our product and vote for our candidate? Are we good citizens?"

But he was caught up in the glory of what we had done. He was dressing in a New York style, rather than his old Western style, and he was gathering new mannerisms like a boxer gathers an entourage. Now, Dr. Crosse waved his arms when he spoke, whereas before, you would not have had to watch two flailing arms, or had to duck now and then, to avoid being hit by his flapping fingers, when you were trying to listen attentively to what he had to say.

Waving his arms, he said: "The basis for wealth and power is not land, is not natural resources, is not weaponry. It is the ability to command the minds and bodies of human beings. In the next war, we'll supply the only dedicated soldiers, we'll send out the only really good troops! You and me, Rennie! Well, gotta catch the shuttle. Meeting at the Pentagon."

Depressed, I no longer wanted to leave my room at the Waldorf. I stayed in bed, watching TV, and the VCR, clicking slowly through scenes of women in the nude, being kissed, smiling, crying, struggling against rape, sitting with their legs crossed, walking away from the camera. I spent days at a time in bed, watching and sleeping.

Chapter 24.
"SEX TALK WON," SEZ FBI.

In January, we went down to Washington on the train, and got drunk, Daphne, Dr. Crosse and myself. We got hotel rooms, and the next day we went to the Inauguration of Mr. Elam as President.

When we got there, our seats had been occupied by someone else. They were VIP seats, only a few feet from the actual podium where the swearing-in would take place. I went to a policeman and showed him our tickets. He looked at them, and said something I couldn't hear, into a walkie-talkie. Then, waiting for a reply, he stood staring at me with what appeared to be hostility. After a few moments, responding to an instruction he got over his earphones, he led us to the far reaches of the viewing stands way down Pennsylvania Avenue. I didn't really care, and it was obvious that Dr. Crosse and Daphne didn't, either. We sat together, waiting for the Inauguration, and we all felt the swelling of pride when we saw the man we had helped so much, President Elam, and his Vice-President, Nimrod Smith, waving from the plastic bubbles that covered the passenger areas of their cars.

Little did we know, as we watched Mr. Elam slowly climb the wooden bleachers to the podium, turning now left, now right, to shake the hands of supporters and government officials, that already, the President had turned away from us. That he had actually set his heart against us. Even me, his dedicated son, and Dr. Crosse, to whom, as much as to any man, he owed his victory.

What had happened, in the short space of time between my last conversation with Mr. Elam - the day before, when he had said he looked forward to seeing me on this day, and spending some talk-time with me - and now, the very next morning?

Answer: the night before, in New York, The FBI had finally concluded its long investigation of the murdered models, totalling eight over the past year or so.

I had watched the news of these killings with a growing certainty that they had something to do with our work. Now, the night before the Inauguration, a man named Ezio Trask had been arrested. Trask was an artist, a painter, who worked for the first advertising agency to experiment with our techniques. Daphne and I had had three meetings with him, when we were first working out our techniques of combining word and image on the invisible plane. I remember him as a nice enough guy. He was the first subliminal cartoonist, creating the dogs and cats, and forest creatures, and little figures of Pan peeking through the subliminal leaves floating in the visible cereal bowls. Also, the gory cartoons of automobile accidents, severed heads and disturbing biological cross-sections of anatomical parts.

It seems, as we later learned, that Ezio fell in love with the models on whose photographs he was assigned to draw his animals and gut-pictures. Perhaps he was drawn to them by the same mechanism with which we hoped to trap the unwary consumer. He would go to them, and make his feelings known. Unfortunately, they all rejected his love, and and when they rejected him he added new embeds to their pictures, that said: KILL ME STAB ME SHOOT ME DEATH MURDER BLOOD KILL ME ETC. - Thus, when the models went out in public, they were among thousands of people whose minds had been embedded with the unconscious urge to kill them. This explained the wide variety of total strangers who had killed our models, and the inability they all had to explain the motives behind their actions. It also explained why in one or two cases, the killers of the models had been forced to push other people away, who were trying to get to the models first, also to kill them.

Since the murders involved people who sold products everyone felt close to, the case had been newsworthy from the beginning. For this reason, the elite FBI VI-CAP Squad, specializing in investigations of serial murders, were followed closely by journalists, and the people who buy rights for film companies, who dogged their every step throughout the investigation.

Each elite FBI investigator was wooed by several well-bankrolled journalists or film producers. Well before the arrest of the suspect, the rights to the story had been sold to so many different corporations that the usually efficient governmental machinery for covering things up couldn't be wheeled into place fast enough. Or so said President Elam, when he explained the predicament to me some time later. When Ezio Trask told his story to the FBI agents who arrested him, that story was leaked almost instantly to the waiting media. The subliminals, the way they were being used in advertising, the part they had taken in the election of President Elam and Vice-President Smith.

By the afternoon of the Inauguration, newspapers were bouncing from trucks onto cold Washington streets with headlines saying: "MIND CONTROL ALLEGED IN ELAM-SMITH VICTORY!" and "SEX TALK WON ELECTION SEZ FBI!"

One immediate result of this shock to the public consciousness was that Dr. Wilson Brian Key, formerly considered a crackpot, was soon seen on many TV shows, explaining the principles of what he so long ago had so accurately named "subliminal seduction." To a series of aghast hosts, he explained the "poisoning of our information stream."

"We must cleanse the information stream, and start over," he said.

Daphne, Dr. Crosse and I missed the news of Ezio's arrest, and the breaking scandal.

We were hung over when we got back from the Inauguration, and all three of us took naps until it was time to get ready for the Inaugural Ball. I had expected a call from one of the President's campaign officials to tell us how we were supposed to get to the Ball, but I wasn't really concerned when he didn't call, or when I couldn't reach him at his home. I called the front desk of our hotel, and arranged for a limo to be waiting for us.

The three of us talked and laughed as we drove through the nighttime streets of Washington. Passing a park, we saw homeless people gathered around their ashcan fires, warming themselves.

We arrived at the party as the guests were still pouring in, and I could see the brightly lit ballroom from the door, and the dancing couples, but the Guard said our names were not on the list. I showed him our invitations, and again we were subjected to the experience of waiting while a man mumbled into his walkie-talkie. Other guests were passing us, and he was waving them right in. I was about to step forward, and make an objection, when I saw Nimrod Smith coming toward us from inside the room. His face was twisted into a shape of tragic incomprehension, as though he were watching a male lion kill lion cubs in the wild.

He reached us, and took me aside.

"Didn't you hear?" he asked me. "Don't you watch the news?"

I said we'd been sleeping most of the day.

He told me about Trask being arrested, and about the widening scandal. He said he was astonished the three of us would show up - He briefly explained the situation, saying people were already calling for the election to be declared invalid. He said, "I don't know if I can ever forgive you for having cheapened the magnificent ritual of America's Presidential election. I told the President when I first heard of these goings-on, I said..."

I interrupted him, asking, "What does the President want us to do, Nimrod?"

He said, "Go back to New York and wait for his call. Talk to no one. Don't try to get in touch with the New York or LA offices of the Party."

I went over to Dr. Crosse and Daphne, who were waiting in their fine clothes a few steps away, and told them what had happened. Dr. Crosse went to Nimrod and tried to hold him from re-entering the party. He said, "Get us in to see the President. I have to talk to him. I can help him. The public will understand when they hear about the centuries of prosperity and peace we can bring them through our new art."

"The public! I said don't talk to anyone. Not one word! You're strictly off the books - remember that," said Nimrod, as he touched himself over the heart, as though he was afraid it would leap out of his chest and run down the street in fear. "Look, if you go home and shut up, we'll do what we can for you - you can be sure, there will always be a place for you in this administration - you won't be in the dog house for long - just disappear for now - Wait here and I'll bring you out some cake and champagne. No reason we can't have our own little shindig right here, is there? Or, over here," he said, stepping into an area pitch black with the multiple shades of many trees.

"No, we're going," said Dr. Crosse. He turned away from the Hotel Ballroom, and started back toward the curb, where the car was parked. He looked tired, beat. His posture changed. He stumbled, and I ran forward to grab his arm, and support him. Daphne held his other side. We went back to the hotel, and tried to get a flight back to New York right away. There were none, so I hired a private plane, and we were back at the Waldorf by two thirty a.m.

When we were finally alone, with all the day's newspapers, Daphne and I discussed what was going on. She cried and said, "We have to go to the press and tell them we had nothing to do with these murders. I don't want them to say my Dad was responsible, when it had nothing to do with him at all!"

I said, "My Dad's the President now. He won't let anything bad happen to your Dad. We owe it to him to keep our mouths shut. Until we talk to him, at least."

"I don't care about your stupid Dad," said Daphne. "All I care about is my Dad. I don't want your stupid Dad and his stupid Party to ruin my Dad's good name."

I said I would appeal to the President, to take special care that Dr. Crosse's reputation was not harmed by whatever statements he made to the press.

She said, "Do you think he'll do that for you?"

I had to admit that I didn't know. "At one time, when I first learned he was my True Dad and he first learned I was his son, I would have said yeah, but now... well... I hope so..."

Daphne and I turned to each other, to forget about the events of the world, and went to sleep.

I woke up before dawn to go back to my own room. Daphne and I were still keeping our love for one another a secret from her father. A couple of hours later, as we had planned the night before, Dr. Crosse and I met in Daphne's room, for breakfast. The light was just being squeezed from that old sponge called the sky over New York, and as we discussed our plans for the coming day, our future looked as bleak and formless as the dawn. I tried to cheer everyone up by telling them, "I will talk to the President today, and I'm sure he won't keep us in limbo concerning our fates. After all," I said, putting jelly on a croisant, "his love for me goes beyond that of a politician for his loyal team. His blood is my blood; my fate is the fate of his family, down the long roads of the coming centuries. And right here, in this room, are the two people I love and care for most in the world - my mentor and my..."

(I didn't want to say future bride) "...my cherished co-worker. Therefore, when I am raised up, as I'm sure I will be, as soon as the President can find a moment to free himself from the pressing needs of his advisers and Party chiefs, there is no doubt that you both will be raised up with me. Then, if there is any scandal, and if the public thinks we have done anything wrong, we will deal with that when the time comes. I'm sure my Dad will stand by us."

I smiled warmly at Dr. Crosse, but he did not return my smile. It seemed to me, though I was no psychologist, he was overcome with shame on hearing my little speech. His face turned red as he turned it toward the yellow sky.

After gulping the rest of his coffee, he went back to his room, at the other end of the hotel, on the same floor. Daphne went to the door with him, and kissed him. We talked about going to a movie that afternoon. Then, she came back into the room, and we ate the breakfast her father had left on the room-service cart. I crossed the room to turn on the TV, to see the news about the subliminal scandal. Something made me turn and look through the window.

I saw, on the iron skeleton of a building that was being built across the street, a construction worker standing on a girder. He was hovering over the street between the construction site and Daphne's room. The girder lurched into motion, bringing the worker closer to the window. For a moment, it looked as though he would fall off, but then I saw he was tied onto the steel cable that held the girder, by a harness of leather. The worker steadied himself, then reached one hand behind him. The hand disappeared into a sort of funnel, about the size of a telescope, and emerged with a stiff green tube, like a documents tube, but thinner. The man made some adjustments to a raised plastic area on one end of the tube and raised it to the level of his waist. Daphne screamed and tackled me from behind, just below the knees. I crashed to the rug, but not before I saw a smudge of flame at the front of the tube, and the emergence from it of a slightly wobbling thin missile. In an instant, the missile came through the window, touching and burning a few strands of the hair at the top of my head before going through the wall behind me, across the corridor, and into the room on the other side of the corridor, where it exploded, demolishing that room and half the corridor between that room and the one we were in.

Daphne got to her feet, took only a moment to assess the situation, then ran through the hole in the wall, toward her father's room. I went after her. The man on the girder was peering through the dust, trying to determine whether or not he needed to take another shot. There was a second shot, moments later, but we were out of the area by then.

As we rounded the corner to Dr. Crosse's room, we saw Dr. Crosse being dragged through his doorway, and down the hall backwards, by two men.

He saw us. "Run! Run!" he called to us. I tried to pull Daphne back around the corner, but she shook me off. Instead of retreating, she walked forward. Slowly, calmly, she approached the agents holding her Dad, speaking to them as she approached, in a voice barely audible, "Fuck cunt prick fuck fuck suck..." and so on.

One of the agents drew his gun. But before it was fully raised, he screwed up his face, and turned it slightly, in an attempt to hear what she was saying. "Wha... H?" he said, or something like it. He looked at the other agent. That one, too, was staring at Daphne, with a strange expression on his face. The one with the gun let it dangle toward the floor. His lips started to move in silent repetition of the phenomes coming from Daphne's mouth, which he and his partner were studying as though for clues to some great mystery. She moved ever forward, saying the words. Her father and I could do nothing but watch her, and wait for the men to act. Daphne's

216

words hypnotized the agents, so they didn't hear the bell ring when their elevator arrived.

They were staring at her. The one who had not yet shown a gun, now had his hand half under his jacket, and was reaching behind him, as though trying to decide whether to pull his gun, but frozen in that position. As a result of her power over them, I was able to approach them, also, crouching behind her like a soldier using a portable tree for cover. Along the route, I was able to reach out and grab a small chair and when I got close enough, I jumped out from behind Daphne and smashed one of the agents, the one with his hand under his jacket, across the arm and ribs with the chair. His gun fell to the rug, and I smashed him again with the chair, and then picked up the gun. The other agent would have shot me, but Dr. Crosse reached up from the floor, lifting himself to a kneeling position in one move, and driving the palm of his hand upward into the bottom of the agent's nose. The agent screamed, then fell to the rug, rolling and holding his face.

Dr. Crosse, Daphne and I got on the elevator. In the lobby, there were police, and guests of the hotel, discussing the explosion everyone had heard, and some had seen. Nobody appeared to notice the three of us. If they did, they thought we were three more guests roused from their morning sleep by what everyone felt must have been a terrorist attack on the hotel.

We got a cab on 59th Street, and sank into its back seat. We went to the building of the condo Daphne and I had long ago bought in this city, but that her father didn't know about. We went to the apartment, used the bathroom, picked up the fifty thousand in cash we kept in the hollow leg of a table there, went down to the basement, and got in one of our cars, a solent blue Jaguar Sovereign.

Gliding majestically from the garage in the climate-controlled, burl-wood-trimmed, leather-faced-seated, still-new-smelling car, I tried to turn left onto 65th. I was surprised when the path was suddenly blocked by a Ford Taurus carrying two men. The passenger turned to face us, and for a moment I thought it was Dr. Huss. The passenger brought a gun up to the open window, and fired into our car. I hit the brake, pulled back a couple of feet, then made a sharp righthand turn, needing the sidewalk to make the turn.

The car had a button to shift it into what is called the "Sport Mode". I hit that button, and flew ahead of the Taurus. They chased us up Third. I lost them when I went across Central Park at 86th Street. We left the city by the George Washington Bridge, into New Jersey.

We fled south to Maryland, to see an old schoolmate of Dr. Crosse's, from his days as an undergraduate at The Johns Hopkins University, in Baltimore.

We ate at a Howard Johnson's in Delaware, and bought some newspapers to read about ourselves. After I looked at each paper for a moment, in amazement, Daphne took it from my hand and read it aloud, though in a low voice, to her father, who sat in his side of the booth with his hands over his head like a madman crushing voices in his skull. The newspapers said we were suspected of blowing up the Waldorf, to destroy evidence of our complicity in the murders of the eight models. They said Ezio was dead, having committed suicide in the custody of the FBI, and that before he died he had made and signed a full confession. In the confession, contrary to what he had said when he was first arrested, he said his love for the models, and their rejection of him, was not the motive behind his plan to enrage a world of strangers to take their lives. This new confession said the murders were part of an experiment run by Dr. Crosse.

Dr. Crosse said, through the forest of his arms, "They're going to kill us. They killed Ezio, forged his so-called confession, all to have an excuse to have us shot on sight."

I said, "Perhaps Ezio went insane at the end, and really did take his own life. Maybe, some lawyer convinced him to implicate us in his crimes, to get himself a lighter sentence. So, he signed that confession. Then, he felt guilty about slandering your name, so he killed himself."

"That would explain everything but the man with the missile outside my window this morning, and the two men in the Ford Taurus who shot at us," said Daphne, seeming to disagree with my suggestion.

I said, "Who has a quarter? I'm going to call the President. Even if I can't get through, I can leave a message, saying, 'Your son is in fear of his life, please make yourself available for another call in one hour,' or something like that. After all, the man is my Dad. I don't think he wants to see my guts spread out on some highway, no matter how embarrassed he may be by his reliance on subliminals to get him elected. A man may be President for eight years, if he's lucky; but fatherhood is a lifelong joy."

Then, I was surprised to see Dr. Crosse grab two fistfuls of his abundant brown hair and tear them, along with some skin, from his scalp. He cried out, "I lied to you, Rennie. President Elam is not your True Dad."

"He's not?" I said.

"The Party came to me. They wanted me to work for Elam's candidacy. But I knew there was no subliminal art without you. You were the genius in the field. You were the creative spark. Along with Daphne, of course," he said, looking forlornly at his daughter.

To me he said, "It was so much money. And more than that, a chance to play a role in history. I couldn't turn them down. But how could I ask you to help Mr. Elam become President, when both you and I thought of him primarily as a person who had walled you in a basement room where he meant for you to die of starvation, thirst, or suffocation? How many young men would vote for such, let alone work diligently for the election of that man? Not many. Except..." and he started to sob brokenly as he finished his short speech, "except... if the candidate... sob sob... is your ... sob sob... True Dad... So I.... Sob ..."

He cried, and I forgive him.

I asked Daphne if she had known of the deceit, but she assured me she had not. She forgave Dr. Crosse, though, and went to the other side of the booth to sit next to him and put his head on her breast, while I held his hands across the table. It was clear he had lost his old confidence and sense of purpose, and we wanted him to know that didn't matter to us. We were all re-seeing one another at that moment, I think, seeing one another as hunted, doomed creatures, and finding that even so, we enjoyed one another's company.

We realized the police would kill us if they got the chance. According to Dr.Crosse, we couldn't give ourselves up, or we would be killed in our cells. We couldn't run, because they would probably shoot us in the back and say we were charging at them with "what appeared to be guns" in our empty hands. We were terrified. When I suggested that perhaps Dr. Crosse was exaggerating the danger of murder by the police, he said, "As any grown person who keeps reasonably well-informed can tell you, the American law-enforcement community is the all-time backshooters' paradise in the history of the known world. Then they slide a pistol under your dead body and say you threatened 'em with it. No, we can't afford to run into the police, kids. We have to get off the road right now."

Daphne said, "Dad, I've never heard you talk like this. You're talking about the police as though you didn't trust them."

Dr. Crosse pressed his lips together for a moment, gathering air in his lungs. Then, he suddenly exhaled with great force, and it was as though he had blown a smile up through his insides, because one now appeared on his lips. He laughed happily, in a voice twenty years younger than any I had ever heard from him, and said, "You're right! We haven't even seen Drummond yet, and already I'm beginning to talk like him again! Ha! Or rather, to talk the way we both used to talk, back at college." Then, his face took on the expression of someone lost in the past.

His face was so happy, so calm, after the strains of the past few hours, that I was hesitant to call him out of his mood of remembrance. Finally, it was Daphne who said, kissing her father's cheek, "Shouldn't we go?"

We took the next exit off the highway onto the local roads. Thus, a trip that might have taken us two hours, took six. Dr. Crosse didn't mind. He spent the time talking about his old college days, and his friendship with Drummond, when the two of them had been the tyros of the psychological community. "Then, after college, and grad school," he said, "I got a huge grant from the U.S. Army, to study the effects of LSD on brain surgeons doing delicate operations. This is not the time or the place to go into detail about that experiment. Suffice it to say LSD is not a good idea for brain surgeons doing delicate operations. Anyway, Drummond could have been on the team, but he said he had certain moral qualms about the experiment. Once that got out, he was through as a scientist. Said he didn't care, he couldn't spend his life in a field that was poised to become the source of new forms of bondage for the human race. He said he was going to earn his living doing something respectable, selling drugs.

"And that's what he did. Became a big pot dealer, started growing it on pieces of land all through Maryland and Pennsylvania."

The entire trip was like that, with Dr. Crosse praising and remembering his old friend, crying over their periods of estrangement, laughing about the tricks they used to play in school, the light stealing they used to do, when they were broke and couldn't afford books, or food. I'm sorry to say, I didn't really listen to most of what he was saying. I was thinking about my loss of President Elam, as my True Dad. No longer was I the son of the President. In my thoughts, I revisited my other possible Dads, and I was happy to have them back again, as possibilities, but at that moment, I don't know if they completely compensated me for the loss of Elam.

As Dr. Crosse spoke, he peered through the front seats, and directed me as best he could, considering he had not been to this place in twenty years.

We finally arrived at a small farming town called One Corner, Maryland. We drove through it, attracting some attention with our huge Jaguar, that took up both sides of the road in many places. We passed groups of Quakers, dressed all in black and driving horse-drawn buggies. We went through some hills, and arrived in a green valley, surrounded by white and blue rocky hills. There were cows standing here and there in the valley. There were lots of trees, and soon we were driving through a cavern of overhung branches so thick it was almost nighttime underneath. When we emerged at the other end, we saw a field of flowers, varieties of roses and tulips and other kinds I didn't recognize. Drummond ran a nursery now, Dr. Crosse said, and this was it.

We drove under more trees, to a large wooden house that was totally hidden from the road. "We're here," said Dr. Crosse. Then, looking anxiously at the house he said, "I hope he still lives here." The moment he said this, I felt against the side of my face, the side that faced my open window, a cold, machined object which I could not identify until I turned my head to face it. It was the barrel of a shotgun. I looked along this barrel and saw at the other end was a woman of about thirty-five, with stringy brown hair, white freckled skin, and thin white lips. I noticed out of the corner of my eye a young girl, striding up to Daphne's side of the car, with a rifle in her hands. The woman holding the shotgun said, "Do you folks want to be buried in your car, or can we keep it?"

Chapter 25. Home Education.

"Don't shoot 'em !" cried a loud, laughing, voice from somewhere behind the car. I didn't have the courage to turn my face toward the shotgun barrel to see who might be calling out, but in the back seat, Dr. Crosse turned and said, "It's Drummond!" A few moments later, the tall, broad figure of a sandy-haired man who had not shaven for three or four days came and scooped up the woman who held the gun on me, the one he called Southpaw, and turned her toward the path to the house, along which she ambled reluctantly. "It's OK, Taffy," the man said to the other woman, and that one lowered her gun, but stood where she was, staring into the car, mostly at Daphne.

"Were you expecting us?" asked Dr. Crosse as Drummond helped him out of the back door of the car. He was referring to the two women with guns.

Drummond said, "Not you. Somebody else. But we'll talk about that later. Now..." and he embraced Dr. Crosse, and the two of them smashed each other on the back for a while, until it became time for Daphne and me to be introduced to Drummond. We shook hands all around, with him and with Taffy. Then, Drummond took us into the kitchen of the house, where he fed us and gave us coffee. Through the kitchen window, we could see men and women walking into the deep woods around the house, all of them armed with guns or, in the case of one or two, bows and arrows. A young man looked toward the house, and Drummond leaned out the window, giving the man a hand-signal that told him where to enter the forest. Seeing this, Daphne became visibly upset, and Dr. Crosse again asked his old friend why the place seemed to be under a state of siege. But Drummond shook his head and said, "Time enough for that later. Right now, I'd like to hear what the fuck *you've* been up to! Man, you three are all over the TV."

"Lies," said Dr. Crosse, as I grabbed some more of the sour bread we were eating.

"I thought so," said Drummond.

Dr. Crosse, with some help from Daphne, told his friend the story of our involvement in the field of subliminal advertising, including the whole truth of our role in the victory of the newly-inaugurated President Elam.

He told Drummond that, despite the news reports, the three of us had had absolutely nothing to do with the deaths of the models, or the destruction of that floor of the Waldorf.

Dr. Crosse's old friend hung his sandy-colored head and looked sad.

He said, "I knew you couldn't have done the things they've been saying you did, but I was afraid the truth would be exactly as you have told it to me."

He looked Dr. Crosse in the eye and said, "What you did was worse than murder. You sold out science for money. Just like when you started out, twenty years ago."

"That's fine for you to say," said Dr. Crosse, becoming angry for the first time since our troubles began. "You haven't done any science. You sell drugs. Good for you. But I wanted to do the work I set out to do, the work we both set out to do. To learn more. That's all I ever cared about. To learn everything. It isn't my fault that you need money to conduct science in this world. Sure, I took money. So what?"

"But from what kind of people? That's the question."

"The kind of people who have money to pay for original research, that's the kind of people. You dropped out, you were pure, you're hot shit. I've done science. If I compromised, at least I didn't compromise my curiosity. How much new knowledge have you uncovered out here in East Mud?"

"At least I learned what shit I won't eat. Sounds like you're still goin' around the shit salad bar, pilin' up your plate."

I thought we were going to leave then, because Dr. Crosse got up and went out the front door. But after a minute or two, Drummond went out there, and we could hear them in the open doorway.

"They'll kill you if they find you, am I right?" asked Drummond. Then, Dr. Crosse must have nodded, because

Drummond said, "You came to the right place, old friend. Stay with us."

When they returned to the kitchen, Dr. Crosse was calmed down, and managed to smile at his friend as he said, "It seemed when we arrived there's some anticipation of trouble here. Violence seems expected at any moment."

Drummond nodded. He made himself another cup of tea, and as he drank it, he told Dr. Crosse what was happening in his life. They had not been in touch for the past ten years. Dr. Crosse knew all about Drummond's drug dealing, which the other said he still did as his main source of income. However, he defended himself, saying, "It's only pot, which George Washington himself not only grew and sold, but smoked every day of his adult life. On his doctor's orders!"

Dr. Crosse smiled. "So, you're expecting the big bust at any moment, is that it?" he asked in a tolerant manner.

"No," said Drummond. "I've been busted, several times, but it was never very serious. Paid a fine, paid off some judge. That's not why we're expecting a siege up here. Nobody really cares about pot. And they don't care that I have four wives."

"Drummond!" said Dr. Crosse in surprise, and his friend smiled sheepishly.

"I believe every man that can support a few women, and have kids with them, and support the kids, should do it. I feel it's our obligation. That's a part of my life that started after you and I lost track of one another. I've got Taffy, Lois, Southpaw and Becky, and Taffy's four kids, Southpaw's three, Becky's four and Lois's twins, Leviticus and Deuteronomy. I'm not denying our family arrangements here are a little unusual for Maryland, but that is not the reason I find myself expecting a visit from the authorities, either.

"No, I lived as an outlaw for years, but I was never bothered much 'til I took our kids out of public school. Decided to teach 'em here at home. Then, they started comin'. The truant officers, the teachers, the principals, the police, the marshalls, the child welfare parasites, everyone drawing pay from the State or the County seemed to find his way to this farm, to tell me about all the laws saying I have to send my kids to their schools to be brainwashed and lied to and made average and docile. But I stuck to my decision. Now, I'm under a state of seige. But don't worry. Even if they come in force, we're ready for 'em."

"Are you telling me you intend to fight it out with the police? Because you don't want your children to go to school!"

"No. Not to the point of suicide. We have a means of egress. I can assure you, all of us, including you and yours will be safe."

"I teach Daphne at home, too," said Dr. Crosse. "I guess they tend to notice more if you have fifteen children, or whatever the number is."

Drummond explained that he believed all public, private and religious schools spread lies, and made children into "godless demons."

He said he was part of a growing movement of people who taught their kids at home:

"We home educators are a weird bunch of coots," he said, "Some people object to that sex education they teach in schools. Some keep their kids at home because they can't stand the teaching of racial integration. I'm not one of those. No, my objection is the damned Darwinians."

"Darwinians?" said Doc Crosse, "You went to Johns Hopkins. You gave the class speech. How can you be so backward?"

Drummond said, "The word of the Bible is true and exact. That's all I'm saying."

Dr. Crosse said with the air of someone who is so tired he can barely push the words through his vocal cords and out to his friend, "But the Bible says the world was created five thousand seven hundred and some odd years ago. Yet the fossils we have show pretty clearly that the world has been here upwards of four billion years. There really doesn't seem to be much room for argument, does there? Have you gone psychotic since our last lunch, ten years ago? Have you had a lobotomy? What's going on?"

But Drummond just laughed good naturedly. "I know, I know," he said, putting his hand up in the stop position. "It sounds crazy. But all I'm saying is, there's a way that the Bible could be taught, and at the same time, science could be taught. But the way they do it, they try to insult the Bible, by making it seem untrue, to our kids, when really the problem is, we don't read it right. Does that make sense?"

"So you're saying you'll keep your children at home until the Biblical story of creation is added to the curriculum of your local school's biology class?"

"That's it!" said Drummond.

"Then I'd say," said Dr. Crosse "that the man or woman who performed your lobotomy should have charged you double."

Drummond said, "Maybe I could write a pamphlet, setting forth some of my ideas, and you folks could teach me how to get those subliminal dirty words in there, just to help put my ideas across? Would you mind helping me with that?"

"Yes!" we all said.

Daphne, speaking for the three of us, added, "We're through with that forever."

Over the next few weeks, we hid out there. I enjoyed being with Drummond and his large family, and was impressed with him, for being the only person I had ever met who had almost as many children as I had fathers.

This question of the True Dad, I could not put to rest. Once the shock wore off, of the attempt on our lives, and our flight to Maryland, and I had mourned the loss of President Elam from my family tree, I found myself once again considering each of my possible Dads as contenders for the role of True Dad. Once again, I would wake from dreams in which I had killed one of my Dads in the name of another of them. I found it painful to be alone in those days, but Daphne didn't have time for me, because she was always with Drummond's wives, cooking and cleaning and reading to the youngest children of that crowded commune.

I spent most of my time trailing after Dr. Crosse and Drummond as they discussed the great changes that had overcome them since college, when they were leftists.

One time Drummond said: "There is no America any more - the social compact that prevailed when we were younger no longer exists. Just look at Reynold's experiences with his Dads - how different they all are, and intolerant of one another. Not one of them

227

is willing to give what used to be called The American Idea, even one more chance. It's over." Nobody said anything.

Another time he said to Dr. Crosse, "Remember when I met you - we were two kids from entirely different backgrounds, but we agreed on almost everything of importance. About how a person should lead his life, our ideals for ourselves and our country. And even when we were protesting the war in Viet Nam, and those other kids were chasing us around the lacrosse field trying to tear up our banners, they and we were, strange as it may sound, in agreement. We agreed that they were worth convincing of our position, they agreed that we were worth chasing and having our banner torn, but not killed. Now, nobody agrees on anything. We're breaking up into primitive gangs of mean sons-of-bitches who hardly admit one another have a right to live. It's over."

I have few opinions of my own, and I always enjoy hearing other people's, no matter what they are. I think of people with opinions as heroes. Of course, Drummond was not a putative, or even a possible Dad of mine, which meant his words could not really carry much weight for me, but some of the things he said stayed with me.

One idea of his especially led me to do a lot of thinking. He and Dr. Crosse had just had one of their discussions about the state of the scientific world, when Drummond turned to me and said, "You have to learn to take what we say with a grain of salt. You have to realize that me and the Doc here, and all your Dads you told me about - we're all part of a certain generation, and everything we say and do, no matter why we think we're saying it or doing it, or what we tell you about why we did it, no matter what - everything we do is because we're in that generation."

"What generation is that?" asked Dr. Crosse, before I had a chance to.

Drummond said, "It's called the Assassination Generation. It was named by our friend Mike, twenty five years ago, and the name is as good today as it was then..."

He said, "All us folks... The Assassination Generation. We were still in school when the President was murdered. Kennedy. Before our very eyes. And we had loved him, because he was young and idealistic, and it looked for a minute there like he was going to lead us on a great mission, a great crusade for humanity. Then, once we had given him our hearts, and we all loved him, he was cut off and taken away from us. And we have been - our whole generation has been - on a certain path, ever since that moment. We might not name it; we might jump in fright if anyone tells us what it is - but in lookin' for your Dads, you've seen that path - you've felt it - the long hard march of my generation on the road to revenge! Because that's what it is. We've called ourselves hippies, but we were really a revenge pact. We called ourselves yuppies, but we were on the tragic revenge juggernaut that will not end until, if we are allowed to, we will destroy this earth. Because somebody killed our President, and we feel we have been betrayed.

"No, kid - don't follow our generation. Turn away from us. Because where will you live, and your children live, after the inconsolable Assassination Generation destroys everything, for the enormity of our grief? We're ruined. We're looking over our shoulder, flinching in our soul. We're mistrustful of our fellow citizens, and we cower as we run the nation, like a man driving a car with his arm thrown over his own eyes, screaming. Talking 'bout my generation... Don't follow us." I looked and saw Dr. Crosse was starting to cry.

When I wasn't helping with farm chores, or standing guard in the forest, to warn the others if the police should come, to take Drummond's children away, I watched the news all the time... Subliminals were being investigated by Congress... The scandal was growing... President Elam was asked about the role of subliminals in his election campaign, and he always laughed as he denied any such shenanigans had been tried by his team...

Meanwhile, it was quite clear that somebody (Dr. Crosse said it was the CIA) was thinking of ways to make subliminals acceptable to the public, should the truth ever finally come out. Suddenly, subliminals were a running gag on TV comedy shows, and on humorous commercials. Of course, the sketches and commercials purposely misrepresented the true nature of subliminals, so the public would not associate the subliminals (and our Government) too closely with the words fuck shit cock cunt and so on.

Companies were formed to publish and distribute subliminal diet and relaxation tapes, and tapes claiming to have subliminal suggestions on them to help people acquire wealth. I bought samples of these tapes at the bookstore in One Corner. Dr.Crosse, Daphne and I listened to them. All these patently false representations of the subliminal arts were designed to soften the blow when the truth finally comes out - to make the idea of it less threatening. The tapes didn't work, but they helped to prepare the public, in case they ever learned what we had actually been doing to their minds.

Though I enjoyed the country setting of our hideout, I did notice in myself a growing fear of being killed by the police, or some other agency working for President Elam, or rather, working for the people who supported President Elam. Dr. Crosse and Daphne and I were frequently on TV. As the Senate Investigating Committee looking into the allegations of election subliminals made its slow progress through months of hearings, our names and faces were flashed almost every day on the network news, always accompanied by the words, "fugitives... suspected killers... alleged serial killers... mad scientists..." The President, in an interview with Barbara Walters, at which he promised to "come clean once and for all with the American electrode, I mean electorate," courageously and forthrightly put all the blame on Dr. Crosse and myself. He said we had somehow wormed our way into his campaign, and set about to murder models and subvert the system, all without the knowledge either of himself or any responsible member of his team. He said, "Barbara, what these people have done, or, are alleged to have done, because we don't want to prejudge them before they've been shot while resisting arrest... well, it's abhorrent, it's abominable, and I don't think anyone can seriously believe that I, or Nimrod Smith, or anyone we would even talk to, could ever have known about, let alone been a party to, such dastardly deeds. No, no, when we catch these three miscreants, and we will, Barbara, I'll be the first to say, let justice be done. But don't tar an entire Administration, mine, with the crimes of a very very very tiny group of floating human turds. I mean, have a heart..."

At the same time, things started happening to my other putative Dads, as a result of their publicly perceived relationships with me, or as a result of my intrusion into their lives.

I read in the papers that the Reverend Minister Faroun's followers turned on him at an African Pride Day Festival, where they beat and almost killed him, because they had seen me with him, and the night before, CBS News had broken the story of my relation with him. He would have been able to deny the whole thing, but he had let the truth slip out once or twice in unguarded moments with some of his trusted bodyguards. The news said the Rev Min Faroun had to be rescued from his followers by the LAPD. Now he was reportedly co-operating with the police on several murder investigations involving members of his group, in exchange for their keeping him in protective custody. I looked at the file footage on the news, and wiped a tear from my eye. The proud, roaring Rev Min Faroun, now despised by his own people, and all because of me!

Then, Dr. Huss showed up on the TV screen.

It seems Mac 'Mac' MacDonald was making quite a good living selling the story of his investigations on my behalf, and when his first-person narrative appeared in <u>Harper's</u>, Dr. Huss's fellow Nazis, instead of being grateful to him for inadvertantly connecting their cause with Reynold Stengrow, who had hurled it out to the wide world through the artfulness of subliminals, instead of thanking him for this, they tortured him in the desert near California City, nailing him to a piece of wood and dragging him head last from the back of a pickup truck. Then, they staked him out over a missile silo, went back to the control room, and would have shot a Trident through his prone form, into space, but were stopped by their Base superiors, who were afraid the incident might publicize the extent and virulence of Nazis and the Nazi ideology throughout the American space program. Those facts came out anyway, but they were vehemently denied. That left only me, feeling sad over my negative effects on the life of yet another putative Dad.

Things got worse. As a minor side-note of the hearings of the Senate Investigating Committee, the world learned that my writer-Dad, Mr. Popper, unknown for many years, had only become famous through subliminally scratched dirty words on the paper he used to submit his work to publishers.

Mr. Popper, learning for the first time that the basis of his popularity was false - falsely gained by my help - tried to kill himself by walking into the lion's veldt at the Bronx Zoo. While women fainted and children screamed, and little carts darted back and forth ineffectually across the great moat that separates the people from the lions in the African Jungle exhibition, Mr. Popper staggered toward the resting felines. They eyed him warily. He stood before a male, with huge mane and spoke to him for a long while before he got tired and fell down and went to sleep. The lions watched him lying there, and then went in for the night, after which, the park police were able to rescue him... Next time, I thought, it might be worse... And seeing him on the news, as he climbed into the rescue wagon, looking so tired, so defeated...

I had to do something, to save my numerous, innocent fathers, but I didn't know what there was for me to do. I could do as Drummond had suggested, and disguise myself for the rest of my life, or I could risk my life, and maybe Daphne's and Dr. Crosse's, by going back to Washington, D.C. to testify. Was it worth the risk of telling the truth? Would that even help my Dads, or just make things worse for them? I was feeling guilty, because my Dads were suffering now, because I had sought them out.

Then, all that guilt fell of its own weight, and I found, to my amazement, that I was angry at them! Yes! Angry at my poor put-upon Dads!

Ashamed as I am to admit it, I wished that none of them had ever fathered me. I fumed in my bed, furious that I should have to feel responsible for the fates of so many Dads.

That night, when I finally fell asleep, I had a dream.

In the dream, I saw myself lifted up in the arms of Mr. Elam, like a child lifted into the air. He held me over his head, and spun me around, like an airplane. Then, he passed me to another pair of hands, the hands of *his* father, who handed me back, in turn, to his father. All the time, I was seeing their lives, the places they had lived, the people they had loved, all through different centuries and ages. Except, at some time - I couldn't tell exactly when it happened - I was passing over the heads of Dr. Huss's ancestors; then, over the heads of the ancestors of the Reverend Minister Faroun; then, over those of those of Mr. Steinstein, and Mr. Persson, and the other Dads, many of whom I had never met, but their ancestors managed somehow to get their hands into the act of passing me around. Then, after all the miles and the continents, centuries, skies and oceans, they set me down in a plain wooden room.

There, as I adjusted my eyes to the earthly light of the room, I saw a man and a woman sitting and talking. They sat side by side, on straight-backed pine chairs, with tall backs. There was a small table between them. On the table was a stack of books and papers, along with crowds of make-up bottles, brushes and combs. They stopped talking when they saw me standing before them. The woman touched the arm of the man, whispering in his ear. I saw then that the woman was Marilyn Monroe, and the man was George Washington, the first President of the United States. They both had white wigs on. The wigs were not the same, but not entirely different.

I walked up to them, I knelt, and kissed the hand of Marilyn Monroe. She smiled at me.

I said, "Everyone is still sad for you. We miss you very much." I was crying.

She said, "I am happy here. From this room, I can look out and see America. I can watch people every day, and I can see for myself how the children are living. I can help them, when they need me."

Then she said, "President Washington has something to say to you."

I looked up and President Washington was putting a chair behind me, like the ones they sat in. I sat in it, and he went back to his chair.

He looked at me intently, and said, "Do you know who I am?"

I answered, "Yes, sir. You're President Washington."

233

He replied, "That's right." Then, he said, "Why have you come here? What do you want?"

I said, "Sir, should I continue to hide out, or should I risk my life by going back, to testify about what I know? The reason I can't decide on my own is, I don't know which of my Dads is my True Dad. I don't want to do anything that will hurt my True Dad, but which one is he?"

President Washington said, "Show me your book." It was only then I realized I had the ledger book with me, with the names of my 36 possible Dads. I gave him the book. He put it on the table, then he opened a drawer on his side of the table. Out of the drawer he took a small hatchet. He raised the hatchet high over my head. I thought he was going to split my head with it, but he brought it down into the cover of the ledger book, through the book, and fixing it to the table with its blade.

President Washington said: "I cannot tell a lie, Reynold. I am your True Dad. Didn't you know that, Reynold? All of your Dads - all of them - when they came to America, I adopted them. They are all my children, and so are you."

I said, "I was looking for you, Father."

After a while, I said, "What should I do, sir?"

He held up some pieces of old paper with ancient writing in a spidery script on their faces. He said, "Read the documents, and tell the truth."

I was trying to see the papers, and I asked him, "What documents, sir?" but before he could answer me, I woke up.

Later that day, I was on guard duty, when a newspaper blew among the trees and fell across the toes of my shoes. I picked it up, and saw an advertisement from a cigarette manufacturer, reminding us it was the anniversary of the Bill of Rights. A photo of the Bill of Rights filled the page. I could see it was like the document which George Washington had shown me in my dream.

I went to the house, and found Daphne. I took her with me, both of us in disguise, and we went to the Smithsonian Museum, in Washington, to the round room where the Declaration of Independence and the Constitution are on display, under tables of glass.

Daphne asked me what we were doing here, but I didn't know what to tell her. We saw the Declaration of Independence, and the Constitution. We stood reading them for a while, as classes of schoolchildren and their teachers came and went. When the huge room was empty, except for the Guards at the doors, Daphne and I performed some tests for the presence of subliminals. With a portable laser, we determined to our own satisfaction that there were no hidden words in the ink or the paper of the documents. or in any wax or powder overlay on the pages themselves. However, a simple moire pattern test revealed that the words "sex" and "death" had recently been etched thousands of times into the glass plates that covered all the documents.

Driving back to One Corner I told Daphne about my dream, and we decided it must mean that we, or at least that I, should testify before Congress.

At dinner,I said I was thinking of giving myself up, in order to be able to tell our side of the story to the world. "They're scratching subliminals on the Constitution and the Declaration of Independence!" I said. "We can't sit by and let them do that!"

Drummond and Dr. Crosse both said I would be shot down in the street. "Like a dog," in the words of Drummond.

But I said, "Drummond, you and Dr. Crosse are both members of that subset of humanity which you yourself have told me to name The Assassination Generation. Could it be that your fears concerning the law-enforcement personnel of the United States are due more to your experiences during the long-ago decade of that long-ago President's death, than to the facts of the situation as they now stand?"

"No," said Drummond. "If you present yourself and offer to tell them the truth, they will bury you deeper than Elam did you the first time."

Instead, Drummond suggested that Dr. Crosse and Daphne and I hide out forever, change our names, learn the simple basics of growing and selling marijuana, which might afford us a decent, honorable living, earned without having to gull our fellow citizens. "What about airbrushing triggering phenomes on the leaves?" asked

235

Dr. Crosse, as though roused from sleep into the midst of a conversation he only partially understood.

"No, buddy, people buy pot because they like it," said Drummond. Dr. Crosse shrugged.

Then, Daphne said, "Reynold is right. He and I will present ourselves to the police, while you, Father, stay here. If there are two of us, we will be that much safer. We have money to hire a good lawyer. We can tell our side of what happened. We made mistakes, we fooled people, but we never did any murders, that's for sure. And what we did for the election was all at the direct request of Mr. Elam, who now pretends not to know us."

But when she said this, I became afraid for her. I didn't want to be the cause of any danger to her. For all I knew, Drummond and Dr. Crosse were right about the police. I had to disagree with my own previous opinion, for Daphne's sake. I said we couldn't risk it.

"However," I said, "I think we can make our lives safer by putting our story on videotape. Then, we can make copies and send them to all the TV shows, magazines and newspapers."

"Fully embedded," said Dr. Crosse, who seemed to be backsliding once again. "Cocks and cunts by the ton! We'll make 'em see the truth! They won't be able to take their eyes off it!"

"Now, Dad," said Daphne, and cuddled close to him as he raved. She, and I and Drummond knew the days of embeds were over for us. For us, everything would have to be on the up and up, from now on.

Drummond got a video camera and we sat in a circle in the forest, in a place Drummond thought would not be recognizable when the tapes were shown on TV, and we told our story. We intended to send one of the first copies directly to Canada, to Dr. Wilson Brian Key, (previously mentioned author of "Subliminal Seduction" and "The Clamplacte Orgy,") as a way of saying to him: "You were right all along, Dr. Key! We're the ones you've been looking for, the technicians of the subliminal."

Drummond manned the camera. Dr.Crosse spoke first, and talked of the first time certain wealthy businessmen had come to him asking him to experiment with mind control, to help them sell their procucts. He then told how he had wrestled with his conscience until, suddenly, Drummond put his hand up and said, "Shh!" and we could see that he was listening into the trees, in the direction of the house.

We all listened, and a bird cry came through the branches. Drummond answered it with a bird cry of his own, and turned to us and said, "That's the southside lookout - it means they're here."

"Who is?"

"State troopers, police, FBI... your guess is as good as mine."

We gathered rushed back to the house through the thick foliage and over the soft fallen leaves, running low past a hedge of white flowers to reach a pair of doors set into the earth about fifty yards from the house, just at the edge of the clearing that surrounded the house. Drummond opened the two doors, we went down some stairs, then walked through a long cellar corridor, that ended inside the house.

In the house, the wives and children of Drummond were already bolting the bolts of their seige-resistant residence. The windows were iron, the doors were thick wood lined with lead. There were slits for rifles in the windows, through which Drummond and his children sighted down the invaders.

The invaders were men in short overcoats and black shoes. The leaders wore baseball caps with the names of beers on their fronts. "Federal agents," said Drummond.

We saw them hoist themselves with difficulty out of four cars and spread out around the house.

Floodlights came on. They were mounted on the roofs of the cars. One of the agents used a megaphone.

"Drummond, we have a court order here, allowing us to take your children, and make sure they get a proper education. We don't want to have to hurt anyone, Drummond! But if we have to we'll kill you, all your wives and most of your kids, so the survivers can have the education to which they are entitled. Come out now, and no one will get hurt."

Drummond said nothing in response. He stuck a rifle barrel through one of the slits in the windows and started firing at the agents. They returned fire. Soon, the walls of the house were shredding over my head, and I could see daylight, or the light of the bright floods, pouring through the bullet gashes. Drummond and his family fought bravely. I didn't see any of the agents go down, so I don't know if any of them were hurt.

Dr. Crosse said, over the din of the battle, "I thought you said we'd be safe, Drummond! I don't want my daughter killed so your children can avoid hearing the Theory of Evolution. Give up! Give up!"

Drummond turned from his shooting-slit to assure his old friend. "Just a few minutes, then we'll get out of here."

Dr. Crosse just shook his head, looked angry, and then crouched between the ancient enamel stove and ice box. I thought Drummond must have a plan, even though I couldn't imagine what it was. I called Drummond, and asked him to meet me under the kitchen table, for a conversation. He fired a couple of shots, then knelt down. Windows were exploding around us. In one place, the wall had taken so many bullets, it could no longer hold its section of the ceiling, and that section started to sag into the kitchen like a huge tattered sail, blowing in the breeze of gunfire.

Under the table, where no one could hear us, I made a deal with Drummond. Part of the deal was that he wouldn't tell Daphne or Dr. Crosse about the deal.

Chapter 26. Short Overcoats.

Drummond returned to his post, and resumed firing. He seemed relaxed as his well-drilled clan kept up a barrage of firepower directed at the Agents. However, Dr. Crosse couldn't keep calm. "We're dead, we're dead," he said over and over.

There was an explosion in the forest, just behind the place where the Agents had left their cars. The trees burst into flames, and lines of fire sped along the ground, through the leaves, into the clearing itself. It was obvious that fuses had been in place around the farm, ready for this moment.

One of the Agents screamed. I peered out through one of the rifle-slits, and saw a man on fire, dancing and then falling, in his short overcoat. Other Agents went to his rescue, and threw their coats over him, to put out the flames. At this moment, I heard the sound of gunshots from the woods, and the Agents were forced to find cover, and direct their attention away from the house, and toward the new threat from the woods.

"That's it," said Drummond, to his family. "Ned's boys are in place. Let's go."

Drummond led us all down into the basement where a man he called "Hosie" was waiting. He was a red haired, grinning fellow, who turned out to be another old friend of Dr. Crosse's, from school days.

After greetings between Hosie and Dr. C., that were necessarily cut short, Drummond and the redhead conferred briefly. Upstairs, the Agents were bursting in. They were on the floor over our heads. A hidden door, previously indistinguishable from the whitewashed cellar wall, slid open, and the first of the clan diasppeared into it. On the other side was a tunnel of earth, re-inforced with timbers. Soon, we were all on the other side of the door, and Drummond and I pushed the door shut again.

There were torches on the walls of the tunnel, which Drummond and his sons lit.

As we walked, Drummond explained that this was part of the tunnel system used by escaping slaves during the Civil War, to get them from Maryland to Pennsylvania, where they wouldn't be executed.

We came out in a field, it was night. A plane was waiting, in the middle of the field. Drummond said he had always kept this escape route available, for this day. The plan was, to fly to a small airstrip in Arizona, on 160 acres owned by Drummond, and to start life over, with new names.

We boarded the plane, twenty-five of us crowding into a space designed for twelve people.

Before the plane took off I told Daphne and Dr. Crosse that I was not going with them.

"I'm going to turn myself over to the FBI, and testify at the Hearings," I said, kneeling beside Daphne. She said she wanted to go with me, but I said we didn't know if they would kill us, and I couldn't let her come with me. I had to do it alone. I was crying. I kissed her, though she turned her face from me.

I turned to Dr. Crosse and said, "I'm sorry, sir. I hope you understand. I can't let you and Daphne risk your lives, but I have to go back and clear my name, all our names, and the names of my Dads."

He said, "You're a good son, Rennie, and when you get a Dad, I'm sure he'll say the same thing." He half-stood in the cramped space and embraced me warmly.

I went to the door of the plane. Daphne tried to follow me out of the plane. I looked at Drummond, reminding him of our deal, and he nodded, moving to her and holding her back, until I had a chance to get out. I heard her screams as the door of the plane was shut, and I saw her beautiful face, crying in the window.

I walked toward the town of One Corner. Just before I reached the one street, I turned left, up a low hill, to the transmission tower of the small local television station, owned by Drummond's friend, and a nursery customer of his, The Reverend Jeffers. The Reverend Jeffers had been a frequent guest at Drummond's farm during the time we were there, and I had grown to like him quite a bit. His TV station was a small cinder block building sitting on a bald-headed hilltop. When I arrived, he was preaching to the cameras. When he saw me standing outside the control booth, he stopped the broadcast, a forecast of those End Times, or Last Days, you hear so much about, and he introduced me to his TV audience.

He said, "Now, brothers and sisters, I gen'rally don't like to interrupt the fundraising portion of our show for anything, anything at all, but today, we have a dear brother, Reynold Stengrow, and I want him to sit and chat with me on camera here, while we wait for the County Sheriff to arrive, and take him to jail..."

The Reverend, a clean-shaven man with white hair and Eskimo eyes, told the audience what we had told him at the farm - about the subliminals, and the election, and President Elam's involvement in our work - saying that I was a very brave young man, to have the courage to tell my story to the world. "Well, Reverend Jeffers," I said, "I'm hoping if I say what I have to say to your audience, the government will have no reason to assassinate me, since the story will already be full public knowledge."

"That's wise thinkin'" said the Reverend. Then, he told his audience that Satan was the true President of the United States, and had been since they took prayer out of the public schools. After he had spoken for a while, he gave me a chance to tell the whole story, giving my side of things, and Dr. Crosse's and Daphne's. I denied any complicity in the murders of the models, and denied the complicity of Dr. Crosse and Daphne, also. I told the truth, that the murderer had been mentally unbalanced.

I also gave an account of the techniques themselves, and the advertising uses to which they had been put, and I told how we got Mr. Elam elected President.

After about an hour and a half, the Sheriff finally arrived, with the FBI, and they arrested me on-camera, with Reverend Jeffers shouting at them the whole time: "My viewers see you takin' this boy here, and if anythin' should happen to him while he's in yo' custody, we got sev'ral hundred folks gonna know you done it."

The FBI Agents dragged me out to a car, and drove me into Washington, DC, which was cold and dusted with white frost. They took me to a jail under the streets. They booked me, photographed me, and put me in a cell, alone.

A few hours later, one of the Agents came to see me, and said that Reverend Jeffers was running all over DC, looking for me, and he was travelling with a cameraman. I was grateful to the Reverend, for I felt his attention was saving my life.

I was taken from the mass cell to a small room where I was questioned concerning the whereabouts of Dr. Crosse and Daphne. I said nothing. Another team of investigators, who didn't care about the subliminals, but only about the fact that Drummond's children had escaped their education, also questioned me, but to them also, I was silent.

Twelve or fourteen hours later, I was allowed to see a lawyer. He said the government had not yet decided whether to charge me for murdering the eight models. For now, I was being held on a Congressional warrant, until I gave testimony to the Senate Committee. The lawyer said by testifying I would probably do myself a lot of good on the murder charges, as well as the interstate flight charges, the tax evasion charges (one of the servants at Dr. Crosse's ranch, threatened with deportation, led them to my hiding place in the garden, where they found $3,765,872.98 in that metal box, and the two canvas artist's bags that were also in the hole.) I told him I would be happy to testify before the Senate Committte, because testifying is what I gave myself up for.

I was moved to a fine, above-ground cell in what seemed to be a hospital or military barracks. The Senate Committee needed two days to prepare themselves for my testimony, according to the newspapers I was given to read every day, and according to the small TV in the bedroom of my cell-suite. They had been meeting in public hearings on this matter for the past five weeks, and my capture was considered to be the biggest boost the hearings could have had. My testimony was eagerly awaited, as I saw the analysts and panelists all say on the weekend political talkshows. They informed me that the whole nation was looking for someone, anyone, who could clear up this issue: Are subliminals real? Were they used in the Presidential election? Did both parties do it, or only one? Did the candidates know, or only the ad agencies that worked for them?

242

Leading ad agency owners and managers had already testified. All of them claimed to know nothing, all of them passed lie detector tests, taken voluntarily at the advice of their attorneys, results presented to the Senate Committee. For all I know, they were sincere. Because of the way the work was organized, I only know about my own involvement, that of Daphne and Dr. Crosse, and some of the technicians and artists we worked with in New York. Once or twice I saw Dr. Crosse with men I thought were probably "his backers," but I had never made any attempt to learn from him who they were, or if they were backers at all. I knew only that I was off the books.

From the articles given to me to read in my cell, it seemed the Committee was pursuing every lead. Dr. Wilson Brian Key was called to testify, but there were ten ad agency people to refute everything Dr. Key said, along with several psychologists, eye-muscle experts, and biochemists.

What it came down to, then, was that they had only one person who knew what had happened and was willing to talk to them. Me.

On the third day, they brought me to a waiting-room which I took to be inside the Senate, although I couldn't tell, because I was brought there before dawn. There I sat with two guards, drinking coffee for about an hour. I heard a lot of noise from the courtroom next door, and then the door was opened and I was led into the Hearing Room.

Flash bulbs went off, there was a burst of light from some other source, that flared then died down again. I went to a table, where I saw my attorney. He stood up when I arrived, and indicated to me the chair I was supposed to sit in. I faced a horse-shoe shaped dais, raised a couple of feet above floor level. I saw the faces of six Senators peering over the edge of the dais, over their name plates. Each one had a microphone in front of him. Sitting behind them, along the wall, were about thirty more people, mostly young, who got up every now and then to hand one of the Senators a piece of paper, or to kneel behind the dais for short conferences.

I recognized two or three of the Senators. I saw Republicans and Democrats, members of President Elam's party and the opposition. I even saw Senator Ted Miller, the plump, handsome liberal on whose shoulders have, for the past 20 years, rested the exhausted hopes of all liberals in America, as Mr. Stengrow and my Mom had told me many times.

Senator Miller, sober for some of the 5 sessions (most lasting all day) during which I testified, asked many probing questions of me, and brought out many harsh criticisms of President Elam, who was in the opposing party. Senator Miller often laughed scornfully at the hypocrisy of a man who claimed to believe in the American Way and yet used cheap psychological parlor tricks - brainwashing, like some Communist, or Fascist - to have himself elected. He was especially interested in my description of how we prepared President Elam for the League of Women Voters' debates, when we had a tiny transmitter surgically implanted in his forehead, just between his eyes and slightly above. The transmitter emitted a high electronic voice, saying "sex mmm sex mmm sex mmm." Hearing this, Senator Miller wept for America.

The Senators from Mr. Elam's party took another tack. They tried to make me say I had sabotaged the campaign at the behest of rich liberals, or that I was a madman, acting alone to fulfill my own twisted fantasies of power and control. They sought to lay the blame on me, Dr. Crosse, Daphne, anyone but the President, or his advisers. They suggested that possibly the dead Ezio, who had precipitated the deaths of the eight models, also designed and ran the entire subliminal election campaign, just another of his lonely crackpot activities. I told them that Ezio had just been an artist, a paste-up man. I didn't know if they believed me.

I told my story with no intention but to rid myself of it, by giving it to them, and to the world at large. As the days filtered along, I became intensely weary of my story, but I knew I must keep telling it. The newspapers delivered to my cell every day were divided on the value of my testimony, and on all other elements of the scandal. I saw the trial footage every day on TV, and it seemed fair enough, true, unbiased, an example in every way of reporting by a free and unfettered press. I was proud of myself for having done my duty. I didn't know what I would ultimately be charged with, or what my sentence might be, but I felt I would be able to handle it. The only thing I minded was that I wouldn't be able to see Daphne for a long time, unless she found a way to contact me without endangering herself and her father. But even this, the separation from the woman I wanted to marry, I could bear. Because I was telling the truth, and that was all that mattered.

As I was taken back to my cell-suite, at the end of the last day of testimony, I looked forward to a pleasant evening watching myself on TV.

Chapter 27. White House, Black Heart.

Imagine then my surprise when I got back to my cell, and found, instead of an empty room and a tray of food, two U.S. Marines, carrying sidearms.

The Marines took me down in the elevator of the building where I had been housed. I still did not know what building it was. They led me to a sub-basement which was brightly lit and covered in green carpet as far as the eye could see. Besides the cinder block walls, painted yellow, there was nothing else in that sub-basement but a round door, like a submarine lock. One of the Marines went to the door, which had a diameter of about five feet, and he referred to a set of handwritten instructions taped to the door itself, in order to get its lock unlocked and its iron handle to screech downward, when he pushed on it. The round steel door popped open about a quarter of an inch. Then, he gestured for the other Marine to join him, and they both threw their shoulders into the door, managing only to budge it. I joined them in pushing. Together, we did heave the massive object back about a foot and a half, enough for us to squeeze through. First went one Marine, then me, then the other Marine. Once on the other side, I was regretful that I had been so co-operative, because we were in what must have been a giant sewer pipe. It stretched before us far, far, and somewhere along the way it curved gently out of sight. Now, I thought they had brought me here to kill me.

I asked, "Is this an assassination?" and the Marines looked at one another and looked grim. We walked on and there was a wall sconce with fresh flowers in it. Behind the flowers, was a small framed picture of a pair of shoes. We walked some more, and came to two more Marines, standing at attention, one on each side of a wooden door set into the curve of the sewer pipe. They opened the door and we went through, to a small elevator lobby. There were two elevator doors, side by side. Between them was a big poster, under a glass door. The poster was for a film called "This Island Earth," starring Rex Reason and Faith Domergue. One of the Marines pushed the Up button, and we waited. When the elevator came, we got in and went to a level called Ground. I still thought I was going to be killed. When the doors opened, we were in an office building, walking past secretaries, mail-boys, a group of men in suits conferring in the middle of the carpeted hallway. I felt I should probably shout out to them, for help, but I didn't.

"Where are we?" I asked my guards.

"In the White House," said one of them.

Then, we climbed a staircase, and at the head of the stairs with his arms stretched out to greet me was none other than The President of the United States of America... Mr. Elam.

He put his arm around my back and patted my stomach. "I hope they've been feeding you well, Rennie. You look thin." He took me into the Oval Office, where we were alone. He sat down and smiled at me from the other side of his desk.

I said, "You don't seem angry at me. How come?"

He said, "Angry at you for what? The fact is, we want you to come back to work again, Rennie. You're too valuable a man to lose. You're a difficult man, that's true. But I just think of you as my Michaelangelo, and I'm that Pope, whatever his name was, and I need the best man for my ceiling, even if he is a pain in the ass. It's the job of a good manager to get the best out of all his people, not just the easy ones. And I consider myself to be a damn fine manager."

I said, "But, President Elam," (showing my respect for the office if not the man) "after the testimony I just gave, how can you or your backers hope to continue the subliminal manipulation of the public? The people know everything!"

But President Elam only smiled, lit a cigarette, inhaled deeply, and said, "None of your testimony was real, none of it existed, none of it was heard by anyone who was not already aware of what was going on. We just wanted to get you to tell us everything you knew. Both to see exactly what you did know, and to help you get it out of your system. Now, you've done that. You've done the right thing. Also, and luckily for you, you've demonstrated to the satisfaction of myself and my wife that you don't know a hell of a lot anyway, about what's been going on, and that's great. Great for us, and great for you, so you can hopefully get off your high horse now, and come back to work for the party. Come play with the big toys, Rennie. Get your money back - we have it for you, you know, everything from your Gene Autry box and canvas bags. You'll still be off the books of course..."

I stopped him, with my hand over my forehead. As I spoke, I used both my hands to search the top of my head for some kind of a hole, or the tiny fibrous end of a wire, trying to determine if I was experiencing some kind of illusory moment, caused by my having had, without my knowledge, an electrode planted in my brain. I said, "What about the newspapers, the TV news, the radio news! What about Senator Miller! Didn't I tell your greatest opponent in the Universe, Senator Miller, every underhanded thing we did to get you elected, and didn't he sit there and call you names and scoff over the remnants of your reputation? Didn't evey paper have an editorial saying you should be tried in a criminal proceding, and if found guilty of the things I said in testimony, you should be taken from this office by force if necessary and thrown in the District Central lockup?"

I kept feeling around the top of my head, furiously now, searching for the wire. I stuck my hands in my ears and nostrils, and then made a systematic search of my teeth and gums, palate and tongue, for telltale whispery thin antennae. The President looked at me a little oddly, I suppose. He didn't know what I was doing.

He continued his explanation, choosing not to comment on what must have appeared to him to be my very unusual behavior.

He said the whole trial had been a hoax, designed to fool only me. The *real* Senate Subcommittee on the Use of Subliminal Messages in the Media was droning on as it always had and would continue to do for six or eight more months, at the end of which time they would issue a report saying that there was no factual basis whatsoever for the suspicion these subliminal messages are being used to sell products. They will add a special section on the election, debunking that truth, too. "We've got the most powerful tool of social management in the history of the world, Rennie," said the President. "How difficult do you think it was to convince the networks, and the print media, to keep our secret. It's their secret, too, after all. It's the key to America's competitiveness in the global marketplace for the next hundred years. Shit, son, we graduate a new class of super-morons every year in this country, each one dumber than the one before. Any European, any Russian, any Japanesio, can speak two or three languages. Our kids can't even speak American! Who's gonna feed and clothe this loveable lop-eared mass of high hopes in a world where everybody else is smarter and willing to work harder? Why, that's my responsibility, and the responsibility of those men you call my "backers." The pillars of our society, the men who see far and set our traps early in the fall. Of course, Senator Miller is one of us. And it's men like him, men who are willing to sit in a real hearing and a false hearing every day for five days, running back and forth between the hearing rooms, not to mention getting on over to the Senate floor for some important votes, it's men like him who know, as I know, and as you would, too, if you weren't so young and (though I love you like a son, and we've all heard about your genius of a Dad till we can't bear it any more) dumb."

I kept searching my mouth for the wire. Was it down my throat? I twisted myself around in my chair and attempted to unobtrusively stick four fingers and my thumb down my throat, as I made a gutteral sound which I hoped would be interpreted by the President as encouragement to continue what he was saying. I did not resent his reference to my lack of intelligence. It was a riddle I had not been able to solve to my own satisfaction, either. Here was I, after all, with one or another genius for a Dad, but I couldn't even find the wire in my own head!

Finally, the President said, "If you're looking for an electrode, Rennie, it isn't there. You're not hallucinating this conversation, I'm simply describing a hoax to you. Cheer up."

I was forced, then, to confront the fact that Mr. Elam, along with friends and associates of his, were willing to do almost anything, to prevserve for themselves the powerful tools of subliminal control.

249

He said, "You saw all those famous journalists at the hearings. A couple of them interviewed you. You poured your heart out to them... Well, nobody read those interviews but you, nobody got that cable feed but you, in your cell. What does it tell you, Rennie, that all these good people have joined us in keeping our secret? These people aren't on some diabolic payroll... Fact is, we worked like hell to put together an ad hoc group to handle this subliminal shit... It's like the atom bomb, or stirrups, or any sudden advance in technology. Every manufacturing entity, and advertising agency has an interest in this, because every citizen does..."

But I said, "I gave myself up to tell the truth. You try to make it sound like you're doing people a favor by lying to them. I don't see it that way. I believe in the words of the documents..."

"What documents?"

"Created equal," I said, "Endowed by their Creator with certain unalienable rights, among these life, liberty, and the pursuit of happiness," I said.

To which the President responded after lighting a new cigarette. "Fine," he said through the bales of smoke. "How are we taking away any of those rights by trying to keep this nation competitive in a hostile world? Do you realize we'll be able to pull ourselves out of recessions by just laying the subliminal fucks and sexes on thicker, and the consumer will buy us back into prosperity? Do you realize we can make parents love their children by simply writing fuck on the kid's forehead so his parents start to look at him as though he were a totem of joy? Are we stealing anyone's equality by doing that? No, because we're fooling everyone equally, if all goes well. Are we stealing their *life*? We give them life, and more abundantly! Are we stealing their liberty? I don't know... maybe that's something we should look into... we could have a conference or something... invite Noam Chomsky... I'm saying, this is a question of national survival... somebody's gonna be fuckin' with everyone's minds and it better fuckin' be us... OK, what about their pursuit of happiness? Can you honestly say we're stealing the public's right to pursue the very happiness we are thrusting toward them?

"Rennie, you're the great technician," he said through puffs, "you're our Einstein, our Al Nobel! Serve your country, serve your self. Join us."

But what about my dream, I thought to myself. I looked around and could see the Oval Office had been thoroughly embedded with triggering phenomes, and I let my eyes roam lazily over them as I thought. I could see the work of one or two of the better subliminal cartoonists. But what about my dream, when President Washington had told me to tell the truth?

Now, the current President was saying just the opposite. Of course, the other had only been a dream. And the interpretation which I had drawn from it. But who was I to draw interpretations that went against the interests of the duly elected Chief Executive of my country? Could it not be that I had only wished that entire dream onto myself in the first place? After all, how flattering to myself to think of President Washington as my True Dad. And what President Elam said made sense, too.

But I asked President Elam, "If you fool someone, aren't you are taking away his liberty? Because liberty is based on the idea that you can do what you want, and doing what you want is based on the idea of knowing what you want..."

"Ah-ha!" said Elam, "But knowing what you want is based on nothing but itself! No one has yet successfully found the source of human desires. They run the show, but what runs them?" To my silence, he said, "Take sex. The purpose of sex, as far as anyone can tell, is to create the next generation. Would anyone engage in the activity even once if that were all it promised? Possibly, but not certainly. Therefore, mother nature writes sex across us one and all, like we do with magazines, and we want it. We know we want it. That should be enough. That, Rennie, should be sacred.

"Help us shape the desires of mankind to propagate the type of world we want for our kids," he said with a hitch in his voice. He took a long drag on his cigarette and stared at me. I had to admit I could not think of reasons right then, to deny his request. I couldn't tell him about my dream, or about President Washington telling me to tell the truth.

Instead, I said I was tempted by his offer but that my fiance, Daphne, had told me she wouldn't let us continue to defraud the public.

He pushed a button on his desk and said, "Send them in."

One of the office's doors opened, and into the room stepped Daphne, along with Dr. Crosse.

I got out of my chair and embraced Daphne, then Dr. Crosse. I said, "How did they catch you? Are you all right? What about Drummond and his family?"

President Elam said, "I think the best thing I can do now is to leave you good people alone, to talk things over."

When he was gone, Dr. Crosse told me what had happened to him and Daphne in the two weeks since we had separated. They had gone to Arizona, but Drummond's hideout was betrayed by a brother of his, who wanted one of Drummond's wives for his own. Again, Drummond had escaped via his private runway but, said Dr. Crosse, "It was obvious to me that we should not go with him, but give ourselves up, and join you, here."

"But why?" I asked. "You were safe."

"My daughter was simply too misereable without you." Daphne put her arms around my waist, saying, "I told my Dad about us, Rennie."

"Fooled me, you did," said Dr. Crosse with a laugh.

"I'm sorry, sir," I said. I had never felt good about the deception.

"It's all right. Daphne had her reasons, and you honored them. Did what you should have done. I never realized how oppressive it could be for a young girl to have a psychologist for a Dad. She had to show that she could keep a secret from me, put some distance between her Dad and herself. And she certainly proved her point. Her old Dad had to admit there was something he didn't know."

Then Daphne said, "I had to tell him, finally. For the same reason we had to stop running from the police. I'm pregnant."

I put my arms around her and looked into her eyes. I kissed her, though it felt strange doing it in front of Dr. Crosse.

Then, we talked about what the President had said. Should we continue to work for him? Dr. Crosse said, considering the powers opposing us, we might as well go along with the President. After all, he said, we would be safe, and have a good life. It was better than being killed. We could go on with our subliminal studies.

I asked, "Will we go back to the ranch?"

Dr. Crosse shook his head. "Only drawback," he said. "We have to go back to One Corner."

Chapter 28.
My True Dad, at Last.

We had no choice but to take their deal.

Our work still has to be kept secret. We are valuable, though not irreplaceable, to the President's plans for a new world system, that will be more amenable to our national needs. We will go on living as long as our existence can be publicly denied, and not a moment more. We are, as they say, off the books. The President, and his team, have so far not allowed anyone to share or threaten their continued secret monoploy on the techniques of mind-control which Dr. Crosse, Daphne, myself, and the other original practitioners, still develop in co-operative harmony with the President.

We all live in peace, in the town and surrounding valley known as One Corner. I still come up with new ideas for Dr. Crosse and the CIA, and in turn they keep me and my family in the style to which we have become accustomed. From time to time I talk to President Elam and he tells me one day they'll have a Pulitzer Prize for subliminal artists, but that will take a few years.

They have turned the town, valley and hills around One Corner into a government installation. The story given out to the press was that the One Corner area had been horribly polluted by the runoff from a chemical plant at the head of the valley. The plant was long-closed, but the idea that its chemicals had leached into the soil and water was far from unbelieveable.

The people who saw me on my TV appearance when I gave myself up have all been informed of their new situation. They can no longer leave the valley, or have any contact with the outside world. Fortunately, not too many people saw the broadcast on the day I gave myself up, and this was always a community of isolated souls - jut a few farms, a couple of stores - so there are few cover stories for the CIA to create. Families (I understand from the men who told me - I can't vouch for their honesty, but they are our only link with the outside world) have been told that their loved ones died from the toxic water or air here, that their bodies could not safely be transported out of the valley, and no one could safely come here, to attend their funerals. The CIA has also bought all the homes and farms from the heirs of the supposedly-dead One Corner residents so there can be no reason for any of them to come here looking for anything.

Here, the Government has also brought all of my possible Dads. It was felt this was the only safe course of action, after I had intruded into their lives, and their connection to me had become known to others. All thirty-six of the possibles, and those of their friends and families they wished to keep with them, have been plucked from the general population, under one pretext or another, and set down here, in our little community. Here, they are able to pursue their former occupations, if there is any need for what they did in the outside world. And if there isn't, the CIA still pays them to carry on, and encourages them in every way to lead normal, productive lives. It isn't always possible.

There is little for a detective to do here, for example, and yet Mac 'Mac' MacDonald for a long time kept himself fairly happy driving around the Valley trying to find the answer to the question of the identity of my True Dad. He did this, even though I told him I would not pay him to keep searching. He said the Government was paying him, and I didn't feel I should stand in his way, or even discourage him, when after all he had been consigned to this place, like the rest of us, because of his connection to me, and he is only really happy when he's on a case. For this reason, I permitted him to question me, hour after hour, and for this reason, the Town Council permitted him to continue his night-long stakeouts of the homes of residents, even after the Citizens' Group for Privacy collected all those signatures asking that he be stopped.

As for me, I like it here in One Corner. It is a me-centered place. Everyone is here because he or she knows me. I have all the Dads anyone could possibly want, although we don't really get

together that often - I being busy with my new inventions and the
kids and Daphne. They, engaged in their various activities, keeping
their journals. The journals of geniuses, after all. Because that's
who my Dads are, except for one of them, about whom more in a
moment...

There is little strife in our community. Some 800 souls live
here in quiet harmony. For a long time the only harsh words I ever
heard, directed by one resident against another, were when they
would fight over the question of my paternity.

"You're his father, you demented wretch!..."

"He looks a lot more like you in the big butt department!..."

"But he's got your weird posture doesn't he, you evil
bastard!"

And similar words of disputation, would waft gently across
the Valley, carried with the pollen on the wind. Sometimes, these
arguments would result in violence, one Dad beating another into
insensibility, or setting fire to the home or barn of another Dad. One
time, Dr. Huss, my Nazi Dad, and the Minister Faroun, my Black
Muslim Dad, became so angry during a routine session of passing off
the responsibility for my genetic composition, that they grabbed each
other by the hair and went rolling down a hill together trying to bite
pieces out of one another's faces. Fortunately, they landed in a soft,
wet pile of horse manure.

Dr. Crosse occupies himself mostly in trying to find out the
equivalents, in animal languages, to the words "fuck," "sex," etc., to
see if he can train animals through the use of triggering phenomes.

We watch the news all the time, and read the papers, but can
only trust our keepers' word, that these are the actual news shows
and papers available to the rest of the country.

Recently, Dr. Crosse was asked - no, begged - by one of the
agents in charge of our valley, to debate Dr. Wilson Brian Key, on a
TV show in Canada. I hoped he would refuse, because doing the
show meant arguing as forcefully as he could against the truth of
everything that we had been doing all those years. Still, I knew he
would go, because the lure of seeing an outside place was so strong
with him. He debated Dr. Key. Dr. Crosse's strategy was to make it
sound like the work we do is still experimental, not likely to be of any

practical use for decades, if not centuries. He laughed in a sparkling way whenever Dr. Key said something true, and tried to make the thing sound absurd.

I felt sorry for Dr. Crosse, and for myself.

President Elam, who calls me now and then, said the Government's idea is not to hide the truth from the people forever, but only to delay it. "By the time America learns the Secret, the shock will have been softened by *The Subliminal Diet Book* (which has already sold 16 million copies, and *The Subliminal Sex Book* ('How to make love to a woman before she knows you're in the room.')"

He said, "You've seen the ads on TV. We're selling furniture, cars and clothes. Make-up and jewelry are making subliminal claims. They claim to have subliminal messages embedded in them, when in fact, they don't. That doesn't matter. All part of the strategy. By the time the truth comes out, every American will think of subliminal messages as his or her God-given right, and people will march and throw stones for the right to have their children's minds controlled."

The President made a commercial for his next election, kidding the rumors that he won the last one via mind control, and we're all sure that will make him even more adorable and puckish. "To be elected by a trick," says President Elam in the commercial, "is well within the structure of what is acceptible throughout the history of Western Civilization. Is it not? Starting with the Trojan Horse. Or Odysseus, when he defeated the Cyclops by introducing himself as Noman, we have always recognized the technology of surprise. Don't hold it against an old guy who loved his country too darned much to let a Democrat be its President. If that's wrong, well I'm sorry."

Who knows? This kind of folksy, semi-honest style may win him his re-election, or alternately, the American people might rise up and tear him, his family and all of us here in One Corner into thin strips of meat jerkie. Only time will tell.

* * * *

Daphne and I were married at the Church of Marilyn. Now, most of us in One Corner belong to the Church, but ours was the first wedding there. Maya performed the service, and since Marilyn Monroe was an orphan, Maya added a sentence to the traditional marriage vows, which we exchanged. After we promised to love, honor and cherish one another, we said, "And we promise to love, honor and cherish our children, no matter how they enter this world, or our home."

We have three kids now - two boys and a girl - and to them I'm not off the books. I am their father, fully in the open and unhidden.

* * * *

As for the question of who is my Actual and True Dad, I had begun to think it would never be known. No one here - myself least of all - is likely to believe anything our captors tell us on the matter. Of course, we all had our theories, and I am still saddened by the occassional fights that break out when two men try to foist the responsibility of my siring onto one another, but these are the price one pays to survive, I suppose.

I myself came to see Mr. Stengrow as my True Dad, because he raised me, and he's the only one I can talk to about my mother. Lately, I talk about her a lot. And to her. I love to sit with her in the kitchen while she cooks, and I remember when I was a child, and I was privileged to spend a few hours with her, shopping for groceries, watching her make dinner, at those times I forgot I had a father at all. Now, after all that had happened to me, I realized that those were the best times, when I could imagine that just Mom and I inhabited my world. Because, when all is said and done, your Mom is a lot more important than your Dad, no matter who he is.

Still, as I went around here in One Corner, visiting with or meeting the men who may have been my True Dad, I began to ask some of the questions that had begun to trouble me. Questions about that great intelligence I was supposed to have, and was told that I had, because I was the product of Dr. Lord's genius sperm bank.

The most interesting question was: If I am so intelligent, how come I never meet anyone stupider than I am?

STENGROW'S DAD

Sure, I met people all the time who knew less about one thing or another than I did, but why in all my life had I never met anyone to whom I could confidently (and affectionately) point, and say, "That one is dumber than I am."

What is intelligence, anyway? Can it really be quantified, like height or weight, or is it a general paste that holds us in the world, meaning that if we are in the world, we have the paste, which sticks to whatever we need to survive, and when the paste dries up, we're dead? How come when I was in school, the kid with the highest IQ and the kid with the lowest IQ could hold the same opinion on any subject concerning which both of them held opinions?

Here was I with this genius Dad. And, on top of that, I had been praised for my high intelligence by Dr. Crosse, President Elam, and many others during the time I had been working with them. I wondered, if I'm so smart, where are all the stupid people?

Maybe you have met them, you who read this. Maybe you feel you are meeting one right here in my prose. That's fine for you. You must be intelligent. But what about me? Where were they - or even, where was he or she - even one person! - whom I could spend some time with and come away with the assurance that there, at least, was a person I was smarter than?

Now, isolated here at One Corner, with not much to do, and finally despairing of ever learning the True Identity of my True Dad, I decided to pass some time in the worthwhile search for one or more people stupider than I was.

No sense looking among my Dads, or their families, all of whom might be suspected of sharing at least some of their greatness of mind. So, I turned my attention to the local residents of One Corner who were trapped here with me. They were a typical cross-section of smalltown folks. People with little ambition (or they long ago would have left One Corner) little accomplishment (a glance around town confirmed this) little reading and much TV watching.

Maybe, among this group, I would find my new grail - the person than whom I am smarter!

The morning I was to start my search, I went out early, filled with the new energy every scientist knows at the start of a new research project. The first person I saw was the milkman.

I took him to be a perfect example of an average citizen of One Corner. Probably out here this morning doing what he's been doing all his adult life. Leaving bottles of milk and cream at the doors of his customers, taking away the empties. I guessed he was one of the unfortunate residents of One Corner who had seen or heard about my appearance on the local TV station, and so, thanks to me, he was now forced to spend the rest of his days right here in our valley. Maybe he didn't mind. I tried not to feel guilty about the One Cornerites who had been trapped here with me and my Dads and the rest of us. They, like me, were now the responsibility of the Government.

Back in Los Angeles, we had had our milk delivered when I was growing up, but a few years ago, I forget when, they stopped delivering, and everyone started getting their milk at the supermarket along with all the other groceries. When I saw this milkman, thoughts of those old days came over me, and I became nostalgic. I said hello to him.

He was an average-looking man, about 45 years old, not very tall, with a somewhat sad, quiet face. He had brown hair, cut short and not well. His ears stood out on the sides of his head like doorknobs. He wore a white dairy uniform and drove a big square truck, with a picture of a cow on the side. The cow had a flower tied over one ear. The milkman reached into the side of the truck, behind the front seats, and pulled out a carrying tray. He deftly loaded the tray with four milk bottles, stood upright, and returned my greeting.

"Mornin'," he said.

"Looks like winter soon," said I.

"Looks like," he agreed, as he walked from his truck to the house outside of which I happened to be standing when I saw him. I watched him put down the milk bottles, pick up the empties, put them in his tray, and start back to his truck. On the way back, he stopped for a moment, right in front of me, and said, "We haven't met. I'm Dan." We shook hands.

"I'm Reynold Stengrow," I said. He smiled, at the unnecessary nature of my announcement.

"Care to come along?" he asked kindly. "Always use the company."

"Sure," I said, with enthusiasm. He seemed like a good fellow to spend a half hour with, and besides, he seemed like a perfect candidate for that elusive prey of mine - the-person-less-smart-than-I for whom I had determined to search. Maybe, I thought, a few minutes of talk with this milkman will put this whole intelligence thing in perspective for me. By studying his lack of genius, I will learn to have a greater appreciation of my own generous helping of it, I hoped.

I hopped on the truck, and so did he. I accompanied him on his rounds. Our conversation was fragmented, because he had to stop and jump out every minute or two, and get the tray, fill it, go to the doors of the houses, put down the bottles, get the empties, and so on.

His conversation, I soon realized, was centered on milk, and on his role as a milkman. I asked him about some trial then big on the news, a murder that had happened in Washington. I said, "What a terrible thing for a man to do," meaning, to kill eight people at a Thanksgiving dinner. His reply was, "The man probably didn't get enough milk when he was growing up." I said, "He poisoned them - eight innocent members of his own family!" to which Dan replied, "If they had all drunk a glass of milk before dinner, it would have coated their stomachs and they probably would have survived the whole thing."

No matter what topic of conversation I started off with, somehow he responded in terms of milk and milk products.

I said, "Maryland is a beautiful state."

He said, "More dairy cows per acre than any other place on earth, except maybe Wisconsin, and I say maybe with good reason, because though a lot of people take it for granted that Wisconsin is the Dairy State, they don't realize that since 1984..." etc.

I asked what he thought of our President, Mr. Elam. He said, "The man's skin shows clear signs of dairy deprivation."

"Maybe he's worried about cholesterol," I suggested.

"Biggest myth in the world," said Dan, seeming to spit at the thought of the word cholesterol. Then, he said in a way that reminded me of a political rabble-rouser: "Dairy for babies, dairy for

261

toddlers, dairy for teens, dairy for grownups - we all need it - milk is life!"

I thought, Well, maybe this is him - the one who is dumber than I am - the one who can prove to me once and for all that some people have more intelligence than others, simply by proving that he has less than I. I was hopeful. The next day, I made sure to be out on the street when he came by, to accompany him once again on his rounds. I broached many subjects with him, and every time, he brought it back to milk. But I wasn't sure yet. Was he really dumb, or was his obsession with dairy products a weird form of intelligence? Possible, I had to admit. And beyond that, what if everything he said was actually some kind of game he was playing, only pretending to have no interests outside of milk while actually using his "simple" speech to weave a consistent and complex critique of the universe? How could I be sure? I had to stick with him, keep notes, gather as much data as I could. For this reason, I started to ride with him every morning. When I sensed he might wish to go back to his old, solo delivery ways, I tried to make myself useful to him, rushing to get the wire mesh tray and fill it, and rushing to the doors to deliver the milk and pick up the empties, all before he even stopped the truck.

I found I enjoyed being with him. I very much enjoyed delivering the milk. I began to agree with him, that every problem we have in America can be pretty clearly traced back to the sad fact that daily milk delivery is no longer available to most of the people in our nation. I remembered so lovingly those old days when I used to open the door of our apartment in the morning and bring in fresh milk for my morning cereal, and for Mr. Stengrow's coffee, that he loved so well. I cried with Dan over the ugliness and unhealthiness of these new cardboard milk containers that have polluted America for the past fifteen years or so. I soon realized I had never enjoyed anything - not school, not being called a genius, not working with subliminals, not helping Mr. Elam to become President - nothing - as well as I enjoyed the simple, neighbor-helping act of delivering the milk in clear, clean bottles, every morning with Dan.

Soon, I forgot my search for the less-smart individual science teaches us must exist somewhere. I forgot my work with Dr. Crosse and I forgot all the scientific and social and philosophical arguments I used to get embroiled in, with my various Dads. All that talk seemed like so much babbling madness to me now, now that I had found this decent, calm job, and this quiet, sensible man to teach me the ropes of it. I saw all my putative Dads in a new light now. No longer did I worry about their strange theories of life, or the odd turns their lives had taken, or even the mixed effect which I myself had had on their existences. Now, Dr. Huss became the man who took two quarts of nonfat on Tuesdays and Fridays. Mr. Steinstein, who woke early every morning to pound out TV scripts no one will ever film, is the man who takes a bottle of milk and one of cream, and who has to be reminded to return his empties.

One morning, about two weeks after I started going on the rounds with Dan, we were talking about the football games coming up that weekend, and Dan was telling me that he had heard a reliable rumor that the Raiders drank more milk and ate more cottage cheese than their opponents, the Giants, and that therefore he could tell me without doubt that they would emerge victorious - when we arrived at the home of my parents (Mr. and Mrs. Stengrow). There were several houses in a row that got milk on this block, so Dan and I both had to carry our mesh trays from the truck, and walk toward the houses together. We were talking happily, when the door of my parents' house opened, and there was my Mom, putting out two empty bottles. One of them had a note rolled up and stuck in the neck of it. My Mom looked very sweet, in her flannel housecoat, her hair in rollers, her eyes bright and shining, as though she never slept.

She had set one bottle down beside the welcome mat and still held one in her hand when I called to her, "Hi, Mom!"

She looked up, slightly startled to hear a voice so early in the morning. For a moment, it was hard to tell what was going through her mind. She saw me, started to smile, then suddenly froze her smile in a half-formed state, and let it melt away to a thin frightened look. She glanced from my face to Dan's, then back to mine, then back to Dan's, then back to mine, then back to Dan's then back to mine, and the bottle in her hand slid to the concrete porch and shattered.

She said to me, "Then, you know."

Then, I knew.

In the kitchen, a few minutes later, Dan and I drank big glasses of milk, served by my mother. Dan said to her, "I didn't say anything to the boy. I hope you believe me."

My mother came and sat down with us. She had a mug of coffee with a picture of an Indian on a pony, shooting an arrow. She said to Dan, "It's all right. I knew he was bound to find out sooner or later."

Then she told me, "Well, Reynold, now you know. Like many children born before around 1970, when home delivery was phased out in most places, your real father, or True Dad as you like to call him, was the milkman."

She smiled briefly at Dan, then looked at me with seriousness. "I just got so tired of going to that Dr. Lord, and his genius sperm bank, over and over, and it never took. I knew I had to get pregnant, somehow, or kill myself from the sheer tedium of talking about it, trying, trying, driving out to Burbank, that Nurse Lilly, talking about geniuses with your father, and he is still your father, Reynold, (she said, waving her hand toward the bedroom, where Mr. Stengrow lay sleeping)... and then, one morning, like today, I was putting out a note to tell the milkman to leave some extra bottles of heavy cream for my Thanksgiving pies, and I went out into the hallway, and there was... Dan..." She put her hand on top of his. "Over the years, we had become acquainted, of course. I had always thought of him as a friend. And on this morning I remembered all those rumors, about women in our building, and up and down the street. I thought, maybe he can help us, too..."

Then Dan said, "That was a great route, my Fourth Street route." He drifted off into memory for a moment. Then, he continued: "I was laid off a few days later. That was the last home delivery in the Santa Monica area..." He paused to think about all that had been lost. "I did a little prospecting out in New Mexico, got in a car wreck, collected a good settlement, and just vegetated out there in Yucaipa. I always missed my route. You never forget your route. Of course, your mother and I didn't see each other for what?

Almost twenty years. Then, I saw your picture in the paper, and had the bright idea of calling her up." He looked at her.

"Just in time to be picked up by the CIA wiretap they had on our condo," said my mother.

I looked downward, full of shame.

Dan hastened to relieve the mood of the moment, saying, "Don't feel bad on my account, Reynold. When I got here, and they told me I could have a route, like I did in the old days, I became the happiest man in the world." Looking at him, I could see he was telling the truth.

Was I looking at a possible answer, I wondered, to the mystery of why I had never really felt like a full-fledged genius? Yes, I was. This was my True Dad, Dan. His interests were my interests, his social class was my social class. He didn't think about being a genius. He had no great vision of the future, toward which he was willing to work, and for which he was willing to do anything in the world, from trickery to murder. He only wanted to deliver good milk, and earn his living like a man.

Already, I could feel any interest I had ever had in geniuses and their doings vanish into thin air, except that I suddenly knew, without the slightest doubt, that all of them, medical, engineering, legal, mathematical, musical and financial, physics-directed and chemistry-driven, wise and hot-tempered, neurotic and insensitive, all of them would lead better and happier lives, no matter what their IQ scores might be, and they would be better family men, and fathers, if they drank more milk. I knew they should also eat large amounts of ice cream, and they would find peace, as I had.

In the near future, I knew, I would tell all my Dads what I had discovered, so they would know the blessings of milk. I felt I owed them that much. After all, I loved every one of them, and wanted them all to be happy.